ALSO BY ERNEST CLINE

READY PLAYER ONE

A NOVEL

ERNEST CLINE

CROWN PUBLISHERS
NEW YORK

Published in the United States by Crown Publishers,
an imprint of the Crown Publishing Group,
a division of Penguin Random House LLC, New York.
www.crownpublishing.com

CROWN and the Crown colophon are registered trademarks of Penguin Random House LLC.

Library of Congress Cataloging-in-Publication Data
Cline, Ernest.
    Armada : a novel / Ernest Cline.
1. High school students—Fiction. 2. Human-alien encounters—Fiction. I. Title.
    PS3603.L548A89 2015
    813'.6—dc23

                          2015009421

ISBN 978-0-8041-3725-6
eBook ISBN 978-0-8041-3726-3

PRINTED IN THE UNITED STATES OF AMERICA

Book design by Ralph Fowler / rlfdesign
Illustrations by Russell Walks
Jacket design by Will Staehle
Inside jacket illustration by Mark Duszkiewicz

10 9 8 7 6 5 4

First Edition

For Major Eric T. Cline, USMC

The bravest person I have ever known

Semper Fi, little brother

PHASE ONE

The only legitimate use of a computer is to play games.

—Eugene Jarvis, creator of *Defender*

1

I WAS STARING OUT THE CLASSROOM WINDOW AND DAYDREAMING OF ADVENTURE WHEN I spotted the flying saucer.

I blinked and looked again—but it was still out there, a shiny chrome disc zigzagging around in the sky. My eyes struggled to track the object through a series of increasingly fast, impossibly sharp turns that would have juiced a human being, had there been any aboard. The disc streaked toward the distant horizon, then came to an instantaneous stop just above it. It hovered there motionless over the distant tree line for a few seconds, as if scanning the area beneath it with an invisible beam, before it abruptly launched itself skyward again, making another series of physics-defying changes to its course and speed.

I tried to keep my cool. I tried to remain skeptical. I reminded myself that I was a man of science, even if I did usually get a C in it.

I looked at it again. I still couldn't tell what it was, but I knew what it wasn't—it wasn't a meteor. Or a weather balloon, or swamp gas, or ball lightning. No, the unidentified flying object I was staring at with my own two eyes was most definitely *not of this earth*.

My first thought was: *Holy fucking shit.*

Followed immediately by: *I can't believe it's finally happening.*

You see, ever since the first day of kindergarten, I had been hoping and waiting for some mind-blowingly fantastic, world-altering event to finally shatter the endless monotony of my public education. I had spent hundreds of hours gazing out at the calm, conquered suburban landscape surrounding my school, silently yearning for the outbreak of a zombie apocalypse, a freak accident that would give me super powers, or perhaps the sudden appearance of a band of time-traveling kleptomaniac dwarves.

I would estimate that approximately one-third of these dark daydreams of mine had involved the unexpected arrival of beings from another world.

Of course, I'd never believed it would really happen. Even if alien visitors *did* decide to drop by this utterly insignificant little blue-green planet, no self-respecting extraterrestrial would ever pick my hometown of Beaverton, Oregon—aka Yawnsville, USA—as their point of first contact. Not unless their plan was to destroy our civilization by wiping out our least interesting locales first. If there was a bright center to the universe, I was on the planet it was farthest from. Please pass the blue milk, Aunt Beru.

But now something miraculous *was* happening here—it was still happening, right now! There was a goddamn flying saucer out there. I was staring right at it.

And I was pretty sure it was getting closer.

I cast a furtive glance back over my shoulder at my two best friends, Cruz and Diehl, who were both seated behind me. But they were currently engaged in a whispered debate and neither of them was looking toward the windows. I considered trying to get their attention, but I was worried the object might vanish any second, and I didn't want to miss my chance to see this for myself.

My gaze shot back outside, just in time to see another bright flash of silver as the craft streaked laterally across the landscape, then halted and hovered over an adjacent patch of terrain before zooming off again. Hover, move. Hover, move.

It was definitely getting closer. I could see its shape in more detail now. The saucer banked sideways for a few seconds, and I got my first clear glimpse of its top-down profile, and I saw that it wasn't really a saucer at all. From this angle, I could see that its symmetrical hull resembled the blade of a two-headed battle-axe, and that a black, octagonal prism lay centered between its long, serrated wings, glinting in the morning sunlight like a dark jewel.

That was when I felt my brain begin to short-circuit, because there was no mistaking the craft's distinctive design. After all, I'd seen it almost every night for the past few years, through a targeting reticle. I was looking at a Sobrukai Glaive, one of the fighter ships piloted by the alien bad guys in *Armada,* my favorite videogame.

Which was, of course, impossible. Like seeing a TIE Fighter or a Klingon Warbird cruising across the sky. The Sobrukai and their Glaive Fighters were fictional videogame creations. They didn't exist in the real world—they *couldn't*. In reality, videogames did *not* come to life and fictional spaceships did *not* buzz your hometown. Implausible shit like that only happened in cheesy '80s movies, like *TRON* or *WarGames* or *The Last Starfighter*. The sorts of movies my late father had been nuts about.

The gleaming craft banked sideways again, and this time I got an even better look—there was no doubt about it. I was looking at a Glaive, right down to the distinctive claw-like grooves along its fuselage and the twin plasma cannons protruding from the front end like two fangs.

There was only one logical explanation for what I was seeing. I had to be hallucinating. And I knew what sort of people suffered from hallucinations in broad daylight without any help from drugs or alcohol. People who were cuckoo for Cocoa Puffs, that's who. Cats with a serious marble deficiency.

I'd long wondered if my father had been one such person, because of what I'd read in one of his old journals. The things I'd seen there had given me the impression that he'd become somewhat delusional near the end of his life. That he may have even lost the ability to differentiate between videogames and reality—the very same problem I now seemed to be experiencing myself. Maybe it was just as I had always secretly feared: The apple had fallen right next to the Crazy Tree.

Had I been drugged? No, impossible. All I'd eaten that morning was a raw strawberry Pop-Tart I'd wolfed down in my car on the way to school—and the only thing crazier than hallucinating a fictional videogame spaceship would be to blame it on a frosted breakfast pastry. Especially if I knew my own DNA was a far more likely culprit.

This was my own fault, I realized. I could've taken precautions. But instead, I'd done the opposite. Like my old man, I'd spent my entire life overdosing on uncut escapism, willingly allowing fantasy to become my reality. And now, like my father before me, I was paying the price for my lack of vision. I was going off the rails on a crazy train. You could practically hear Ozzy screaming "All aboard!"

Don't do this, I pleaded with myself. *Don't crack up now, when we've only got two months to go until graduation! This is the home stretch, Lightman! Keep it together!*

Outside the window, the Glaive Fighter streaked laterally again. As it zoomed over a cluster of tall trees, I saw their branches rustle in its wake. Then it zipped through another cloud bank, moving so fast it punched a perfect circular hole through its center, dragging several long wisps of cloud vapor along with it as it tore out the other side.

A second later, the craft froze in midair one last time before it streaked straight upward in a silver blur, vanishing from sight as quickly as it had appeared.

I just sat there for a moment, unable to do more than stare at the empty patch of sky where it had been a second earlier. Then I glanced around at the other students seated nearby. No one else was looking in the direction of the windows. If that Glaive Fighter had really been out there, no one else had seen it.

I turned back and scanned the empty sky once again, praying for the strange silver craft to reappear. But it was long gone, and now here I was, forced to deal with the aftermath.

Seeing that Glaive Fighter, or imagining I'd seen it, had triggered a small rock slide in my mind that was already growing into a crushing avalanche of conflicting emotions and fragmented memories—all of them linked to my father, and that old journal I'd found among his things.

Actually, I wasn't even sure it had been a journal. I'd never finished reading it. I'd been too disturbed by its contents, and what they'd seemed to imply about the author's mental state. So I'd put the old notebook back where I found it and tried to forget that it even existed—and until a few seconds ago, I had succeeded.

But now I couldn't seem to think about anything else.

I felt a sudden compulsion to run out of the school, drive home, and find it. It wouldn't take long. My house was only a few minutes away.

I glanced over at the exit, and the man guarding it, Mr. Sayles, our elderly Integrated Mathematics II teacher. He had a silver buzz cut, thick horn-rimmed glasses, and wore the same monochromatic outfit he always did: black loafers, black slacks, a white short-sleeve dress shirt, and a black clip-on necktie. He'd been teaching at this high school for over forty-five years now, and the old yearbook photos in the library were proof that he'd been rocking this same retro ensemble the entire time. Mr. S was finally retiring this year, which was a good thing, because he appeared to have run out of shits to give sometime in the previous century. Today, he'd spent the first five minutes going over our homework assignment, then given us the rest of the period to work on it, while he shut off his hearing aid and did his crosswords. But he would still spot me if I tried to sneak out.

My eyes moved to the ancient clock embedded in the lime green brick wall above the obsolete chalkboard. With its usual lack of pity, it informed me there were still thirty-two minutes remaining until the bell.

There was no way I could take thirty-two more minutes of this. After what I'd just seen, I'd be lucky if I managed to keep my shit together for another thirty-two seconds.

Off to my left, Douglas Knotcher was currently engaged in his daily humiliation of Casey Cox, the shy, acne-plagued kid unfortunate enough to be seated in front of him. Knotcher usually limited himself to lobbing verbal insults at the poor guy, but today he'd decided to go old-school and lob spitballs at him instead. Knotcher had a stack of moist projectiles piled on his desk like cannonballs, and he was currently firing them at the back of Casey's head, one after another. The back of the poor kid's hair was already damp with spit from Knotcher's previous attacks. A couple of Knotcher's pals were watching from the back of the room, and they snickered each time he nailed Casey with another projectile, egging him on.

It drove me nuts when Knotcher bullied Casey like this—which, I suspected, was one of the reasons Knotcher enjoyed doing it so much. He knew I couldn't do a damn thing about it.

I glanced at Mr. Sayles, but he was still lost in his crossword, clueless as always—a fact that Knotcher took advantage of on a daily basis. And on a daily basis, I had to resist the urge to knock his teeth down his throat.

Doug Knotcher and I had managed to avoid each other, for the most part, ever since "the Incident" back in junior high. Until this year, when a cruel act of fate had landed us both in the same math class. Seated in adjacent rows, no less. It was almost as if the universe *wanted* my last semester of high school to be as hellish as possible.

That would have also explained why my ex-girlfriend, Ellen Adams, was in this class, too. Three rows to my right and two rows back, sitting just beyond the reach of my peripheral vision.

Ellen was my first love, and we'd lost our virginity to each other. It had been nearly two years since she'd dumped me for some wrestler from a neighboring school, but every time I saw those freckles across the bridge of her nose—or caught sight of her tossing that curly red hair out of her eyes—I felt my heart breaking all over again. I usually spent the entire class period trying to forget she was in the room.

Being forced to sit between my mortal enemy and my ex-girlfriend every afternoon made seventh-period math feel like my own private Kobayashi Maru, a brutal no-win scenario designed to test my emotional fortitude.

Thankfully fate had balanced out the nightmare equation slightly by placing my two best friends in this class, too. If Cruz and Diehl hadn't been assigned here, I probably would've snapped and started hallucinating shit midway through my first week.

I glanced back at them again. Diehl, who was tall and thin, and Cruz, who was short and stocky, both shared the same first name, Michael. Ever since grade school I had been calling them by their last names to avoid confusion. The Mikes were still engaged in the same whispered conversation they'd been having earlier, before I'd zoned out and started seeing things—a debate over the "coolest melee weapon in the history of cinema." I tried to focus in on their voices again now.

"Sting wasn't even really a *sword*," Diehl was saying. "It was more like a glow-in-the-dark Hobbit butter knife, used to spread jam on scones and lembas bread and shit."

Cruz rolled his eyes. " 'Your love of the halflings' leaf has clearly slowed your mind,'" he quoted. "Sting was an *Elvish* blade, forged in Gondolin in the First Age! It could cut through almost anything! And its blade only glowed when it detected the presence of orcs or goblins nearby. What does Mjolnir detect? Fake accents and frosted hair?"

I wanted to tell them what I'd just seen, but best friends or not, there was no way in hell they'd believe me. They'd think of it as another symptom of their pal Zack's psychological instability.

And maybe it was, too.

"Thor doesn't need to detect his enemies so he can run off and hide in his little Hobbit hole!" Diehl whispered. "Mjolnir is powerful enough to destroy mountains, and it can also emit energy blasts, create force fields, and summon lightning. The hammer also always returns to Thor's hand after he throws it, even if it has to tear through an entire planet to get back to him! And only Thor can wield it!" He leaned back.

"Dude, Mjolnir is a bullshit magical Swiss Army knife!" Cruz said. "Even worse than Green Lantern's ring! They give that hammer a new power every other week, just to get Thor out of whatever asinine fix they've written him into." He smirked. "By the way, lots of other people have wielded Mjolnir, including *Wonder Woman* in a crossover issue! Google it! Your whole argument is invalid, Diehl!"

For the record, my own personal choice would have probably been Excalibur, as depicted in the film of the same name. But I didn't have the heart to join the debate. Instead, my attention drifted back over to Knotcher, who was in the process of lobbing another giant spitball at Casey. It nailed him in the back of his already damp head, then fell to the floor, where it joined the soggy pile of previously fired missiles that had already collected there.

Casey went rigid for a second on impact, but he didn't turn around. He just sank back down into his seat while his tormenter prepared another saliva salvo.

There was an obvious connection between Knotcher's behavior and the abusive drunk he had for a father, but the cause of his sadistic behavior didn't excuse it in my opinion. I clearly had a few daddy issues myself, but you didn't see me pulling the wings off of flies.

On the other hand, I did have a slight anger-management problem, and a related history of physical violence, both well documented by the public school system.

And, oh yeah, that whole "hallucinating alien spacecraft from my favorite videogame" thing.

So perhaps I wasn't in the best position to judge the sanity of others.

I looked around at my classmates. Everyone in the vicinity was staring at Casey now, probably wondering if this would be the day he'd finally stand up to Knotcher. But Casey just kept glancing up at Mr. Sayles, who was still engrossed in his crossword, oblivious to the intense adolescent drama unfolding in front of him.

Knotcher launched another spitball, and Casey sank even lower into his seat, almost like he was melting.

I tried to do what I'd been doing all semester. I tried to manage my anger. To focus my attention elsewhere and mind my own business. But I couldn't and I didn't.

Watching Knotcher torment Casey while the rest of us just sat and watched filled me not only with self-loathing, but with disgust for my whole species. If there were other civilizations out there, why would they ever want to make contact with humanity? If this was how we treated each other, how much kindness could we possibly show to some race of bug-eyed beings from beyond?

A clear image of the Glaive Fighter reappeared in my mind, cranking up the tension in my nerves a few more notches. I tried to calm them once again—this time by reminding myself of the Drake equation, and the Fermi paradox. I knew there was probably life elsewhere. But given the vast size and age of the universe, I also knew how astronomically unlikely it was we would ever make contact with it, much less within the narrow window of my own lifetime. We were all probably stuck here for the duration, on the third rock from our sun. Boldly going extinct.

I felt a sharp pain in my jaw and realized I was clenching my teeth—hard enough to crack my back molars. With some effort, I unclenched them. Then I glanced back at Ellen, to see if she was watching all of this. She was staring at Casey with a helpless expression, and her eyes were filled with pity.

That was what finally pushed me over the edge.

"Zack, what are you doing?" I heard Diehl ask in a panicked whisper. "Sit down!"

I glanced down. Without realizing it, I'd gotten up from my desk. My eyes were still locked on Knotcher and Casey.

"Yeah, stay out of it!" Cruz whispered over my other shoulder. "Come on, man."

But by that point, a red film of rage had already slipped down across my vision.

When I reached Knotcher, I didn't do what I wanted to, which was to grab him by his hair and slam his face into his desktop as hard as I could, again and again.

Instead, I reached down and scooped up the soggy pile of gray spitballs resting on the floor behind Casey's chair. I used both hands to pack them all together in a single wet ball, then slapped it down directly on the top of Knotcher's head. It made an extremely satisfying *splat* sound.

Knotcher jumped up and spun around to face his attacker, but he froze when he saw my face staring back at him. His eyes went wide, and he seemed to turn slightly pale.

A collective "*Ooooooh!*" emanated from our classmates. Everyone knew what had happened between me and Knotcher back in junior high, and they were all electrified by the possibility of a rematch. Seventh period Integrated Math had just gotten a hell of a lot more exciting.

Knotcher reached up and clawed the wet ball of chewed-up napkins off his head. Then he hurled it angrily across the room, unintentionally pelting half a dozen people. We locked eyes. I noticed a rivulet of Knotcher's own spittle dripping down the left side of his face. He wiped it away, still keeping his eyes on me.

"Finally decided to stick up for your boyfriend, Lightman?" he muttered, doing a poor job of concealing the unsteadiness in his voice.

I bared my teeth and lunged a step forward, cocking my right fist back. It had the desired effect. Knotcher didn't just flinch—he lurched backward, tripping over his own chair and nearly falling to the floor. But then he righted himself and faced off with me again, his cheeks now flushed in embarrassment.

The classroom was now dead silent, save for the incessant click of the electric wall clock, ticking off the seconds.

Do it, I thought. *Give me an excuse. Throw a punch.*

But I could see the fear growing in Knotcher's eyes, subsuming his anger. Maybe he could tell from the look in my own eyes that I was on the verge of coming unhinged.

"Psycho," he muttered under his breath. Then he turned and sat down, flipping me the bird over his shoulder.

I realized my right fist was still raised. When I finally lowered it, the entire class seemed to exhale in unison. I glanced at Casey, expecting him to offer me a nod of thanks. But he was still cowering at his desk like a whipped dog, and he wouldn't make eye contact with me.

I stole another glance at Ellen. She was staring right at me this time, but she immediately looked away, refusing to meet my gaze. I scanned the rest of the classroom. The only two people who would make eye contact with me were Cruz and Diehl, and they both wore expressions of concern.

That was when Mr. Sayles finally looked up from his crossword and noticed me hovering over Knotcher like an axe murderer. He fumbled with his hearing aid and powered it back on; then he looked back at me, then at Knotcher, then back at me again.

"What's going on, Lightman?" he asked, leveling a crooked finger at me. When I didn't respond, he frowned. "Back in your seat—now."

But I couldn't do that. If I stayed here one second longer my skull was going to implode. So I walked out of the classroom, passing right in front of Mr. Sayles' desk on my way out the open door. He watched me go, eyebrows raised in disbelief.

"You better be on your way to the office, mister!" he shouted after me.

I was already sprinting for the nearest exit, disrupting one class after another with the staccato screech of my sneaker soles on the waxed corridor floor.

After what seemed like an eternity, I finally burst out of the school's main entrance. As I ran for the student parking lot, I swept my gaze back and forth across the sky, from one horizon to the other. To anyone watching from inside the school, I must've looked like a complete mental case, spectating some tennis match between giants that I alone could see—or maybe like Don Quixote, tilting at a few windmills before he gave them the La Mancha beatdown.

My car was parked near the back of the lot. It was a white 1989 Dodge Omni that had once belonged to my father, covered in dents, dings, peeling paint, and large patches of rust. It had sat neglected under a tarp in our garage throughout my childhood, until my mother had tossed me the keys on my sixteenth birthday. I'd accepted the gift with mixed feelings—and not just because it was a rusted-out eyesore that barely ran. It also happened to be the car in which I was conceived—while it was parked in the very same lot where I now stood, coincidentally. An unfortunate bit of trivia that my mother let slip one Valentine's Day, after too much wine, and one too many back-to-back viewings of *Say Anything. In vino veritas*—doubly true in my mother's case when a Cameron Crowe movie was added to the mix.

Anyway, now the Omni belonged to me. Life is a circle, I suppose. And free wheels are free wheels, especially to a broke high school kid. I just did my best not to think about my teenage parents going at in the backseat while Peter Gabriel crooned to them on the tape deck.

Yes—the car still had a functioning tape deck. I had an adapter cable for it, so I could play music off my phone, but I preferred to listen to my father's old mixtapes instead. His favorite bands had become my favorites, too: ZZ Top, AC/DC, Van Halen, Queen. I fired up the Omni's mighty four-cylinder engine, and Power Station's cover of "Get It On (Bang a Gong)" began to blare out of its half-blown speakers.

I hauled ass home as fast as I could, weaving through the maze of shady suburban streets at what was probably an unsafe speed—especially since I spent most of the trip looking up instead of at the road in front of me. It was still only midafternoon, but a nearly full moon was already faintly visible overhead, and my gaze kept locking onto it as I scanned the heavens. As a result, I almost ran two stop signs during the short drive home, then came within a few inches of getting broadsided by an SUV when I coasted through a red light.

After that, I put on my hazard lights and drove the last few miles at a crawl—still craning my neck out the window, unable to keep my eyes off the sky.

2

I PARKED IN THE EMPTY DRIVEWAY AND KILLED THE ENGINE, BUT I DIDN'T GET OUT OF THE car right away. Instead I sat there gripping the wheel with both hands, peering silently up at the attic window of our little ivy-covered brick house, thinking about the first time I'd gone up there to dig through my father's old possessions. I'd felt like a young Clark Kent, preparing to finally learn the truth about his origins from the holographic ghost of his own long-dead father. But now I was thinking of a young Jedi-in-training named Luke Skywalker, looking into the mouth of that cave on Dagobah while Master Yoda told him about today's activity lesson: *Strong with the Dark Side of the Force that place is. In you must go, mofo.*

So in I went.

When I unlocked the front door of our house and stepped into the living room, Muffit, our ancient beagle, glanced up at me sleepily from where he was stretched out on the rug. A few years earlier he would have been waiting for me just inside the door, yapping like a madman. But the poor guy had now grown so old and deaf that my arrival barely woke him. Muffit rolled onto his back, and I gave his tummy a few quick rubs before heading upstairs. The old dog watched me go, but didn't follow.

When I finally reached the attic door, I just stood there at the top of the stairs, with one hand on the doorknob. I didn't open the door. I didn't go in. Not right away.

First I needed a moment to prepare myself.

HIS NAME WAS XAVIER ULYSSES LIGHTMAN, AND HE DIED WHEN HE WAS ONLY NINETEEN years old. I was still just a baby at the time, so I didn't remember him. Growing up, I'd always told myself that was lucky. Because you can't miss someone you don't even remember.

But the truth was, I *did* miss him. And I'd attempted to fill the void created by his absence with data, by absorbing every scrap of information about him that I could. Sometimes, it felt like I was trying to earn the right to miss him with the same intensity my mom and his parents had always seemed to.

When I was around ten years old, I entered what I thought of now as my "Garp phase." That was when my lifelong curiosity about my late father gradually blossomed into a full-blown obsession.

Up until that point, I'd made do with a vague, idealized image of my young father that had gradually formed in my mind over the years. But in actuality, I really only knew four basic facts about him—the same four things I'd heard over and over again throughout my childhood, mostly from my grandparents:

1. I looked just like him when he was (insert my current age).

2. He had loved me and my mother very much.

3. He died in an on-the-job accident at the local wastewater treatment plant.

4. The accident supposedly wasn't his fault.

But once my age reached double digits, these vague details were no longer sufficient to satisfy my growing curiosity about him. So, naturally, I began to barrage his widow with questions. Daily. Incessantly. At the time, I was too young and clueless to realize how painful it was for my mother to be endlessly interrogated about her dead husband by his ten-year-old clone. No, my self-involved ass couldn't seem to connect those glowing neon dots, so I kept right on asking questions, and my mother, trooper that she was, answered them to the best of her ability, for as long as she could.

Then, one day, she handed me a small brass key and told me about the boxes up in our attic.

Until then, I'd always assumed that my mother had donated all of my dad's stuff to charity after he died, because that seemed like the first thing a young, widowed single mother who was trying to start her life over would do. But that summer day, my mother explained that this was not the case. Instead, she had packed everything he'd owned into cardboard boxes, and when we moved into our current house a few months later—purchased with the payout from the accident settlement—she'd stored all of them up in our attic. She had done this for me, she said, so that when I grew up and wanted to know more about my father, those boxes would be up there waiting for me.

When I finally got the door unlocked and burst into the attic, they were really there—a dozen pristine cardboard moving boxes stacked neatly in a corner beneath the sloping rafters, illuminated by a bright shaft of sunlight. For a long time all I could do was stand there frozen, staring at this tower of time capsules waiting for me to unlock their secrets.

I'd spent the rest of the summer up in that attic, sorting through it all, like an archaeologist unearthing relics in an ancient tomb. It took some time. For a guy who had only made it to the age of nineteen, my dad had managed to amass an awful lot of stuff.

About a third of the boxes were filled with my father's collection of old videogames—which was actually more of a hoard than a collection. He'd owned five different videogame consoles, along with hundreds of games for each of them. I found the real stockpile, however, on his old PC, which contained thousands of classic arcade and console videogame emulators and ROM files—more games than one person could have possibly played in a single lifetime. My father appeared to have given it a shot, though.

In another box, I found an ancient top-loading VCR. I figured out how to hook it up to the small TV in my bedroom and started watching his old videotapes, one after the other, in whatever order I pulled them out of the box. Most of them contained old science fiction movies and TV shows, along with a lot of science programs taped off of PBS.

There were boxes filled with my father's old clothes, too. Everything had been way too big on me, but that hadn't stopped me from trying on every last stitch he'd owned, breathing in the smell as I stared at myself in the dusty attic mirror.

I got really excited when I found a box of old cards and letters among his things, along with a shoebox overflowing with carefully folded love notes my mother had passed him during their classroom courtship. I shamelessly read through them all, gulping down new details about the man who had sired me.

The last box I'd looked through had been the one that contained all of my father's old role-playing game materials. It was filled with rulebooks, bags of polyhedral dice, character sheets, and a large stack of his old campaign notebooks, each one outlining the minutiae of some fictional reality intended to serve as the setting for one of his role-playing games—and each one providing a small glimpse into my father's famously overactive imagination.

But one of those notebooks had been different from the others. It had a worn blue cover, and my father had carefully block-printed a single cryptic word in the center of it: PHAËTON.

The yellowing pages within contained a strange list of dates and names, followed by what appeared to be a series of fragmented journal entries, which outlined the details of a global conspiracy my father believed he'd uncovered—a top-secret project involving all four branches of the US military, which he claimed were working in collusion with the entertainment and videogame industries, as well as select members of the United Nations.

At first, I tried to convince myself I was reading an outline for some role-playing game scenario my father had concocted, or notes for some short story he'd never gotten around to writing. But the further I read, the more disturbed I got. It wasn't written like a piece of fiction. It was more like a long, rambling letter written by a highly delusional mental patient—one who happened to have contributed half of my DNA.

The journal had helped shatter the idealized image I'd constructed of my young father. That was one reason I'd vowed never to look at it again.

But now, the same thing that had happened to him was happening to me. Videogames were infecting my reality too. Had my father also experienced hallucinations? Was he—was *I*—schizophrenic? I *had* to know what he'd been thinking, had to dive back into his delusions and learn how they might be linked to my own.

WHEN I FINALLY WORKED UP THE COURAGE TO OPEN THE ATTIC DOOR AND STEP INSIDE, I spotted the boxes right away. I'd restacked them in the dusty corner where I'd first found them. They were unlabeled, so it took me a few minutes of shuffling them around before I found the one filled with my father's old role-playing games.

I put it down on the floor and began to dig through it, pulling out rulebooks and supplements for games with names like *Advanced Dungeons & Dragons, GURPs, Champions, Star Frontiers,* and *Spacemaster.* Beneath those was a stack of about a dozen of my father's old campaign notebooks. The notebook I was looking for was at the very bottom—where I'd hidden it from view over eight years earlier. I pulled it out and held it in my hands and looked at it. It was a battered blue three-subject notebook with 120 college-ruled pages. I brushed my fingertips over the name my father had written on the cover—a name that had haunted me ever since I'd first looked it up: PHAËTON.

In Greek mythology, Phaëton, aka Phaethon, is an idiot kid who guilt-trips his dad, the god Helios, into letting him take his sun chariot for a joy ride. Phaëton doesn't even have his learner's permit, so he promptly loses control of the sun, and Zeus has to smite him with a thunderbolt to prevent him from scorching the Earth.

I sat down cross-legged and placed the notebook on my lap, then examined its cover a bit more closely. In the bottom right corner, very small, my father had also printed *Property of Xavier Lightman,* followed by his home address at the time.

Seeing that address triggered another flood of memories, because it was the same tiny house on Oak Park Avenue where my Grammy and Grampy Lightman had lived. The same house where I used to visit them almost every weekend when I was growing up. I would sit on their ancient sofa, eat homemade peanut butter cookies, and listen raptly as they told stories in tandem about their lost son, my lost father. And even though these stories they told about their only child were always laced with an undercurrent of sadness and loss, I still kept coming back to hear them again and again—until they both passed away, too, within a year of each other. Since then, my mother had been forced to bear the terrible burden of being my main living link to my father.

I took a deep breath and flipped the notebook open.

On the inside of its front cover, my father had created some sort of elaborate timeline—or as he'd labeled it, a "Chronology." This densely packed list of names and dates filled up every centimeter of the cover's white cardstock backing, and it looked as if my father had created it over a period of months or years, using a variety of pens, pencils, and markers. (No crayons, thankfully.) He'd also circled some of the entries before connecting them to other entries elsewhere on the timeline, using an overlapping web of lines and arrows that made the whole thing look more like an elaborate flowchart than a timeline:

CHRONOLOGY

> 1962—Spacewar!—First videogame (after OXO and Tennis for Two)
>
> 1966—Star Trek premieres on NBC TV (airs from 9/8/66–6/3/69)
>
> 1968—2001: A Space Odyssey
>
> 1971—Computer Space—First coin-op arcade game—port of Spacewar!

1972—Star Trek Text Game—BASIC program for early home computers

1975—Interceptor—Taito—combat flight sim with 1st person perspective

1975—Panther—First tank sim? PLATO network

1976—Starship 1—earliest FPS space combat videogame—Trek inspired

1977—Star Wars is released on 5/25/77. Highest grossing movie in history. First wave of brainwashing in prep for invaders arrival?

1977—Close Encounters released. Used to program the populace not to fear their impending arrival?

1977—Atari 2600 video computer system released, placing a combat training simulator in millions of homes! Ships with the game COMBAT!

1977—Starhawk. First of many videogames inspired by Star Wars

1977—Ender's Game short story. First instance of videogames as training simulators in SF? Published same year as Star Wars—coincidence?

1978—Space Invaders—inspired by Star Wars—first blockbuster game

1979—Tail Gunner, Asteroids, Galaxian, and Starfire all released.

1979—Star Raiders—released for Atari 400/800—ported to other systems.

1980—Empire Strikes Back released in movie theaters.

1980—Battlezone by Atari—first realistic tank simulator game

1981—March—US Army contracts Atari to convert Battlezone into "Bradley Trainer," a tank training simulator. Army claims only one prototype was ever made, but control yoke design used in many future games including Star Wars and PHAËTON!

1981—July—First Polybius sightings at MGP in Beaverton. Mid-July.

1982—E.T.: The Extra-Terrestrial—out-grosses Star Wars.

1982—The Thing, Star Trek II: Wrath of Khan

1983—Return of the Jedi!

1983—Starmaster—space combat simulator for the Atari 2600

1983—Star Wars: The Arcade Game by Atari & Star Trek: Strategic Operations Simulator by Sega—cabinets simulate cockpit

1984—Elite—released on 9/20/84

1984—2010: The Year We Make Contact—sequel to 2001

1984—The Last Starfighter released on 7/13! Videogame tie-in canceled?

1985—Explorers, Enemy Mine

1985—Ender's Game (novel) published—same premise as '77 short story

1986—Iron Eagle, Aliens, Flight of the Navigator, Invaders from Mars

1987—The Hidden, Predator

1988—Alien Nation, They Live

1989—The Abyss!

1989— PHAËTON cabinet sighted at MGP on 8/8/89. Never seen again.

1989—MechWarrior released—another training sim for military use?

1990—Wing Commander—released by Origin Systems—training sim?

1991—Wing Commander II

1993—Star Wars Rebel Assault, X-Wing, Privateer, Doom

1993—The X-Files—fictional alien cover-up created to conceal real one?

1994—Star Wars: TIE Fighter, Wing Commander III, Doom II

1994—The Puppet Masters, Stargate

1995—Absolute Zero, Shockwave, Wing Commander IV

1996—Marine Doom—Doom II modified for use by the USMC

1996—Star Trek: First Contact, Independence Day

1997—Men in Black, Starship Troopers, Contact

1997—Independence Day videogame tie-in released—Playstation and PC

1997—X-Wing vs. TIE Fighter

1998—Dark City, The Faculty, Lost in Space

1998—Wing Commander Secret Ops, Star Wars Trilogy Arcade

1999—Star Wars: Episode I

1999—Galaxy Quest

The release of the first *Star Wars* film in 1977 seemed to be the timeline's focal point. My father had circled that entry several times and drawn a series of arrows linking it to at least a dozen other items further down the timeline—including a bunch of videogames that the *Star Wars* franchise had helped inspire, like *Space Invaders, Starhawk, Elite,* and *Wing Commander.*

Armada wasn't listed on my father's timeline, of course—nor was any other game released in the past eighteen years. His final entry was the one noting the release of *Galaxy Quest* in 1999. I was born a few months later, and by the time I reached my first birthday, my poor father was already fertilizing daffodils at the local cemetery.

I spent a few more minutes puzzling over the timeline before turning my attention to the notebook's first page, which contained a pencil drawing of an old-school coin-operated arcade game—one I didn't recognize. Its control panel featured a single joystick and one unlabeled white button, and its cabinet was entirely black, with no side art or other markings anywhere on it, save for the game's strange title, which was printed in all capital green letters across its jet black marquee: POLYBIUS.

Below his drawing of the game, my father had made the following notations:

- No copyright or manufacturer info anywhere on game cabinet.

- Reportedly only seen for 1–2 weeks in July 1981 at MGP.

- Gameplay was similar to Tempest. Vector graphics. Ten levels?

- Higher levels caused players to have seizures, hallucinations, and nightmares. In some cases, subject committed murder and/or suicide.

- "Men in Black" would download scores from the game each night.

- Possible early military prototype created to train gamers for war?

- Created by same covert op behind Bradley Trainer?

Back when I'd first discovered the journal, I'd done a quick Internet search and learned that *Polybius* was an urban legend that had been circulating on the Internet for decades. It was the title of a strange videogame that only appeared in one Portland arcade during the summer of 1981. According to the story, the game drove several kids who played it insane; then the machine mysteriously vanished, never to be seen again. In some versions of the story, "Men in Black" were also seen visiting the arcade after closing time, to open up the *Polybius* machine and download the high scores from its data banks.

But according to the Internet, the *Polybius* urban legend had already been debunked. Its origins had been traced back to an incident in the summer of 1981, at a now-defunct arcade right here in Beaverton called the Malibu Grand Prix. Some kid collapsed from exhaustion after an *Asteroids* high score attempt and got taken away in an ambulance. Accounts of this incident were apparently conflated with another rumor circulating in the arcades at that time, about how the Atari arcade game *Tempest* caused some of the kids who played it to have epileptic seizures—which was actually true.

The Men in Black part of the urban legend also appeared to have roots in reality. In the early '80s, there had been an ongoing federal investigation into illegal gambling at various Portland-area arcades, and so during that time there really had been FBI agents spotted around local game rooms after closing time, opening up game machines—but this was to check for gambling devices, not to monitor gamers' high scores.

Of course, none of this information had come to light yet when my father had drawn his sketch of the *Polybius* game in his notebook sometime in the early '90s. Back then, *Polybius* would've just been a local urban legend—circulating around the very arcade where it had been born, Malibu Grand Prix. The same arcade my father had frequented when he was growing up.

On the second page of the notebook my father had drawn an illustration of another fictional arcade game, called *Phaëton*. My father's sketch of its cabinet was far more elaborate and detailed than his sketch of *Polybius*—perhaps because he claimed to have seen the game in person. Across the top of the page he'd written: "I saw this game with my own eyes on 8-9-1989 at Malibu Grand Prix in Beaverton, Oregon."

Then he'd signed his name.

According to his drawing, *Phaëton* had a sit-down cockpit-style game cabinet, which was sort of capsule shaped, like a *TRON* light cycle, with fake laser cannons built into each side of it, making the game itself look like a starship. Weirdest of all, it had *doors*. According to my father's sketch, the cabinet had two clamshell-shaped hatches made of tinted plexiglass, one on either side of the cockpit seat, which opened straight up, like the doors on a Lamborghini, and sealed you inside while you played the game. He'd also drawn a schematic of its control panel, which featured a four-trigger flight yoke, buttons mounted on each armrest, and another bank of switches on the cockpit ceiling. To me, it looked more like a flight simulator than a videogame. The entire cabinet was black, except for the game's title—printed in stylized white letters across its side: *PHAËTON*.

I hadn't been able to find any mention of a videogame by that name when I'd tried looking it up on the Internet eight years ago. I took out my phone and did another quick search on it. Still, nothing. According to the Internet, there had never been a videogame called *Phaëton* released anywhere, for any platform. That name had been appropriated for lots of other things, including cars and comic book characters. But there had never been an arcade game released with that title. Which meant the whole thing was probably a figment of my father's imagination—just like the Glaive Fighter I'd seen just half an hour ago was a figment of mine.

I glanced back at my father's illustration of the *Phaëton* cabinet. He'd drawn an arrow to the umlaut over the capital *E* in the word *PHAËTON* printed on its side. Next to the arrow he wrote: "Umlaut conceals hidden data port plug for downloading scores!"

As with his *Polybius* drawing, he'd made several bulleted notations down below—an apparent list of "facts" about the fictional game:

- Only seen at MGP on 8-9-1989—removed and never seen again.

- No copyright or manufacturer information anywhere. Plain black game cabinet—just like the eyewitness descriptions of Polybius.

- First-person space combat simulator—gameplay similar to Battlezone and Tail Gunner 2. Color vector graphics.

- "Men in Black" arrived at closing time and took game away in a black cargo van—also very similar to Polybius stories.

- Link between Bradley Trainer and Polybius and Phaëton? All prototypes created to train/test gamers for military recruitment?

I studied both the *Polybius* and *Phaëton* illustration for several more minutes. Then I flipped ahead to the journal entry describing *Battlezone*.

> 1981—US Army contracts Atari to convert Battlezone into "Bradley Trainer," a training simulator for the Bradley Fighting Vehicle. It was unveiled at a worldwide TRADOC conference in March 1981. After that, Atari claims project was "abandoned" and only one prototype was ever produced. But the new six-axis controller Atari created for Bradley Trainer was used in many of their upcoming games, including Star Wars.

This part of my father's conspiracy theory, at least, was true. From what I'd read online, a group of "US Army consultants" really had paid Atari to rework *Battlezone* into a training simulator for the Bradley Fighting Vehicle, and the United States Army really had pursued the idea of using videogames to train real soldiers, as early as 1980. As my father had also noted on his strange timeline, the Marine Corps had run a similar operation back in 1996, when they'd modified the groundbreaking first-person shooter *Doom II* and used it to train soldiers for real combat.

If he'd lived to see it, my father's timeline probably would have also listed the release of *America's Army* in 2002, a free-to-play videogame that had been one of the US Army's most valuable recruiting tools for over a decade now. An army recruiter had even let us spend a half hour playing it at school, just after we'd finished taking the mandatory ASVAB test—the Armed Services Vocational Aptitude Battery. I remembered thinking it was pretty weird that we were being encouraged to play a videogame simulation of warfare, right after being tested on our aptitude for it.

I continued to flip through the faded pages of my father's notebook, marveling at the time and energy he'd spent researching and puzzling over the details of the elaborate conspiracy he'd believed he was uncovering. Lists of names, dates, movie titles, and half-formed theories were scribbled across every page. But, I realized now, my ten-year-old self had been too hasty in dismissing it as gibberish. There was at least a hint of method lurking behind his seeming madness.

It looked as though the existence of *Bradley Trainer* and *Marine Doom* were two of the key pieces of "evidence" behind his vague, half-formed conspiracy theory, along with the classic science fiction novel *Ender's Game,* and two old movies, *The Last Starfighter* and *Iron Eagle.* My father had highlighted the release dates of these items on his timeline, and later on in the notebook he'd devoted several pages to describing and dissecting their storylines—as if they held crucial clues about the grand mystery he was trying to solve.

I smiled down at the list. I'd never even heard of *Iron Eagle* until I saw it mentioned in my father's journal and watched the VHS copy of it I found among his things. The film had instantly become one of my go-to guilty-pleasure movies. The hero of *Iron Eagle* is an Air Force brat named Doug Masters who learns to pilot an F-16 by cutting class to sneak into the base flight simulator—really just an incredibly expensive videogame. Doug is a natural pilot, but only if he's rocking out to his favorite tunes. When his dad gets shot down overseas and is taken captive, Doug steals two F-16s and flies over to rescue him, with a little help from Lou Gossett Jr., his Walkman, Twisted Sister, and Queen.

The result was a cinematic masterpiece—although sadly, it appeared to be recognized as such by me alone. Cruz and Diehl had both vowed never to sit through another screening of it. Muffit was still always happy to curl up and watch it with me, though, and our repeated viewings of the film, along with the *Snoopy vs. the Red Baron* album my mother insisted on playing every Christmas, had served as the inspiration for my *Armada* pilot call sign: *IronBeagle.* (When I posted in the *Armada* player forums, my avatar was an image of Snoopy in his World War I flying ace getup.)

I glanced back at his timeline once again. My father had drawn circles around the entries for *Iron Eagle, Ender's Game,* and *The Last Starfighter;* then he'd added lines connecting them all to each other—and now for the first time I finally understood why. All three stories were about a kid who trained for real-life combat by playing a videogame simulation of it.

I kept flipping pages until I came to the journal's second-to-last entry. In the center of an empty page my father had written the following question:

> What if they're using videogames to train us to fight without us even knowing it? Like Mr. Miyagi in *The Karate Kid,* when he

made Daniel-san paint his house, sand his deck, and wax all of his cars—he was training him and he didn't even realize it!

Wax on, wax off—but on a global scale!

The journal's final entry was an undated, rambling, half-illegible, four-page-long essay in which my father attempted to summarize the threads of his half-formed conspiracy theory and link them together.

"The entire videogame industry is secretly under the control of the US military," he wrote. "They may have even invented the videogame industry! WHY?"

Aside from his fictional *Polybius* and *Phaëton* drawings, he never gave much in the way of evidence. Just his own wild theories.

"The military—or some shadow organization within the military—is tracking and profiling all of the world's highest-scoring videogamers, using a variety of methods." Then he detailed one example—Activision's high-score patches.

Back in the '80s, the game company Activision had run a popular promotion in which players who mailed in proof of a high score—in the form of a Polaroid of the high score on their TV screen—received cool embroidered patches as a reward. My father believed Activision's patch promotion had actually been an elaborate ruse designed to obtain the names and addresses of the world's highest-scoring gamers.

At the end of the entry, using a different-colored pen, my father had added: "Much easier to track elite gamers now via the Internet! Was this one of the reasons it was created?"

Of course, my father never actually got around to specifying exactly what he believed the military was going to recruit all of the world's most gifted gamers to *do*. But his timeline and journal entries were filled with ominous references to games, films, and shows about alien visitors, both friendly and hostile: *Space Invaders, E.T., The Thing, Explorers, Enemy Mine, Aliens, The Abyss, Alien Nation, They Live. . . .*

I shook my head vigorously, as if it were possible to shake out the crazy.

Nearly two decades had elapsed since my father had first written all of this stuff in his journal, and in all that time, no secret government videogame conspiracy had ever come to light. And that was because the whole idea had been a product of my late father's overactive—perhaps even borderline delusional—imagination. The guy had grown up wanting to be Luke Skywalker or Ender Wiggin or Alex Rogan so badly that he'd concocted this elaborate, delusional fantasy in an attempt to make it so.

And that, I told myself, was probably the exact same sort of starry-eyed wanderlust that had triggered my Glaive Fighter hallucination. Maybe the whole incident had even been inspired by the contents of the very journal I now held in my hands. Maybe the memory of my father's conspiracy theory had been sitting up in a forgotten corner of my brain all these years, like a discarded crate of dynamite sticks sweating drops of nitroglycerin onto my subconscious.

I took a deep breath and exhaled it slowly, comforted by my half-assed self-diagnosis. Nothing but a mild flare-up of inherited nuttiness, brought on by my lifelong dead-dad fixation and somewhat related self-instituted overexposure to science fiction.

And I *had* been spending way too much time playing videogames lately—especially *Armada*. I played it every night and all day on the weekends. I'd even ditched school a few times to play elite missions on servers in Asia that were scheduled in the middle of the day over here. Clearly I had been overdoing it for some time now. But that was easy enough to remedy. I would just go cold turkey for a while, to clear my head.

Sitting there in the dusty attic, I made a silent vow to quit playing *Armada* entirely for two full weeks—starting right after the elite mission scheduled later that night, of course. Bailing on that wasn't even really an option. Elite missions only rolled out a few times a year, and they usually revealed new plot developments in the game's ongoing storyline.

In fact, I had spent the past week practicing and preparing for tonight's mission, playing *Armada* even more than I normally did. I'd probably been seeing Glaive Fighters in my sleep. No wonder I was seeing them when I was awake now, too. I just needed to cut myself off. To take a break. Then everything would be fine. I would be fine.

I was still repeating those words to myself, like a mantra, when my phone buzzed a reminder at me. *Shit.* I'd spent so long up here screwing around that I'd made myself late for work.

I got to my feet and tossed my father's journal back into its cardboard coffin. Enough was enough. The time had come for me to stop living in the past—my father's past, especially. A lot of his old stuff had migrated downstairs to my bedroom—an embarrassing amount, I now realized. My room was practically a shrine to his memory. It was high time I grew up and moved some—if not all—of that crap back up here, where I'd found it. Where it belonged.

I'd get started on that tonight, I told myself as I shut the attic door behind me.

3

WHEN I PULLED INTO THE HALF-DESERTED STRIP MALL WHERE "THE Base" was located, I parked a few spots away from my boss Ray's gas-guzzling pride and joy, a red 1964 Ford Galaxie with a faded bumper sticker that read: STARSHIP CAPTAINS DO IT ON IMPULSE.

As usual, the rest of the customer parking lot was empty, except for a small cluster of cars in front of THAI, the generically named Thai food restaurant at the other end of the strip mall, where Ray and I ordered copious amounts of takeout. We'd nicknamed the place "Thai Fighter," because the capital *H* on their sign had a circular bulge at its center that made the letter resemble an imperial fighter with Twin Ion Engines.

The sign mounted over the entrance of Starbase Ace was a bit fancier. Ray had designed it to look like a real Starbase was bursting out of the building's brick façade. It had cost him a fortune, but it did look cool as hell.

As I pushed through the front door, the electronic chime Ray had rigged up to it activated, playing a sliding-door sound effect from the original *Star Trek* TV series, making it sound like I was walking onto the bridge of the *Enterprise*. It still made me smile every time I arrived at work—even today.

As I walked into the store, a pair of toy laser turrets mounted on the ceiling swiveled around to track me, activated by their primitive motion sensors. Ray had taped a sign to the wall beside them that read WARNING: ANYONE CAUGHT SHOPLIFTING WILL BE VAPORIZED BY OUR TURBO-LASERS!

Ray was in his usual spot behind the counter, hunched over "Big Bootay," his ancient overclocked gaming PC. His left hand danced across its keyboard while he clicked the mouse with his right.

"Zack is back for the attack!" Ray bellowed, keeping his eyes on the game. "How was school, my man?"

"Uneventful," I lied, joining him behind the counter. "How's business today?"

"Nice and slow, just like we like it," he said. "Dost thou care for a Funyun?"

He proffered a giant bag of the simulated onion rings, and I took one to be polite. Ray seemed to subsist primarily on a diet of high-fructose junk food and old videogames. It was hard not to love the guy.

Back before I was old enough to drive, I used to ride my bike over to Starbase Ace every day after school, just to bullshit about old videogames with Ray and kill time until my mom got off work at the hospital. Either he recognized me as a kindred spirit, or he just got tired of my chronic latchkey kid loitering and eventually offered me a job. I was overjoyed—even before I discovered that my new position as assistant sales clerk involved about ten percent actual work and about ninety percent hanging out with Ray while we played videogames, cracked jokes, and ate junk food on the clock.

Ray once told me that he operated Starbase Ace "for kicks." After making a boatload of dough on tech stocks during the dot-com boom, he now wanted to enjoy his early retirement at the helm of his own private nerd lair, where he got to spend all day playing and talking about videogames with his like-minded clientele.

He was always saying he didn't give a damn if the store ever turned a profit—which was good, because it rarely did. Ray paid way too much for the used games we bought, and then immediately priced them for less than he'd just paid for them. He put everything on sale, all the time. He sold consoles, controllers, and hardware at no markup—to, as he put it, "foster customer loyalty and promote the gaming industry."

Ray was also terrible at customer service. He made people wait at the register if he was in the middle of playing a game. He also loved to talk shit about people's game selections while he was ringing them up, if he thought they were buying a lame or easy title, and I'd seen him drive both children and adults out of the store with his opinions on everything from cheat codes to crop circles. He didn't seem to care if his rude behavior drove him out of business. I did, though, which made for a strange employee-employer relationship, since I was usually the one who had to scold him for not being more polite to our customers.

I fished my Starbase Ace nametag out of a drawer and pinned it on. A few years ago, as a joke, Ray had put his nickname for me on there, so now it read: *Hello! My name is ZACK ATTACK.* He didn't know that "Zack Attack" was also the name my peers had saddled me with after "the Incident" back in junior high.

I stood there stalling for a few more minutes, then forced myself to walk over to Smallberries, our second enormous sales PC. I clicked its mouse a few times and opened a search engine. I glanced at Ray to make sure he wasn't looking my way, then typed in the words: *Beaverton, Oregon, UFO,* and *flying saucer.*

The only hits that came back were references to Flying Saucer Pizza, a local restaurant. There were no recent UFO sightings mentioned on the local TV station or newspaper websites. If anyone else had seen the same ship I had, they still hadn't reported it. Or maybe there had been a report, but no one had taken it seriously?

I sighed and closed the browser window, then glanced back over at Ray. If there was anyone I could have told about the Glaive Fighter, it was him. Ray seemed to believe that everything happening in the world was somehow connected to Roswell, Area 51, or Hangar 18. He'd told me on numerous occasions that he believed aliens had already made first contact with humanity decades ago, and that our leaders were still covering it up all these years later because "the sheeple of Earth" weren't ready to hear the truth yet.

But UFO cover-ups and alien abductions were one thing. Seeing a fictional alien spacecraft from a bestselling videogame series buzzing your town made even the craziest Roswell conspiracy theories seem sane by comparison. Besides, how was I supposed to walk over to Ray and tell him with a straight face that I'd seen a Sobrukai fighter buzzing our town—when he was, at that very moment, doing battle with that very same fictional alien race?

I walked over to get a better view of his huge monitor. Ray was playing the same videogame he'd been playing pretty much nonstop for the past few years—*Terra Firma,* a wildly popular first-person shooter published by Chaos Terrain, the same developer behind *Armada.* Both games shared the same near-future alien invasion storyline, in which Earth was being attacked by the "Sobrukai," a race of ill-tempered anthropomorphic squid-like creatures from Tau Ceti V who were hell-bent on exterminating all of humanity, for one of the usual bullshit reasons—they wanted our sweet-ass M-Class planet, and sharing shit just wasn't in their cephalopod nature.

Like nearly every race of evil alien invaders in the history of science fiction, the Sobrukai were somehow technologically advanced enough to construct huge warships capable of crossing interstellar space, and yet still not smart enough to terraform a lifeless world to suit their needs, instead of going through the huge hassle of trying to conquer one that was already inhabited—especially one inhabited by billions of nuke-wielding apes who generally don't cotton to strangers being on their land. No, the Sobrukai just had to have *Earth* for some reason, and they were determined to Kill All Humans before they took possession. Luckily for us, like so many made-up evil alien invaders before them, the Sobrukai also seemed intent on exterminating us as slowly and inefficiently as possible. Instead of just wiping out humanity with a meteor or a killer virus or a few old-fashioned long-range nuclear weapons, the squids had opted to wage a prolonged World War II–style air and ground war against us—while somehow allowing all of their advanced weapons, propulsion, and communications technology to fall into their primitive enemy's hands.

In both *Armada* and *Terra Firma,* you played a human recruit in the Earth Defense Alliance, tasked with using a variety of ground-based combat drones to fight off the invasion. Each drone in the EDA's arsenal was designed to serve as a direct match for a similar type of drone used by the alien enemy.

Terra Firma focused on humanity's ground war against the Sobrukai after their drones had reached Earth. *Armada* was an aerospace combat sim released the following year, allowing players to remotely control humanity's global stockpile of defense drones, and use them to battle the Sobrukai invaders out in space and over the besieged cities of Earth. Since their release, *Terra Firma* and *Armada* had become two of the most popular multiplayer action games in the world. I'd played *TF* religiously when it came out—until Chaos Terrain released *Armada* the following year, and then it had become my primary videogame obsession. I still played *Terra Firma* with Cruz and Diehl a few times a week—usually in return for them agreeing to play an *Armada* mission with me.

Ray also frequently coerced me into playing *TF* with him here at work, so my infantry drone skills were still sharp. This was essential, because in *Terra Firma,* the size and power of the drones you were allowed to control during each mission was based on your overall combat skill rating. Newbie players were only authorized to operate the smallest and cheapest combat drones in the EDA's arsenal. Once you increased in rank and skill, you were allowed to pilot increasingly bigger and more advanced drones—Spartan hover tanks, Nautiloid attack submarines, Sentinels (ten-foot-tall super-ATHIDs with more firepower), and the EDA's largest and most impressive weapon, the Titan Warmech—a giant humanoid robot that looked like something out of an old Japanese anime.

Ray happened to be controlling a Warmech at that very moment, and he was in trouble. I watched as a horde of alien Spider Fighters closed in on him. His mech finally succumbed to the incoming barrage of laser fire and toppled backward into a large tenement building, demolishing it. He and I both winced—in *Terra Firma,* players got penalized for all of the property damage caused by their drones in combat—intentional or otherwise.

Although the game's backstory embraced a lot of tired alien invasion tropes, it subverted many of them, too. For example, the Sobrukai weren't actually invading Earth in person—they were using drones to do it. And humanity had constructed its own stockpile of drones to repel them. So all of the aerospace fighters, mechs, tanks, subs, and ground troops used by both sides were remotely controlled war machines—each one operated by an alien or human who was physically located somewhere far from the battlefield.

From a purely tactical standpoint, using drones made a hell of a lot more sense than using manned (or aliened) ships and vehicles to wage an interplanetary war. Why risk the lives of your best pilots by sending them into combat? Now whenever I watched a *Star Wars* film, I found myself wondering how the Empire had the technology to make long-distance holographic phone calls between planets light-years apart, and yet no one had figured out how to make a remote-controlled TIE Fighter or X-Wing yet.

A warning message flashed on Ray's HUD: YOUR DRONE HAS BEEN DESTROYED! Then his display went dark for a second before a new message flashed on his HUD, informing him that he had just been given control of a new drone. But since all of his unit's larger drones and tanks had already been destroyed, Ray was forced to take control of the only thing they had left. An ATHID—Armored Tactical Humanoid Infantry Drone.

From the neck down, an ATHID looked similar to the original Terminator, after all of Arnie's cyborg flesh got burned away, leaving only its armored chrome skeleton underneath. But in place of a human-shaped head, each ATHID had a stereoscopic camera encased inside an armored acrylic dome, giving it a vaguely insect-like appearance. Every ATHID was armed with a Gauss mini-gun mounted on each forearm, a pair of shoulder-mounted missile launchers, and a laser cannon embedded in its chest plate.

I watched over Ray's shoulder as he used his ATHID's twin mini-guns to mow down an onslaught of Sobrukai Spider Fighters—eight-legged antipersonnel robots—that were attacking him on the roof of a burning tenement building, somewhere near the center of the besieged city he was helping defend. He was bobbing his head in time to his favorite *TF* battle soundtrack song, "Vital Signs" by Rush. Ray claimed that its unique time signature matched up perfectly with the alien Spider Fighter drones' erratic swarming patterns, making it easier for him to anticipate their movements and rate of attack. He also claimed that each of the other songs on Rush's *Moving Pictures* album was perfect for battling a different Sobrukai drone. Personally, I'd always assumed this was just an excuse he'd concocted for playing that same album on a continuous loop, day after day.

On Ray's monitor, dozens of Sobrukai troopships were descending from the sky. These massive, gunmetal gray octahedrons were what the enemy used to deploy their ground forces once they reached Earth's orbit. Each one had automated sentry guns mounted all over its heavily armored hull, which was nearly invulnerable to laser fire. Of course, in typical videogame fashion, these ships had been engineered with a glaring weak spot: their engines were unshielded and vulnerable to attack—a fact I knew well from playing *Armada*. When one of these diamond-shaped troopships made landfall, it would impact with enough velocity to bury its lower half into the surface, like a giant spike. Then the pyramid-shaped top half would open like an enormous four-petaled metal flower, and the thousands of Sobrukai drones packed inside it would pour out, like an army of newborn insects bursting from a broken egg sac, intent on devouring everything in sight.

In the distance, a swarm of Sobrukai Glaive Fighters streaked across the sky, banking in unison to change course, like a school of piranha in search of prey. Viewed from above, the Glaive's symmetrical fuselage resembled the blade of a double-headed axe, but seen edge-on, its profile distinctly resembled that of a flying saucer from an old sci-fi film—a detail that had worked its way into my earlier hallucination.

I'd destroyed countless Glaive Fighters during the three years I'd been playing *Armada*. Until now, I'd never found them especially frightening or ominous. But today, just seeing the background animations on Ray's screen filled me with a sense of dread, as if the ships really were somehow a threat to everything I held dear and not a harmless collection of textured polygons rendered on a computer display.

Ray power-leaped his ATHID off of the burning rooftop and onto the back of a Sobrukai Basilisk, a reptilian-looking robot tank with laser cannons for eyes. Ray power-jumped into the air again, spinning his

ATHID around 180 degrees just before he brought the huge metal Basilisk down with a single well-placed missile shot to its segmented abdomen. It exploded beneath him in a huge orange fireball, and Ray had to fire his ATHID's jump jets again to land clear of it.

"Bravo, Sergeant," I said, using his rank in the fictional Earth Defense Alliance.

"Thank you, Lieutenant," he replied. "I'm doing my best, sir!"

He grinned and raised his right hand off of his mouse long enough to snap me a salute before refocusing on the battle.

According to the readouts on his HUD, his squadron had already lost all six of their hover tanks, and both of their Titans. They only had seven ATHIDs left in reserve, and the pulsing icons on his tactical map indicated these were stored inside a nearby EDA weapons cache that was already under attack by a swarm of Spider Fighters. Ray's squadron was fighting a losing battle at this point. The city would fall to the Sobrukai any minute now. But as usual, Ray kept on fighting, even in the face of certain defeat. It was one of his most endearing qualities.

Ray was, by far, the best *Terra Firma* player I'd ever seen in person. A few months ago, he'd finally managed to earn membership in "The Thirty Dozen," an elite clan of the best 360 players in the game. Since then, I'd seen him logged on to *Terra Firma*'s servers every day, playing one high-level mission after another. And since he wasn't burdened with distractions like school or homework, Ray could devote his every waking moment to the game, so he'd logged more combat time than me, Cruz, and Diehl all put together.

"Son of a bitch!" Ray shouted, hitting the side of his monitor. I glanced over and saw that the Sobrukai were currently overrunning the surviving members of his squadron and exterminating the last of their drones. A few seconds after Ray's last reserve ATHID was crushed between a Spider Fighter's vise-like mandibles, the words MISSION FAILED flashed on his display, and then he was treated to a cut-scene animation of the Sobrukai's forces destroying downtown Newark.

"Oh well," he muttered, shoving another mouthful of Funyuns into his face as he pondered the city's smoking ruins. "At least it's only Newark, right? No big loss."

He chuckled to himself as he wiped simulated-onion dust off his fingers and onto the legs of his jeans; then he gave me an excited grin.

"Hey, guess what came in today?" he asked. Then he produced a large box from underneath the counter and set it in front of me.

If I'd been a cartoon character, my eyes would have bulged out of their sockets.

It was a brand-new *Armada* Interceptor Flight Control System—the most advanced (and expensive) videogame controller ever made.

"No way!" I whispered, examining the photos and stats printed on its glossy black box. "I thought these things weren't supposed to hit the market until next month!"

"It looks like Chaos Terrain decided to ship them early," he said, rubbing his hands together excitedly. "Want to unbox this bad boy?"

I nodded my head vigorously, and Ray grabbed a packing knife. He cut the box open and then instructed me to hold on to its sides as he pulled out the Styrofoam cube housing the controller's various components. A few seconds later, everything was freed from the packaging and laid out on the glass countertop in front of us.

The *Armada* Interceptor Flight Control System (IFCS) contained an Interceptor pilot helmet (incorporating a set of built-in VR goggles, noise-canceling headphones, and a retractable microphone) and a two-piece HOTAS (Hands-On Throttle and Stick) rig, comprised of an all-metal force-feedback flight stick and a separate dual-throttle controller with a built-in weapons control panel. The stick, throttle, and weapons panel all bristled with ergonomic buttons, triggers, indicators, mode selectors, rotary dials, and eight-way hat studs, each of which could be configured to give you total control of your *Armada* Interceptor's flight, navigation, and weapons systems.

"You likey, Zack?" Ray asked, after watching me drool over it for a while.

"Ray, I want to marry this thing."

"We've got over a dozen more back in the stockroom," he said. "Maybe we can build a display pyramid out of them or something."

I picked up the helmet and hefted it, impressed by its weight and detail. It looked and felt like a real fighter pilot helmet, and its Oculus Rift components were state-of-the-art. (I had a half-decent VR headset at home that Ray had gifted me, but it was a few years old, and the display resolution had increased drastically since then.)

"These new helmets can read your thoughts, too," Ray joked. "But you have to think in Russian."

I laughed and set the helmet back on the counter, resisting the urge to try it on. Then I reached out and rested my left hand on the throttle controller while I wrapped my right hand around the cold metal of the attached flight stick. Both seemed like a perfect fit, as if they'd been machined to match my hands. I'd been playing *Armada* for years, and the whole time I'd been using a cheap plastic flight stick and throttle controller. I'd had no idea what I'd been missing. I'd coveted an IFCS ever since I heard they were coming out on the *Armada* forums. But the price tag was somewhere north of five hundred bucks—even with my ten percent employee discount, that was still way too rich for my blood.

I reluctantly slid my hands off the controllers and shoved them into my pockets. "If I start saving up now, I might be able to afford one by the end of the summer," I muttered. "That is, if my crapmobile doesn't break down again."

Ray mimed playing a violin. Then he smiled and slid the helmet across the counter to me.

"You can have this one," he said. "Consider it an early graduation gift." He elbowed me playfully. "You *are* going to graduate, right?"

"No way!" I said, staring at the controller in disbelief. Then I looked up at Ray. "I mean—yes, I'll graduate—but, you're not kidding? I can have this one? For reals?"

Ray nodded solemnly. "For reals."

I felt like hugging him, so I did—throwing my arms around his thick midsection in a fierce embrace. He laughed uncomfortably and patted me on the back until I finally let go of him.

"I'm only doing it because it's good for the war effort!" he said, straightening his flannel shirt and then ruffling my hair in retaliation. "Having your own flight control system might make you an even better Interceptor pilot. If that's even possible."

"Ray, this is way too generous," I said. "Thank you."

"Ah, don't mention it, kid."

Although I'd been worrying for years that Ray's runaway altruism would drive him bankrupt, and that I'd be forced to go find a real job somewhere, it didn't stop me from accepting his latest extravagant gift.

"Want to head back in the War Room and give it a spin?" He motioned to the small, cramped back room where dozens of linked PCs and gaming consoles were set up. Customers rented the War Room out for LAN parties and clan events. "You could work out the kinks before that big elite mission later tonight. . . ."

"No thanks," I said. "I think I'll just wait and try it out then, on my home setup." *Because I might flip out or start foaming at the mouth the next time I see a Glaive Fighter coming at me, and I'd rather be alone in my bedroom if and when it happens.*

He cocked an eyebrow at me. "What's wrong with you?" he said. "You sick?"

I looked away. "No, I'm fine," I replied. "Why?"

"Your boss just offered you a chance to play your favorite videogame at work, on the clock, and you turn it down?" He reached out to touch my forehead. "You got a brain fever or something, kid?"

I laughed uneasily and shook my head. "No, it's just—I recently vowed to stop goofing off so much here at work, regardless of how much you encourage me to."

"Why in the hell would you do *that*?"

"It's all part of my master plan," I said. "To show you how responsible and reliable I've become, so you'll hire me on as a full-time employee after I graduate."

He shot me the same perturbed look he always seemed to give me whenever I brought up this subject.

"Zack, you can work here for as long as we manage to stay in business," he said. "Honestly, though, you have to know you're destined for much bigger things. Right?"

"Thanks, Ray," I said, struggling not to roll my eyes. If today was any indication, the only thing I was destined for was a straitjacket. Maybe a padded helmet, too.

"'You cannot escape your destiny,'" he said in his best Obi-Wan. Then he collapsed back onto his stool and fired up another *Terra Firma* mission with a click of his mouse. Chaos Terrain manufactured a wide variety of *Terra Firma* controllers, including the bestselling Titan Control System, a dual flight-stick rig that we sold right here in the store. But Ray never played with anything but a keyboard and mouse. He also still preferred a two-dimensional computer monitor to VR goggles, which he claimed gave him vertigo. Like a lot of gamers his age, Ray was set in his ways.

In spite of what I'd just said to him, I walked back over to Smallberries and clicked the *Terra Firma* icon on its desktop. The game's opening cut scene began, and I almost hit "Skip Intro" out of habit. But then I let it play, rewatching it for the first time in years.

The intro's somber opening voice-over (performed by Morgan Freeman, killing it like always) briefly laid out the game's basic storyline. It was set sometime "in the mid twenty-first century," roughly ten years after Earth was first invaded by the Sobrukai, an aquatic race hailing from the Tau Ceti star system, a popular point-of-origin for aliens since the dawn of sci-fi, due to its close proximity to Earth. The Sobrukai somewhat resembled the giant squids of Earth, but with an added mane of spiked tentacles and a vertical shark-like mouth ringed by six soulless black eyes.

The game's intro segued into a video transmission the invaders had sent to humanity on the day of their arrival, containing a threatening message from the Sobrukai overlord, whose Weta designers had gone way too Giger in my humble opinion. The gray translucent-skinned creature was shown floating in its dark underwater lair, its tentacles splayed out behind it, addressing the camera in its grating native language, which sounded sort of like a whale's song, if the whale in question was into death metal.

Thankfully, someone turned on the English subtitles just before the overlord began to make his evil alien species' somewhat clichéd intentions known.

"We are the Sobrukai," it said. "And we declare your pitiful species to be unworthy of survival. You shall therefore be eradicated—"

There was more to the overlord's message, but I hit the space bar to skip over it. I remembered the highlights. These malevolent unfeeling inkfish had traveled twelve light-years across interstellar space to wipe out humanity and then knock down all of our Pizza Huts, so that they could seize our rare blue jewel of a world as their own. It was my mission to use my baller videogame skills to stop them. Boo-yah. Press FIRE to continue.

The whole convoluted backstory behind humanity's ongoing war with the Sobrukai was available online, but gamers had to piece it together by digging through an elaborate network of Earth Defense Alliance websites—an alternate-reality game element meant to help players immerse themselves in the game's narrative. According to the information buried on those sites, at some point during the onset of the Sobrukai invasion a decade ago, the EDA had somehow managed to capture one of the aliens' ships undamaged, and then they had reverse-engineered all of its incredibly advanced weaponry, communication, life support, and propulsion technology—seemingly overnight—and then used it to construct a massive global arsenal of combat drones that were capable of going toe-to-toe with the Sobrukai.

Of course, the developers never bothered to explain how the EDA's scientists managed to accomplish these amazing feats in such a short time span while fending off constant attacks from the Sobrukai's vastly superior technology—but the way I saw it, if you were willing to suspend your disbelief enough to believe that a race of anthropomorphic extraterrestrial squids from Tau Ceti had been using an armada of remote-controlled robots to wage war on humanity for the past decade, it was pretty silly to nitpick over plot holes and scientific inaccuracies. Especially if they justified evil alien overlords and dogfighting in space.

I closed the *Terra Firma* client and opened a web browser; then I pulled up Chaos Terrain's website. I clicked through to their website's "About Us" page and scanned it. As a longtime CT super fan, I already knew quite a lot about the company's history. It had been founded back in 2010 by a Bay Area videogame developer named Finn Arbogast, who quit a lucrative job working on the *Battlefield* series for Electronic Arts to venture out on his own. He founded Chaos Terrain with the lofty goal of "creating the next generation of multiplayer VR games."

Arbogast had then assembled a dream team of creative consultants and contractors to help make his bold claim a reality, luring some of the videogame industry's brightest stars away from their own companies and projects, with the sole promise of collaborating on his groundbreaking new

MMOs. That was how gaming legends like Chris Roberts, Richard Garriott, Hidetaka Miyazaki, Gabe Newell, and Shigeru Miyamoto had all wound up as consultants on both *Terra Firma* and *Armada*—along with several big Hollywood filmmakers, including James Cameron, who had contributed to the EDA's realistic ship and mech designs, and Peter Jackson, whose Weta Workshop had rendered all of the in-game cinematics.

Chaos Terrain had created its own custom games engine for both *Terra Firma* and *Armada,* using many of the same programmers who had worked on previous combat-simulation game series like *Battlefield, Call of Duty,* and *Modern Warfare,* and on existing aerial and space combat simulators like *Star Citizen, Elite: Dangerous,* and *EVE Online.*

This plagiaristic, Frankenstein-like development strategy proved wildly successful. *Terra Firma* and *Armada* were two of the bestselling multiplayer videogames in the world, and with good reason. Their stripped-down arcade-style gameplay made both titles easy to learn and fun for casual players, but they were also scalable and dynamic enough to be challenging for everyday players like myself. Both games also had killer production values, and they could be played on any modern gaming platform, including smartphones and tablets. Best of all, the games weren't overpriced, like most MMOs. Sure, Chaos Terrain charged a low monthly subscription fee to play both *Terra Firma* and *Armada,* but once you got good enough to achieve the rank of officer in either game, CT waived your monthly fee and you played for free from then on. And they didn't use in-game microtransactions to milk players for extra revenue, either.

I closed the window and stared at the icons on the desktop, trying to sort out my thoughts. Until today, it had never occurred to me to make a connection between the alien invasion plotline of Chaos Terrain's games and the conspiracy theory outlined in my father's notebook. There were hundreds of alien-invasion-themed movies, shows, books, and videogames released every year, and *Armada* was just one of them. Besides, the game had only been out for a few years, so how could it possibly be connected to the stuff my father had written in his notebook decades ago?

On the other hand, if the government really did want to train average citizens to operate drones in combat, then multiplayer combat games like

Armada and *Terra Firma* would be exactly the sort of games you'd create to do it....

When the *Star Trek* door chime sounded a few minutes later and a gaggle of semi-regulars from the nearby junior high filed into the store, I shoved my new helmet, throttle, and flight-stick controllers back into their box and stowed it under the counter before any of the prepubescent hooligans could lay their covetous eyes upon it.

"Welcome to Starbase Ace, where the game is never over," I said, reciting the store's canned greeting with as much enthusiasm as I could muster. "How may I help you young gentlemen this evening?"

4

WHEN I GOT BACK HOME, MY MOTHER'S CAR WAS PARKED IN THE driveway. This was a pleasant surprise, because she'd had to work a lot of overtime at the hospital this past year, and most nights she didn't get home until I'd already crashed.

But knowing she was home also put me on edge, because she'd always been able to tell when something was bothering me. When I was younger, I was convinced she possessed some sort of mutant maternal telepathy that allowed her to read my mind, especially when there was crazy shit going on inside it.

I found my mother stretched out on the living-room sofa, with Muffit curled up at her feet, watching the latest episode of *Doctor Who*, one of her many televised addictions. Neither of them heard me come in, so I set my *Armada* controller box on the stairs and then just stood there for a moment, watching my mother watch her show.

Pamela Lightman (née Crandall) was the coolest woman I'd ever met, as well as the toughest. She reminded me a lot of Sarah Connor or Ellen Ripley—sure, she might have a few issues, but she was also the kind of single mom who would strap on heavy artillery and mow down killer cyborgs, if that was what it took to protect her offspring.

My mother was also ridiculously beautiful. I know people are supposed to say things like that about their mothers, but in my case it happened to be a fact. Few young men know the Oedipal torment of growing up with an insanely hot, perpetually single mom. Watching men constantly flip out over her looks before they'd even bothered to get to know her had made me faintly disgusted by my own gender—as if I didn't already have enough psychological baggage strapped to my luggage rack.

Raising me all by herself had been difficult for my mother, in lots of ways that probably weren't obvious to most people. For one thing, she'd done it without any assistance from her own parents. She'd lost her own father to cancer when she was still in grade school, and then her ultra-religious mother had disowned her for getting knocked up while she was still a senior in high school and then marrying the no-good Nintendo nerd who'd defiled her.

My mom had told me that her mother only tried to reconcile with her once, a few months after my father died. It didn't go well. She'd made the mistake of telling my mom his death was "a blessing in disguise" because it meant that now she could find herself a "respectable husband—one with some prospects."

After that, my mom had disowned *her*.

I secretly worried that one of the toughest things for my mother was the simple necessity of being forced to look at my face every day. I looked just like my father, and so far, the similarity had only seemed to increase as I got older. Now I was nearing the age he'd been at the time of his death, and I tried not to wonder how awful it must be for my mom to see her dead husband's doppelganger smiling at her from across the breakfast table every morning. Part of me even wondered if that might be why she'd become such a workaholic the past few years.

My mom had never played the part of the lonely widow—she went out dancing with her friends all the time, and I knew she dated occasionally, too. But she always seemed to end her relationships before they got serious. I'd never bothered to ask her why. The reason was obvious—she was still in love with my father, or at least with the memory of him.

In my younger years, I'd drawn a kind of perverse satisfaction from knowing how much she missed him, because it was proof my parents really had been in love, but now that I'd grown up a little, I was beginning to worry she might stay single forever. I didn't like the idea of her living here all alone in this house after I graduated and moved out.

"Hi, Mom," I said, speaking softly so as not to startle her.

"Oh hey, honey!" she said, muting the TV and sitting up slowly. "I didn't hear you come in." She pointed at her right cheek, and I dutifully went over and planted a kiss there. "Thank you!" she said, ruffling my hair. Then she patted the couch beside her and I sat down, pulling Muffit onto my lap. "How was your day, kiddo?" she asked.

"Not too bad," I said, punctuating the lie with a casual shrug to help sell it. "How was your day, Ma?"

"Oh, it was pretty good," she replied, mimicking my voice—and my casual shrug.

"Glad to hear it," I said, even though I suspected she was fibbing, too. She spent her days taking care of cancer patients, many of them terminally ill. I wasn't sure how she ever managed to have a good day at that job.

"You're not working late tonight?" I asked. "It's a Christmas miracle."

She laughed at our old family joke. Everything was a Christmas miracle at our house, all year round.

"I decided to take a night off." She swung her feet off the couch and turned to face me. "You hungry, babe? Because I'm craving cinnamon French toast." She stood up. "How about it, kid? Feel like having some breakfast-for-dinner with your mom?"

Her question made my spider-sense tingle. My mom only offered to make me breakfast-for-dinner when she wanted to have a "serious talk" with me.

"Thanks, but I had pizza at work," I said, inching backward. "I'm kinda stuffed."

She moved between me and the staircase, blocking my escape.

"You shall not pass!" she declared, stomping her foot down theatrically on the carpet.

"Your vice principal called me a little while ago," she said. "He told me you ditched math class early today—right after you tried to pick a fight with Douglas Knotcher."

I looked at her face and fought down a wave of anger, instead forcing myself to see how worried and upset she was, and how much she was trying to hide it.

"I wasn't trying to pick a fight, Mom," I said. "He was tormenting this other kid who sits near me. He's been bullying him for weeks. And I ran out of there because it was the only way to stop myself from tearing Knotcher's head off. You should be proud of me."

She studied my face for a moment; then she sighed and kissed me on the cheek.

"Okay, kiddo," she said, hugging me. "I know it isn't easy being stuck in that zoo. Just tough it out for a few more months and then you'll be free. Captain of your own destiny."

"I know, Ma," I said. "Two months. I'll make it. No worries."

"Remember," she added, biting her lip. "You're not a minor anymore. . . ."

"I know," I said. "Don't worry. Nothing like that will ever happen again, okay?"

She nodded. I could see that she was thinking about the Incident. The Incident that I'd just promised her, for the thousandth time, would never happen again.

Here's what would never happen again:

One morning, a few weeks after I started seventh grade, I was walking past Knotcher and a few of his friends in the hallway when he smiled at me and said, "Hey, Lightman! Is it true your old man was dumb enough to die in a shit-factory explosion?"

I'm not paraphrasing. That's a direct quote. There were eyewitnesses.

The next thing I remember, I was sitting on Knotcher's chest, staring down at his motionless, blood-drenched face, amid a cacophony of screams from our classmates. Then I felt a tangle of strong arms around my neck and torso, pulling me up and off of him—and found myself wondering why my knuckles were in agony, and why Knotcher was now curled in a bleeding heap on the waxed marble floor in front of me.

Afterward, they said I attacked him "like a wild animal" and beat him unconscious. They said I kept right on beating him, even after he went limp.

Apparently it took two other boys and a teacher to finally pull me off of him.

Knotcher spent a week in the hospital recovering from a mild concussion and a fractured jaw. I got off pretty light, considering—a two-week suspension and mandatory anger-management therapy the remainder of the school year, along with the nickname "Zack Attack" and a permanent reputation as the class psycho.

Far worse than any of that was the terrible ten-second gap the Incident had left in my memory, and the question it'd forced me to ask myself nearly every day since: What would I have done if there had been no one there to stop me?

Knotcher had probably seen a scan of my father's old newspaper obituary online. It was one of the only results that came up when you searched for his name. That was the way I'd learned how he'd died. My mother and grandparents had kept the details of his death from me while I was growing up—and I'm thankful they did, because that obituary had haunted me since the moment I'd first read it. I still had every word memorized:

Beaverton Man Dies in Wastewater Treatment Plant Accident

Beaverton Valley Times—October 6, 2000

A Beaverton man was killed at approximately 9am Friday in an accident at the city's wastewater treatment plant on South River Road. Dead is Xavier Ulysses Lightman, 19, of 603 Bluebonnet Ave., an employee of the city of Beaverton. The Washington County Coroner pronounced Lightman dead at the scene. Lightman was working near a storage tank when an undetected methane leak rendered him unconscious. Investigators surmised a spark from an exposed electrical circuit ignited the gas, and Lightman was killed instantly in the subsequent explosion. A lifetime resident of Beaverton, Lightman is survived by his wife, Pamela, and son, Zackary. Funeral arrangements—

"Zack, are you even listening to me right now?"

"Of course I am, Mom," I lied. "What were you saying?"

"I said that your guidance counselor, Mr. Russell, left me a voicemail, too." She folded her arms. "He said you missed your last two career counseling sessions."

"Sorry—I must have forgotten," I said. "I'll go to the next one, okay? I promise."

I tried to slip past her again, but she blocked my path and then stomped her foot down in front of me again, pretending like she was Gandalf and I was the balrog.

"Did you finally make a decision?" she asked, eyeing me.

"You mean, did I decide what I want to do with the rest of my life?"

She nodded. I took a deep breath and said the first thing that came to mind.

"Well, I have thought about this quite a bit, and after careful consideration, I've decided that I don't want to buy anything, sell anything, or process anything."

She frowned and began to shake her head in protest, but I kept going.

"You know, as a career, I don't want to do that," I went on. "I don't want to buy anything sold or processed, I don't want to sell anything bought or processed—"

"—or process anything sold, bought, or processed," she finished, cutting me off. "Who do you think you're messing with? Lloyd, Lloyd, all-null-and-void?"

"Busted," I said, raising my hands in a gesture of guilt. "That's what you get for making me watch that flick seven gajillion times."

She folded her arms.

"Zack, there's more than enough money set aside in your college fund to cover four years of tuition at most schools. You can go anywhere you want—and study anything you want. Do you know how lucky you are?"

Yep. I was lucky, all right. My mom had started that college fund for me when I was still just a baby, using some of the settlement money from my father's death that was left over after she bought our house. There had been enough to cover her tuition for nursing school, too.

Lucky, right?

Want to hear another stroke of great luck? My father's corpse was so badly burned in the explosion that the coroner had to use his dental records to identify the body, saving my mom from having to go to the morgue and identify his corpse herself.

How much good fortune can one family stand?

"Did you think over what we discussed last time?" she asked. "You promised to consider going to college to study how to make videogames, like Mike Cruz is planning to do?"

"I'm good at *playing* videogames, Mom," I said. "Not at making them. You need to be really good at programming or digital art, and I suck at both." I sighed and looked at my feet.

"The important thing is that you love gaming," she said. "You'd figure out the rest. You'd enjoy it." She smiled and touched my face. "You know I'm right. You've got gamer geek DNA on both sides."

It was true. You'd never know it to look at her, but my mom was a hardcore gamer in her day, too. She'd had a serious *World of Warcraft* habit for a few years. She was more of a casual gamer now, but she played *Terra Firma* missions with me sometimes.

"Aren't there people who get paid to play the videogames to test them out?"

"Yeah, they're called quality-assurance testers," I said. "The job sounds good in theory, but in reality it sucks. The pay is crap, and all you do is play the same level of the same game over and over thousands of times to try and find bugs in the code. That would drive me nuts."

She sighed and nodded. "Yeah, me too." She lowered her voice to a conspiratorial whisper, then smiled. "You know, Zack," she said, "you can enroll in college even if you're still not sure what you want to study. You just take a bunch of different courses and see what interests you. You'll figure out what you want to do eventually."

I smiled and nodded in agreement. But she still didn't budge.

"I'm not trying to pressure you, honey," she said. "I just want you to have a plan."

"My plan for right now," I slowly told my mother, "is to keep on working at Starbase Ace. Maybe switch from part-time to full-time—"

"That's an after-school job, Zack, not a long-term career plan. Think about what it would be like five years from now. Everyone else will be finishing college and starting a career, and you—"

"I'll still be sitting on my ass all day, five blocks from where I graduated, working the same crappy retail job I had when I was sixteen?" I finished for her.

"Exactly."

I tried to look hurt. "I find your lack of faith disturbing."

"You're going to find my foot jammed disturbingly far up your ass if you don't stop screwing around and start making a serious plan for your future, mister."

"When you call me 'mister' I know you're being super serious," I said.

"I'm not saying that you have to go to college, honey. Join a monastery! Join the Peace Corps! Join the fucking X-Men—I don't care what you do, as long as you do something. Okay?"

I pretended to sigh heavily in relief.

"In that case, maybe I'll run off and join the circus," I said. "I could start out as a weight guesser, then maybe work my way up to operating the Tilt-A-Whirl."

"I think you might have a few too many teeth for that line of work, smart-ass," she said, giving me a playful shove. "I'm not trying to give you a hard time, ace. I just want the best for you. You're so smart and talented, honey. You can do great things." She looked me in the eyes. "You know that, right?"

"Yeah, I know, Ma," I said. "Try not to worry, okay?"

She frowned and continued to block my path, arms folded to indicate that getting past her wasn't going to be that easy. But then, like a gift from the gods, my phone chimed to inform me I had a new text message. I fumbled it out of my pocket and studied its display: *Urgent Reminder—Earth Defense Alliance Command—Lt. Lightman, you are ordered to log in for your mission briefing at 8pm PST.*

I also saw that Cruz and Diehl had each sent me multiple text messages, asking what the hell had happened in class, and if I was still down for our *Armada* mission.

"Sorry, Ma, I gotta run!" I said, holding up my phone like it was some sort of hall pass. "I'm late for my *Armada* mission—it starts in just a few minutes!"

"Yeah, yeah," she said, rolling her eyes. "I know. Late for a videogame." She stepped out of my way. "Go on. Go get 'em, Maverick."

"Thanks!" I gave her a quick kiss on the cheek, which briefly inverted her frown. Then I grabbed the *Armada* controller box as I ran up the stairs and then down the hall, eager to reach the safety of my bedroom and the portal to another reality that lay beyond it.

But my mother's voice traveled faster than I did, and her final shouted warning reached my ears before I could clear the Neutral Zone. It was something I'd heard her say countless times growing up, and usually it made me want to roll my eyes at her. But this time, her words filled me with a genuine sense of dread.

"I know the future is scary at times, sweetheart. But there's just no escaping it."

5

LOCKED THE DOOR AND PRESSED MY BACK TO IT, AND WITH MY MOTHER'S WARNING about the inescapable nature of the future still echoing in my ears, I scanned the interior of my room, for the first time feeling a sense of shame over how I'd chosen to decorate it. The posters on my walls, the books and comics and toys on my shelves—nearly all of them had once belonged to my late father. The room couldn't even be classified as a shrine to his memory, because I didn't even remember the guy. This was more like a museum exhibit—a really sad, fucked-up one, devoted to a man I'd never even known, and never would.

No wonder my mother avoided coming in here. Seeing the décor probably broke her heart two or three different ways.

A small fleet of model spacecraft hung suspended from the ceiling on fishing line, and as I crossed my room, I brushed each of them with my fingertips, setting them in motion one after the other. First the starship *Enterprise,* then the *Sulaco* from *Aliens,* followed by an X-Wing, a Y-Wing, the *Millennium Falcon,* a Veritech Fighter from *Robotech*—and finally, a carefully painted Gunstar from *The Last Starfighter.*

I pulled the window shades down, plunging the room into darkness save for a narrow shaft of moonlight that fell on my battered leather gaming chair in the corner, casting it in an otherworldly glow. As I collapsed into the chair, I sang the first five bars of "Duel of the Fates" to myself in anticipation: *Dunt-dunt-dah-dah-dah!*

I grabbed my dusty game console and disconnected my old plastic flight stick and throttle controllers, along with my bulky first-generation VR headset, which was held together with copious amounts of black electrical tape. Once the old gear was set aside, I connected the various components of my new Interceptor Flight Control System and positioned them around my chair, placing the heavy metal flight stick on an old milk crate in front of me, directly between my knees, with the separate throttle controller on the flat armrest of my chair, within easy reach of my left hand.

This setup was supposed to re-create the exact layout of the Interceptor cockpit controls seen in the game. My own private starship simulator. Sitting there inside it, I remembered building a spaceship cockpit out of couch pillows in front of the television when I was a kid, in an effort to make the experience of playing *Star Fox* on my Nintendo 64 more realistic. I'd had the idea after seeing some kids do it in an old Atari commercial for *Cosmic Ark* on one of my father's videotapes.

Once I had my new controllers arranged properly, I synced my phone to the Bluetooth headphones built into my new *Armada* VR flight helmet. Then I cued up my *Raid the Arcade* playlist—my digital re-creation of an old analog mixtape I'd found among my father's things with that title carefully printed on its label in my father's handwriting. The title led me to assume it was a compilation of his favorite gaming music, and I'd grown up listening to those songs while I played videogames, too. As a result, listening to my father's old digital combat compilation had become an essential part of my *Armada* gaming ritual. Trying to play without my *Raid the Arcade* playlist on in the background invariably threw off my aim and my rhythm. That's why I made sure I had it cued up before the start of every mission.

I put on the faux Interceptor pilot helmet and adjusted its built-in noise-canceling headphones, which completely covered each of my ears. After I adjusted the VR goggles to make sure they fit snugly over my eyes, I thumbed the small button that extended the helmet's retractable microphone—a completely pointless, yet undeniably cool feature. Then I retracted and extended the microphone a few more times, just to hear the sound it made.

Once the game finished loading, I spent a few minutes customizing the button configuration on my new throttle and flight-stick controllers, then logged on to the *Armada* multiplayer server.

I immediately checked the EDA pilot rankings, to make sure my ranking hadn't slipped since my last login. But my so-cheesy-it-was-cool call sign was still there, in sixth place. I'd held that spot for over two months now, but a part of me was always still shocked to see it there, listed among the top ten, alongside the game's most famous—and infamous—players. I scanned the familiar collection of call signs, listed in what had now become a familiar order:

01. RedJive

02. MaxJenius

03. Withnailed

04. Viper

05. Rostam

06. IronBeagle

07. Whoadie

08. CrazyJi

09. AtomicMom

10. Kushmaster5000

I had been seeing these ten call signs almost every night for years, but I didn't actually know who any of those people really were—or where they lived, either. Aside from a few casual acquaintances at school and work, Cruz and Diehl were the only *Armada* pilots I'd ever met in real life.

The game had over nine million active players in dozens of countries, so clawing my way up into the top ten had been no easy feat. Even with what I've been told is a natural talent for videogames, it had still taken me over three years of daily practice before I even managed to crack the top one hundred. Once I'd crossed that threshold, I finally seemed to find my groove, and in the months that followed, I made a meteoric rise into the top ten while also rising up the ranks of the Earth Defense Alliance, earning one field promotion after another until I was promoted all the way up to lieutenant.

I knew *Armada* was only a videogame, but I'd never been one of the "best of the best" at anything before, and my accomplishment gave me a real sense of pride.

Admittedly, all the time I'd had to devote to the game had shaved a full point off my grade average, and it had probably cost me my relationship with Ellen, too. But I'd already vowed to turn over a new leaf, I reminded myself. After tonight's mission, no more *Armada* for at least two full weeks—even if that meant sacrificing my position in the top ten. No great loss, I told myself. The higher you were ranked, the more trash talk, friendly fire, and accusations of cheating you had to endure from the other players.

Case in point—the *Armada* pilots currently ranked in the top five were easily the most loathed players in the game's brief history. This was partly because the top five ranked pilots had the honor of "painting" their drones with their own customized multicolored designs, while the rest of us flew plain old stainless steel ones. That was how the top five had earned their nickname "The Flying Circus."

A lot of posters in the Chaos Terrain forums seemed to believe the top five pilots were just too good to be real players, and that they had to be NPC bots or Chaos Terrain employees. Others theorized they were an elitist gamer clan, because the five of them never responded to messages or in-game chat requests. Of course, that may have been because N00bs were always accusing them of cheating, by using some sort of client hack to auto-aim or give their shields infinite energy. But it was all bullshit sour grapes. I'd been going head-to-head with RedJive (aka "The Red Baron") and the other members of the Flying Circus on the free-for-all death-match servers for over a year now, and I'd never once seen any sign they were cheating. They were just better than everyone else. In fact, studying their moves and learning from them was how I'd climbed into the top ten.

I still found their general arrogance obnoxious, though—especially Red-Jive, who had an infuriating habit of sending the same text message every time he shot someone else down in the game's player-versus-player practice mode: *You're welcome.*

Those two words would flash on your screen, accompanied by a blood-boiling *BEEP!* RedJive obviously had a macro set up to fire that message like a missile, right after he blasted your ship to bits—literally adding insult to injury. I knew why he (or she) did it, too. It was a tactical move designed to anger his opponents and throw them even further off balance right before they respawned in another ship. And it worked, too. On everyone. Including me. But one of these days, when I finally got RedJive between my crosshairs, it would be my turn to send one of those infuriating texts: *No, no, no, RedJive. You're welcome.*

Of course, now I constantly got accused of hacking all the time, too. To quote my wizened boss, Ray Wierzbowski: "That's how you know you've mastered a videogame—when a bunch of butt-hurt crybabies start to accuse you of cheating in an effort to cope with the beatdown they've just suffered at your hands."

When I pulled up my friends list, I saw that Cruz and Diehl were both already logged in, their player rankings listed beside their call signs. Cruz (whose call sign was "Kvothe") was currently in 6791st place, and Diehl (aka "Dealio") was ranked 7445th. Their *Terra Firma* player rankings were much higher, but they were both still a long way from making it into the Thirty Dozen like Ray.

I switched on my helmet microphone and joined Kvothe and Dealio on their private voice-chat line.

"You still won't admit you're wrong?" Cruz was shouting as I logged in.

"I told you, your Wonder Woman argument proves nothing!" Diehl said. "Yes, Princess Diana of Themyscira did once wield Mjolnir in some obscure bullshit crossover issue! That only proves my point, Cruz! Do you think Wonder Woman would ever be caught dead wielding Sting?"

"No, but she's a superhero, and they don't use swords, do they?" Cruz said—clearly without thinking his statement through.

"Superheroes don't use swords?" Diehl said gleefully. "What about Nightcrawler? Deadpool? Electra, Shatterstar, Green Arrow,

Hawkeye—oh, and then there's *Blade* and *Katana*! Two superheroes who are actually *named* after swords! Oh, and Wolverine had that idiotic Muramasa Blade made with part of his soul. Which, while incredibly lame, was still a far cooler magical weapon than Sting!"

"Sorry to interrupt, ladies," I said. "I think you should just agree to disagree."

"Iron Seagull!" Cruz called out. "I didn't see you log in!"

"You're late, fool," Diehl said. "And Cruz won't shut up about Wonder Woman!"

"I'm right on time," I said. "The briefing doesn't start for another thirty seconds."

"What the hell happened with you and Herr Knotcher today?" Diehl asked. He said it with a thick German accent.

"Nothing happened," I said. "Because I split before anything did."

"Well, he was making threats toward you to his idiot friends after the bell rang," he said. "Vengeance in his eyes and all that. Plan accordingly."

I cleared my throat. "Time is short. Let's talk mission, guys."

"If this is another Disrupter takedown, I'm out, y'all," Cruz said. "I'll bail and play *Terra Firma* instead. I'm serious, guys."

"What's the matter, Kvothe?" I asked. "Don't you enjoy a challenge?"

"I enjoy balanced gameplay," Cruz replied. "I'm not a masochist like you."

I felt a brief impulse to defend the game, but it was hard to argue the point. The Disrupter was a powerful new weapon the Sobrukai had unveiled after one of the game's most recent content updates. It was capable of disrupting the quantum communication link to all of Earth's defensive drones, rendering them useless. For the past few months, all of the game's most devoted players—myself included—had been trying to figure out how to disable a Disrupter's defenses and destroy the damn thing. But so far the Sobrukai's new super weapon had proven to be indestructible, and that made many of the game's higher-level missions more or less unwinnable.

Despite the endless barrage of complaints claiming that Chaos Terrain had broken and/or ruined their own game, the company refused to remove the Disrupter from the enemy's arsenal or make it easier to destroy.

As a result, a lot of *Armada* players were defecting to play *Terra Firma*. The Disrupter never showed up in any *TF* mission—maybe because by the time one made landfall, there was nothing the EDA's ground troops could do to stop it.

"It's a new mission," I said. "Be optimistic. There might not be a Disrupter in it."

"Yeah," Diehl said. "Maybe the devs have cooked up something even worse."

"What could possibly be worse?" Cruz asked. "A mission where you have to blow up a Death Star while being attacked by two Borg Cubes inside an asteroid field?"

"Cruz," Diehl immediately chimed in. "I highly doubt that either the Borg or—"

Thankfully, an alert sounded in our headphones just then, signaling the start of the mission briefing. All of the data display windows vanished and I found myself seated in a packed briefing room, with Cruz's and Diehl's uniformed avatars Kvothe and Dealio sitting on either side of me. We had each customized our avatars so that they vaguely resembled our real selves—only slightly taller, more muscular, and less pale. The avatars of a few other last-minute arrivals were materializing in the tiered seats around us.

In the fictional near-future reality of *Armada,* Cruz, Diehl, and I were drone pilots stationed at Moon Base Alpha, a top-secret military outpost on the moon's far side. They were both lowly corporals, while I held the coveted rank of lieutenant.

The lights in the virtual briefing room dimmed, and the spinning crest of the Earth Defense Alliance appeared on the view screen in front of us. As the crest faded away, it was replaced by the familiar face of Admiral Archibald Vance, the Earth Defense Alliance's highest-ranking officer. The actor Chaos Terrain had hired to portray the admiral totally nailed the part. His jagged facial scar and eye patch might have seemed over the top on another actor, but this guy somehow managed to sell the whole look and make you believe he really was a battle-hardened military commander facing impossible odds with weary determination and grim resolve.

"Greetings, pilots," the admiral said, addressing us from the view screen.

"This evening's mission will not be an easy one—but it's one I know many of you have been hoping and waiting for since this war first began. Humanity has suffered countless unprovoked attacks from these alien invaders over the years, but now we're finally going to take this fight to them."

The corners of the admiral's mouth turned upward in the faintest hint of a smile—the closest I'd ever seen him come to displaying an emotion.

"Tonight, we're finally going to hit them where they live—literally."

The view screen window displaying the admiral's face shrank and moved to the top right-hand corner, while the rest of the screen displayed a technical diagram of a ship model I'd never seen before. Its design reminded me a little of the *Sulaco* from *Aliens*. Its elongated, armored hull made it look like a heavy-caliber machine gun drifting through the void of space.

"This is the EDA's first Interstellar Drone Carrier, the SS *Doolittle*. After traveling for over two years at nearly seven times the speed of light, the *Doolittle* has finally reached its target—and your target for this mission—the enemy's home planet of Sobrukai."

"Finally!" Cruz shouted over the comm, perfectly echoing my own reaction.

All of the previous *Armada* missions had been focused on defense, and the game's action had always been confined to our own solar system, oftentimes on Earth itself, in the skies over a major city or military outpost the Sobrukai were attacking, although we'd also locked horns with them out beyond the orbit of Mars, near the edge of the asteroid belt, and on the far side of the moon. This was the first mission that had ever involved an offensive against our enemy—and we'd hit the mother lode.

"As soon as the *Doolittle* reaches Sobrukai's orbit," the admiral went on, "it will deactivate its cloaking device before launching the Icebreaker, our weapon of last resort, along with an escort of fighters that will be under your control."

The admiral began to play the tactical pre-vis on the screen. The computer animation showed the cloaked *Doolittle* swinging into orbit above Sobrukai, and the armada of glittering warships that encircled its equator, like an artificial planetary ring. Spaced out evenly along this ring were six massive chrome orbs—Sobrukai Dreadnaught Spheres. The players had nicknamed them "muthaships." This was the first time we'd ever had to go up against more than one of them.

The bay doors embedded on the starboard side of the *Doolittle*'s bow irised open and the Icebreaker launched out of it, accompanied by a dense escort of three dozen fighters. The Icebreaker looked like what it was—a giant focused beam-laser bolted to an orbital nuclear weapons platform. The moment it began to fire its powerful melt laser down at the thick layer of ice covering the planet's surface, Sobrukai fighters began to pour out of the six Dreadnaught spheres, streaming forth from glowing, slit-like hangar doors that had opened in their armored skins, to engage with the comparatively tiny group of EDA fighters protecting the doomsday weapon being fired directly down at the icy roof of their squid crib.

"Eat it!" Diehl cried in mock triumph. "How does it feel, assholes? You like that?"

I smiled under my helmet. Diehl was right. After months of getting our asses handed to us on our home court, this chance to strike back at the Sobrukai on theirs was going to be hugely cathartic.

"Your mission is to keep the Icebreaker operational for approximately three minutes—just long enough for it to melt through the ice and launch its warheads into the planet's subsurface ocean, destroying the enemy's underwater lair, an aquatic hive located on the ocean floor."

The tactical animation showed our drone fighters handily defending the Icebreaker from the enraged enemy armada just long enough for it to finish melting its giant hole and launch its warheads through it, into the planet's subsurface ocean. At this point, the ICBMs transformed into guided nuclear torpedoes, which quickly homed in on the Sobrukai's underwater cave city, which looked like a high-tech hive built into the ocean's rocky floor.

"Now I feel bad," Diehl said. "Like we're about to nuke Aquaman. Or the Little Mermaid. . . ."

"Pretend they're Gungans," Cruz suggested. "And that we get to nuke Jar Jar."

They both laughed, but I was still focused on the tactical animation. It showed the EDA's torpedo nukes closing in on the Sobrukai's aquatic hive like a volley of squid-seeking missiles. A few of them were knocked out by the hive's defense turrets, but the vast majority reached their target.

The ensuing detonations lit up the view screen like an old-school game of *Missile Command*. Sobrukai Central was obliterated, and the force of the subsequent thermonuclear explosions rocked the planet so violently that cracks spread across the entire circumference of its icy surface, making it resemble a shattered hardboiled egg. There were no mushroom clouds—only a massive column of red steam rising from the massive hole burned in the surface, which shot straight up into orbit as if the planet were spraying blood from a gunshot wound.

"It's another suicide mission," Cruz said. "But it still looks fun. I'm in."

It looked as if our inept alien enemy had made another colossal tactical mistake. They had not only let their faster-than-light propulsion technology fall into our reverse-engineering monkey hands, they had *then* given us enough time to build an interstellar warship of our own and send it all the way across the vast gulf of space to launch a counterattack against them.

As usual, the alien invaders' tactics didn't make a whole lot of sense—and as usual, I didn't care. I just wanted to kill me some aliens, and this was the juiciest setup for a balls-out kamikaze mission in the history of the game—maybe *any* game.

In my headset, the admiral's voice was drowned out by the sound of Diehl pretending to snore. "Come on, old man!" he shouted. "Less talk, more rock!"

"Yeah, I wish we could skip this storyline crap," Cruz said. "Bor-ing."

"See, this is exactly why you two always get killed within the first two minutes," I said. "You never pay attention during the admiral's briefing."

"No, we always get killed because of *you*, Leeroy Jenkins!"

"I've asked you repeatedly to stop calling me that."

"If the shoe fits, Smack Attack!" Cruz said. "Why don't you try being a team player for once? Just once?"

"Interplanetary warfare isn't a team sport," I replied. "Never has been."

"Actually, it kinda *is*, if you think about it," Diehl chimed in. "The home team versus the visitors. Get it? Visitors?" After a pause, he added. "Because they're aliens."

"Yeah, we got it," I said. "Will everybody shut up so I can hear the rest of this?"

"This mission must succeed," the admiral was telling us now. "That armada is preparing to depart for Earth, so this is our one and only chance to destroy the Sobrukai before they come here to destroy us. The fate of humanity depends on the Icebreaker reaching its target." He paused to clasp his hands behind his back. "We're only going to get one shot at this, people, so let's make it count."

"Are you kidding?" Cruz shouted, as if the prerecorded actor could hear him. "This better not be a single-play mission. It's way too awesome!"

"He was just saying that for dramatic effect," I said. "I'm sure we'll be able to replay it—just like with the Disrupter scenarios."

"You better be right," Diehl said. "Because there's no way in hell we're going to pull this mission off on our first try—or our second or third, either. They've got six Dreadnaught Spheres! Each one loaded with over a billion killer alien drones—and a Disrupter to boot!"

"They won't activate one of their Disrupters here," Cruz pointed out. "It wouldn't have any effect. For a quantum link to be disrupted, both the transmitting and receiving ends have to be inside the sphere." That was the reason the EDA had drones and humans stationed on the far side of the moon.

"With no Disrupter to worry about, this should be doable," I said. "All we have to do is protect that Icebreaker for three minutes. No problemo."

"No problem?" Cruz repeated. "Really? You think so?"

"Yeah. We just—you know—create a blockade."

"With what?" Cruz said. "Did you check the mission stats? Our carrier only brought two hundred drones along! The admiral failed to mention that."

"Maybe he did it when you two were snoring?" I suggested.

"Like I said before, this is yet another example of unbalanced, poorly thought out gameplay," he continued. "The devs at Chaos Terrain are *trying* to piss us off now. We're gonna get slaughtered—again!"

"Yeah, yeah," Diehl said. "How do I get out of this chickenshit outfit?"

I laughed. Before Cruz could reply, we realized that Admiral Vance was bringing his chalk talk to a close.

"Good luck, pilots. Everyone down here on Earth is counting on you."

He snapped us a farewell salute, and his image winked out on the view screen, once again replaced by the Earth Defense Alliance crest.

Then, while the mission loaded, we were all treated to a familiar cut scene showing our squadron of heroic-looking, slightly out-of-focus EDA pilots sprinting out the briefing room's exit, down a brightly lit access corridor, and on into the Moon Base Alpha Drone Operations Control Center, a large circular room with dozens of oval hatchways embedded in the floor, spaced only a few meters apart—each containing a drone controller pod. Their hatches hissed open, revealing simulated Interceptor cockpits—each one a pilot seat surrounded by an array of controls and readouts, along with a wraparound view screen shaped like a cockpit canopy window.

The cut scene ended, and my perspective shifted back to my avatar's POV—only now I was sitting inside my own drone controller pod.

A second later, the hatch hissed closed above me just as all of the control panels around me lit up, as did the wraparound view screen. This created a second layer of simulation—the illusion that I was now sitting inside an ADI-88 Aerospace Drone Interceptor, powered up and waiting in its coiled launch rack in the *Doolittle*'s drone hangar.

I reached out to blindly place my hands on the new controllers in front of me, adjusting their placement to match the layout of my virtual cockpit inside the game. Then I took a deep breath and exhaled it slowly, trying to relax. This was usually the best part of my day, when I got to escape my suburban existence for a few hours and become a crack fighter pilot duking it out with evil alien invaders.

But tonight, I didn't feel like I was escaping anything. I felt anxious. Excited. Righteous. Maybe even a little bloodthirsty.

Like I was going to war.

6

THE GOGGLES INSIDE MY NEW *ARMADA* VR HELMET PROVIDED ME WITH AN immersive 360-degree view from inside my drone's simulated cockpit. Looking out through its wraparound canopy, I could see the *Doolittle*'s drone launch hangar. I glanced left and then right, taking in the row of identical Interceptors lined up on either side of me, gleaming under the hangar dome's floodlights, ready for launch.

My heads-up display appeared, superimposed over my wraparound view out of the cockpit, providing readouts of my starship's flight, weapon, and communication systems, along with radar, sensor, and navigation data.

I cleared my throat and addressed TAC, my ship's Tactical Avionics Computer. TAC served as a virtual copilot, managing my ship's navigation, weapons, and communication systems and providing me with verbal status updates. TAC could also give novice pilots helpful on-the-fly recommendations on how to improve their maneuvering techniques and weapon usage, but I'd disabled that feature long ago.

"TAC, prepare all systems for launch," I said.

"Compliance!" TAC chirped brightly. At the default setting, the computer spoke in a perpetually calm, synthesized female voice that I found unnerving in the heat of battle. So I'd installed several other custom sound profiles, including one called Trimaxion, which gave it the voice of the ship's computer in *Flight of the Navigator*. It made my ship's voice sound like Pee-wee Herman yelling through a vocoder, but this amused me and kept me on my toes.

Each Interceptor's thrusters, weapons, and shields were powered by a fusion reactor that constantly recharged its drone's power cells. But it did so at a very slow rate, so you needed to use your power sparingly during battle—otherwise you'd end up floating through space, a sitting duck with a dead stick.

It was easy to run out of juice during the heat of combat, because every time you moved or fired your weapons it used up some of your power, and whenever your shields took a direct hit, that drained your power cells, too. When they started to get too low, your drone would lose its shields first, then its weapons, and finally its thrusters. Then your drone would crash and burn—or, if you were lucky enough to be fighting in space, it would just begin to drift helplessly through the void while you waited for the power cells to recharge enough for your thrusters to come back online, praying that an enemy ship didn't pick you off first—which it almost always did.

The enemy Glaive Fighters had blaster turrets mounted on each of their wingtips that could rotate in any direction, giving them an almost unlimited field of fire. But my Interceptor's plasma cannons (aka "sun guns") and Macross missiles were both forward-firing weapons, so my target needed to be in front of me if I was going to be able to hit it. My ship had a laser turret, however, that was able to fire in any direction, but unlike my sun guns, the turret used up a lot of power and had to be used sparingly.

Our ships were also each equipped with a self-destruct mechanism, which also served as a weapon of last resort. As long as your drone had even a tiny bit of power remaining, you could detonate its reactor core in an explosion that could vaporize everything within a tenth of a kilometer. If you timed it right, you could take out nearly a dozen enemy ships at once with this tactic. Unfortunately, the enemy also had the ability to detonate their power cores—and they didn't care about taking out friendlies when they did it. A lot of players didn't either, of course. For some, it was their only real strategy. The only major downside to pulling this self-destruct move was that it meant you would miss at least part of the battle, because before you could fly back out to rejoin the fight, you had to wait to take control of another drone back inside the hangar, and then wait for it to reach the front of the launch queue—all of which could take up to a minute or more, depending on how fast the enemy was dropping our drones.

A klaxon began to sound as the hangar's belt-fed launch rack whirred into action and began to deploy the Interceptors slotted ahead of mine one after the other, firing them out of the belly of the *Doolittle* like bullets from a machine gun.

"Huzzah!" I heard Dealio say. "Now I finally get to kill some aliens!"

"Not if you get waxed before you fire a single shot," Cruz said. "Like last time."

"I told you, my Internet connection went out!" Dealio shouted.

"Dude, we heard you cursing on the comm *after* you got killed," I reminded him.

"That proves nothing," he said cheerfully. Then he shouted, "Cry havoc!"

When neither of us followed suit, he cleared his throat loudly over the comm.

"Uh, why didn't either of you cry havoc with me just now?" he asked. "You bitches best be crying me some havoc! You want to jinx us?"

"Sorry, Dealio," I said. Then, as loud as I could, I shouted, "Cry havoc!"

"I'll leaving the crying to you guys," Cruz said, before muttering his own personal pre-throw-down mantra to himself. "Led's-do-dis."

I cracked my knuckles, then pressed play on the best "ass-kicking track" on my father's old *Raid the Arcade* mix. As the opening bass line of Queen's "Another One Bites the Dust" began to thud over my helmet's built-in headphones, I felt myself begin to slip into the zone.

The song's machine gun beat was a perfect match for the timing and rhythm of the enemy's ships, in nearly every kind of mission. ("We Will Rock You" worked really well for me during shooting gallery scenarios like this one, too.) When Freddie Mercury's vocals kicked in a few seconds later, I cranked up the volume in my headset—apparently loud enough for my microphone to pick it up.

"Oh, great," Cruz said. "Sounds like DJ Geriatric is spinning again tonight. What a surprise."

"If it's too loud, you're too old, Kvothe," I shot back. "Why don't you mute me and put on the latest Kidz Bop compilation instead?"

"Perhaps I will," he replied. "They're unappreciated musical geniuses, you know."

The two drones Cruz and Diehl were controlling launched out of the hangar just ahead of me, each labeled with their call sign on my HUD.

"Attention, your drone is next in the launch queue!" my computer announced, with far too much enthusiasm. "Prepare to engage the enemy!"

The belt cycled forward again, feeding my drone into the launch tunnel and then blasting it out in space.

And then it was on like *Red Dawn*.

The first wave of responding enemy ships was already pouring out of the bottom of the nearest Dreadnaught Sphere like hornets from a metal hive and streaking down on us out of the blackness, approaching fast along our twelve o'clock.

A split second later, the space in front of my drone was filled with hundreds of Sobrukai Glaive Fighters, along with dozens of dragon-like Wyverns uncoiling and snaking through their swarming ranks, all of them moving in unison as they moved to attack the Icebreaker. I held my breath as I targeted one of the lead Glaives. I felt like I had a grudge to settle with the damn thing, for escaping from my fantasy life to invade my reality—and for making me question my own sanity in the process.

My three-dimensional tactical display flashed, warning me of a reactor detonation directly behind me, and I accelerated just in time to escape being caught in the blast.

Lasting longer than a few minutes in a battle of this size wasn't easy. Evading enemy fire required lightning-fast reflexes, wicked spatial awareness, and a gift for pattern recognition. You had to learn how to find the best route to cut through the enemy's ranks, retreating and attacking simultaneously.

Once I'd spent enough hours studying how the Sobrukai ships moved and attacked as a group, I gradually began to see the patterns hidden in all that chaos. Sometimes they moved like a flock of birds, chasing its own tail as it circled for a landing. Other times, they made sharp turns in the sky, like a school of predatory fish. But there was always a pattern to it, and recognizing it allowed me to anticipate the enemy's movements and reactions, and that made it relatively easy for me to get them in my sights—as long as I was listening to the right music. Music was key. The old rock songs on my father's old mixtapes were perfect, because they had a steady, hard-driving beat that served as my mental combat metronome.

I cut my engines and fired my retro-thrusters, swinging my ship around 180 degrees without altering or slowing my forward momentum. Then I opened fire on the swarm of Glaives converging on the Icebreaker's tail with a series of bursts from my sun guns.

When I hit my first target, it imploded into collapsing fireballs of super-heated plasma in front of me, and a message flashed on my HUD informing me I'd made the first kill of the engagement.

"One down, a few million to go," I announced over the comm, already buzzing with adrenaline. Killing videogame aliens had always been an outlet for my adolescent frustrations—but tonight it felt as though I was venting compressed rage each time I pulled the trigger.

It didn't matter that the Sobrukai were fictional—I still wanted to kill every last one of them.

"Guys, I've got two Glaives on my tail," Diehl announced. "Any help?"

"Help yourself, pal!" I heard Cruz say. "We're all getting our asses handed to us!"

"Not me," I replied. "I am officially in the zone."

I scanned my scopes, but neither Kvothe nor Dealio was currently visible, because the Icebreaker was now directly between us. I fired my lateral thrusters and did a series of diving barrel rolls to evade the incoming barrage of plasma bolts streaking past me on all sides. I also teased the throttle to vary my ship's speed and angle of ascent, while I lined up my omnidirectional laser turret's targeting reticle with a new threat—a train of three Glaives I'd just picked up on my tail, looming on my HUD's aft display.

The moment I got a targeting lock on the leader, I thumbed the laser turret's trigger. The beam only lasted for a split second and it wasn't visible with the naked eye, but its exact trajectory appeared on my HUD.

I watched as it burned through the hull of the Glaive closest to my tail, then continued burning on through the other two Glaives directly behind that one, destroying them in a rapid chain of explosions: *Boom! Boom! Ba-Boom!*

I powered down my already overheating laser, then switched back to my plasma cannons, which automatically reoriented my HUD so that it showed what was in front of my ship, instead of the dissipating fireball in its wake. Then I threw the throttle wide open. But as I passed under the Icebreaker and prepared to swing up on its opposite side, two more Glaives reappeared on my tail. They dropped in directly behind me and I started to take heavy fire, knocking my shields down by half and putting even more of a drain on my power cells, which were already dangerously low.

According to my HUD, the Icebreaker had been firing its melt laser for less than a minute, and the Sobrukai had already destroyed nearly half of our Interceptors. Reinforcements were still pouring out of the *Doolittle*'s hangar, but these drones were all piloted by players who had already gotten themselves killed once, and most of them would be destroyed a second time within seconds of rejoining the battle.

Cruz was right—we weren't going to be able to hold them off long enough.

"Screw this," I said. "I'm gonna try and create a diversion."

"Where are you going?" Cruz said over the comm. "Protect the Icebreaker, dumb ass!"

"Sorry, Cruz!" I said, pushing my throttle forward. "But you'll never guess who just showed up. *Leeeeeeroyyy—*"

"Oh, Lightman, don't you even dare!"

"*—mmm-Jenkinsss!*"

I broke formation with the others, leaving the Icebreaker behind as I moved to attack the nearest Dreadnaught. I slammed my throttle forward and crossed in front of it, strafing the turrets spaced along the sphere's equator, taking out one or two of them.

"Goddammit, Zack!" Cruz shouted. "Every time! Every goddamn time!"

I grinned and fired my thrusters, putting my fighter into an instantaneous vertical dive, with the intention of slipping under the sphere to strafe its shield. This maneuver cost me nearly a third of my remaining power, because my Interceptor had to momentarily activate its inertia-cancellation field to execute it. But I shook several of the Sobrukai fighters off my tail, because they needed to execute the same move to stay on me, and most of them didn't have enough power. Instead, they had to fishhook around behind me, then try to get a bead on my Interceptor again—when I was already gone.

Another swarm of Glaives emerged from the nearby Dreadnaught, all diving at the Icebreaker in a straight line, firing in tandem. I shredded them with a single sustained burst from my sun guns, bringing my Sobrukai kill count up to nine. Not bad, but also not up to my usual standards. My aim was a bit off.

"Shit!" I heard Diehl shout over the comm. "I just lost my gorram shields because I'm already out of frakkin' power!"

"Dude," Cruz said. "You shouldn't mix swears from different universes."

"Says who?" Diehl shot back. "Besides, what if *BSG* and *Firefly* took place in the *same universe*? You ever consider *that*?"

I heard a thunderous series of explosions behind me and swung my head around just in time to see the IDC *Doolittle* erupt into a huge fireball amid a hail of enemy plasma fire.

"What did I tell you?" Cruz muttered into his headset. "There goes the carrier, and the rest of our drone reserves."

"Yeah, and that goddamn Icebreaker still isn't finished making its stupid ice-fishing hole, either," Diehl added. "Game over, man. Game-the-fuck-over."

"Not yet," I muttered.

Clenching my teeth, I swung my Interceptor back around and returned to try to help defend the Icebreaker, targeting the cluster of Glaives attacking its aft thrusters—but I couldn't get a lock on any of the targets flashing on my HUD, because I kept having to dodge incoming enemy fire, as well as friendly fire from the sentry guns on the Icebreaker's armored skin as my drone skimmed over it.

My drone took two more direct hits, knocking my shields down to fifteen percent. One more hit and they would fail, and my weapons would follow soon after. Not good.

I jammed my flight stick forward, cutting into a sharp dive to avoid flying right into the beam of the Icebreaker's pulsing melt laser. Ignoring TAC's warnings about my drone's imminent power failure, I gunned the throttle and continued turning into a barrel roll, both sun guns still blazing.

"Shit!" I heard Diehl curse. "They got me, guys. I'm out."

I glanced at my HUD just in time to see Diehl's Interceptor vanish off my scopes.

"Me too," Cruz added a second later. He unleashed a colorful stream of profanity on his comm and logged out of the game completely.

The digital deaths of my two best friends distracted me just long enough to take another series of direct hits, causing my shields and weapons to fail. I immediately initiated the self-destruct sequence on my drone's power core, even though I knew it was unlikely I would last the seven seconds required for it to complete.

All of the Glaive Fighters in the vicinity began to redirect their fire at me, hoping to destroy my core before it could complete its countdown and go critical. But in doing so, they were momentarily forced to take their focus off the Icebreaker, just as I'd hoped.

Five seconds remaining on my drone's self-destruct sequence. Then four, three—

But that was when the inevitable happened—the Icebreaker finally took one hit too many and exploded directly beneath me. The ensuing fireball destroyed my drone, along with every ship within its blast radius.

Ominous music began to play in my headphones as the words MISSION FAILED appeared, superimposed over my now disembodied view of the Sobrukai armada, as each of the six Dreadnaught spheres began to recall their remaining drones and return to their original formation in orbit, with this minor threat to their world now vanquished.

I BLINDLY POWERED OFF MY GAME CONSOLE AND SAT IN THE DARKNESS FOR A MOMENT BEfore pulling off my VR helmet and returning to the real world with a sigh.

My phone rang a few seconds later. Cruz was on the line—he had already checked, and wanted to let me know that *Attack on Sobrukai* wasn't on the list of replayable missions—at least not yet. Then he conferenced Diehl in for his traditional post-mission bitch fest. After, the Mikes tried to cajole me into joining them for a *Terra Firma* mission, but I mumbled something about having homework and said I'd see them at school tomorrow.

Then I got up and went over to my closet. When I opened the door, a small avalanche of stuff spilled out onto my feet. I rummaged through the dense forest of dress shirts and winter coats on plastic hangers until I found my father's old jacket way at the back. It was an old black baseball jacket with leather sleeves, and it was completely covered, front and back, with embroidered patches, all somehow science fiction or videogame related, including several high-score-award patches for old Activision games like *Starmaster, Dreadnaught Destroyer, Laser Blast,* and *Kaboom!* Running down both sleeves were logos and military insignia from the Rebel Alliance, the Star League, the United Federation of Planets, the Colonial Fleet from *BSG,* and the Robotech Defense Force, among others.

I studied each one in turn, running my fingertips over the embroidery. When I'd last tried this jacket on a few years ago, it had still been too big on me. But when I slipped it on now, it fit me perfectly, almost as if it had been tailor-made.

I found myself itching to wear it to school tomorrow—despite my earlier vow to stop living in the past and obsessing over the father I had never known.

I looked around at the posters, toys, and models that filled my room and felt a pang in my chest at the thought of moving all my dad's prized possessions up into the attic. Despite my good intentions, it seemed I wasn't quite ready to let go of my father. Not yet.

I leaned back in my chair, stifling a yawn that did not wish to be stifled. I did a quick systems-wide status check, the results of which confirmed that my wagon was draggin'. Plutonium chamber empty. Sleep required immediately.

I took three steps toward my bed and collapsed facefirst onto my vintage *Star Wars* bed sheets, where I immediately fell into a fitful sleep.

My dreams that night were plagued by visions of a giant Sobrukai overlord constricting its enormous tentacles around a defenseless planet Earth as if preparing to swallow it whole.

7

WHEN I WALKED OUT TO MY CAR THE NEXT MORNING AND GLANCED down to unlock it, I saw the long sine-wave gouge that now ran bumper to bumper down the driver's side.

Someone had keyed my car. I turned to scan the surrounding houses, on the off chance Knotcher was still in the vicinity. But he was nowhere to be seen, and it occurred to me he had probably done this last night, while the Omni was parked outside Starbase Ace. I just hadn't noticed after work because it was dark out, and my car's paint job wasn't exactly unblemished to begin with.

I turned back to resurvey the damage, this time in the context of the vehicle's overall condition. The long scratch Knotcher had added would be barely noticeable to anyone else. One of the few perks of driving an ancient, rusted-out shit wagon was that it took real effort to make it look any less aesthetically pleasing than it already was.

This realization allowed me to calm myself enough to heed the whispered advice of Master Yoda now on repeat in my head: *Let go of your anger.*

I often tried to calm myself with Yoda's voice (which sounded nothing like Fozzie Bear, damn you) during moments of distress. Obi-Wan or Qui-Gon or Mace Windu sometimes had calming movie-quote wisdom to share too.

That was only on good days, of course. On the bad ones, I found myself drawing on equally compelling advice from Lords Vader or Palpatine.

But it wasn't their dark influence that motivated me to get the tire iron out of the Omni's trunk and place it inside my backpack. It was the voice of my friend Diehl, recounting his warning last night about Knotcher's threat to seek revenge.

I PARKED MY CAR IN THE STUDENT LOT AND TRUDGED TOWARD MY SCHOOL'S FRONT EN-trance while counting off the number of days remaining in my sentence—only forty-five more to go.

But when I reached the open grassy area bordering the parking lot, Knotcher was there waiting for me, along with two of his brain-trust buddies. All three were grinning, arms folded across their chests like goons in some *Power Rangers* episode.

My gaze shot over to the school's front entrance, calculating the distance. If I tried, I could probably make it there before they stopped me. But I found that I didn't want to.

Knotcher was standing out in front. As I'd feared, keying my car wasn't enough. He'd decided that his manhood was now in question, and that he had no choice but to corner me and deliver a beating—with some help, of course.

Knotcher's two gargantuan pals were known around school as "the Lennys," even though neither of them was actually named Lenny. They'd been saddled with this nickname after our class read *Of Mice and Men* in sophomore English. I didn't think the moniker really fit. Yes, they were both big and dumb, like the character in the book, but deep down, Steinbeck's Lenny had been a kindhearted soul. The two Lennys standing in front of me now (who I thought of as Skinhead Lenny and Neck-Tattoo Lenny, respectively) were both as mean as they were massive. But their size was dwarfed by the epic scope of their stupidity.

"Love your new jacket!" Knotcher said. He made a show of slowly circling me to examine each of the patches sewn onto it. "These are *really* impressive. Is there a little rainbow patch on there somewhere, too?"

After a few seconds of processing time, both of the Lennys chuckled—that was how long it took their reptilian brains to complete Knotcher's elegant rainbow-equals-gay equation.

When I failed to respond, Knotcher tried again.

"You know, that *sorta* looks like a varsity letterman's jacket," he said. "If being a videogame nerd who can't get laid was a sport." He laughed. "Then I suppose you'd be our star quarterback—eh, Lightman?"

I could already feel my anger spiraling out of control. What had made me think it was a good idea to wear my father's old jacket to school? I'd basically been inviting public ridicule on the one topic guaranteed to set me off—and of course Knotcher would be the one to take the bait. Maybe that was why I'd done it in the first place—the same reason I'd confronted Knotcher yesterday. Some angry caveman lobe of my brain was itching for a fight—and so I had orchestrated this confrontation. This was my doing.

Knotcher and the Lennys took a step toward me. But I stood my ground.

"At least you were smart enough to bring backup this time," I said as I slipped off my backpack and took both of its shoulder straps in my right hand, feeling the comforting weight of the tire iron inside.

Knotcher's smile momentarily faltered, then twisted into a sneer.

"They're just here to make sure you don't fight dirty," he said. "Like last time."

Then, in direct contradiction to what he'd just said, Knotcher nodded at the Lennys, and all three of them began to spread out, forming a rough semicircle around me.

In my head, I thought I could hear the cracked-but-commanding voice of Emperor Palpatine, saying, *"Use your aggressive feelings, boy. Let the hate flow through you!"*

"You're in deep shit now, eh, Lightman?" Knotcher sneered. "Kinda like your old man."

I knew Knotcher was trying to push my buttons. Unfortunately, he'd pushed the big red one first. The ICBMs had just left their silos, and now there was no recalling them.

I didn't remember unzipping my backpack, or taking out the tire iron, but I must have, because now I had the cold steel rod clenched in my hand, and I was raising it to strike.

All three of my opponents stood frozen for a moment, their eyes wide. The Lennys threw up their hands and started backing away. Knotcher's eyes flicked over to them, and I saw him registering that his simian pals had bowed out of the fight. He started moving backward too.

I looked at the curb a few feet behind him, had a nasty thought, and followed through on it by lunging at Knotcher with the tire iron. He lurched backward and—just as I'd hoped—caught a heel on the concrete rise and landed flat on his back.

And then I was standing over him, looking down at the tire iron clutched in my hands.

Off to my left, someone screamed. My head snapped around and I saw that an audience had gathered—a handful of students on their way in to first period. Among them one girl, too young and deer-in-the-headlights to be anything but a freshman, slapped a hand over her mouth and flinched backward as I looked her way. As if she was terrified that I—Zack the school psycho—would choose her as my next target.

I glanced back at the Lennys, who were now standing among the students who had gathered to watch the fight. All of the onlookers seemed to be wearing the same expression of horrified anticipation, as if they believed they might be seconds away from witnessing their first homicide.

A wave of cold shame washed over me as the intensity of my rage faded away. I looked down at the tire iron clutched in my hands and let it clatter to the pavement. I heard a chorus of nervous laughter behind me, along with more than one relieved sigh.

I stepped away from Knotcher. He slowly got to his feet. We stared at each other for a moment, and he looked as if he was about to say something when his gaze shot upward, focused on something in the sky behind me.

When I turned around, I saw a strange-looking aircraft approaching from the east, moving at an incredible speed. The closer it got, the more familiar it looked. My brain still refused to accept what my eyes were seeing—until a few seconds later, when the craft braked to a dead stop and hovered directly over us, close enough for me to make out the Earth Defense Alliance crest stenciled on the side of its armored hull.

"No *way*," I heard someone whisper. A second later, I realized it was me.

It was an ATS-31 Aerospace Troop Shuttle, one of the ships used by the Earth Defense Alliance in both *Armada* and *Terra Firma*. And it was about to land in front of my high school.

I definitely wasn't hallucinating this time: Dozens of other people were staring up at the shuttle in amazement, too. And I could hear the rumble of the shuttle's fusion engines and feel the heat from their exhaust buffeting my face. It was really up there.

As the shuttle began to descend, everyone in my vicinity scattered like roaches, heading for the safety of the school.

I just stood there like a statue, unable to look away. The ship was identical to the troop shuttles I'd piloted while playing *Armada,* right down to the EDA crest and identification bar code stamped on the underside of its hull.

The Earth Defense Alliance can't be real, Zack, I assured myself. *And neither can that shuttle you think you're looking at right now. You* are *hallucinating again, only it's much worse this time. This time, you're having a full-on psychotic break.*

But I couldn't make myself believe that. There was too much evidence to the contrary.

Okay, then you might be trapped inside a lucid dream, like Tom Cruise in Vanilla Sky. *Or maybe your reality is really just an incredibly convincing computer simulation, like in* The Matrix. *Or maybe you just died in a car accident, and this is all just an elaborate fantasy playing out in your brain during the last few seconds of your life—like in that one old* Twilight Zone *episode.*

As I continued to watch the Earth Defense Alliance shuttle land, I told myself that I had no choice but to roll with the situation as best I could—at least until I woke up, ran into Agent Smith, or heard Rod Serling begin his closing voice-over.

The shuttle lowered its landing gear and touched down softly on the broad sidewalk leading up to the school's main entrance. I glanced back at the school and saw faces filling the windows in every classroom while hundreds of students poured out of every school exit, eager to get a better look at the strange ship and find out what the hell was happening.

It was easy to tell which of them recognized the Earth Defense Alliance shuttle. They, like me, were the ones looking the most shocked right now. To everyone else, it probably looked like some new kind of military aircraft, a slightly futuristic cross between a helicopter and a Harrier jet, like the drop ships in *Avatar* or *Edge of Tomorrow*.

The shuttle's automatic doors slid open, and three men wearing dark suits jumped out. They looked like Secret Service agents. Our principal, Mr. Wood, stood there frozen for a few seconds, then rushed forward to greet them, his hand outstretched. After he shook hands with all of them, the shortest of the three men removed his sunglasses, and I heard myself gasp. It was Ray Wierzbowski, my boss at Starbase Ace.

What the hell was Ray doing here, dressed like one of the Men in Black? And where the hell had he obtained a working Earth Defense Alliance tactical shuttle?

I watched in a daze as Ray flashed some form of ID at Principal Wood. They conferred briefly and shook hands again; then Ray raised a small bullhorn and used it to address the growing crowd.

"We apologize for interrupting your morning, everyone," Ray said, in an uncharacteristically commanding voice that echoed across the school grounds. "But we desperately need to locate Zack Lightman. Does anyone know where he is right now? Zack Lightman? Please look around and point him out if you see him. We require his assistance with an urgent matter of national security. Zack! Zack Lightman!"

I realized Ray was saying *my* name about the same time I realized that everyone within my field of vision was now staring and pointing at me—including Knotcher and both Lennys. It was like that scene from *Invasion of the Body Snatchers*. Eventually, my public school training took over and I raised my hand and shouted "Here!"

When he spotted me, Ray grinned and started running across the grass toward me like his life depended on it. It was the fastest I'd ever seen him move.

"Hey there, Zack!" he said when he reached me, only slightly out of breath. Then he rested a hand on my shoulder and nodded at the gleaming shuttle behind him. "Wanna go for a ride?"

It's finally happening, Zack. The Call to Adventure you've been waiting for your whole life. It's standing right in front of you.

And I was scared shitless.

But I still managed to nod my head and mumble, "Yes."

Ray grinned—proudly, I think—and squeezed my shoulder.

"I thought so!" he said. "Follow me, pal. There's no time to lose."

As the entire school looked on, I followed Ray back across the lawn and over to the waiting Earth Defense Alliance shuttle. As the crowd parted to clear a path for us, I spotted my ex-girlfriend, Ellen, staring at me in disbelief from amid the sea of faces. The crowd swelled forward and I lost sight of her. I spotted Cruz and Diehl a few seconds later. They'd managed to push their way to the front of the crowd and were standing a few feet away from the two Secret Service types, who were now standing guard in front of the shuttle, holding the throng at bay with the force-field-like power of their buzz cuts and Ray-Bans.

"Zack!" Cruz shouted when we made eye contact. "What's happening? This is crazy!"

Diehl shoved him aside and tried to lunge in my direction, his arms flailing like a drowning man. "You lucky bastard!" he cried. "Tell them to take us, too!"

Then I found myself inside the shuttle, in the jump seat directly across from Ray and his two suited companions. The hatch slid closed, silencing the roar of the crowd. Following Ray's example, I buckled my safety harness across my chest and pulled it tight.

As soon as he saw that I was safely strapped in, Ray gave a thumbs-up to the lone pilot sitting up in the cockpit, who was wearing an honest-to-God Earth Defense Alliance uniform. For a few absurd seconds, I caught myself appreciating the attention to detail this dude had obviously put into his cosplay. Then he completed the shuttle's ignition sequence and fired its engines.

As we ascended, my internal monologue went something like this: *That isn't some guy cosplaying at SobruCon IV, Zack. To me, he looks like a real-life EDA pilot, in a real-life EDA uniform, who is currently piloting the real-life EDA shuttle you appear to be aboard. So, let me see now—multiply by two and carry the one—hey, that's really weird, but if my math is correct then THE EARTH DEFENSE ALLIANCE IS FUCKING REAL!*

I pressed my face to the curved window beside my seat and gazed down at my peers and teachers, still gathered in front of the school far below, already shrinking to the size of ants as we zoomed upward in a surreal blur of speed.

But when I closed my eyes, it didn't even feel like we were moving. No g-forces were pushing me back into my seat. The shuttle wasn't even shimmying or vibrating from turbulence as it climbed through the atmosphere.

Then I remembered—according to *Armada*'s backstory, all Earth Defense Alliance ships were outfitted with reverse-engineered alien technology, including a Trägheitslosigkeit Field Generator, which created a small inertia-cancellation field around a spacecraft, by "harnessing the aligned spin of gyromagnetic particles to alter the curvature of space-time" or something. I'd always assumed this was just more phlebotinum-powered pseudoscientific handwavium, concocted by Chaos Terrain's writers to make their game's impossibly kick-ass outer space dogfights seem mildly plausible, just as *Star Trek* and *Star Wars* used "inertial dampers" and "inertial compensators" so that Han Solo and Captain Kirk didn't get squished into heroic jelly every time they made the jump to light/warp speed.

I clamped my eyes shut again. It still felt like I was sitting in a car idling at a red light. So much for Sir Isaac Newton.

A DENSE LAYER OF CLOUDS OBSCURED THE STUNNING VIEW, AND I FINALLY MANAGED TO TEAR my eyes away from the window. I turned to face Ray. He was still smiling. His two stoic companions remained stonily silent and expressionless.

"Nice jacket," Ray said. But unlike when Knotcher had commented about it, there was no sarcasm in his voice. He leaned forward to admire the patches running down both of my sleeves. "I used to have a few of those Activision patches, you know. Not easy to get."

I stared back at him in disbelief. He was making small talk with me, as if we were still behind the counter at Starbase Ace. As if he hadn't just turned my whole notion of reality upside down and inside out.

I felt a wave of anger. Mild-mannered, middle-aged Raymond Wierzbowski—my employer, close friend, and surrogate father figure—had clearly lied to me about a great many things. The deceitful bastard obviously knew what was going on—and had for quite some time now.

"What the fuck is happening right now, Ray?" I asked, unnerved by the amount of fear in my own voice.

"'Somebody set up us the bomb,' pal," he quoted. "Now it's time to take off every zig for great justice."

He chuckled softly. I wanted to sock him in the face. Instead, I started shouting.

"Where did you get an Earth Defense Alliance tactical shuttle? How can this thing even be real? And where is it taking us?"

Before he could answer, I pointed at the two men seated beside him. "Who are those two clowns? For that matter, who the hell are *you*, asshole! Huh?"

"Okay, okay!" Ray said, throwing up his hands. "I'll try to answer your questions—but first you need to take a deep breath and calm down a little bit, all right?"

"Fuck calming down!" I shouted, straining against my safety harness. "And fuck you, too, Ray, you lying sack of shit! Tell me what's going on, or I'll lose it, I swear!"

"Okay," he said in a soothing voice. "But first, I need you to breathe, Zack."

He studied my face anxiously. I realized then that I did not, in fact, appear to be breathing. So I took a deep, gasping breath, then exhaled slowly. I felt a little better then, and my breathing began to normalize. Ray nodded, satisfied.

"Good," he said. "Thank you. Now go ahead and ask your questions again, one at a time, and I'll do my best to answer them, if I can."

"Where the hell did this shuttle come from? Who built it?"

"Isn't that obvious?" he said. "The Earth Defense Alliance built it." He nodded at his two companions. "And to answer your earlier question, these two men are EDA field agents, here to ensure your safe transport."

"No way," I said. "There's no way the EDA can be real."

"It's real," he said. "The Earth Defense Alliance is a top-secret global military coalition formed over four decades ago."

"Formed to do what? To 'defend Earth,' I suppose?"

He nodded. "Hence the name."

"To defend it from what?" I wanted to hear him say it. Out loud.

"From an alien invasion."

I studied Ray's face for any hint of irony, but his expression was now gravely serious. I glanced at his two companions to gauge their reaction, but they didn't even seem to be listening to our conversation. Both of them had taken out smartphones and were studying their displays.

I looked back at Ray. "An alien invasion? By who? The Sobrukai? Evil humanoid squids from Tau Ceti? You're gonna tell me they're real, too?"

"No, not exactly," he said. "The Sobrukai are fictional, invented by Chaos Terrain to serve as the alien antagonists in their videogames. But, as you're probably now realizing, *Armada* and *Terra Firma* aren't just games. They are simulators designed for a very specific purpose—to train citizens all over this planet to operate the drones that will defend it."

"Defend it from who? You just said the Sobrukai aren't real. . . ."

"They aren't," he said. "But they're stand-ins for a *real* alien threat, whose existence had to be kept secret until now to prevent global panic." He gave me an odd smile. "The name Sobrukai is actually a play on the word *sobriquet,* which is just a fancy term for *nickname*. Sneaky, eh?"

A terrible thought occurred to me. "Yesterday morning, I was sure I saw a Glaive Fighter. . . ."

"That was the real deal," he said. "You spotted a real enemy scout ship. EDA intel says a bunch of them have been spotted over the past twenty-four hours, all over the world. We think they're conducting surveillance on all of our hard-line intranet nodes—"

"But it looked exactly like a Sobrukai Glaive!"

"Of course it did," he said. "That's what I'm trying to tell you. Chaos Terrain modeled all of the Sobrukai's forces after our real enemy. They re-created their ships and drones as accurately as possible inside the sim—in the games. To make them as realistic as possible."

"So these aliens, they really have Glaive Fighters? And Wyverns—"

"And Dreadnaught Spheres, Spider Fighters, Basilisks—they all really exist," he said. "Chaos Terrain made up those names, but everything else about the enemy's drones in *Armada* is completely accurate. Their appearance, weaponry, maneuverability, tactics, and strategy—all were based on direct observations of our real enemy's forces and technology, made during our previous engagements with them."

"Previous engagements?" I asked. "How long have we been fighting them? Where are they from? What do they look like? When did they make first contact? If—"

He held up a hand to cut me off, sensing the hysteria creeping back into my voice.

"I can't tell you any of that yet," he said. "The information we've gathered on the enemy is still classified." He checked his watch. "But not for very much longer. You'll be fully briefed as soon as we reach Nebraska."

"Nebraska," I said. "What's in Nebraska?"

"A top-secret Earth Defense Alliance base."

I opened my mouth to reply, then closed it again. Then I repeated this process a few more times, until I actually managed to form words again.

"You said the EDA was formed over four decades ago. So we've known this alien invasion was coming for that long?"

He nodded. "Since the mid-seventies," he said. "That was when the EDA first began using certain elements of pop culture to subliminally prepare the world's population for the invasion. That's why the EDA secretly poured billions into the fledgling videogame industry back then—they recognized its potential military training applications." He smiled. "They helped get *Star Wars* made back in 1977 for pretty much the same reason."

"Pardon me?"

Ray held up three fingers—Scout's Honor. "I didn't believe it either, when I first found out. But it's true. *Star Wars* was one of the first movie projects the EDA helped finance, because their think tanks told them its unique subject matter could help the war effort. George Lucas never even found out about it. He always thought Alan Ladd Jr. deserved all the credit for green-lighting *Star Wars,* but in reality, the EDA put up a large chunk of the budget through a bogus network of film and television financing companies that could never be traced back to—"

"Hold on. You're telling me that *Star Wars* was secretly financed by the Earth Defense Alliance to serve as anti-alien propaganda?"

He nodded. "That's a gross oversimplification, but yeah—more or less."

I thought about the timeline my father had made in his old journal.

"What about all of the other science fiction movies and shows released over the past forty years?" I asked. "You're telling me they were all created as anti-alien propaganda, too?"

"Of course not," he said. "Not *all* of them. Just certain key properties, like *Star Wars,* which played a key role in the militarization of science fiction films, TV shows, and videogames in the late seventies. *Space Invaders* came out the year after *Star Wars* was released, and humanity has been fighting off videogame aliens ever since. Now you know why. The EDA made sure of it."

"Bullshit."

"It's true," he said. "All of the recent *Star Trek* reboots and *Star Wars* sequels were a key part of the final wave of the EDA's subliminal preparation of the world's population. I doubt that Viacom, Disney, or J. J. Abrams ever knew what was really going on, or who was pulling the strings."

I was quiet for a long time as I took all of this in.

"Why didn't you ever tell me about any of this?" I finally asked.

He gave me a sad smile. "Sorry about that, Zack," he said. "It wasn't up to me."

That suddenly drove it home. I had known this man for over six years, and that entire time he had been lying to me—probably about everything, including his identity.

"Who are you? Is Ray Wierzbowski even your real name?"

"Actually, no," he said. "My real name is Raymond Habashaw. I borrowed 'Wierzbowski' from one of the Colonial Marines in *Aliens*."

"I mentioned that once, and you told me it was a fucking coincidence!"

He shrugged and looked sheepish. It made me want to strangle him.

"I was given a new identity when the EDA stationed me in Beaverton in the first place—to keep an eye on you."

"To keep an eye on *me*? Why?"

"Why do you think?" he said. "You possess a very rare and valuable talent, Zack. The EDA has been tracking and profiling you ever since you first played a videogame online. That's why I was assigned to watch over you, and to help facilitate your training." He grinned. "You know, sort of like Obi-Wan, watching over Luke while he was growing up on Tatooine."

"You're a bold-faced liar like Obi-Wan, too!" I shot back. "That's for sure."

Ray's smile vanished, and his eyes narrowed.

"And you're being a whiny little bitch, just like Luke!"

The other two EDA agents snickered—they were apparently listening after all. I shot them a glare, and they conspicuously returned their attention to their smartphones. I glanced down at the devices they were holding, wondering how they were even getting a signal up here. Each phone was slighter larger and thicker than a normal mobile phone, and hinged so that it opened like a portable gaming console. One of the agents appeared to be playing a game of some kind on his, but I couldn't see his display well enough to tell what it was. I looked back up at Ray.

"Listen, I'm sorry," he said. "I didn't mean that. I just thought you'd be a little more appreciative, that's all. Do you think I enjoyed living in Beaverton all this time?"

Now I was beginning to understand. Ray had spent the past six years of his life stuck with what soldiers referred to as a "shit detail." Trapped behind the counter of a used videogame shop in a desolate suburban strip mall, with nothing to do but watch me play *Armada,* listen to all of my pointless adolescent bitching, or pass the time by ranting to me about alien abductions and government cover-ups—

All of his *X-Files*-inspired alien conspiracy rants over the years had probably been his own way of trying to psychologically prepare me for the truth, whenever the EDA finally decided that I deserved to hear it—which was right now, evidently. At the last possible fucking moment.

Of course, the truth—or at least some of it—had already been revealed to me years ago, back when I'd first read my father's journal. I'd just been incapable of believing it.

That led me to finally ask the question I'd been working up the courage to ask ever since I'd first boarded the shuttle.

"Was my father ever recruited by the Earth Defense Alliance?"

He let out a sigh, as if he'd been waiting for this question—and dreading it.

"I honestly don't know," he said. Before I could call him a liar again, he went on. "I'm telling you the truth, so just hold on now and listen to me!" He took a deep breath. "This isn't about your father, Zack. Try to understand what's happening—what's at stake. The entire future of the human race—"

"Just answer me! I read his journal—he knew about the EDA. He was starting to figure out what they were, and what they were up to, right before he died in some bizarre on-the-job accident. So what really happened? Did the EDA have him killed to keep him quiet?"

Ray was silent for what seemed like an eternity. But it may have only been a second.

"I told you, I don't know what happened to your father," he said. "I'm a lowly field agent, with equally low security clearance." He held up a finger to keep me from interrupting him again. "Here's what I *do* know: The EDA does have a file on him in their database. But it's classified, and I've never been able to access it. So I don't know what his connection was to the EDA, if there was one at all. But the EDA wasn't created to murder people. It was formed to save them."

I was hyperventilating now.

"Please, Ray," I heard myself say. "You know how important this is to me. . . ."

"Yes, I do," he said. "That's why you need to pull yourself together right now and focus; otherwise you'll ruin any chance to find out what they know about your father."

"What do you mean? What chance?"

"You're being transported to an enlistment briefing," he said. "Afterward, you'll be offered the opportunity to enlist in the Earth Defense Alliance."

"But—"

"If you take it, you'll be made a flight officer," he said, continuing to talk over me. "And then you'll outrank me." He looked me directly in the eyes. "You'll also have a higher security clearance than I do. You might be able to access your father's file."

Ray seemed about to say something more when a boom shook the entire shuttle. I felt a rush of panic, thinking we'd just come under attack. Then I realized we'd just broken the sound barrier.

"Hold on to your seat," Ray said, taking his own advice. "We're about to go suborbital."

Dozens of questions were still ricocheting around in my head, but I managed to put them out of my mind, at least for the moment. Then I forced myself to sit back and try to enjoy the rest of this surreal ride I now found myself on.

This was a smart move, because I was about to make my first trip into space.

PHASE TWO

All war is deception.

—Sun Tzu

8

CLUTCHED MY JUMP SEAT'S ARMRESTS, WATCHING ANXIOUSLY AS THE COBALT BLUE SKY outside the shuttle's porthole windows darkened to a deep shade of indigo, then on to pitch black just a few heartbeats later.

We were at the edge of space. The boundary I'd dreamed of crossing my entire life. I'd never really believed I'd get the chance to do it during my lifetime—let alone today, when I should've been in my first-period civics class.

I strained against my safety harness and craned my neck toward the curved window, trying to take in the entire radiant blue curve of Earth now visible beyond it. The sight was overwhelming, and made the little kid inside me involuntarily whisper, *"Wow!"*

Unfortunately, he must have whispered it out loud, because Ray was now staring at me with the same amused smirk he gave me every time he schooled me in a *Terra Firma* death match. I nearly flipped him the bird out of force of habit. Some thick part of my brain still thought Ray was my boss and friend.

We were only in low-Earth orbit for a minute. I kept waiting for the gravity to cut out, right up until the shuttle reached its apogee. No such luck. I still felt no indication that we were even moving—not even when we began to fall back to Earth and the blackness outside my window returned to a deep, dark blue and continued to grow lighter in hue every second until daylight flooded in again.

We sliced down through another dense layer of clouds, and suddenly the ground was rushing upward in a terrifying blur of speed. But then, in the space of a few seconds, we decelerated to a dead stop. I felt momentarily nauseous, but only because my eyes and my body were sending my brain conflicting information about whether or not I was in motion.

When I recovered a second later, I looked back out the window. Directly below us was a large white ranch house flanked by several barns and outbuildings and a long row of tower grain silos topped with steel domes that glinted in the morning sun, like rockets waiting to be launched. The farm was surrounded on all sides by a vast sea of fields and rolling green hills and prairies, broken only by a single dirt road that snaked away across the northern horizon. I also spotted three other EDA shuttles drifting in the sky around us, all descending on a course similar to our own.

As our shuttle continued its descent, one of the plowed fields adjacent to the farm collapsed in on itself, like a perfectly rectangular sinkhole, then split in two and slid apart, like two massive elevator doors set into the earth. They revealed an enormous circular shaft leading deep underground—like an empty missile silo, but much larger in diameter. The blue runway lights that lined its curved concrete walls pulsed in sequence as they receded into the depths below, guiding our shuttle down into the darkness.

"The EDA has bases like this one hidden all over the world," Ray said. "Some are in remote, unpopulated areas like this one. But we also have hidden drone caches and control bunkers located throughout every major city."

"Just like in *Armada*," I said. "And *Terra Firma*."

Ray nodded. "Everything is hidden in plain sight." He pointed below us. "Those outbuildings actually conceal the entrance of an underground infantry drone bunker. And those grain silos are camouflaged Interceptor launch tunnels. Amazing, eh? It's astounding how much the EDA has accomplished while working in secret all these years."

I nodded, still trying to rein in my conflicting emotions. Everything

I'd ever been told or taught about the state of the world had been a lie. I'd grown up believing that despite our aspirations, humans were still just a bunch of bipedal apes, divided into arbitrary tribes that were constantly at war over their ruined planet's dwindling natural resources. I'd always assumed that our future would end up looking more like *Mad Max* than *Star Trek*. But now I was forced to see our rampant fossil fuel consumption—and our seeming disregard for its effect on our already-changing climate—in an entirely new light. We hadn't used up all of our oil and ravaged our planet in a mindless pursuit of consumerism, but in preparation for a dark day that most of us hadn't even known was coming.

Even humanity's lack of concern for its rampant overpopulation problem now made a terrible kind of sense. What difference did it make if our planet was capable of supporting all seven billion of us in the long term when a far greater threat to our numbers was waiting in the wings? And despite the overwhelming odds, humanity had done what was necessary to ensure its own survival. It filled me with a strange new sense of pride in my own species. We weren't a bunch of primitive monkeys teetering on the brink of self-destruction after all—this appeared to be an altogether different kind of destruction we were teetering on the brink of.

Our shuttle was racing down the tunnel now, blurring the lights embedded in its walls into strobing neon bands as we plunged deep underground.

When we reached the bottom of the shaft a few seconds later, it widened into an enormous subterranean hangar, with a large circular runway that was now spread out below us. Our shuttle landed at its northern edge, joining a long line of identical EDA tactical shuttles parked along the runway's glowing perimeter.

As soon as the doors slid open, Ray unbuckled his harness, jumped out onto the runway, and motioned for me to follow. My fingers fumbled with the latch of my safety harness for a few seconds; then I finally slipped free of it. After I tested my legs to make sure they were both still working, I climbed outside to join Ray. The pilot and the other two EDA agents remained on board. Like an idiot, I awkwardly waved goodbye to them just before the shuttle doors closed again with a pneumatic hiss.

I checked the time on my phone and saw that the trip here from

Beaverton had taken less than twenty minutes. I also noticed that I wasn't getting a signal down here. Which meant I wouldn't be able to call my mom and tell her I was all right. Suddenly, I wanted very badly to hear her voice. Had the school called her yet? What had they told her? She had to be going crazy with worry right now.

Earlier that morning, when I'd stumbled downstairs, she'd surprised me with dinner-for-breakfast waiting on the kitchen table. Her "monstrous meatloaf" and mashed potatoes—my absolute favorite. She'd watched me stuff my face, grinning from ear to ear and pausing every few minutes to tell me to slow down and chew my food. I'd given her a quick kiss on the cheek and rushed out the door, worried that she might decide to revisit the dreaded subject of my academic future at any moment. She'd called out "I love you," and I'd mumbled it back to her as I continued hurrying out to my car. Had she heard me? I felt like kicking myself for not making sure.

"Welcome to Crystal Palace," Ray said. "That's the EDA's code name for this place."

"Why?" I asked.

He shook his head. "Because it's easier to say than 'Earth Defense Alliance Strategic Command Post Number Fourteen,'" he said. "Sounds cooler, too."

As we stepped away from the shuttle, I took in my new surroundings. Hundreds of people were hurrying around the runway in what appeared to be a state of highly organized chaos. Most of them wore Earth Defense Alliance combat fatigues like our shuttle pilot, and I found myself wondering if I was going to be issued a uniform, too.

I heard a rush of air over our heads and looked up to see a procession of four more shuttles descending through the entry shaft. As each one set down on the runway and discharged its passengers, other civilians like me emerged, escorted by one or more EDA agents wearing dark suits. Most of them appeared to be holding it together pretty well. A few of them looked terrified, like lambs being led to the slaughter, but the vast majority appeared to be having the time of their lives. I took quick stock of my own emotions, and I decided I fell somewhere in the middle.

There was a loud *whoosh* behind us as our shuttle lifted off again, and

Ray and I turned to watch it slowly rise and then rocket back up through the circular shaft to the surface.

"Follow me, pal," Ray said before striding off toward a pair of large armored doors set into the stone wall at the opposite end of the runway. They were already sliding open to reveal a broad, downward-sloping corridor that led even farther underground.

I stopped and called out to Ray, who turned and walked back to me as the other agents and recruits began to stream past us, continuing through the massive armored doors.

"What if I decide I don't want to enlist?" I asked. "What if I sit through this big briefing of yours and then decide I want to go back home?"

Ray smiled, as if he'd been waiting for me to ask this, too.

"Then I would remind you, Zackary Ulysses Lightman, that you are an eighteen-year-old citizen of the United States of America and therefore legally subject to military conscription."

This possibility hadn't occurred to me. "Wait, so—I'm being drafted right now?"

"Not really," Ray said. "No one's going to force you to fight. If you still want to go home after the briefing, just say the word. They'll put you on another shuttle to take you straight back to Beaverton—a first-class seat on the *Chickenshit Express*."

I didn't respond—I was already too busy nursing my wounded pride.

"I know you, Zack," Ray said. "You've been waiting your whole life for something like this to happen. Something important. Something meaningful. A *dare to be great* situation. Right?" He took me by the shoulders. "Well, this is it, ace! The universe has given you a chance to use your gifts to help save the world. Do you really expect me to believe that you're gonna pass it up to run home, sit on your ass, and watch the end of the world on TV?"

Ray let go of me and set off again. His footsteps echoed off the high stone walls as he passed through the open doors and down into the corridor beyond, disappearing from view.

I took one last look up at the tiny circle of sky still visible through the open shaft entrance high overhead. Then I ran after Ray.

―――――

THE ENTRANCE CORRIDOR LED DOWN TO A SECURITY CHECKPOINT WHERE A UNIFORMED EDA corporal named Foyle scanned my handprints and retinas to verify my identity, then stood me in front of a blue screen to snap a digital photo of my face. A few seconds later, the printer behind him spat out a photo ID badge with a holographic EDA crest on it, which he handed to me. Printed beneath my picture were my full name, social security number, and the words *Elite Recruit Candidate*.

As I clipped it onto my shirt, the corporal handed another badge to Ray. It had an old photo of Ray on it, along with: *Sergeant Raymond Habashaw—Field Operative*.

I wondered why our call signs weren't printed on our badges, but then it occurred to me that the EDA probably didn't want any of its recruits walking around with handles like "Moar Dakka" or "PercyJackoff69" printed onto their official identification cards.

Corporal Foyle reached under the counter and handed me a small hand-held device that resembled an extra-thick smartphone—the same sort of device I'd seen Ray and his two companions using during the shuttle ride here. The device was inside a protective case with a thick Velcro wrist strap attached to the back, which the corporal used to fasten the device to my right forearm, like an oversized wristwatch.

"This is your QComm," he explained. "It's a Quantum Communicator—basically a smartphone with unlimited range. It will work anywhere in the world—or in outer space." He smiled. "They also have insanely fast Internet access and Bluetooth capability. I already imported all of your contacts, photos, and music from your iPhone, so you're all set up."

I pulled my iPhone from the front pocket of my jeans. It still had no signal, and the battery was about to die. "How the hell were you able to do that?"

"Don't worry," the corporal said, ignoring my question. "Your QComm is far more secure—and versatile." He tapped its display. "It's like an iPhone, a tricorder, and a small laser pistol, all rolled into one device."

"Whoa, seriously?" I unsnapped it from my wrist to examine it more closely.

"Yeah," Foyle said, smiling proudly. "I'm sort of like Q in the James Bond films. Except, you know, I only get to hand out this one thing."

I turned the QComm over in my palm, trying to accept that I was holding a piece of reverse-engineered alien technology. I tapped the touch-screen and it lit up, displaying a large collection of icons. Email, Internet, GPS, and what looked like a normal phone dialer, along with other applications I didn't recognize.

"Can I call home with this?" I asked.

"Not yet," the corporal replied. "Your QComm's outside phone and Internet access will remain disabled until the big news goes public later today. But you're already connected to the EDA's quantum network, so you can call any other QComm in existence, if you have its contact code. Your code is printed on the back of the case."

I flipped it over in my hands and saw a ten-digit number etched onto the case. Ray pulled out his own QComm and touched the edge of his device to mine. I heard a soft electronic *ding,* and Ray's name and number appeared on my QComm's contact list.

"Now you can call me anytime, from anywhere," he said. "Even from the opposite side of the galaxy." He laughed an unsettling little laugh. "Not that it's likely to happen."

I gazed down at the QComm. It was hinged along one side, like a flip phone, and it opened up into what looked like a portable gaming device, with another display screen on top and a game controller beneath it, with two thumb-pads and six lettered buttons.

"What, can I play *Sonic the Hedgehog* on this thing, too?"

"Actually, yes," Foyle said. "Your QComm also doubles as a portable drone-control platform. In emergency situations, it can be used to control an Interceptor, an ATHID, or any of our other drones." He lowered his voice, as if imparting a secret. "They're a real bitch to use, though. Take a lot of practice."

Still leaning forward conspiratorially, the corporal whispered, "Each one also has a built-in weirding module." He raised his own QComm and crossed his wrists as he held it out in front of him. "By using sound and motion, you will be able to paralyze nerves, shatter bones, set fires, suffo-cate an enemy, or burst his organs."

I laughed out loud.

"That's the first weirding-module joke I've ever heard," I said. "Bravo."

"There were no weirding modules in the original *Dune* books, you know," Ray muttered, shaking his head. "David Lynch made that shit up."

"So what, Ray?" I said, feeling like we were back at the store. "They're cool as hell. I'm not saying it makes up for that super-creepy heart-plug scene—"

Foyle was seemingly all business again. "You should be all set," he said. "Your QComm's laser is currently disabled, but your commanding officer will activate it after you enlist."

"*If* I enlist," I said. "They still haven't even told me who or what is invading us."

"Right," he said, shooting Ray a surprised look. "Anyway, the laser will drain your battery after three or four shots, so if you have to use it, try to do so sparingly."

"Got it," I told the corporal. "So I'm all set?"

"Yes sir," he replied. "Good to go."

We all saluted each other again instead of waving goodbye; then the corporal remained at attention as we walked out of sight. I followed Ray through a pair of automatic doors into another downward-sloping hallway.

"Why didn't the EDA introduce all of this new technology into the mainstream?" I asked, studying the QComm on my wrist. "Ultrafast travel, quantum communication—it seems like that would have given a boost to the global economy and the war effort..."

"Our scientists spent decades reverse-engineering all of this alien technology, but they've only managed to perfect it in the last few years," he said. "I think the EDA would have gradually released it into the mainstream, if there'd been enough time."

We passed through two more security checkpoints, then proceeded down a long tubular corridor with lots of smaller corridors branching off of it, each lined with numbered doors spaced just a few feet apart. I was just about to ask Ray what was behind them when one hissed open and a female EDA officer emerged. Before the door closed behind her, I caught a glimpse of a tiny closet-sized room. In its center was a rotating chair bolted to the floor, surrounded by an array of ergonomic control panels and game controllers, along with a wraparound monitor displaying a first-person cockpit view from inside a giant EDA Warmech. "Drone controller stations," Ray said, following my gaze. "There are thousands of them located throughout the base. Each one can be used to remote-pilot an Interceptor, an ATHID, or any other drone in the EDA's arsenal—with no lag and no range limitations."

"You mean . . . real drones?"

"Real ones." He pointed behind me. "Here come a few right now." I turned to see a column of ten ATHIDs marching down the corridor toward us. I stood frozen as the robots lumbered by, joints clanking and servos whining. By the time they rounded the corner and vanished, Ray was already moving again and I hurried to catch up, still trying to get my bearings.

"Lieutenant Lightman?" a male voice called out.

Ray and I both stopped and turned around to confront the voice's owner. He was just a kid, even younger than me, with dark brown skin, hair, and eyes. There were captain's bars on his lapel and an Iranian flag was stitched onto the shoulder of his uniform. The young man held up a QComm and appeared to scan my face with it. Then an enormous smile appeared on his face when he saw my name appear on its display. He abruptly snapped to attention and saluted me.

"It's such an honor to finally meet you in person!" he said. "Captain Arjang Dagh, at your service. I'm a huge fan of your work, Lieutenant!"

"My work?" I repeated, glancing over at Ray uncertainly. "Lieutenant?"

"Sorry, sir," Ray said, returning Dagh's salute. "Mr. Lightman here hasn't been sworn in yet."

"Of course!" he said. "I knew that!" He grinned apologetically. "Sorry for stalking you with my QComm, 'Mr.' Lightman, but I've always wanted to meet you." He began to shake my hand and didn't stop. "The two of us have flown dozens of missions together over the years, so you might recognize my call sign." He put out his hand. I shook his hand as firmly as I could. "I'm Rostam."

My smile faltered and I let go of his hand. I recognized the name, all right.

"Wow, really?" I said, trying to recover by mustering a fake grin. "It's great to finally meet you, too. I always assumed I was the youngest pilot in the top ten."

"That honor appears to be mine," he replied, flashing me an infuriatingly humble smile. Then he turned to address Ray. "I'm currently ranked fifth," he said. "The IronBeagle here is in sixth." He smiled back at me. "But that's a recent development. For a long time I was chasing your tail."

"You deserve to be in the top five," I said, trying to hide how much his compliments were irking me. "You've trounced me on the player-versus-player servers more than once. You're an ace, man. Elite."

"Very kind of you to say," he replied. "That means a lot, coming from you."

Ray cleared his throat impatiently and pointed to his nonexistent watch. Captain Dagh gave him a perturbed glare, then jerked a thumb at the captain's bars on his lapel.

"Chillax, Sergeant," Dagh said. "The grownups are talking."

When Dagh turned back to face me, Ray reached out and mimed snapping his neck. "Yes, sir, Captain, sir."

Dagh smiled at me again; then he produced a glossy eight-by-ten photo from a plastic folder stuffed under his arm. It was a photo of me—an enlarged version of the one they'd just taken for my ID badge. He held it out to me sheepishly, along with a black felt-tip pen.

"Would you mind terribly signing this?" he asked. "I'm trying to collect autographs from all of the other pilots in the top ten, and I figured this might be my only chance to get yours."

I ignored the ominous subtext of what he'd just said and then used his pen to sign my first ever autograph. Then I handed the photo back to Dagh, wondering how many other *Armada* pilot autographs he'd collected so far today, and from whom.

"Thank you so much, Mr. Lightman," Dagh said. "Like I said, it was an honor."

He started to salute me again, then stuck out his hand instead. We shook.

"The honor was all mine, sir," I said. "I hope we run into each other again."

He reached out and touched his QComm to mine. Both devices beeped.

"I added my QComm number to your contact list," he said. "Don't hesitate to call me if I can help you with anything."

"I won't," I said. "Thanks."

He turned and hurried off in another direction. Once he was out of sight, Ray and I continued walking. We passed through another set of automatic armored doors.

"How old was that kid?"

"Who, Captain Dagh?" he said. "Seventeen. But he was only fifteen when the EDA first recruited him. He's a prodigy, though." He stopped walking and gave me a nervous glance. "Not to imply that you weren't—or aren't."

I felt like I'd just been picked last for the world's biggest game of kickball.

"I was ranked in the top ten, too," I said. "Why wasn't I recruited at age fifteen?"

He frowned and gave me an incredulous look.

"Your psych profile indicated you weren't suitable for early recruitment."

"Why not? Why wasn't I suitable?"

"Don't play dumb, 'Zack Attack,'" he said. "You know why."

Before I could respond, Ray turned his back on me and continued walking.

But before he could get out of sight, I swallowed my pride and hurried after him.

EVENTUALLY, WE ARRIVED IN A CIRCULAR LOBBY CONTAINING A LARGE BANK OF ELEVATORS. There were already several other "Elite Recruit Candidates" milling around, waiting for the next car to arrive. I was about to walk over and join them when Ray tapped me on the shoulder.

"This is as far as I go," he said. Then he looked me up and down, as if he were sending me off to my first day of school. He reached for my backpack, which was now mostly empty, and I handed it to him. Then before I could protest, he slipped my father's jacket off of me and began to fold it up.

"Hey, that's mine!" I said, hating how much I sounded like an angry child.

"Yeah, I know," he said. "And it's a very cool jacket—no argument. But wearing it into this briefing won't help you make the best first impression."

He stuffed the jacket into my backpack and forced the zipper closed, then put the pack back on my shoulders.

"Those elevators will take you down to the briefing auditorium," he said, pointing behind me. "Just follow those other recruit candidates."

I glanced across the lobby, over at the recruits forming a line at the elevators. Then I turned back to face Ray. "When will I see you again?"

"I'm not sure, pal," he said, meeting my gaze. "Things are happening very fast now. I'm departing on another shuttle in just a few minutes."

"Why?" I asked. "Where are they sending you?"

"To help defend the Big Apple," he said. "I'm one of the Thirty Dozen, remember?" He smiled and straightened his posture, then his lapels. "I've been assigned to the EDA's First Armored Drone Battalion," he said. "We'll be defending the Eastern Seaboard. So I'll be down here fighting them on the ground while you're up there, fighting them in the sky."

We stood there in silence for a moment; then Ray stuck out his hand. I hesitated for a moment, but then I shook it. In spite of everything, I still didn't want Ray to leave. He was the only familiar face in this place. While I was fumbling for a way to say goodbye to him without expressing any hint of forgiveness, Ray surprised me by throwing his arms around me in a fierce bear hug. Then I surprised myself by hugging him back, just as tightly.

"You've got a gift, Zack," he said, stepping back. "You really can make a difference in this war. Remember that, okay? No matter how frightening things get these next few hours . . ."

I nodded, but didn't reply. I had absolutely no idea how to respond to that—or to anything that was happening right now. I wasn't a soldier. I was just a kid from the suburbs who played a shitload of videogames. I wasn't prepared to fight an interplanetary war! At the moment, I didn't feel prepared for much of anything—not even to say goodbye to Ray.

"Okay, let's not make a scene," Ray said. "Take care of yourself for me, okay? And—" His voice caught. He cleared his throat and went on. "And when this is all over, let's make a pact to meet back at Starbase Ace. We'll order some Thai Fighter takeout and swap war stories. Deal?"

"Deal," I said around the lump rising in my throat.

Ray saluted me, and I saluted him back, even though I felt like a kid playing soldier.

"The Force will be with you," Ray said, giving my shoulder one last squeeze. "Always."

That was it. He turned and walked off, disappearing back the way we came. I stood for a moment, staring after him; then I glanced back over at the bank of elevators, where my fellow "Elite Recruit Candidates" continued to form an anxious queue.

9

FILED ONTO AN ELEVATOR WITH FIFTEEN OTHER RECRUITS. THEY VARIED DRASTICALLY IN age, gender, and ethnicity, but all of them wore a variation of the same dazed expression, which I knew was probably also mirrored on my own face.

As the elevator descended, we all stood there in silence, staring at the ceiling, our shoes, or at the closed doors in front of us—anything to avoid making eye contact. I wondered where each of them had been and what they'd been doing earlier that morning, when an Earth Defense Alliance shuttle had appeared out of nowhere to shatter their notion of reality, yank them out of their lives, and bring them here.

I also found myself wondering if I'd ever played *Terra Firma* or *Armada* with any of these people. It seemed possible—even probable. Hell, for all I knew, one of the people beside me could be the famed RedJive, in the flesh.

The elevator car had no floor indicator or control panel, just a single down arrow that lit up and beeped about twice every second as the car descended deeper and deeper belowground. I counted over twenty of those beeps before the doors finally opened again.

We stepped off the elevator into a large circular lobby that was already clogged with a procession of disoriented recruit candidates like ourselves.

Most were dressed in their normal street clothes like me, but for a wide variety of different climates. I also spotted people in business suits, fast food uniforms, surgical scrubs, and one dazed-looking middle-aged woman who was wearing a wedding dress and still clutching her bridal bouquet.

A line of EDA soldiers stationed around the lobby herded everyone through a long row of doors, into the adjacent sunken auditorium. As I filed into it with the others, I swiveled my head around to survey the layout. The enormous bowl-shaped auditorium had stadium-style seating that faced an enormous curved projection screen, making it look more like an IMAX theater than a top-secret underground briefing room. But the ceiling was a different story—it was a long, sloping grid of concrete waffle slabs, each reinforced with shock-absorption springs at its center. Like the rest of the base, the auditorium looked as if it had been built to withstand a direct nuclear blast on the surface above.

I swept my gaze around the auditorium, trying to decide where I should sit. At the foot of the giant screen, I noticed a low rectangular stage with a podium at its center. The first thirty or so rows in front of it were already filled with nervous recruits, and a steady stream of new ones were filing in and filling up the rows behind them, one after another, the way we did at school assemblies. But a few dozen less conformist (or more antisocial) individuals had chosen to sit much farther back, either by themselves or in scattered small groups.

I began to climb the nearest staircase, heading for the least populated seats in the upper third of the auditorium. Once I reached the nosebleed section, I began to look for a sufficiently isolated seat—then I froze in midstep.

She was just off to my right, sitting all alone in a deserted row near the back, taking brazen pulls from a chrome hip flask painted to look like R2-D2. Even seated, I could tell she must be a few inches taller than me. Her pale, alabaster skin contrasted sharply with her dark clothing—black combat boots, black jeans, and a black tank top (which didn't fully conceal the black bra she was wearing underneath). She had a spiky wave of black hair that was buzzed down one side and chin-length on the other. But the real kicker was her tattoos, on each arm: on the left was a beautiful seminude rendering of the comic book heroine Tank Girl, adorned in postapocalyptic rock lingerie and smooching an M16. On her right bicep, in stylized capital letters, were the words EL RIESGO SIEMPRE VIVE.

Seeing her was almost as jarring as when I'd first glimpsed that Glaive Fighter the previous afternoon. I had fallen for Ellen gradually, over a period of months. But this—this was like taking a lightning bolt from Mjolnir straight to the forehead.

I was still wondering if I had the courage to go sit near her when I realized I was already moving in that direction, as fast as my feet would carry me. As I climbed the stairs, it occurred to me that my emotions were probably not to be trusted under these heightened circumstances, but that thought was lost amid the influx of hormones flooding my brain as I made my way to the center of the row where she was sitting. I tried to convince myself that she looked like she could use some company—even though everything about her demeanor indicated the opposite.

When I reached her seat, she ignored me, leaving me standing there waiting for her to acknowledge my existence. As she continued to stare at her lap, I looked down at what was holding her attention and saw that she'd cracked open her QComm and had its electronic innards arrayed on her thighs, like she was performing an autopsy on the device—which I figured she was, since it seemed doubtful she would ever be able to put it back together.

But then she began to do just that, reassembling the QComm in seconds, with the speed and dexterity of a Marine field-stripping a weapon. When she finished putting it back together, she powered it on and watched the operating system reboot.

Then she finally raised her eyes to meet mine. I pointed to the seat beside her.

"Is it okay if I sit here?"

I know it's hard to believe, but I improvised this opening line right on the spot.

She gave me a quick once-over before answering.

"Sorry," she said. "I'm having a private conversation with my droid. Isn't that right, R2?" She raised her flask to her lips again, then waved it at the sea of empty seats spread out below us. "Why don't you go find another female of the species to mack on?"

"Don't flatter yourself, Vasquez." I nodded at her flask. "I'm just here to bum some of your booze."

She laughed, and I felt a sharp pain in the center of my chest. She glanced down at her *El Riesgo Siempre Vive* tattoo, clearly impressed that I knew its origin.

"All right," she said with an amused sigh. "Have a seat, baby face."

"Thanks, Grandma." I took the seat next to her and propped my feet up on the seat back in front of me, like she was doing.

"Did you just call me 'Grandma'?"

"Yeah, because just you called me 'baby face.' And it wounded my masculine pride."

She laughed again, louder this time, increasing the intensity of my chest pains.

She was even more gorgeous up close, and her eyes, which I'd thought were brown, actually appeared to be more amber colored, and her gold irises were shot through with streaks of copper.

"Sorry," she said. "You have a young face. How old are you?"

"Eighteen last month."

She smirked. "Too bad," she said. "I kinda have a thing for jailbait."

"Great," I said. "A pedophile with a drinking habit."

That got a third laugh—a snorting, girlish chuckle that disrupted my heart rate yet again. Then she glanced back down at her flask and addressed it in a confidential tone.

"R2," she muttered. "This dream just keeps getting weirder. Now a cute, wisecracking boy has shown up in it. What are the odds?"

I almost asked if she meant me. Disaster averted.

"I hate to break it to you," I said. "But you're not dreaming this."

"I'm not? How can you be so sure?"

"Because *I'm* clearly the one who's dreaming all of this," I said. "How could you be dreaming this, when you're just another figment of my imagination, like everyone else here?"

"Well, I hate to break it to *you*," she said, poking me with her flask and splashing some of its contents on my leg, "but I am not a figment of anyone's imagination."

That's a relief, I thought. But what I actually said was, "Unfortunately, neither am I." Then I offered her a smile. "So all of this must really be happening right now. To both of us."

She nodded and took another drink. "Yeah," she said. "That's what I was afraid of." Then she held out her flask, finally offering me a drink. But I shook my head.

"You know, on second thought, maybe I should keep a clear head for the briefing," I said. Then, as if that weren't lame enough, I added, "I'm not old enough to drink, anyway."

She rolled her eyes at me. "They're about to tell us the world is ending, you realize?" she said. "You don't want to be stone-cold sober for that shit, do you?"

"You make a compelling argument," I said, taking the flask from her.

As I raised it to my lips, she began to chant "Breakin'-the-law-breakin'-the-law."

I gave her a pleading look. "Please—don't make me shoot this out my nose, okay?"

She nodded solemnly and raised three fingers. "Girl Scout's honor."

I rolled my eyes. "I find it hard to believe that you were ever a Girl Scout."

Her eyes narrowed, then she reached out and rolled down her striped knee sock, revealing a dark green Girl Scouts of America logo tattooed on her left calf.

"I stand corrected," I said. "Are you hiding any other cool tattoos?"

She punched me in the shoulder—hard—then pointed at the flask, still in my hand. "Quit stalling, baby face. Bottoms up."

I took a small sip—but I still swallowed enough of the burning liquid to make me wince and cough. I didn't know enough about liquor to discern what she had in there, but my guess would have been rocket fuel mixed with a finger or two of paint thinner. I knew she was still watching me, so I forced myself to choke down a second, longer drink. Then I passed the flask back to her, all smooth-like, even though my eyes were watering and my throat felt like I'd just downed a shot of molten lava.

"Thank you," I said hoarsely.

"I'm Alexis Larkin." She stuck out her hand. "But my friends call me Lex."

"Nice to meet you, Lex." I felt a small static shock as we shook hands. "I'm Zack—Zack Lightman," I said, stuttering through my own name.

She grinned and reached for the flask, which I gladly handed back to her. "So, where do you hail from, Zack-Zack Lightman?"

"It's just one *Zack*," I said, laughing. "I'm from Portland, Oregon. What about you?"

"Texas," she said softly. "I live in Austin." Her expression darkened, and she took another drink—wincing at this one. "And I was just there, less than an hour ago, debugging subroutines in my cubicle, when a mother-fucking Earth Defense Alliance shuttle suddenly shows up and lands right outside my office building! I figured I must be losing it. Now I'm not sure what to think."

She shivered and rubbed her bare shoulders.

"It's cold as balls in here!" she said. "And I left my sweater in a different time zone."

I offered up a silent prayer of thanks to Crom, then opened my backpack and handed her my father's jacket.

"Wow," she said. "Badass. Thank you." She spent a few seconds admiring the patches; then she drew the jacket across her shoulders like a shawl.

"Where do you work?"

"At a software company. We make apps and operating systems for mobile devices. It was surreal when the shuttle landed outside our offices, because a lot of my coworkers are gamers, too. So a lot of us recognized the shuttle right away, even before we saw the Earth Defense Alliance crest on its hull. None of us could believe what we were seeing."

"What happened?"

"We all ran outside to the parking lot. Then two people wearing suits—a man and a woman—stepped out of the shuttle and asked for me by my full name, which was weirdly humiliating, like getting called to the principal's office or something. They said they needed my 'assistance with a matter of urgent national security.' What was I supposed to do? They were riding around in a spaceship from a videogame, and I knew I couldn't spend the rest of my life wondering what it looked like on the inside, or where it was going to take me—so I went with them." She nodded at our surroundings. "Now I'm in a top-secret government base somewhere in the middle of fucking Iowa, waiting to find out what the hell is happening. In short— I'm totally losing my shit."

She said all of this in a very calm, steady voice.

I nodded. "I think we're actually somewhere in the middle of fucking Nebraska."

"Yeah? How do you know?"

"Because Ray—the EDA agent who brought me here—said this was Nebraska."

"The jokers who brought me here wouldn't tell me shit," she said.

It hadn't occurred to me until now that I may have been given special treatment, but it seemed doubtful that all of the other recruit candidates in that auditorium had been mentored and watched over by an undercover EDA agent who had been stationed in their hometown for the past six years.

Lex glanced back down at her QComm, which had finished rebooting, and thumbed through the icons on its display.

"They better make good on their promise to unlock these things," she said. "I don't want my grandma to get too worried about me. She tends to do that if I don't call her every day—" Lex dialed a number on the QComm from memory, but a red X appeared on the display, along with a message that said, "Access to Civilian Networks Locked."

"We'll see about that," she muttered, scowling at the QComm before she slid it into her pocket.

"Are you and your grandma close?" I asked, just to hear her talk some more.

She nodded. "My folks both died in a car crash when I was little. My grandpa had already passed, so my grandma raised me by herself." She met my gaze. "How about you, Zack? Anyone back at home you're worried about? Anybody who'll be worried about you?"

I nodded. "My mom." I pictured her face. "She's a nurse. It's just the two of us."

Lex nodded, as if I'd explained everything. We both fell silent for a moment. I suddenly found myself wishing Cruz and Diehl were there with me. The insanity of this experience would have been much easier to handle with my two best friends around.

But even though the Mikes were skilled at both *Terra Firma* and *Armada,* their rankings apparently weren't high enough in either game to merit an invitation to these strange proceedings.

"Lex?"

"Zack?"

"Do you play *Terra Firma* and *Armada*?"

"TF."

"How good are you at it?" I asked. "Are you one of the Thirty Dozen?"

She nodded. "I'm currently ranked seventeenth," she said, far too nonchalantly. "But I've been as high as fifteenth. Those standings fluctuate a lot."

I whistled low, impressed. "Damn, woman," I said. "What's your call sign?"

"Lexecutioner," she said. "It's a portmanteau. What's yours?"

"IronBeagle," I told her, wincing at how dorky it sounded in my ears. "It's a—"

"It's fantastic!" she said. "I love that flick, as cheesy as it is. And my grandma used to play that *Snoopy vs. the Red Baron* album every Christmas."

I did a double-take at her. No one had ever gotten the *Iron Eagle/Peanuts* mash-up in my call sign without me first having to explain it to them—including Cruz and Diehl. I felt a strong urge to reach out and touch her shoulder, to confirm that she was real.

"You're not in the Thirty Dozen, otherwise I'd recognize your call sign," she said. "You must play *Armada*?"

I nodded, trying to hide my disappointment. "Not your game?"

She shook her head. "Flight simulators give me vertigo. I prefer to throw down with my feet on the ground." She pointed a thumb at herself. "You put me at the controls of a giant battle mech, I will crush my enemies and see them driven before me."

I grinned. "What about the lamentations of their women?"

"Oh yeah," she said, chuckling. "Their women lamentate all over the place. That goes without saying, doesn't it?"

We both laughed loudly, drawing annoyed stares from those seated within earshot. We appeared to be the only two people in that auditorium who were in a laughing mood—which made us laugh even louder.

When we regained our composure, Lex upended her flask and let the last few drops inside fall onto her outstretched tongue. Then she screwed the cap back on and stowed the flask in her jeans.

"'I've lost R2,'" she quoted, before mimicking the little blue droid's famous whistling sigh. This time, I was the one who snorted out an unexpected laugh.

"So spill it, Star Lord," she said. "What's your player ranking?"

"My *Terra Firma* ranking is too abysmal to say out loud," I said, laying on the false modesty with a trowel. "But in the *Armada* rankings I'm currently sixth."

Her eyes widened, and she swiveled her head around to stare at me.

"Sixth place?" she repeated. "In *the world*? No bullshit?"

I crossed my heart, but did not hope to die.

"That's some serious bill-paying skillage," she said. "Color me impressed, Zack-Zack Lightman."

"Color me flattered, Miss Larkin," I replied. "But you'd be a lot less impressed if you'd ever seen me play *Terra Firma*. I'm okay in an ATHID, but I can't drive a Sentinel to save my ass. I always end up stomping on a tenement full of civilians; then I get demoted back to the infantry."

"Doh! Collateral *and* property damage! You like to double down, eh?"

Before I could answer, the lights in the auditorium dimmed and a hush fell over the audience. I felt Lex grab my forearm and squeeze it tightly enough to cut off my circulation. I stared straight ahead, clutching the armrests of my seat, trembling with a lifetime's worth of accumulated anticipation as the screen in front of us was illuminated.

Then they showed us the most disturbing government training film in history.

10

N ANIMATED EARTH DEFENSE ALLIANCE LOGO APPEARED ON THE SCREEN, with the capital *E* and *D* in *EDA* morphing into a transparent shield that encircled a spinning blue Earth. The negative space between the legs of the stylized capital *A* formed the domed head of a Sentinel mech, while the space at the *A*'s center contained a lidded cyclopean eye, which I knew was meant to represent Moon Base Alpha, the secret Earth Defense Alliance installation on the far side of the moon. I wondered why the real EDA had chosen to include Moon Base Alpha in the crest, since the base itself obviously couldn't be real. Then I reminded myself—just a few hours ago, I'd thought the same exact thing about the EDA itself.

The EDA's Latin motto, *Si Vis Pacem Para Bellum,* appeared below the crest, then both faded away, leaving a vast field of stars on the screen, as ominous music swelled on the soundtrack. It was the opening track of the orchestral score for *Armada,* composed by none other than John Williams. When the London Symphony Orchestra's string section kicked in, I felt the hair on the back of my neck stand up.

I reminded myself that this was real life.

I reminded myself to keep breathing.

On the screen, an early NASA probe drifted into the shot, hurtling through the starry void. It looked like an old backyard satellite dish with three long outdoor TV antennas bolted to its base at right angles. I recognized it as one of the twin *Pioneer 10* and *Pioneer 11* spacecraft, the first two probes NASA sent to survey our outer solar system. They were launched in the early 1970s, so I knew the footage we were seeing had to be computer generated.

The camera swung around behind the spacecraft, revealing that it was fast approaching Jupiter. As the gas giant loomed on the screen, a voice began to speak over the music on the soundtrack. Lex and I both gasped with recognition, along with a chorus of others in the auditorium. We all recognized the voice instantly, even though its owner had been dead for nearly twenty years.

It was Carl Sagan.

And the first words he spoke contradicted nearly everything I'd ever been told about our current understanding of the universe.

"In 1973, NASA discovered the first evidence of a nonterrestrial intelligence, right here in our very own solar system, when the *Pioneer 10* spacecraft sent back the first close-up image of Europa, Jupiter's fourth-largest moon. It was received and decoded at the Jet Propulsion Laboratory in Pasadena, California, on December 3rd at 7:26 p.m. Pacific standard time."

It was immediately obvious to me why the EDA had recruited Dr. Sagan to narrate this film. Sagan's assured and familiar baritone imbued each word he spoke with the weight of cold, hard scientific fact—which was incredibly unsettling, because Sagan had been a driving force in humanity's search for extraterrestrial intelligence since the 1960s. If NASA had discovered aliens back in 1973 and Sagan had helped conceal it from the world for the rest of his life, he must have had an incredibly compelling reason for doing so—but for the life of me, I couldn't imagine what it could have been.

Maybe the EDA had somehow edited or simulated Sagan's voice for this film? Or maybe they had blackmailed him into doing it? Shit, for all I knew, the EDA might have a secret lab beneath the Pentagon filled with Axlotl Tanks, where they mass-produced Sagan and Einstein clones around the clock like Honda Accords.

Then a video image of Dr. Sagan himself appeared on the screen, and I stopped wondering whether it was really his voice. The footage was clearly from the '70s: Sagan looked younger than he did in the original *Cosmos* miniseries. He was standing in a crowded JPL control room with a dozen or so shaggy-looking scientists, all of whom were clustered around a tiny black-and-white TV monitor, watching anxiously as humanity's first close-up photo of Europa slowly appeared on it, a single line of pixels at a time. The right half of the Jovian moon lay in shadow, but the hemisphere on the left was currently in full sunlight, and some faint surface features were already visible there, despite the image's low resolution.

As the download approached completion and the rest of Europa's surface gradually became visible, Sagan and the other scientists began to study the image with an increasing air of confusion and alarm. When the last row of pixels formed and the complete image appeared on the monitor, it revealed that an enormous section of Europa's icy surface was covered with a giant swastika.

Frightened whispers and murmured expletives swept through the auditorium. Beside me, I heard Lex whisper, *"What the fuck?"*

I nodded in agreement. This was undoubtedly the most unsettling history lesson I'd ever been subjected to—and I couldn't imagine what could be coming next.

"That first close-up image revealed the existence of an enormous symbol etched onto the Jovian moon's surface," Sagan's voice calmly explained. "An equilateral cross with all four of its arms bent at perfect right angles—known here on Earth as a swastika—was clearly visible in the southern hemisphere, covering an area of over a million square kilometers. The swastika was so large, in fact, that it appeared slightly warped in that first *Pioneer* photo, due to the curvature of the moon's surface.

"The discovery of this symbol was immediately recognized by NASA scientists as the first concrete evidence of an extraterrestrial intelligence. However, the excitement over this landmark discovery was eclipsed by the debate over the symbol's potential meaning. For thousands of years the swastika had been used by peaceful cultures around the world as both an ornamental symbol and a good luck charm, until it was adopted by the

Nazi Party in 1920, and the atrocities they subsequently committed forever transformed it into an icon of humanity at its absolute worst."

"Yeah, why didn't they slap a yin-yang symbol on Europa instead?" Lex whispered beside me, slurring her speech a bit. "That would've *blown NASA's mind.*"

I shushed her, and she let out a short hysterical laugh, then seemed to regain her composure. We both returned our attention to the screen.

"We had no way of knowing whether or not the beings who had defaced Europa were aware of the meaning the symbol held for us," Sagan's voice continued. "Until we had more information, all we could do was speculate about the symbol's origin and meaning. Our nation's political and military leaders made the decision to conceal it from the world, fearing that news of its existence would create a panic that might plunge our entire civilization into religious, political, and economic chaos. President Richard Nixon issued a secret executive order that NASA's dark discovery on Europa would remain a highly classified national secret until it could be studied further."

Now I understood why Dr. Sagan and the other JPL scientists had gone along with the government's cover-up. The alternative would have been to tell the fragile citizens of planet Earth that they'd just discovered a giant Nazi Post-it note orbiting Jupiter. If Walter Cronkite had dropped a bomb like that on the evening news back in 1973, human civilization would have gone collectively apeshit. Planning another mission to Europa under those circumstances would have been problematic—maybe even impossible.

But there were still a lot of things about this story that bothered me. For one, the details of NASA's discovery on Europa were giving me a strange sense of déjà vu. It took me a moment to figure out why.

Since the late '70s, the official word on Europa from our scientists had been that it was one of the most promising *potential* habitats for extraterrestrial life in our solar system, due the vast ocean of liquid water beneath its surface. As a result, Europa had been a popular setting with science fiction writers ever since. I could think of at least half a dozen stories that involved the discovery of alien life on Europa—most notably the Arthur C. Clarke novel *2010,* his sequel to *2001: A Space Odyssey.* Peter Hyams had directed an excellent film adaptation of *2010* back in the '80s, and the movie version ended with a highly advanced alien intelligence using HAL-9000 to send humanity a mass text message warning us to stay the hell away from Europa.

Attempt no landing there.

There was also something familiar about an alien first-contact message that contained a swastika. After racking my brain for what seemed like an eternity, I realized the answer was staring me in the face—Carl Sagan himself had written a similar scenario into his first and only science fiction novel, *Contact*. In Sagan's story, SETI researchers receive a message from an extraterrestrial intelligence that contains a copy of the first television broadcast from Earth the aliens ever intercepted, which turns out to be footage of Adolf Hitler's opening speech at the 1936 Summer Olympics in Berlin. One of the most memorable moments in both the book and the film adaptation occurs when the SETI scientists decode the first frame of the alien video transmission and discover that it contains a close-up image of a Nazi swastika.

The events unfolding on the screen in front of me were different from the tales of first contact described in either *2010* or *Contact,* granted—but surely those similarities couldn't be mere coincidence?

Like Sagan, Clarke had been a NASA insider. It made sense that he too had learned of *Pioneer 10*'s discovery on Europa and agreed to take part in the cover-up. But then why had both men subsequently hidden kernels of the top-secret truth in their bestselling science fiction novels? And why had the EDA let them get away with it? Especially considering that both of their novels were then adapted into blockbuster films that had exposed this classified information to a global audience?

As it occurred to me that I'd probably just answered my own question, several high-resolution images of Europa began to appear on the screen, showing its surface in much greater detail. Up close, the moon looked like a dirty snowball crisscrossed with reddish orange cracks and streaks that were thousands of kilometers long. The giant black swastika stood out in stark relief against the moon's surface.

"When *Pioneer 11* reached Jupiter a year later in December of 1974,"

Sagan's voice-over continued, "its course was adjusted to make a close flyby of Europa, and it sent back much clearer images of the moon and its surface anomaly, putting to rest any lingering suspicions that the earlier *Pioneer 10* image had been faked in some way. By this time, NASA was already rushing the construction of a new top-secret probe designed to travel to Europa and land on its surface to study the swastika anomaly up close, and hopefully collect enough data to ascertain its origin or purpose. NASA dubbed this spacecraft the *Envoy I,* and it reached Europa on the 9th of July, 1976—the day humanity made its first direct contact with an alien intelligence."

I had never been so glued to a movie screen in my life.

A shot of the *Envoy I*—or rather, another CGI simulation—appeared on the screen, showing the probe as it maneuvered into orbit around Europa, with majestic Jupiter looming behind it. It looked like a larger, less streamlined version of the two *Voyager* spacecraft NASA launched the following year, with giant fuel tanks and a lander cobbled onto its frame.

As the spacecraft passed over the huge black symbol, the orbiter deployed its landing module and it began to descend toward the frozen surface.

The image cut to what appeared to be actual video footage shot by the *Envoy* lander's on-board camera during its final approach.

Seen directly from above and in full sunlight, the giant swastika on Europa's surface appeared to consist of nothing more than long bands of discolored ice. The blackened sections of ice still reflected sunlight, and aside from the change in its color, there appeared to be no disruption in the pattern of striated cracks and frozen ridges covering the moon's surface. It looked like someone had slapped the solar system's largest swastika stencil on the side of Europa and then hit it with a Star Destroyer–sized can of black acrylic spray paint.

"The *Envoy* lander set down near the southernmost tip of the anomaly, near what would later become known as the Thera Macula region," Sagan's voice-over continued, just as the lander completed its controlled descent and touched down on the surface, with its landing gear straddling the border between the swastika's edge and the unblemished ice beside it.

To my shock, a familiar gold disc was attached to the base of the lander. It looked identical to the famous gold records NASA had attached to both of its Voyager spacecraft.

"A twelve-inch gold-plated copper disc was attached to the *Envoy* lander," Sagan explained. "This phonograph record was encoded with sound recordings and images selected to portray the diversity of life and culture on Earth, to serve as a token of peace from our species."

After the lander finished unfolding its solar panel array, a jointed robotic arm extended from its underside and began to collect a sample of the blackened surface. The heated metal scoop at the end of the arm dug a furrow into the ice about a foot deep, revealing that it was black at that depth, too. Once the arm retracted, the body of the lander opened up like a metal flower, revealing a torpedo-shaped probe within, with its nose pointed straight down at the ice.

"The heat generated by Jupiter's tidal flexing of Europa causes most of the moon's subsurface ice to remain liquid, resulting in a subterranean ocean that we knew could possibly harbor life, which made it the first logical place for us to search for the beings responsible for creating the symbol on the moon's surface."

I once again marveled at the powerfully calming effect of Sagan's voice. If James Earl Jones had been chosen to narrate this briefing film, it would have been even more terrifying to watch.

"Shortly after it touched down, the *Envoy* lander deployed a cryobot, an experimental nuclear-powered melt probe designed to burn down through the moon's surface ice and explore the ocean hidden beneath it for signs of extraterrestrial life."

The lander slowly lowered the torpedo-shaped cryobot, pressing its superheated nose down into the blackened ice. An explosive column of steam shot up high into Europa's nearly nonexistent atmosphere as the probe began to melt through the onyx surface, burning a perfect cylindrical tunnel through the ice as it descended, pulled downward by gravity.

In a few seconds, the tail of the cryobot disappeared beneath the surface, unspooling a long fiber-optic tether behind it that would keep it connected to the lander and its transmitter. Then a cutaway animation of

Europa appeared on the screen, showing the cryobot's progress as it burrowed down through several kilometers of solid ice before it finally made it all the way through the crust and then plunged into Europa's dark ocean.

"We lost contact with the cryobot just a few seconds after it cleared the underside of the moon's ice layer. At first, NASA suspected an equipment malfunction, because we also lost contact with the lander up on the surface at the same moment. But when the *Envoy* orbiter passed over the landing site again a few hours later, the satellite images it sent back revealed two things: The lander had completely vanished from the surface, and so had the swastika."

The film cut to a rapid slideshow of still photos taken by the orbiter. The swastika had indeed disappeared, leaving no sign it had ever been there in the first place. Then the image magnified to show a detailed view of the probe's landing site. The four impressions left by the lander's feet were still visible, as was the circular hole the cryobot had burned into the ice—ice that had miraculously reverted to its natural color.

"Forty-two hours after NASA lost contact with the lander, its radio transmitter came back online, broadcasting on the same top-secret NASA frequency. When its signal reached Earth, we discovered that it contained a brief voice message, apparently sent by the inhabitants of Europa. To our surprise, it was worded in plain English, and spoken in the voice of a human child."

A recording of a young girl's voice began to play on the soundtrack.

"You have desecrated our most sacred temple," the child's voice intoned in a flat, inflectionless tone. *"For this there can be no forgiveness. We are coming to kill you all."*

Even as I shuddered in my seat, something about the message struck me as oddly familiar. It was like something out of a bad science fiction movie.

Then Carl Sagan's calming voice-over continued.

"It was quickly determined that the female voice heard in the alien transmission had been synthesized from one of the brief audio recordings included on the gold record we had attached to the lander.

"To our dismay, this twenty-one-word message began to repeat on a continuous loop, hour after hour, day after day. The Europans, as we began to refer to them, ignored all of our attempts to respond or explain our actions. For reasons we still don't understand, it appears they viewed our first attempt to make contact with them as an unforgivable act of war. By sending a melt probe to explore beneath their moon's surface, we may have unknowingly violated some territorial or religious boundary their species holds sacred. Or the Europans may simply view our species as a threat to their own. We still aren't sure of their motivations, because all of our subsequent efforts to communicate with them have met with failure."

Another wave of nervous chattering swept through the auditorium. I scanned the audience, half expecting someone to flip out, but everyone remained calm and in their seats—including me. The revelation that evil aliens were coming to try to wipe us out didn't send anyone into hysterics or create a panic—and I thought I understood why. For decades, we had all been inundated with a steady barrage of science fiction novels, movies, cartoons, and television shows about aliens of one kind or another. Extraterrestrial visitors had permeated pop culture for so long that they were now embedded in humanity's collective unconscious, preparing us to deal with the real thing, now that it was actually happening.

"We began to send more probes to Europa, numbering in the hundreds, but nearly all of them were lost or destroyed shortly after they reached the moon's orbit. However, through trial and error, we were eventually able to place a handful of remote surveillance platforms on several of Jupiter's neighboring moons, allowing us to closely monitor Europa without being detected. Their cameras sent back the following orbital surveillance images."

Thousands of satellite images of Europa began to appear on the screen, displayed rapidly in chronological order, so that they created a rough stop-motion video, showing what appeared to be a thin ring of metallic debris forming around the moon near its equator. When these photos were magnified and enhanced, millions of construction robots became visible, crawling along orbital scaffolds and the skeletal hulls of the spacecraft they were building.

It looked just like the Sobrukai homeworld during our mission last night, except that Europa's surface was mostly white, instead of red. And instead of the purplish gas giant named Tau Ceti V looming behind it, it was the familiar cyclopean eye of Jupiter.

The Europans were building an armada, just like the Sobrukai. But much closer to Earth. They had Foundry Ships orbiting their moon, cranking out fighters and drones—just like those I'd spotted above Sobrukai last night. The Europans had also towed several large asteroids and meteorites into safe orbits around their moon, and now hordes of those spider-like construction robots could be seen swarming over and burrowing into their surfaces, to mine them for metals and other raw materials. When an asteroid was all mined out, another would be towed into orbit.

As the time-lapsed footage continued to play, flying through weeks, months, and years of incessant construction by these self-replicating machines, a small fleet of glittering spaceships began to form around Europa. It continued to grow until the alien war vessels grew so numerous they formed a Saturn-like ring that encircled the equator.

As the asteroids were towed in and mined out, six massive Dreadnaught Spheres began to take shape in orbit above Europa. "Despite all of our ongoing efforts to negotiate a truce with the Europans, they continued to make their preparations for war, constructing drones that then went on to build other drones," the voice-over explained. "We watched with growing concern as their numbers began to multiply exponentially right before our eyes, month after month, and then year after year.

"In the mid-1980s, the Europans began to send scout ships to Earth," Sagan continued. "Our military forces managed to capture and study several of the enemy's spacecraft. That was when we discovered that they were all drones, which the Europans were controlling from hundreds of thousands of miles away, using some form of instantaneous quantum communication. For this reason, we still know almost nothing about the Europans' biological makeup or physical appearance."

I shifted uncomfortably in my seat, feeling a strange combination of frustration and relief. I'd half expected Sagan to reveal that the Europans looked just like the anthropomorphic squid-like Sobrukai depicted in *Armada*. It was a relief to learn this was not the case, but equally frustrating to be told that, after four decades, we still didn't know anything about our enemy's biology.

"However, after years of effort, our scientists were able to reverse-engineer the aliens' quantum communication technology, along with certain facets of their ships' propulsion and weapons systems. We have since used these newfound technologies to construct a global stockpile of our own defense drones, which we believe will give humanity a fighting chance against the invaders."

I heard myself let out an uneasy sigh. I'd been willing to suspend my disbelief for the EDA's "we reverse-engineered the aliens' technology in just a few years" explanation back when I'd thought it was just a fictional videogame backstory. But I definitely didn't buy it now that the EDA was trying to pass it off as a historical fact—even if they were using Carl Sagan's voice to do it. It seemed utterly impossible that the EDA had managed to reverse-engineer vastly superior communication, propulsion, and weapons technology in just a few years while concealing this endeavor from the whole world—let alone mass-produce it into millions of drones. And even if that was possible, why had our enemy made the task so easy for us? According to what we'd just been told, the Europans had not only let us capture several of their vessels, they'd then given us enough time to figure out how they worked, to build our own fleet of ships with the same capabilities. And by constructing their armada in orbit around their moon, in full view of our satellites, they'd basically given humanity a detailed video of what to expect when their attack came.

There had to be some truth to what the EDA was telling us. The shuttle ride I'd just taken to get here was proof of that, as were my current surroundings. But I was sure there was more to this story than they were telling us. A lot more.

"Gradually, it became evident to humanity's leaders that we faced certain extinction if we didn't set aside our differences and unite as one species to defend ourselves and our home. This prompted select members of the United Nations to form a secret global military coalition for that very purpose, known as the Earth Defense Alliance, in the event that our worst fears are one day realized, and the entire Europan armada disembarks for Earth."

The animated EDA logo reappeared on the screen.

"Until then, we continue to work toward peace, while preparing for the possibility of war."

As Sagan finished the closing voice-over, the screen went dark and the film ended abruptly. Lex realized she was still clutching my forearm and let go of it. There were marks where she'd dug her nails into my skin, but I hadn't even noticed. I'd been too busy having my whole perception of reality shattered into a million pieces.

When the lights came up a few seconds later, they hit us with the really bad news.

TALL MAN IN A HEAVILY DECORATED EDA UNIFORM MOUNTED THE SMALL stage down below and walked to the podium at its center. When he reached it, his face appeared on the giant view screen behind him, and I gasped in unison with Lex and a chorus of others in the audience.

It was Admiral Archibald Vance, the cyclopean EDA commander who gave players their mission briefings in both *Armada* and *Terra Firma*.

I'd always assumed he was just an actor who had been hired to play that role, but it appeared I'd been wrong about that, too.

The admiral rested his hands on the podium and cast a long appraising gaze over his audience.

"Greetings, recruit candidates," he said. "My name is Admiral Archibald Vance, and I've been a field commander in the Earth Defense Alliance for over a decade now. I'm sure many of you are surprised to learn that I'm a real person, and not a fictional character. But rest assured, I am real, and so is the Earth Defense Alliance."

There were scattered cheers and some muted laughter. The admiral waited for total silence before he continued.

"You've all been summoned here today because we need your help. You people are among the most skilled and highly trained drone pilots in the world. The videogames you've each mastered, *Terra Firma* and *Armada*, are both actually combat training simulations created by the EDA to help us locate and train individuals like each of you—who possess the rare talents required to help us defend our planet from the impending Europan invasion.

"As you just saw, our alien enemy's existence has been kept a guarded secret since its initial discovery," he went on. "This was done out of necessity, so that humanity would keep calm and carry on long enough for our leaders to organize and mount a defense against the invaders." He slid his hands off the podium and scanned his audience again.

"But we've finally run out of time. The day we've been dreading all these years is now at hand. And you people are the EDA's most promising recruit candidates, from dozens of different countries all over the world," he told us. "Which is why we've taken the precaution of relocating you here, to a secure location, before the truth of our circumstances is revealed to the entire world."

"Holy fucking shit," Lex whispered beside me.

"The briefing film you just saw was first prepared in the early 1990s," Admiral Vance said. "We've updated the computer-generated imagery over the years, but its contents have changed very little. The EDA has always intended to release this film to the world when the threat of invasion could no longer be concealed. Sadly, that day is now at hand. After threatening us with extinction for over forty years, it appears the Europans have finally completed their preparations for war."

He gripped the edges of the podium, as if to steady himself. It made me realize that I was doing the same thing with the armrests of my chair.

"Here is our satellite imagery from early yesterday morning." A new high-resolution image of Europa appeared on the screen behind him. The armada we'd seen under construction in the canned video was now complete. The six Dreadnaught Spheres had flowered open to take on their deadly cargo, and their long spiral storage racks were nearly filled to capacity with over a billion individual drones, ready for transport and deployment.

"This next image was taken just a few hours ago," the admiral said as another image of Europa appeared on the screen. The band of gleaming alien construction ships that had been orbiting the icy moon was now gone—and so were the six massive Dreadnaught Spheres. And there was a giant circle burned in Europa's southern hemisphere—in the exact same spot on the moon's surface where the Icebreaker had aimed its melt laser during our assault on Sobrukai last night during the *Armada* mission.

"Holy shit!" I shouted, and I wasn't alone. "That mission was *real*?"

"What do you mean?" Lex asked.

Before I could answer, the admiral spoke again.

"The EDA launched an attack on Europa last night," he said. "Many of you *Armada* pilots took part in that mission, which was our one shot at destroying them before they launched their drones to destroy us. But the Icebreaker mission failed. And now their armada is on its way to Earth."

I couldn't keep my doubts to myself any longer. "This story doesn't make any damn sense," I whispered to Lex. "If these aliens want to wipe us out, why wait forty years to attack? Why give us that long to figure out their technology and prepare to fight them off, when they could have wiped us out back in the seventies? Why wait?" I shook my head. "It didn't make sense when it was backstory for the game, and it doesn't make sense now either. I mean, why send a fleet of robotic drones? Why not hit us with a virus or a killer asteroid or—"

"Christ, who the fuck cares, man?" Lex hissed back. Out of the corner of my eye, I saw her attempt to take another sip from her already-empty flask with a trembling hand. Then she cursed and retightened its cap. "Maybe they live for thousands of years? Four decades might seem like a long weekend to them." Her eyes narrowed at the glowing image on the screen. "It doesn't matter now, does it? They're obviously through waiting."

She turned her attention back to the admiral, and I tried to do the same.

"This is the enemy fleet's current position and trajectory," Vance said, just as an animated map of our solar system appeared on the screen behind him. The current location of the Europan armada was indicated by a chain of three amoeba-shaped blobs, each one larger than the last. They were stretched out in a line between Jupiter and Earth, inching their way through the asteroid belt like an interplanetary wagon train.

The Europan armada appeared to be approaching Earth in three separate attack waves. Their overall trajectory was indicated by a glowing yellow line that left no doubt as to their destination.

"Oh my God," Lex whispered. "They're already more than halfway here."

She was right. The first wave was already approaching the asteroid belt out beyond Mars' orbit.

The display zoomed in on the vanguard—the blob in the lead—showing that it was comprised of a dense cloud of thousands of tiny green triangles swarming around a dark green circle in their midst—a Dreadnaught Sphere, surrounded by its fighter escort. The admiral then adjusted the tactical display to zoom in on the two even-larger blobs of ships trailing it. The second blob contained two Dreadnaught Spheres and twice as many Glaive Fighters escorting it. The third blob contained three Dreadnaught Spheres, and triple the number of fighters escorting them.

The admiral used a laser pointer to highlight the three clusters of ships.

"For reasons we still don't understand, the enemy has divided its invasion force into three attack waves, each progressively larger than the last," he said. "We estimate that each one of those Dreadnaught Spheres is carrying a payload of approximately one billion individual drones."

Even I was able to do arithmetic that simple. The admiral had just told us that there were six billion killer alien drones on their way here to wipe us out. This obviously wasn't going to be a fair fight—not after that second wave got here.

The admiral moved his laser pointer back to the arrow-shaped cluster of ships out in front. "If it continues on its current course at the same speed, the vanguard—this first wave of ships out front—will reach our lunar perimeter less than eight hours from now."

A digital countdown clock appeared in the bottom right-hand corner of the screen, showing the time remaining until the vanguard's arrival: 07:54:07.

A second later, my QComm beeped and its display lit up on my wrist, just as every other QComm in the auditorium did the same thing, creating a single loud beep that echoed through the crowd. I glanced down at my wrist and saw that the same invasion countdown clock now appeared on my QComm's display, perfectly in sync with the one on the giant projection screen behind the admiral.

07:54:05

07:54:04

07:54:03

"Jesus," Lex muttered, staring at the QComm strapped to her wrist, watching the seconds tick down. "Now I feel like Snake Plissken."

I snorted out a wholly inappropriate laugh that echoed through the silent auditorium before I quickly stifled it as the sea of faces below us turned to scowl in our general direction. Lex snickered, and I raised a finger to my lips and shushed her.

"If we manage to survive the vanguard's attack, the second wave of enemy drones will reach Earth approximately three hours later, with the final wave reaching us roughly three hours after that."

Every time he said the word *vanguard,* all I could think of was an old arcade game with that title. *Vanguard* was a great side-scrolling space shooter from the mid-1980s that I'd discovered in my father's collection. In the game, when you reached the last of the game's five increasingly difficult waves, you faced the final boss, known as "The Gond." In my head, I was already imagining that the Gond and the Europan overlord looked more or less identical. Then I reminded myself there might not even be a Europan overlord—the briefing film said we still didn't know anything about their biology or social structure. Maybe they didn't even have a leader. Maybe they were a hive mind?

When the admiral finished speaking and turned away from the screen, a rumble of anxious murmuring spread through the audience, gradually increasing in volume, until Vance finally motioned for silence.

"You're right to be alarmed," he said. "A full-scale invasion of our planet is now under way, and our enemy has us vastly outnumbered. Thankfully, the odds aren't nearly as hopeless as they seem. The Earth Defense Alliance has been preparing the world for this moment for decades, and when it begins, humanity will be ready to fight back and defend our home."

A desperate cheer went up as the Earth Defense Alliance crest reappeared on the screen, accompanied by another piece of music from John Williams' score for *Armada*. As skeptical as I was about everything I'd just been told, hearing the music in that context gave me goose bumps.

A hangar full of ADI-88 Interceptors appeared on the screen, and I felt my jaw go involuntarily slack. They looked exactly like the drones I'd piloted in *Armada,* down to the last detail. Another photo appeared, showing thousands of ATHIDs standing in formation under powerful floodlights in some secret concrete bunker. Finally, a photo of a single Sentinel mech was displayed, and I heard Lex mutter "*whoa*" under her breath. It looked just like one of the Sentinels in the game, and just as huge.

"You're looking at the real reason for the recent global financial crisis— all of human civilization's technology, industry, and natural resources have been leveraged to the hilt in our effort to ensure that we have the firepower necessary to repel the invaders' superior numbers and advanced weaponry. And now, at long last, our forces are ready for deployment."

More photos were displayed on the screen, showing thousands of real Interceptors, Sentinels, and ATHIDs stored in hidden locations around the world, waiting for battle. I felt an involuntary surge of pride for my species, and the technological miracles we had accomplished in an effort to ensure our own survival.

"We have constructed millions of these drones and hidden them in strategic locations all over the globe," the admiral continued. "When the invasion begins, civilian recruits around the world will be able to use their gaming platforms to take control of these stockpiled drone forces using the enemy's instantaneous quantum communication link technology. This global network of military defense drones will be our only hope to even the odds that are stacked against us all."

The EDA crest appeared on the screen behind the admiral once again.

"The Alliance's international forces have already managed to thwart dozens of enemy scouting missions to Earth, and these engagements have helped us collect an enormous amount of data on their ships, weapons, and tactics," he said. "And we've fed every ounce of that data into the *Terra Firma* and *Armada* training simulations, to ensure that they would be effective in preparing you to face real enemy drones in combat. So all of you people have been fighting a simulated version of this war for years." He smiled grimly. "Now it's time for the real thing."

He clasped his hands behind his back, and his expression softened. "I know how frightening all of this must be for some of you," he said. "We can't force you to risk your lives and join our ranks. But you should all know by now that you won't be able to hide from this war by running back to your homes. And your friends and families won't be able to hide from it either. No one anywhere on Earth can hide. These creatures, whatever they are, are coming to exterminate us all. If we don't stop them, humanity will cease to exist."

He rested both hands on the podium and angled his gaze downward, as if addressing the recruits seated in the first row.

"But we *are* going to stop them. If all seven billion members of the human race unite in the face of this threat, and we fight back as one species and one planet, with every ounce of strength we have, we can win this war. I know it. And that starts right now, with each of you."

A cheer slowly rose from the audience. I didn't add my voice to it, and neither did Lex. But she nodded slowly, as if resigning herself to Admiral Vance's call to action. Down on the stage, the admiral paused to straighten his posture, and when he spoke again, the calm edge had returned to his voice.

"Even though the Europan vanguard won't reach our lunar perimeter for another eight hours, we have reason to believe the enemy may be preparing to launch a sneak attack sometime today, before the rest of the fleet begins to arrive. Over the past few days, dozens of Europan scout ships have been spotted in our atmosphere, and several of them were observed conducting surveillance on EDA installations and outposts like this one."

He pointed to a map of the world that had just appeared on the screen behind him, which was scattered with flashing red dots indicating the locations of the scout ship sightings. Most of them were near largely populated cities, but one was flashing right over my hometown.

"We still have no way of tracking these Europan scout ships, so their current position remains unknown. However, we—"

We heard a low, rumbling boom from somewhere far above us, like a muffled detonation, followed by a fierce tremor that shook the entire auditorium, like a brief earthquake. A few people screamed; then a warning klaxon began to wail.

"Red alert. This installation is under attack," a synthesized female voice announced over the PA system. "All personnel report to your battle stations immediately. Repeat—this installation is under attack. Red alert."

Lex and I exchanged looks of disbelief.

"Seriously?" she said. "This can't really be happening right now, can it?"

"No way," I said. "They're screwing with us. This has to be a drill or something. . . ."

Another blast up on the surface shook the stone floor beneath our feet once again—more fiercely this time—and there was another volley of panicked screams and shouting. The map projected on the auditorium's giant screen was suddenly replaced with eight live video feeds from cameras up on the surface, showing Crystal Palace's dairy farm façade from various angles around its outer perimeter. All of the buildings were in flames, and the sky overhead was filled with a swarm of dozens of Glaive Fighters. I could see their blade-shaped hulls flashing like mirrors in the morning sun as they rained lasers and plasma bombs down on the base.

The auditorium fell eerily silent for a moment as everyone stared up at the images on the screen. Then the screaming and the shouting continued, now at a much higher volume.

Up on the screen, a squadron of Glaive Fighters swooped down and carpet-bombed the armored doors over the docking bay entrance.

Another tremor rocked the auditorium, and silt began to rain down from cracks in the reinforced concrete ceiling. I wondered how much more abuse it could take before it collapsed.

"Remain calm, people!" the admiral ordered, shouting to be heard over the growing din of panic in the audience. "If you want to live, I need you to pull it together and follow orders!"

The fear in the admiral's voice was almost as unsettling as the video on the screen behind him.

"Repeat—this installation is under attack," the computerized female voice repeated over the PA. "All personnel report to your drone controller station immediately. Check your QComm for further instructions. All personnel report to your drone controller station immediately—"

Lex whipped out her QComm. Its display lit up with another GPS-style map of the base, showing a green path from where we were sitting at the back of the auditorium, down the steps to the nearest exit, then down a series of corridors to a circular room labeled Controller Hub 3. I checked my QComm and saw that I was assigned to Hub 5, which was along the same route, but slightly farther away from us.

"Let's go!" Lex said, dropping my jacket in my lap as she squeezed past me. I didn't rise from my seat. My eyes were still fixed on the chaos unfolding on the screen, but my brain was churning through everything I'd learned today—and how little sense any of it made. Something was wrong here. And I still didn't know if my dad's—

"Zack?"

I looked over and saw Lex staring back at me from the end of the row, her eyes burning with impatience. "Well? Are you just gonna sit here and let these things kill us?"

She was right. This wasn't the EDA's fault. It was the Europans'. Here, revealed at last, was my true enemy—the cause of all the loss and hardship that had plagued me since birth. These invaders from another world—they were the reason all of this was happening. By declaring war on us all those decades ago, the Europans had disrupted human history and robbed us of our future. And now they were here to rob us of everything else, too.

Suddenly, the only thing I cared about was making them pay. Every last one of them.

"Yeah, I'm coming," I said, jumping to my feet. I shoved the jacket back into my pack, then ran to catch up with Lex, who was already bounding down the tiered steps three and four at a time.

LEX AND I SQUEEZED THROUGH THE BOTTLENECK OF PEOPLE AT THE NEAREST EXIT. AS SOON as we cleared it and burst into the corridor outside the auditorium, Lex took off running again, pushing past other, less-eager recruits until she was out in front, leading the charge. I raced to keep up with her, following the machine-gun-like sound of her combat boots hitting the stone floor up ahead of me.

We heard another concussive explosion impact up on the surface, and the shockwave shook the floor. Dust and silt began to rain down from the tile seams in the corridor ceiling as the people around us continued to sprint in all directions, following maps on the glowing screens of their QComms.

I ignored mine and just focused on keeping up with Lex as she continued to run down a seemingly endless series of corridors, until finally she stopped outside a set of armored doors labeled CONTROLLER HUB 3.

"This is me," she said, pointing down the corridor. "Hub Five is farther down."

I nodded and opened my mouth to wish her good luck, but I'd only managed to get out "Goo—" when she turned and planted a kiss on my cheek. This may have caused a slight drop in the structural integrity of my knee joints, but I managed to stay upright.

"Give 'em hell, IronBeagle," she said, just before she ran through the armored doors and they slammed shut behind her.

As soon as I was able to will my legs back into motion, I took off running again. At the end of that same corridor, I reached a pair of doors labeled CONTROLLER HUB 5 and bolted through them. They opened onto an enormous barrel-shaped room with hundreds of drone controller stations honeycombed into its curved walls, to which were bolted a network of narrow ladders and access ramps. It looked like a larger version of the drone-control centers in *Armada*'s cut scenes. My QComm display switched to a three-dimensional diagram of the room, then highlighted my station assignment—DCS537. I scaled the nearest ladder up to level three, then sprinted down the metal access ramp to my station. A scanner beeped as I approached, and the door hissed open. I hurried inside.

As soon as I sat down in the leather chair, the door hissed closed and the control panels around me lit up, along with the wraparound view screen, which currently displayed the Earth Defense Alliance insignia.

I looked around at the familiar array of controls and wrapped my right hand around the flight stick directly in front of me, which appeared identical to the *Armada* flight-stick controller Ray had given me the previous day. The dual-throttle controller by my left hand also appeared identical to Chaos Terrain's home version, except that it was bolted to the armrest of my ergonomic pilot seat.

The station was also outfitted with several other controller options, including a pair of *Terra Firma* battle gauntlets, used for operating an ATHID or Sentinel, along with more mundane options like a keyboard and mouse setup or a standard Xbox, Nintendo, or PlayStation controller—enough choices to make almost any gamer feel right at home.

I saw a brief flash of red as my retinas were scanned; then a red *X* flashed on my display, along with the words *DRONE CONTROLLER ACCESS NOT AUTHORIZED.*

"Attention, recruit candidate," the same synthesized female voice said as her words appeared on the display screen in front of me. "Only Earth Defense Alliance personnel are authorized to operate drones or engage in combat. Do you wish to enlist in the Earth Defense Alliance at this time?"

Several paragraphs of dense text began to scroll across the screen, an unreadable blur of legalese outlining all the details of enlistment. It would have taken hours to read it all, and then I still probably wouldn't have understood a word of it.

"Are you fucking kidding me?" I shouted. "I have to enlist before I can fight?"

"Only Earth Defense Alliance personnel are authorized to operate drones or engage in combat," the computer repeated.

"That's a little manipulative, don't you think?"

"Please rephrase your question."

"This is fucking ridiculous!" I cried, punching the console again.

"If you do not wish to enlist in the Earth Defense Alliance at this time, please exit this drone controller station and proceed to the nearest out-processing station."

When I didn't respond to this right away, the computer said, "I'm sorry, I didn't hear your answer. Do you wish to enlist in the Earth Defense Alliance at this time?"

Another tremor rocked the base to its foundations. The lights embedded in the ceiling of my station dimmed for half a second.

"Okay, yes!" I began repeatedly tapping the ACCEPT button at the bottom of the screen. "I want to fucking enlist! Sign my ass up!"

"Please raise your right hand and read the enlistment oath aloud."

A paragraph of text appeared on my display, with my name already inserted at the beginning. I began to read it, and each word dimmed once I'd said it aloud:

> I, Zackary Ulysses Lightman, having been appointed an officer in the Earth Defense Alliance, do solemnly swear that I will support and defend my home planet and its citizens against all enemies, that I will bear true faith and allegiance to the same; that I take this obligation freely, without any mental reservation or purpose of evasion; that I will obey the orders of the officers appointed over me; and that I will well and faithfully discharge the duties of the office upon which I am about to enter. So help me God.

That last line was marked as "optional," but I was in a hurry, so I said it anyway, even though I'd always been a devout agnostic. Besides, now I was thinking there just might be a God after all—that would explain who was currently fucking with my whole notion of reality.

"Congratulations!" the computer said. "You are now a flight officer in the Earth Defense Alliance with the rank of lieutenant. Your EDA skill profile and *Armada* pilot ranking have both been verified. Flight status—authorized. Combat status—authorized. Drone controller station access granted. User preferences imported. Interceptor synchronization engaged. Good luck, Lieutenant Lightman!"

My view screen suddenly switched to a familiar first-person view, from inside an ADI-88 Aerospace Drone Interceptor, prepped for launch. The song "You Really Got Me" by Van Halen began to blast out of the drone controller station's surround sound system, making me jerk back in my chair. I relaxed as I realized that the computer had just made a Bluetooth connection to my QComm and automatically started playing the next song on my father's old *Raid the Arcade* playlist.

I didn't hesitate. I hit the launch release and my Interceptor rocketed forward, out of its launch tunnel—one of those disguised grain silos—and into the clear blue sky.

A real sky, filled with real clouds.

That was when I realized my view from inside the cockpit was slightly different from the one I was used to seeing when I played *Armada*. The HUD readouts and targeting reticle were identical, but they were superimposed over a live high-definition video feed of my drone's surroundings, seen from the stereoscopic camera mounted inside the real drone Interceptor I was now piloting. With the door of my drone controller station closed, the illusion of being inside an actual cockpit was almost total. I could even see the fang-like tips of its sun guns protruding from the ship in front of me.

A split second later, my view of the sky was filled with another familiar sight: a swarm of Glaive Fighters firing in all directions, including directly at me. Thanks to Lex's prodding, mine was the first Interceptor drone to be launched. Which meant I was also currently the only aerial target for the enemy.

As I banked to take evasive action, I got my first glimpse of the landscape below. The farmhouses, barns, and silos—everything was on fire. Including the ground itself, which had already been scorched black by sweeping laser fire from above.

According to my HUD, there were exactly a hundred Glaive Fighters attacking the base.

And this time it's for real, Zack. If you don't stop them, you die.

I had to make a few adjustments to my controller setup, but it only took seconds because the interface was so familiar. Then I took a deep breath and scanned the field of battle. Down below me, other Interceptor drones were beginning to rocket up out of the open tops of rows of disguised launch tunnels along the farm's northern edge, all of which were now on fire. Hundreds of ATHIDs and several Sentinel mechs were beginning to stream out of the underground bunkers concealed beneath the flaming barns and utility buildings nearby.

My HUD confirmed that the lone Sentinel running out in front, leading the charge, was being operated by Lex—her call sign and rank were superimposed over her mech on my display. I watched as she launched her Sentinel into a power leap while simultaneously unloading both of its wrist cannons at a line of Glaive Fighters as they zoomed overhead, strafing the ground on either side of her drone with laser fire.

I banked my Interceptor around and scanned the sky directly over the base. Most of the Glaive Fighters appeared to be focusing their attacks on the entrance—those two large armored doors set into the earth, which were already starting to glow red and warp under the intense barrage of laser fire and plasma bombs. Once they made it through those doors, they would storm down the base and rain molten fire down on everything, killing me, and Lex, and everyone else inside Crystal Palace.

But I didn't feel uncertain or afraid. I'd been preparing for this moment my whole life—since the first time I ever picked up a videogame controller.

I knew what had to be done.

I pulled back on my flight stick and firewalled the throttle, launching my drone into the mass of Glaive Fighters swarming across the sky directly in front of it. My HUD highlighted the ship closest to my position, and I took a bead on it, leading the target just enough to compensate for its speed and distance before I squeezed the trigger, firing off a sustained burst from my sun guns, scoring two direct hits. The first knocked out the Glaive Fighter's shields, and the second destroyed it in a brilliant fireball a millisecond later.

Unbeknownst to me, I had just scored the first enemy kill of the battle, and the war.

After that, though, things began to go downhill.

12

THE BATTLE OF CRYSTAL PALACE, AS IT CAME TO BE KNOWN, WAS MY FIRST taste of real life-or-death combat. Even though I wasn't physically inside my Interceptor, my body was only a few hundred yards away, somewhere deep within the underground base I was fighting to protect. If the aliens managed to breach our surface defenses and get inside, I would be killed, along with Lex, the admiral, and everyone else.

I wasn't going to let that happen.

I also wasn't going to wait around until RedJive got his or her drone launched and then proceeded to steal all the glory.

I cleared my throat. "TAC?" I said. "Are you there?"

I expected to hear the default synthesized female voice respond, but to my surprise the system had also imported my customized *Armada* sound profile, so I heard a familiar sound bite from *Flight of the Navigator* instead.

"Compliance!" my TAC said, using its digitized version of Paul Reubens' faux computer voice. "How may I assist you, Lieutenant Lightman?"

"Engage autopilot," I said, tapping the screen of my tactical display. I dragged my finger across it, indicating an S-shaped trajectory through the highest concentration of enemy fighters. "Take me right into the middle of that mess. You fly; I'll shoot."

"Compliance!"

Now that I was in a real battle, my *Flight of the Navigator* sound profile seemed inappropriate and distracting, so I switched back to the default female, which—fun fact—had been recorded by the actress Candice Bergen. Chaos Terrain had spared no expense.

With the autopilot engaged, I changed my controller configurations so that my throttle and flight stick now functioned as dual-joystick multiaxis firing controls for the Interceptor's omnidirectional laser turret. As I did so, the turret's three-dimensional targeting system activated, highlighting the enemy ships around me in an ever-widening spiral of overlapping red targeting brackets.

"Hello, fish," I whispered, reciting an old incantation. "Welcome to my barrel."

TAC piloted my Interceptor along the corkscrewing arc I'd laid out, plunging it directly into the enemy's chaotic midst. A swirling whorl of highlight targets appeared on my HUD overlay. I cranked my music up even louder, took a bead on one of the leaders, and opened fire.

To my surprise, I managed to take out seven enemy ships in rapid succession, with precise, sustained bursts from my laser turret, before any of them even had time to take evasive action. Then the other ships on my HUD broke from their attack formations and scattered in all directions, all while firing back at me—or at where my Interceptor had been a millisecond earlier. Just as I'd planned, when my Interceptor passed directly through the center of the enemy's symmetrical gauntlet, their ships were caught in their own crossfire for two or three glorious seconds, resulting in the destruction of at least a dozen more of their fighters. Then, as if controlled by some hive mind, they all ceased their friendly fire in unison, allowing my drone to escape and slip out the other side.

I'd executed this maneuver hundreds of times in simulated *Armada* dogfights, and if I got the timing just right, it always worked like a charm, because the enemy ships reacted to it the same way every single time—the way videogame enemies often tend to do.

But why would the same tactics work now, in the real world? If these were real alien attack drones, under the control of sentient beings living in the subsurface oceans of Europa, half a billion kilometers away, why would they fly and fight exactly like their videogame counterparts?

How could Chaos Terrain have been able to simulate the enemy's maneuvers and tactics with such a high level of precision and accuracy? That shouldn't be possible, unless the Europan drones were being controlled by some form of artificial intelligence or some sort of linked hive mind, instead of being piloted by individual sentient beings.

My Interceptor took a glancing hit to its shields and a warning klaxon sounded, drawing all of my attention back to the battle. The haptic feedback system in my chair vibrated to simulate the impact of the enemy plasma bolt against my shields, and I watched their strength indicator bar decrease by half. I highlighted another course on my tactical display and tapped the commit icon.

"Affirmative," TAC said calmly as the computer pulled us into a steep climb. On my HUD, I saw a long chain of enemy Glaives converge on my tail and arc upward to follow me.

My laser turret had already drained most of my power core's reserves, so I switched back to my sun guns, then swung my targeting reticle over the leader, taking careful aim. I closed one eye, took a breath, held it—and then fired. And fired again. And again. BOOM! KA-BOOM! BOOM! Three more Glaives exploded brilliantly in front of me, one after the other, just as I'd seen their videogame counterparts do countless time before, from the safety of my suburban bedroom, and I heard the words of a young Luke Skywalker echo in my mind: *It'll be just like Beggar's Canyon back home.*

I nailed another Glaive, and then another. I was on fire. Everything about the way these Glaive Fighters were moving and attacking was familiar—in some ways, even predictable.

And it still felt too easy. Like many fictional alien bad guys, the Sobrukai fighters I'd faced off against in *Armada* had always suffered from Stormtrooper Syndrome. They couldn't aim for shit, and they were way too easy to kill. But those had been fictional aliens in a videogame. These were real extraterrestrial ships in a real-life battle. So why did the same tactics still work?

I mouthed the lyrics to the Queen song playing on my headset as I blasted one Glaive after another right out of the sky. *And another one gone, another one gone, another one bites the dust.*

I took out three more Glaives with a volley of plasma bolts, bringing my total kills up to seventeen. According to the mission timer on my HUD, my Interceptor had only been in the sky for seventy-three seconds.

Then, just as I was beginning to feel invincible, my ship took a series of direct hits from behind and my shields failed completely. Warning indicators began to flash on my HUD as TAC put my Interceptor into an evasive barrel roll and we swooped in low over the base.

The ground below was already littered with the burning, skeletal remains of hundreds of downed ATHIDs. I zeroed in on one that was legless and decapitated, but still flailing and firing its guns blindly at the sky. Then its operator finally activated the drone's self-destruct sequence, and the detonation caused one of the flaming buildings nearby to collapse.

A rapid series of piercing shrieks, each followed by what sounded like a brief thunderclap, erupted from the surround-sound speakers lining the walls, floor, and ceiling of my drone controller station. It was a sound I knew well from playing *Armada*—EDA surface-to-air cannons being fired. During the game's online co-op missions, I'd learned to react to this sound by checking for friendly fire, because the players relegated to operating surface guns during these battles were usually those with the worst aim.

I tilted my ship starboard and scanned the ground below, tracking the sound to its source. Several long, concealed trenches had opened in the terrain surrounding the farm on all sides. They were each lined with dozens of antiaircraft plasma cannons and surface-to-air laser turrets. Each one of them was already moving and firing in its own unique pattern, and I knew these guns must now be under the control of other Earth Defense Alliance recruits like me, who were also fighting for their lives from a darkened drone controller station somewhere deep underground.

I reoriented my tactical display to a two-dimensional view, and it instantly reminded me of the classic arcade game *Missile Command*. Squadrons of Glaive Fighters were making repeated, swooping attacks on the armored blast doors set into the surface, diving toward them in tight groups of four and five, raining plasma bombs as they came—while also trying to evade the steady barrage of fire from the base's surface guns, with only marginal success.

The number of enemy ships was already beginning to dwindle, and they were coming under more fire every second, as an intermittent stream of reserve Interceptor drones continued to emerge from the grain silo launch tunnels and join the fight.

Infantry reserves were beginning to arrive, too. New ATHIDs and Sentinels were pouring out of their underground bunkers in a steady stream, firing their weapons at the invaders as they came.

My shields were coming back up now, so I deactivated the autopilot and nosed my Interceptor over into a spiraling dive, attempting to engage another squadron of Glaive Fighters as they arced down to make another carpet-bombing run on the already red-hot blast doors, which were now beginning to warp and buckle in their massive earthen frame, creating gaps along their edges that were growing wider every second. Soon, they'd be wide enough for a fighter to get inside—and that was all it would take.

I adjusted my ship's angle of approach and closed in on the Glaive squadron from above, swinging my targeting reticle over with their silhouettes on my HUD. I thumbed my weapons selector and armed my Interceptor's Macross missile pod. But just as I was about to fire it, my targets stopped firing and accelerated their dive.

For a split second I was certain all five of them were going to crash into one of the blast doors in some sort of kamikaze run. But then I realized that they weren't going to impact on the doors. They were aiming for a spot several dozen yards away, near the center of the farm—near a cluster of our remaining infantry drones, which were already scattering to get out of their way.

But the squadron slid to an abrupt halt just before impact, then began to hover a few feet above the ground. In the space of a few seconds, the five Glaive Fighters turned and rotated themselves into a star-shaped formation, so that their wingtips barely touched, linking themselves together in a circular chain. Then the curved, blade-like wings of the five Glaive Fighters began to interlock and merge with each other, rapidly combining and then reconfiguring to form a single giant humanoid robot, roughly the same size as one of our own Sentinels—like a makeshift Basilisk.

The giant junkyard golem began to bound across the solitary paved road leading up to the isolated farm house façade, uprooting the line of utility poles adjacent to it, until the power lines snapped across its chest like Godzilla. Tines of electricity briefly erupted across its shambling torso, but that didn't slow its progress. It kept on coming, as other Glaives began to combine and make landfall behind it.

That was when I stopped feeling cocky, and started feeling afraid— terrified, really. None of the Sobrukai ships had ever exhibited behavior like this in *Armada* or *Terra Firma*. This was something new. Nearby squadrons of ATHIDs and Sentinels were already converging on the threat, scrambling to attack this new enemy in their midst.

"You've got to be kidding me!" I heard a female voice shout over the open comlink channel. It was Lex. "Since when did these things learn how to form into Voltron?"

She said something else after that, but her voice was drowned out by the chainsaw-like roar of her Sentinel's Gauss guns as she unloaded both of them at the thing.

Hearing Lex's voice seemed to remind all of the other drone operators that *they* had access to a comlink, too, because the public channel was suddenly flooded with overlapping voices. Several of them were ground troops screaming for more air support, as the giant five-Glaive mech thing began to wade through their comparatively Lilliputian ranks, strafing them with plasma bolts from the photon cannons that bristled on each of its armored limbs. Blue flame roared from the thrusters at its feet as it flexed its knees and leapt forward, propelling itself a hundred meters across the burning landscape, toward the base's massive armored blast doors, which had both warped and buckled free of their frame, creating huge gaps along their edges—several of which looked wide enough to allow the giant alien mech to squeeze through and get inside.

I scanned the wave of ATHIDs and Sentinels storming across the landscape below me. Each operator's call sign was superimposed over the drone they were controlling on my HUD, but it still took me several seconds to locate Lex. She was power-leaping toward the newly assembled Glaive mechs, but her drone and those around her were fighting through a hail of plasma fire from above as the remaining Glaive squadrons swooped in to lay down cover fire for their comrades on the surface.

I jinked my ship down and to the left, joining a line of Interceptors beginning an attack run on the remaining mass of Glaives. We rocketed straight into their midst, unloading everything we had at them. I nailed at least two enemy fighters myself and saw at least a dozen more get bull's-eyed by my comrades in the space of as many seconds, but we lost several of our Interceptors during the charge.

Down on the surface, I saw Lex's Sentinel overtake the lead Glaive mech. The two towering opponents began to grapple with each other at the edge of the widest breach in the blast doors. The Sentinel executed an impressive move, spinning counterclockwise and bringing up one of its massive arms in a clothesline maneuver that knocked the enemy mech's leg completely off of its hodgepodge torso. Lex power-jumped her Sentinel clear of it just before two other Sentinels unloaded on the immobilized metal beast. This barrage was joined by hundreds of ATHIDs who began to fire on it, too. Within seconds, the five-Glaive mech exploded, raining wreckage and debris down onto the smoking blast doors, which pinged and clanged as each piece impacted on it.

I swung my Interceptor up and around again, intending to make another pass at the remaining Glaives. But then I scanned my HUD and saw that only five Glaive Fighters remained, a small cluster of green triangles on my tactical display moving into some kind of attack formation high above me.

I angled my ship toward the remaining squadron, just in time to see them all simultaneously turn into a sharp dive, streaking straight down toward the base, as if they intended to make one final kamikaze run. But it looked to me like their angle was wrong—they weren't diving toward the breach in the warped blast doors. Instead, they were descending toward the long row of Interceptor launch tunnels nearby—the ones that had been disguised as grain silos until a few minutes ago. Now most of that false exterior was burned and blasted away, leaving nothing but scarred armor plating underneath.

The diving line of Glaive Fighters began to spread out, each one lining up with a different launch tunnel. And each of those tunnels—which, I suddenly realized, were all sitting wide open at their tops—led directly down into the drone reserve hangar. According to the diagram on my HUD, that hangar was deep inside the base, not too far from where I was currently sitting.

They intended to make a final kamikaze run into the base, through the open mouths of those drone launch tunnels. The simulated alien invaders in *Armada* had never tried this move. How had the rocket scientists who designed this base not seen this massive hole in its defenses?

Luckily, I happened to be there to save the day.

I jammed my throttle forward and moved to swing in above them, firing my weapons before I was even within range. I got lucky and took two of them out. Then a few of the other Interceptors loitering nearby finally began to fire on them, too, taking out two more of the enemy ships just before they reached the open mouths of the launch tunnels.

But the last remaining Glaive Fighter managed to get through, and I continued to pursue it as it rocketed downward, closing in on the row of launch silos jutting up from the charred and blackened earth like a row of skeletal fingers.

"Attention, all Interceptor pilots, this is Palace Command," Admiral Vance's familiar voice barked over the comlink. "Disengage and cease fire! Do not attempt to pursue that ship into the launch tunnels! I repeat, disengage and cease fire! We have automatic security fail-safes in place that will—"

I muted the admiral's voice on my comlink.

On my tactical display, I saw the wing of Interceptors trailing me break off and disengage, just as Vance had instructed, and for a brief second I almost did the same: The years I'd spent playing *Armada* had conditioned me to follow orders, and Vance's orders in particular, because the game's mechanics rewarded officer obedience.

But that had been in a videogame, and this was real life, and the admiral's last-minute order to break off my pursuit seemed like certain suicide. If I didn't destroy this last remaining Glaive Fighter before it reached the other end of the launch tunnel, nothing would prevent it from overloading its power core inside the drone hangar. The detonation could cause the entire underground base to collapse in on itself, killing me and Lex and everyone else inside before any of us got our big chance to save the world. I wasn't willing to take that risk—or to trust my life to the same moronically designed "automatic security fail-safe" that had just allowed this massive enemy breach in our defenses.

So I made the snap decision to disobey a direct order and continued to pursue the kamikaze Glaive as it made its nosedive down through the silo's open mouth and into the launch tunnel beyond it, ignoring the insistent, looping voice of Master Yoda in my head: *Told you, I have! Regret this, you will!*

We both streaked farther through the narrow launch tunnel, like one bullet chasing another down the barrel of a gun, both headed the wrong direction. Just as I was about to open fire on the enemy ship again, it turned into a barrel roll and began to scrape the bladed edge of its right wingtip against the tunnel wall, and I pitched clockwise to dodge the shower of sparks it threw up in its wake. Once I righted myself, I managed to get the Glaive back in my sights for a moment, and I fired a short burst at it with my sun guns. But they glanced off its shields and it kept right on trucking. Meanwhile, overfiring my weapons had caused my drone to decelerate in speed, so the Glaive had increased its lead, making it even more difficult for me to get a bead on it. It reminded me of playing *Space Invaders*—the last alien alive was always the bitch of the bunch, and the hardest to kill, because it moved faster than all of the others. Was it just my imagination, or did this Glaive suddenly seem a whole lot harder to kill than all of its cannon-fodder brethren?

I had to stop firing for a second to focus on keeping my Interceptor from crashing into the tunnel walls as I inched my speed back up, trying to get the enemy back in my sights. Its metal hull glinted up ahead as the pulsing collision lights embedded in the concrete walls of the shaft streaked past in a neon blur.

The power in my Interceptor was nearly depleted. Soon, I would have to choose between firing and keeping up. I only had enough juice for a couple sun gun shots.

As our two ships continued to hurtle downward in a diving chase, I saw the tunnel begin to broaden slightly, and I fired another burst from my sun guns. But it didn't connect, and my cockiness now turned to panic, because the lone Glaive had just cleared the tunnel and come out the other side, zooming on into the cavernous drone hangar.

I followed it inside, and then slammed on my Interceptor's inertia brakes, because it appeared that I now had my enemy cornered. I continued firing plasma bolts at the Glaive, and shooting from a standstill drastically improved my aim. I scored two directs hits on its shields in rapid succession, causing them to flicker and then fail.

The second the Glaive's shields dropped, it slid to an instantaneous stop out ahead of me, near the hangar's cavernous center. I'd seen Glaive Fighters and EDA Interceptors execute this maneuver countless times while playing *Armada*. I'd executed it plenty of times myself—the drone had just initiated its self-destruct sequence. Its reactor core would overload in approximately seven seconds.

I fired a last volley of plasma bolts at the unprotected enemy ship, which was already vibrating from the buildup of power in its reactor core, and held my breath as they streaked toward it, silently praying to Crom that they would reach the Glaive and destroy it before it finished transforming itself into a weapon of mass destruction.

Time seemed to stop. I caught a second-long glimpse of the hangar around us and noticed that it was still over half-full. Thousands of brand-new, unused Interceptors were nestled into belt-fed launch racks that lined the hangar's curved reinforced concrete walls.

I watched in slow motion as the shots I'd fired closed in on the Glaive's quivering metal hull. They finally seemed to reach their mark at last, and I saw a blinding white flash across my cockpit's wraparound screens.

Then they all went black, and my entire drone controller station powered down, throwing the tiny room into total darkness. Somewhere above me, I heard the muffled atomic boom of a power core detonation, followed by a horrible rumbling that could only be several levels of the base collapsing in on each other.

I don't know how long I sat there in the pitch-black darkness, listening to the aftermath of my mistake. But at some point the door of my controller station hissed open, and a terrible flood of light poured in, momentarily blinding me. As my eyesight slowly returned, I saw a female silhouette resolve in the doorway. Lex was standing there, with one hand cocked on her hip.

"Did you see what happened?" she said, shaking her head. "Some moron Interceptor pilot chased that last Glaive Fighter into one of the launch tunnels, right before the whole hangar went up."

I nodded and got to my feet unsteadily; then I stepped out of my control pod, feeling almost as if I'd just emerged from a real Interceptor—and a real battle. Which, of course, I had.

"I'm still not even sure what happened up there," I lied.

"We'd already won," she said. "We'd just destroyed all but one of their drones—but then somehow the last Glaive Fighter got inside the drone hangar before it self-destructed," she said. "Somebody screwed up."

When I didn't respond, she studied my face for a moment.

"It was you, wasn't it?" she said. "Didn't you hear Admiral Vance screaming at you to break off over the comlink? Everyone else sure did!"

She pursed her lips and gave me two thumbs-up.

Before I could begin to formulate my defense, my QComm beeped and vibrated against my forearm; then its display began flashing red to get my attention. A text message appeared, ordering me to report to Admiral Vance in the command center. An interactive map of the base below it appeared, and a green path lit up, leading from my current location in the drone controller hub out into the corridor outside, then down to another bank of elevators.

Just as I finished reading the message, that synthesized female voice spoke over the base PA system. "Lieutenant Zack Lightman. You are ordered to report to Admiral Vance in the command center on level three immediately."

As Lex stepped aside to clear my path, she softly sang, *"You're in trouble."*

13

THE THREE-DIMENSIONAL MAP ON MY QCOMM TOOK ME ON A CIRCUITOUS multilevel route through the base. It seemed to be detouring me around the sections most heavily damaged by the hangar explosion, but I still saw signs of its aftermath everywhere.

As I made my way down half-collapsed corridors filled with smoke and sparking electrical fires, several ATHID emergency response teams marched past me, coming the other direction. I also saw a few of my fellow drone operators, many of them covered in dust or ash. Some shuffled along like zombies, while others ran past me in hysterics. At every turn, I expected to see a corpse—someone who had died because of me.

The dreamlike euphoria I'd felt during my arrival here had now completely subsided—replaced with a cocktail of confusion, uncertainty, and, most of all, doom.

When I passed through the security doors leading into the Crystal Palace command center, the two guards at the entrance seemed to know who I was and what I was doing there. In fact, it seemed as if everyone who saw me fixed me with a withering glare. But I glared back at each of them defiantly.

When I finally reached Admiral Vance's office, I paused outside in the corridor and practiced saluting a few times, mimicking the way I'd seen soldiers do it in the movies. Then I took a deep breath and pressed my hand to the scanner plate on the wall. A tone sounded and the doors slid open. With some effort, I stepped inside, and the doors hissed shut again behind me.

Admiral Vance was sitting behind his desk, but he stood up when I walked in. I halted just inside the entrance and gave him the amateur salute I'd just finished rehearsing.

He surprised me by straightening his posture and returning it, raising a rigid right hand to his brow in a blur, then dropping it like the blade of a guillotine a half-second later. That was when I noticed the sidearm on his right hip. An old-fashioned nine-millimeter Beretta. I was pretty sure he hadn't been wearing it earlier in the briefing auditorium.

I lowered my salute, but made sure to remain at rigid attention, while doing my best to avoid making direct eye contact with the admiral—which was surprisingly difficult, considering he was only rocking one eye. The admiral let the silence wear on, and I realized that he was waiting for me to speak first.

"Lieutenant Zack Lightman," I said, clearing my throat. "Reporting as ordered . . . sir."

"At ease, Lieutenant," the admiral replied, sounding surprisingly calm. "Sit."

He motioned to a metal chair beside his desk. As he took his own seat, the admiral reached over to shut off one of the computer monitors arrayed around his desk in a semicircle, but just before the screen went dark, I caught a glimpse of what was displayed on it—the same mug shot that was on my EDA security badge was clearly visible at the top, along with my senior yearbook photo and a lot of densely packed text—all of my private information, including my school records. Before I'd walked into his office, the admiral had been skimming my entire life story—and he'd made no effort to conceal this from me.

"You had quite a first day, Mr. Lightman," he said. "You're going to be the first recruit in EDA history to be court-martialed less than an hour after they enlisted." He smiled. "You might make *The Guinness Book of World Records,* provided it still exists after tomorrow."

"Admiral, sir—I'm still not even sure what it was I did wrong," I said, and that was mostly true. "I was trying to stop that ship from getting inside the base before it self-destructed! What did you expect me to do?"

"To follow orders, Lieutenant," the admiral said, and I thought I finally detected a hint of anger in his voice. He tapped a key on his computer, and his display screen lit up. He clicked his mouse a few times and my Interceptor appeared on the monitor, turning into a steep dive to pursue the last remaining Glaive Fighter as it streaked down into the open mouth of the drone launch tunnel while the admiral shouted over the comlink: *"Disengage and cease fire! Do not attempt to pursue that ship into the launch tunnels! I repeat, disengage and cease fire!"* "Hey, you skipped right over all the footage of me kicking ass," I protested. "Can't we watch a little of that? You know, for context?"

The admiral ignored me. The clip cut to another camera angle, which showed the last Glaive Fighter as it emerged from the opposite end of the drone launch tunnel and entered the hangar, with my ship close on its tail, still firing at it. The admiral paused the footage again.

"I issued that order for a good reason, Lieutenant," he said calmly. "If you'd followed it and broken off your pursuit, an armored safety blockade would have locked into place over that launch tunnel at both ends, preventing the enemy ship from flying into it. Like this—see?"

On another monitor, the admiral pointed to an animated wire-frame graphic that showed a Glaive Fighter approaching the launch tunnel's open mouth. But just before it got there, a thick circular disc slammed into place, covering the launch tunnel's entrance. A second later the enemy ship crashed into it and exploded in a simulated fireball.

"But that's not what happened, is it?" the admiral said. "Because you ignored my order and continued to pursue the enemy ship at close range, the transponder inside your Interceptor disabled the tunnel's safety blockades to allow it safe passage. Unfortunately, this also allowed the Glaive Fighter you were chasing to do the very same thing. Thanks to you, it was able to breach our defenses and enter our drone hangar, where it promptly detonated its reactor core."

He hit Play on the footage again, and I watched in silence as the Glaive Fighter completed its self-destruct sequence and detonated.

"Bravo, IronBeagle," the admiral said, giving me a sarcastic round of applause. "By some miracle no personnel were killed in that explosion," he said. "But we lost over five hundred brand-new ADI-88 Interceptors."

I winced. That was a lot.

"I did shoot down more enemy fighters than any of the other pilots," I said.

"True," he replied. "But your little screwup did more damage to this base than the enemy's sneak attack managed to." He frowned at me. "Whose side are you on?"

I didn't have a response for that. The even-tempered disappointment in his voice was somehow far worse than the *Full Metal Jacket*–style bawling-out I'd expected. "Those drones took years to build, at a cost of millions," he said. "But that's just money. To humanity, they were priceless, since we've run out of time to build any more of them."

"But, sir—how was I supposed to know about those automatic security blockades?" I said. "That was never a part of the game. In *Armada*, the Sobrukai never tried to fly one of their fighters into an EDA base through its drone launch tunnels."

"That's because we didn't think there was any way for the enemy's fighters to get past the launch tunnel security blockades." He sighed. "Apparently, no one believed one of our own pilots would be dumb enough to tail an enemy ship making a suicide run into our drone hangar."

"It's not fair to pin that on me," I shot back. "I've never even been in combat before—and I never wanted to be! You brought me here and told me we were being invaded by aliens about ten minutes before they attacked this fucking place! I'm a high school kid! I'm supposed to be in school right now!"

The admiral nodded, raising both hands in a calming gesture.

"You're right," he said. "I apologize. This isn't your fault." He smirked. "Not entirely."

His answer threw me. I didn't respond.

"The EDA always knew the risks of using a videogame simulation as the sole method of training civilian recruits," he said. "But under the circumstances there was no other option. It was the only way to locate and train millions of average people to operate combat drones in a short period of time without anyone knowing it. Your act of insubordination today—and its disastrous aftermath—are inevitable results of putting an unstable, undisciplined civilian like you on the front lines. But you're one of our most gifted pilots, so in your case, I was told the benefits would outweigh the risks." He let out a weary sigh. "Obviously, that turned out not to be the case."

He paused, giving me another chance to speak up in my own defense. I didn't take it.

"If you act without thinking in an *Armada* dogfight, there are no real consequences," he went on. "Your player ranking drops a few places and the game gives you a canned cut-scene lecture that you promptly ignore." He leaned forward. "But things have changed. This isn't a game anymore. We can't afford any more mistakes like the one you just made. Understood?"

"So does this mean you're not going to court-martial me?"

"Of course not," Vance said. "We need you, Lieutenant. Once the European armada begins to arrive, we're going to need every able-bodied human being on Earth to take up arms and help us fight them off. And that may still not be enough."

His gaze drifted back up to the countdown clock mounted on the wall above his desk, and mine followed: 7 hours 02 minutes and 11 seconds remaining. I glanced down at my QComm and saw the countdown mirrored there. It was hard to believe the attack and subsequent battle had all occurred in less than an hour. I watched the seconds tick off.

"But this was your first and only warning," the admiral said. "You screw up like this again . . . you'll be flying a cargo plane full of rubber dog shit out of Hong Kong."

I stared at him in surprise. He glared back at me for several seconds, then gave me an almost imperceptible smile. I suddenly realized who I was talking to—Admiral Vance was also Viper, the *Armada* pilot currently ranked in fourth place, just above Rostam. Viper was also the name of a character in *Top Gun*, the film he'd just quoted.

Until now, I hadn't known that Viper and Admiral Vance were the same guy. This little detail had yet to be revealed in *Armada*'s ongoing storyline—which now seemed to have spilled over into reality.

The admiral was still staring at me, waiting for a response. His grin was gone.

"Do we understand each other, son?"

I winced at the admiral's choice of words.

"Yes sir," I said through clenched teeth. "But I'm not your son."

He stared at me for a moment; then he smiled and nodded.

"I know," he said. "You're Xavier Lightman's kid."

We locked eyes.

"You look just like him," the admiral said, matter-of-factly. "You fly like him, too."

The office seemed to be spinning now, whirling around me with increasing velocity.

"You knew my father?" I finally managed to ask.

"I still know him," he said. He pointed to his QComm. "I just spoke with General Lightman before you arrived in my office. We talked about you, naturally."

The words fell on me like an avalanche.

Since I was a boy, I had imagined countless absurd scenarios in which my father had somehow faked his own death, or lost his memory, or been kidnapped by the CIA and brainwashed into becoming an assassin like Jason Bourne. But the fantasies had been just that—fantasies. I'd never really doubted that he was dead. Not until this moment.

"My father is dead," I said hollowly. "He didn't live to see my first birthday."

"Your father is alive," the admiral said. He reached up to touch the jagged scar on his right cheek. "And I owe him my life. We all do."

My mind kept rejecting that any of this was even possible. That any of this was really happening. My father wasn't just alive, but a general in the Earth Defense Alliance? A war hero, tasked with saving the world?

I opened my mouth, but Vance seemed to anticipate my next question before I asked it.

"The EDA faked your father's death when he was first recruited. All our early recruits were forced to cut off all contact with their old lives. In return, the EDA promised to take measures to help support each of their families financially, while they were off saving the world."

So my father had knowingly and willingly deceived and abandoned us? How could he have—

Admiral Vance cut into my thoughts again. "Try not to be angry at your father. He did it to protect *you*. To protect the *world*. And don't feel too sorry for yourself, either. Your family wasn't the only one that had to make sacrifices." He glanced down at the wedding ring on his left hand. "Trust me, Zack. Your father never forgot about you. He was actually kind of a crybaby over how much he missed you, to be honest." He studied me. "And even though you weren't aware of it, he actually reentered your life several years ago, albeit in a very limited way.

"General Lightman has been supervising your training ever since the *Armada* simulation first went online," Vance said. "He took part in nearly all of your training missions. He also happens to be *Armada*'s highest-ranking pilot. His call sign—"

"RedJive!" I blurted out. "My father is The Red Baron?"

The admiral nodded.

"Is he here?" I asked, glancing behind me, wondering if he was about to walk in. "When can I see him?" I jumped to my feet. "I want to talk to him, right now!"

"Calm down, Lieutenant," he said. "The general isn't stationed here at the Palace."

He flipped open a clear plastic folder on his desk and handed me the single sheet of paper inside. It appeared to be some kind of office memo printed on Earth Defense Alliance stationery. My full name, rank, and other vital statistics were printed neatly across the top, followed by several lines of text that contained a lot of abbreviations and acronyms I didn't recognize. The admiral's name and signature were at the bottom.

"What is this?" I asked, still trying to decipher the text.

"Your orders," he said. "Along with your duty station assignment. A digital copy has also been sent to your QComm."

I looked up at him. "I'm not staying here?"

He shook his head. "Most of Crystal Palace's personnel are being relocated to other outposts as we speak," he said. "The location of this base is obviously no longer a secret to the enemy—if it ever was to begin with. Besides, as you know, nearly all of our remaining aerial drones were destroyed when the reserve hangar went up."

I continued to scan my orders, trying to figure out where I was being sent—then I saw it, printed near the top. DUTY STATION ASSIGNMENT: MBA—LUNAR DCS.

"No way. You're sending me to *Moon Base Alpha*?"

He nodded.

"It's really up there?" I asked. "The EDA really built a secret defense base in a crater on the far side of the moon? Just like in the game?"

"Yes, Lightman," he said. "Just like in the game. Try to keep up."

His QComm buzzed on the desk in front of him, and he checked its display. Then he spun around in his chair and began to study the half-dozen display screens arrayed behind him.

"That will be all, Lieutenant," he said. He pointed to the exit. "Get your uniform and report to the shuttle bay immediately."

I stared back at him, not moving.

"I'm not going anywhere until you let me see my father, sir."

"Can't you read, Lieutenant?" he said. "He's your new commanding officer."

I glanced back down at the printout in my hand. There it was, printed just below my duty station: CO: GEN LIGHTMAN, X.

"Give your old man my best when you get to the far side of the moon," Admiral Vance said, in a voice that suddenly sounded light-years away. "And tell him we're even."

THE MAP ON MY QCOMM'S DISPLAY SCREEN LED ME BACK THROUGH THE UNDAMAGED SEC-tions of the base, down to level four. When I stepped off of one of the turbo elevators that was still operational, I joined the procession of recruits filing into the New Recruit Induction Center, an enormous carpeted room filled with a maze of high-walled office cubicles. It reminded me of the DMV offices in Portland—although, thank Zod, the line here appeared to be moving much more quickly. When I reached the front of it, a uniformed technician gave my retinas another scan. Then he retrieved a crisp new EDA flight officer's uniform from the long rack behind him and presented it to me, on a hanger draped in clear plastic, along with a pair of black running shoes with dark gray soles, Velcro laces, and no manufacturer's logo anywhere on them. The two-piece EDA uniform was dark blue, and its zippered jacket had gold piping along the shoulders and down each sleeve. My name and rank were stitched over the jacket's left breast pocket, above the Earth Defense Alliance insignia.

I filed into the adjacent changing rooms, then found an empty stall and got undressed. After I finished stuffing my civilian clothes into my backpack, I put my EDA uniform on. Everything was just my size.

I avoided looking in the mirror until I was finished, then turned to face my reflection. I hadn't worn a uniform since Cub Scouts, and I was concerned that this one might look equally unflattering on me. But when I checked my profile in the mirror, I thought I actually looked pretty sharp, like an intrepid young space hero about to embark on an epic adventure. Then I realized—that was more or less my new job description.

I stared at my face in the mirror, taking in the strange mix of fear and anticipation battling each other for supremacy there.

Then I straightened my uniform one last time, picked up my backpack, and exited the dressing room, feeling several inches taller now than when I'd first stepped inside. The map on my QComm directed me back through the base, again highlighting a circuitous route that took me around the areas damaged during the enemy's sneak attack.

When I reached the shuttle bay, I was surprised to see that aside from some rocky debris scattering the runway, it seemed to have escaped the attack—and my monumental screwup—unscathed.

Several EDA shuttles were parked on numbered landing pads around the perimeter of the hangar's oval-shaped runway, and I walked down the line until I spotted the one specified in my orders. Its cabin doors were open, and through them I could see that several people were already sitting on board, waiting for departure.

"Look at you," I heard a female voice say behind me. "An officer and a gentleman!"

I turned to see Lex, standing at rigid attention in her new EDA uniform, which looked as if it had been tailored to accentuate her frame.

"Well?" she said. "What do you think?"

I think you might be the girl of my dreams and I'll probably never see you again. That was what I was thinking. But I couldn't bring myself to say it out loud, so instead I took a step, straightened my spine, and snapped her a sharp salute.

"Lieutenant Zack Lightman," I said. "Reporting for duty, ma'am!"

"Lieutenant Alexis Larkin," she replied, returning the salute. "Ready to save the world!"

I dropped my hand and took a step back. "You look outstanding, Lieutenant."

"Why, thank you, Lieutenant," she said. "You don't look too shabby yourself." She studied the rank on my uniform. "So I take it the admiral decided not to court-martial your insubordinate ass?"

I shook my head. "He let me off with a warning."

She shook her head. "See what I mean?" she said. "You're clearly getting special treatment." She gave me a shove. "Is your old man a senator or a mob boss or something?"

I wasn't sure how to answer that, so I didn't. "Where are they sending you?" I asked.

"Sapphire Station," she said. "That's the code name for another base like this one, located just outside Billings, Montana. How about you?"

I handed her the printout of my orders that Vance had given to me. When she finally located my destination, her eyes went wide and she looked back up at me.

"Moon Base Alpha?" she said. "It's real?"

"Apparently."

She shoved the sheet of paper back at me in disgust. "What a bunch of horseshit!" she said. "I get stationed in Montana, and you get to go to the fucking moon. That's real fair." She gave me another playful shove. "Maybe I need to start being insubordinate, like you."

I knew she was joking, so I didn't respond. An awkward silence descended.

Lex unsnapped her QComm from the strap on her forearm. "Hold your arm out for a second."

I did as she asked. She touched her QComm to mine and both devices beeped.

"Now I've got your number, and you've got mine," she said. "We can stay in touch." She pointed to the countdown clock on her QComm and smiled. "We'll probably only be able to stay in touch for another six hours and forty-three minutes, so it's no big deal."

"Thank you," I said, staring down at her name on my own QComm's display, and then at the countdown timer next to it.

"Wow, you're a popular guy," Lex said, staring down at her QComm screen. She tapped it a few times, then tilted it toward me again, and I saw the three names listed on my own contact list mirrored there: Arjang Dagh, Alexis Larkin, and Ray Habashaw. Then she tapped the music icon, and I saw that she had somehow pulled all of the music off of my device, too.

"Hey, how did you do that?" I said, making a halfhearted grab for her QComm. She snatched it out of my reach.

"I was pissed when they hacked into my old phone, so I decided to try hacking theirs. It was shockingly easy." She smiled. "They may have used alien technology in these things," she said. "But the software they installed to run it all was clearly created by humans—overworked, underpaid programmers like me who take all kinds of shortcuts. The security protocols on the file-sharing system are a total joke. It only took me about five minutes to jailbreak this thing."

She tossed her QComm behind her back with one hand, then caught it effortlessly with the other, keeping her eyes on me the whole time. Then she held it back up in front of me.

"Access to the public phone network is still disabled, so I wasn't able to call my grandma," she said. "However, I did figure out how to enable admin privileges on the QComm network. Now I can pull private data stored on another QComm, just by calling it or touching it with mine. Contacts, text messages, emails, everything."

"But why would those features even be included in the software?"

"Why do you think?" she said. "So Big Brother can keep on spying on each of us, right up to the bitter end." She grabbed my phone. "Here, I'll jailbreak yours, too."

I handed my QComm back to her, then watched as her thumbs danced across the keyboard on its display for a moment.

"You're kind of amazing," I blurted out—because that was what I was thinking, and I'd recently been told the world was about to end. "Did you know that?"

She blushed, but didn't avert her gaze from my QComm display.

"Yeah, well," she said, playfully rolling her eyes. "That's just, like, your *opinion,* man."

I laughed and moved a step closer to her. She didn't move away.

"Listen," I said, as if she weren't quite obviously already doing so, "I know we just met, but I just wanted to let you know that I wish we'd met each other a long time ago, under different circumstances. . . ."

She smiled. "Don't go getting all mushy on me now, Princess," she said, stepping back. "So long."

She turned as if to walk away—then she abruptly turned again, spinning back around on her heel, grabbed me by my lapels, and then she kissed me—right on the lips, with tongue and everything. When we both finally came up for air, Lex wrapped her arms around me in a fierce hug. Then she stepped back and jerked a thumb over her shoulder, toward the lone shuttle on the opposite side of the bay.

"That's my ride over there," I said. "I think they're probably waiting on me."

"Yeah, we should both get going."

"Yes. We should."

Neither of us moved.

"Good luck, Lex," I said finally.

"Give 'em hell, Zack," she replied, grinning. "Call me from the far side of the moon. Let me know if you spot any Decepticons or secret Nazi bases hidden up there."

"Will do."

We saluted each other again; then she hoisted her new EDA backpack and ran over to her shuttle. I watched until she disappeared inside and its doors hissed closed. A few seconds later the shuttle lifted off and ascended through the narrow gap between the armored blast doors high above, which were now too warped and damaged to open all the way.

Then Lex's shuttle tilted skyward and rocketed away, out of sight.

I took a deep breath, hoisted my own pack onto my shoulder, and turned to walk toward my own shuttle, wondering how long it would take to fly me to the moon.

14

S I APPROACHED THE SHUTTLE, I COULD HEAR SEVERAL LOUD, OVERLAP-
ping voices coming through its open hatchway.

"Why does everyone always automatically assume that
RedJive is a man?" a woman asked in a thick, Fargo-esque accent. "That's
pretty damn sexist, if you ask me."

"Yeah," a younger female voice chimed in. "The Red Baroness might be
a better nickname—for *her*."

Female laughter followed. I paused a few yards from the shuttle and
crouched, pretending to adjust the Velcro straps of my new EDA sneakers
so that I could continue to eavesdrop.

"People assume RedJive is a guy because Red Five was a guy," a male
voice replied. He had some sort of East Coast accent that sounded equally
thick to my Pacific-Northwestern ears. "Hate to tell ya, but the Red Baron
was a dude, too—just like Maverick, Goose, Iceman, and every other ace
fighter pilot in history."

"You're aware that those are all fictional characters, right?" the younger
woman asked, talking over the man's chuckling. "For your information,
there have been female fighter pilots for over a hundred years now. I wrote
a report about it for school. A woman named Marie Marvingt flew combat missions over France way back in World War I, and the Russians

used female fighter pilots in World War II. And the US military has had women fighter pilots since the seventies."

After a pregnant pause, the male voice responded with an annoyed "Yeah, whatever."

This was followed by another round of high-pitched laughter and some scattered applause. I took it as my cue and stood up, then mounted the shuttle's small retractable staircase.

The laughter died out as soon as the cabin's four occupants saw me appear in the open hatchway and turned to face me. I stood there for an awkward beat, letting them size me up, while I did the same to them.

They were all dressed in newly pressed EDA flight officer uniforms like mine. To my immediate left sat a pretty middle-aged woman with tanned skin and dark hair, and the name LT. WINN stitched onto her uniform. There was an empty seat to her right while on her left sat a heavyset guy with an unruly beard who seemed to be eying me suspiciously. Seated across from him was a teenaged African-American girl who looked like she probably wasn't old enough to drive yet. A young Asian man sat beside her. He looked like he was in his early twenties, and there was a small Chinese flag beneath the EDA emblem on his uniform, instead of the tiny embroidered version of Old Glory that adorned everyone else's uniform, and instead of the words *Earth Defense Alliance* there was a string of characters in Chinese.

After the five of us had stared at each other in silence for what I felt was a sufficient length of time, I stowed my pack in the overhead compartment and took the empty seat next to the older woman, because she was the only one who had smiled at me.

"Hi," I said, offering her my hand. "I'm Zack Lightman. From Portland, Oregon." As dazed as I was, I still remembered to say I was from Portland instead of Beaverton, to avoid sounding like a hick—or having to endure any beaver-related attempts at humor.

"Welcome aboard, Zack," she said, squeezing my hand between both of her own. "I'm Debbie Winn." Something about her demeanor and tone made me guess that she was a schoolteacher.

"It's nice to meet you, Debbie."

"It's nice to meet you—even under such terrifying circumstances." She laughed and gave me an anxious smile. I returned it with one of my own.

"That's Milo," she said, gesturing to the bear-like man to her left, who was still staring at me with open hostility. The name patch on his uniform identified him as LT. DOBSON.

"Hi there, Milo," I said, reaching over to offer him my hand. "How goes it?"

He just stared at my hand without replying, until I finally shrugged and lowered it.

"Oh, ignore him—he's from Philly," Debbie said, as if that explained his rude behavior. Then she nodded at the young woman across from her. "Zack, that's Lila. Lila, meet Zack."

"Nobody actually calls me that," the girl said. "Everyone calls me by my nickname, Whoadie. That's my *Armada* call sign, too."

We shook hands, and I was about to tell her that I recognized her call sign, but then the young man beside her cleared his throat. The name LT. CHÉN was stitched onto his uniform.

"This is Jiang Chén—better known as CrazyJi," Whoadie said. "He's Chinese, and doesn't speak much English."

Chén smiled and shook my hand. He had spiky red hair that obscured the right half of his face, but the look seemed to work for him. Chén glanced down at the QComm strapped to his right wrist, where a string of Mandarin characters was appearing on his display. It must've been translating what Whoadie had said, because after Chén read over them, he looked up and gave me an exhausted smile.

"Hell-oh," he said with a thick accent. *"It goo to mee you."*

"It's good to meet you, too," I replied slowly. "I know your call sign well, CrazyJi. Yours too, Whoadie. We've flown lots of missions together. It's an honor to finally meet you in person." I stood up and held out my hand. "I'm Zack—also known as IronBeagle."

As soon as they heard my call sign, the tension in the tiny cabin evaporated, and all four of my new companions visibly relaxed—especially Milo, who actually smiled in my direction for the first time since I'd stepped aboard.

"The Beagle!" Whoadie repeated, smiling with recognition. "Good to finally meet you. You're a fucking legend, man!"

I saw Debbie wince when Whoadie dropped her F-bomb.

"IronBeagle?" Chén repeated with raised eyebrows, in what sounded like perfect English.

When I nodded, he lunged out of his seat to shake my hand, talking excitedly in Chinese. An English translation appeared on my QComm—a garbled string of compliments, for which I thanked him profusely. Once he finally calmed down and let go of me, we both retook our seats.

"What's your call sign, Debbie?" I asked, even though I already had a good guess, just due to the process of elimination.

She laid a hand on her chest and bowed her head. "AtomicMom, at your service." She smiled nervously. "You know, like 'Atomic Bomb'?"

"Yeah, lady, we get it," Milo said, rolling his bloodshot eyes.

"Let me guess," I said, leveling a finger at him. "You're Kushmaster5000, right?"

He smiled, looking immensely pleased. "The one and only."

The Kushmaster, also known as "KM5K" to his many detractors, was a pilot known for his incessant (and often unintentionally hilarious) boasting and trash talk on the Chaos Terrain player forums, where he used a prismatic cannabis leaf for his avatar. He also loved to do a running voice commentary of the battles over the public comm channel, like Jack Burton broadcasting on his CB. I usually muted him, but I still recognized his Philly accent, and the cocky attitude that seemed to come along with it. I wasn't sure I liked him, and he seemed to like it that way.

But in a strange way, learning their call signs suddenly made me feel as though I was among old friends—or at least familiar allies. AtomicMom, Whoadie, CrazyJi, and Kushmaster5000 were all names that I'd been seeing daily for the past year, because they were four of the call signs always listed among the top ten *Armada* pilot rankings—at first above, and then eventually below, my own. When I'd checked the rankings last night, Whoadie's call sign had been listed right after mine in seventh place, followed by CrazyJi in eighth, AtomicMom in ninth, and Kushmaster5000 in tenth.

"Sorry if I acted like a prick before," Milo said, solemnly offering me his fist to bump, which I did. "I thought you might be RedJive, or one of those other elitist dicks in the top five."

Chén read the translation, then whispered a response into his QComm in Chinese. The device instantly translated his words and repeated them in English.

"I was thinking the same thing," the computer said, in a synthesized male voice that sounded exactly like the one used by Stephen Hawking.

I suddenly found myself wondering if Hawking had been a part of the EDA's big cover-up, too. And what about Neil deGrasse Tyson? If Carl Sagan had been let in on the secret, it seemed possible that other prominent scientists had, too. I added this to the list of unanswered questions whirling around inside my head, which seemed to only be growing longer as this insane day progressed.

"I am not liking RedJive also," Chén's translator went on to declare loudly in its uninflected monotone. "He is an asshole total!"

Whoadie laughed and mimicked the translator's voice while she made stiff robotic motions with her arms. "Yes!" she intoned. "The Baron is complete face-fuck!"

The others laughed, but I shifted uncomfortably in my seat. Luckily, my dad's impromptu roast was interrupted a second later, when the hatchway leading to the cockpit slid open and an ATHID clanked through it on metal feet. The drone's head split open and extended a small flatscreen telepresence monitor that displayed a live video image of the drone's operator, a middle-aged EDA officer with an impressive Sam Elliott–gauge mustache.

"Welcome aboard," he said. "I'll be your shuttle pilot today: Captain Meadows."

The second he finished introducing himself, he was bombarded with questions from all sides, in a variety of accents, and in at least two languages. I wanted to ask him a few thousand of my own, but he was already holding up one of his drone's clawed hands, motioning for silence. It took a minute.

"I'm not authorized to answer your questions," he said. "Your new commanding officer will brief you as soon as we arrive at the moon base. If you have any other questions and the answers aren't classified, you can find them using the EDA Recruit Orientation Manual app on your QComm. Understood?"

Everyone nodded and glanced down at their QComms.

"Outstanding," the captain said in response to our silent compliance. "We'll depart in just a few minutes. But before we leave, I'm told there's someone who wants to see you off."

He motioned to the open hatchway just as a familiar-looking middle-aged man with red hair stepped through it, leaning into the shuttle's crowded cabin. He greeted everyone with a gleaming, press-photo-friendly smile.

"Finn Arbogast?" several of us said in unison.

"Guilty as charged," he said, grinning and slightly out of breath. "I ran all the way down here from the Op Center so I wouldn't miss my chance to finally meet all of you." He went around the cabin, giving each of us a firm handshake in turn. "You five people have been the pride and joy of the Chaos Terrain project for a long time now. In fact, your talent and dedication were what helped us convince the higher-ups that our civilian simulator training initiative could actually work on a global scale, so thank you!"

I'd seen plenty of photos and video interviews with Chaos Terrain's founder, but in person he was shorter than I expected. He shook my hand last, and when our eyes met, he cocked his head at me sideways.

"You're Zack Lightman, aren't you?" he said, shaking his head as he studied my face. "The famous IronBeagle?"

I nodded. He glanced around at the others, then gave me a sheepish grin.

"Listen, Lieutenant," Arbogast said. "I hope Admiral Vance wasn't too hard on you earlier. There was no way you could have known about the security blockade doors on those drone launch tunnels. No enemy ship ever attempted that maneuver during any of their attacks against our moon base, so we never included it as a possibility in any of your *Armada* training missions." He shrugged. "Live and learn, I guess."

I glanced around the cabin. Everyone was staring at me in wide-eyed surprise.

"That was you?" Milo said, laughing. "You're the kamikaze dumbass who chased that Glaive Fighter into the hangar before it went kaboom?"

I nodded.

Everyone stared at me for an awkward beat; then Arbogast clapped his hands.

"Well—I know you're about to depart for MBA, so I don't want to hold you up," he said. "I just wanted to thank each of you, and commend you on your bravery—"

"Excuse me, sir," Milo said, in his thick Philly accent. "But where the hell is RedJive? You know, The Red Baron? He's the top-ranked *Armada* pilot in the world, right? So why ain't he here? Aren't you gonna recruit him, too?"

Arbogast shot a glance at me, then looked back at Milo.

"RedJive was recruited decades ago," he said. "He's our most decorated pilot."

Arbogast studied my reaction while the others exchanged looks of surprise.

"But who the hell is he?" Milo asked. "Or she?" He gave Whoadie and Debbie a placating smile.

Arbogast nodded. "RedJive is the call sign used by General Xavier Lightman."

One at a time, the others each turned to look at the name patch sewn onto my uniform. Then they all stared at me for a few seconds. When I failed to say anything, Debbie finally broke the silence.

"Any relation, Zack?" she asked quietly.

I looked at Arbogast. He seemed interested in hearing how I would answer, too.

"He's my father," I said. "But I never knew him. I grew up believing he died when I was still just a baby. I just found out the EDA faked his death when they recruited him."

They all stared back at me in silence, taking this in—except for Chén, who had to read the translation off his QComm before he understood what I'd just said. When he looked up from its display a few seconds later, he let out a long low whistle.

"And now you're on your way to the moon to meet him for the first time?" Debbie said.

I nodded.

"Jesus, kid!" Milo said, shaking his head. "And I thought *my* day was turning out weird."

I turned back to Arbogast. "Do you know him?"

"A little," he said. "I had the honor of working with General Lightman briefly a few years ago. He was one of our primary military consultants on *Armada*." He studied my face for a second, then shook his head. "You look just like him."

I nodded. "Yeah, so I keep hearing."

We heard a low whine as the shuttle engines began to power up. Arbogast stood up straight and snapped us all a clumsy salute.

"Thank you again for your service," he said. "And good luck up there!"

Then he exited the shuttle before anyone could even return his salute. After he left, the ATHID Meadows was controlling turned to slap a large red button on the bulkhead. The shuttle's doors slid closed with a pressurized hiss, barely audible over the growing roar of the engines.

"Strap in, recruits," Meadows told us over his comm. "We're cleared for departure."

I pulled on my safety harness and fumbled with the buckle until it finally clicked into place; then I pulled the straps tight against my chest. Once everyone was properly buckled in, Meadows' ATHID gave us all a robotic thumbs-up.

"The journey to Moon Base Alpha should only take about forty minutes," he said. "Once we clear the Earth's atmosphere, we'll be moving extremely fast. If we run into any hostiles along the way, you'll each be able to use your QComms to control one of the omnidirectional laser turrets mounted on the underside of the hull. But our scopes are clear right now, so it should be smooth sailing. Just sit back and try to enjoy the ride."

The drone returned to the cockpit, and I saw it dock with its charging station just before the hatch closed. When I glanced around the cabin, I found that my companions were once again staring at me. Debbie and Whoadie quickly averted their eyes, but Milo and Chén both just kept right on staring, as if a sparkly horn had suddenly sprouted from my forehead. I ignored them as long as I could; then I slowly mimed cranking up the middle finger of my right hand. When it reached full mast, they both finally seemed to get the hint and looked away.

I took out my QComm and tried punching my mother's mobile number into the keypad, but the call didn't go through, and a notice popped up informing me that access to the civilian phone system was still restricted.

I sighed and snapped the QComm back onto my wrist.

WE LIFTED OFF A FEW MINUTES LATER. AS BEFORE, THE RIDE REMAINED PERFECTLY SMOOTH, even as the shuttle climbed through the atmosphere and accelerated to escape velocity—and the sky outside our windows gradually began to turn from light blue to pitch black.

And this time, when we reached the edge of all that blackness, the shuttle didn't turn around and begin to fall back to Earth. We kept right on going, out into space. As on my first shuttle trip, the gravity inside the cabin never wavered, and when I closed my eyes, it felt as if we were motionless, even though we were moving so fast that within just a few minutes, we'd already traveled far enough away from Earth for me to be able to see the entire planet all at once, something I'd dreamed of doing for as long as I could remember.

I stared down at the radiant blue-white sphere that was home to everything and everyone I loved and scanned the gaps in the swirling cloud layer until I located the western coastline of North America, then followed it until I spotted the familiar inlet of Portland, just barely visible. I realized then just how far away I already was from home. And it was getting farther and farther away every second.

That's what we're fighting for, I thought. *That's what they're trying to take from us.*

I pressed my face against the window beside me, craning my neck to see as far ahead of us as possible. And there it was: a radiant gray-white bulb, shining in the darkness far ahead of us. I'd spent my entire life believing that no human being had set foot on its surface since the last Apollo mission in 1972. Now I was headed there myself, aboard a spacecraft that incorporated reverse-engineered alien technology, to meet the father I had never known. What was he like now? What would he say when he saw me? How would I react?

Across from me, I noticed that Debbie had her head down, and her hands were clasped together in her lap. Her eyes were closed, and she was moving her lips in silence.

"What are you doing?" Milo asked, sounding genuinely curious.

Debbie silently whispered *"Amen"* to herself, then opened her eyes and looked over at him.

"I was obviously trying to pray, Milo," she said.

"You were *praying*?" he said, his voice dripping with sarcasm. "To who?"

Debbie stared at him in disbelief. "To Jesus, Our Lord and Savior, of course."

"Oh, yeah, of course," Milo said, chuckling. "Just one question, church lady—in what part of the Bible did Jesus warn us about this alien invasion?" He glanced around the cabin at the rest of us for support. "Because I must have missed that verse!"

Debbie stared back at him, instantly livid. She opened her mouth, but his question seemed to have her so flustered that she didn't know how to respond.

Whoadie did, though.

"'And the fifth angel sounded,'" she recited, locking eyes with Milo, "'and I saw a star fall from heaven unto the earth: and to him was given the key of the bottomless pit. And he opened the bottomless pit; and there arose a smoke out of the pit, as the smoke of a great furnace.... And the sun and the air were darkened by reason of the smoke of the pit.'"

"What pit?" Milo asked. His smile was gone. "What are you talking about, kid?"

I'd been raised to believe there was no real difference between religion and mythology, but Whoadie's words spooked me nevertheless. The verse she quoted conjured up a vivid memory of the cataclysmic fire and smoke roiling off the Crystal Palace blast doors as they buckled and warped under a hail of alien laser fire.

"'And they worshipped the dragon which gave power unto the beast,'" she said, "'and they worshipped the beast, saying, who is like unto the beast? Who is able to make war with him?'"

When she finished, everyone just stared at her for a moment. Then Debbie began to applaud, and Chén and I joined in. Whoadie blushed and looked down at her feet.

"My uncle Franklin loves to quote Scripture," she said, shrugging. "I been hearing him recite Revelations since before I could walk."

"Well, I vote for no more Bible verses," Milo said, raising his right hand. "That seriously creeped me out."

Debbie nodded. "Quoting Revelations is probably a bad idea right now," she said. "I think we're all terrified enough already."

Whoadie gave Milo and Debbie a look of disappointment before she replied.

"'He which hath no stomach to this fight, let him depart,'" she recited, still glaring at the two adults. "'His passport shall be made, and crowns for convoy put into his purse—we would not die in that man's company, that fears his fellowship to die with us.'"

They both stared back at her for a long moment.

"What is it with you, anyway, kid?" Milo asked finally.

Whoadie shrugged again. "The only thing my uncle Franklin loves more than quoting Scripture is quoting Shakespeare." She smiled to herself. "I seen all those Branagh and Zeffirelli movies about a zillion times each, so I know every word by heart."

Chén typed something into his QComm's translator, then tilted it toward her.

"You are very smart and you have an amazing memory," the synthesized voice said.

Even though his compliment came via a computer, it was enough to make her blush again as she whispered, "Thank you." She and Chén shared another glance. They seemed smitten with each other already, despite the language barrier.

"How old are you, Whoadie?" Debbie asked, clearly trying to change the subject.

"I just turned sixteen last week," she said. "But I don't have my license yet."

"You sound like you're from New Orleans," Debbie told her, doing her best to pronounce it *N'Awlins*.

Whoadie nodded. "I live in the Ninth Ward," she said. "That's actually where my nickname comes from. *Whoadie* is how the locals say *wardie*. That's a person who lives in the same ward as you," she explained. "My parents called me Whoadie ever since I was a baby. I didn't always like it, because there were some boys at school used to call me Whoadie the Toadie all the time. But then I punched their fucking lights out and they stopped."

She said this in such a sweet, girlish voice that I burst out laughing. So did Milo. But Debbie looked absolutely horrified.

"Lila!" she said, wincing again. "Such language, honey! Your parents don't let you swear like that around them, do they?"

Whoadie folded her arms. "Well, no, they didn't used to," she said. "But they both died in a hurricane when I was little, so now I get to say whatever the fuck I want."

"Oh, snap!" Milo muttered under his breath.

"You poor dear," Debbie said, looking embarrassed. "I'm sorry. I didn't know."

Whoadie nodded and looked away, leaving Debbie to squirm in the silence that followed. That was when Milo decided to try to help salvage the conversation.

"Hey," he said, nodding at me. "Zack over there thought his father was dead, too—but he's not. Maybe your folks are still alive, too?"

Whoadie glared back at him, then shook her head slowly.

"They drowned," she said. "I saw their bodies."

She didn't elaborate. Milo was too taken aback to even respond. Whoadie turned to look out the window, and I watched her, recalling what Admiral Vance had told me about not feeling too sorry for myself.

"How about you, Debbie?" I asked, desperate to change the subject. "Where do you hail from?"

"Duluth, Minnesota," she said, giving me a grateful smile. "I'm a school librarian there. I also have three boys, all teenagers now. The oldest is only fifteen." Her smile faded. "I didn't even get to say goodbye to any of them. They let me send my sister a text message, asking her to pick them up, but I obviously couldn't say why."

"Can't your husband take care of them?" Whoadie asked.

Debbie glanced down at the wedding ring on her left hand, then smiled at Whoadie.

"I'm afraid not, dear," she said, meeting Whoadie's gaze. "Howard died of a heart attack last year."

Now it was Whoadie's turn to look embarrassed. "Sorry."

"It's all right," she said. "My boys are tough as nails. I'm sure they'll get through this fine. I just hope—" Her voice hitched, but she went on. "When I'm allowed to call them later, I just hope they understand why I couldn't stay with them through all of this."

"They'll understand," I said, with as much assurance as I could. "Your sons are gamers, too, right?"

She nodded. "They all play *Terra Firma* together every night, while their mom is playing *Armada*," she said. "We all have our computers set up next to each other in the living room."

"Then your boys will be fighting right alongside us," I said, smiling at her. "Right?"

Debbie nodded, and wiped her eyes on her sleeve.

"Right," she said. "That's right, I forgot."

"Fucking-A!" Milo shouted. "We're gonna have AtomicMom's boys whipping ass for our team, too?" He smiled at Debbie. "Those alien dip-shits won't stand a chance."

To my surprise, Debbie returned his smile, and I found myself reconsidering my first impression of Milo. His Rocky Balboa–esque method of speaking somehow made his cocky enthusiasm seem endearing.

Chén—who had just now caught up with the conversation via his translator—nodded vigorously in agreement with Milo, then spoke into his translator.

"I know my friends and family back home will be helping us fight, too," the software said for him—finally giving a coherent translation for once. "And that is very comforting to me."

"Thank you, Chén," Debbie said. "You too, Milo. You're right, that is comforting." She twisted her hands into knots in her lap. "But I'm still frightened for my family—and for all of us." She shook her head. "I never believed something like this could really happen. It's a nightmare."

"I don't know," Milo said, leaning back. "It seems more like a dream come true to me."

Debbie stared at him. "Are you insane?" she asked. "How could you possibly think that?"

Milo shrugged. "Yesterday I was living in a shitty basement apartment and working a soul-crushingly boring cubicle job." He motioned to the surreal view out the shuttle window. "Look at me now! I'm an officer in the Earth Defense Alliance, and I'm on my way to the fucking moon to help save Earth from an alien invasion!" He turned back to Debbie. "Now please explain to me how this isn't the greatest day *ever*? Like, in history?"

"Because we're all about to get killed, moron!" she shouted back, with a tremor of hysteria creeping into her voice. "Were you even paying attention during the admiral's briefing? Did you see the size of their armada? We're going to be ridiculously outnumbered!"

Milo seemed genuinely surprised. "I may have missed that part of the briefing," he said. Then, under her withering glare, he added, "I have ADD! My mind wanders during long meetings!" For the first time, I detected genuine fear in his voice. "Are the odds really that bad? The admiral never said—"

"What?" Debbie asked, interrupting him. "That we're probably doomed? Why would he say that out loud?" She turned to look out the window. "He doesn't need to. It's obvious. I mean, how desperate must the odds be if *we're* the Alliance's best hope? We're a bunch of gamer geeks, not soldiers."

"Yes we are!" Milo replied. "We all just enlisted, remember?" He shook his head at her. "Come on, lady—can't you try and be a little more positive? This isn't over yet. We can still win this thing!"

Debbie studied him for a moment before she replied. "Don't you get it, Milo? No matter who wins, millions of people are going to die when the fighting starts a few hours from now."

He waved a hand at her dismissively. "Oh, grow some balls! If killing these alien dipshits is half as easy as it is in the game, we're gonna kick their European asses!"

"*Europan,* Milo," I said. "You. Rope. An. Not 'European.'"

"Whatever the fuck you wanna call them," he sighed. "You know what I mean."

"I hate to say it," Whoadie said. "But I agree with Milo. If we beat them in the game, we can beat them in real life." She looked around at the three of us hopefully. "After all, we are the best of the best, right?"

Before his QComm even had time to finish translating for him, Chén jumped to his feet and shouted "Right!" with a raised fist. Then he bared his teeth and shouted something that sounded like "Sheng-lee!"

His QComm repeated the word in synthesized English: "Victory!"

Whoadie grinned and raised a fist of her own, then repeated after Chén, shouting "Sheng-lee!" at nearly the same volume.

"Hell yeah!" Milo shouted, throwing up a pair of heavy-metal horns. "Sheng-lee!"

Debbie glanced at me, waiting to see if I would take up their battle cry, too. Privately, I shared her grim appraisal of our chances. But feigning optimism seemed like it would be better for everyone's morale—including my own.

I raised a fist like the others, then, with as much enthusiasm as I could muster, I repeated their cry of "Sheng-lee!" I nudged Debbie with my elbow, and she sighed in resignation.

"Sheng-lee!" she echoed, halfheartedly pumping her fist in the air. "Woo."

Chén grinned at all of us, leaned forward, and stretched out his right hand, with his palm facing down. Whoadie smiled back and stacked her hand on top of his; then Milo, Debbie, and I each did the same thing. Then, in unison, we all shouted "Sheng-lee!" one more time.

A second later, we heard Captain Meadows' voice on the intercom again, announcing that we were on final approach to Moon Base Alpha. This seemed to make us self-conscious, and we all quickly withdrew our hands.

The shuttle banked sharply, and the moon's cratered surface suddenly filled the portside windows as we rocketed into orbit. I caught a brief glimpse of the Tycho impact crater as we zoomed over it on our way around to the far side, which was mostly in shadow. This hemisphere of the moon always faced away from Earth, so it was the first time any of us were seeing it with our own eyes. The surface was marred by a few small blackened regions, which looked like burn marks, but there were no ocean-sized dark patches or "seas" like those that marred the moon's more familiar hemisphere. The landscape here on the far side of the moon was far more uniform in color and appearance, but that didn't make it seem any more inviting.

As we sailed over the cratered and barren lunar surface, I was struck by a brief vision of Earth after the coming conflict. The battle had left our world ravaged and dead, as devoid of life and color as its own moon, its oceans and atmosphere burned away, its mighty cities replaced with impact craters, and the whole of its once-beautiful surface scorched black by the fire of war.

I shook my head and rubbed my eyes with the palms of my hands before looking back down at the lunar surface.

The sun was low in the sky, causing the more prominent craters to cast long shadows that stretched out across the pockmarked surface like crooked black fingers. Far below, an enormous bowl-shaped crater slid into view, and the sight sent a chill cascading down my spine. I recognized this place. I was looking down at the Daedalus crater complex, the secret location of Moon Base Alpha. I'd known this was our destination, but I still hadn't been able to convince myself that it really existed until that moment, when I saw it with my own eyes.

The large crater, Daedalus, had a much smaller, steeper crater named Daedalus B immediately adjacent to it, and a third, even smaller crater adjacent to that, known as Daedalus C. The lips of all three craters touched, and when viewed from directly above, their outlines somewhat resembled the shape of a pocket watch, with Daedalus B standing in for the small round knob on top, and Daedalus C serving as the even smaller chain ring attached to it. These three craters immediately stood out from the thousands of others on the lunar surface because even at this distance, they all contained obvious evidence of human construction.

The walls of the big crater had been smoothed out and curved into a perfect bowl shape to create a dish antenna for an enormous radio telescope. Its design was similar to that of the Arecibo Observatory in the mountains of Puerto Rico, but several hundred times larger. The two smaller craters each had an armored sphere nestled inside, like a golf ball sitting atop a shot glass. They were made of armored metal plating that had been painted gray to match the lunar surface.

"Moon Base Alpha!" Chén shouted as he spotted it, too. Then he began to talk excitedly in Chinese as he pointed out things down on the surface. The others craned their necks to see out the nearest window, and they each gasped at their first glimpse of our destination.

"There it is!" Whoadie said, bouncing in her seat. "It's really there. It's really real!"

Moon Base Alpha was a familiar sight to all of us, because we'd flown our Interceptors into and out of a simulated version of it hundreds of times while playing *Armada*. Our shuttle was even approaching along the same trajectory, giving me a strange sense of déjà vu.

As we made our final approach, the dome at the top of the smaller sphere split apart into equal segments, like an orange, and retracted far enough to permit our shuttle entrance. As soon as we descended inside the dome, its armored segments slammed back together above us, sealing the hangar bay once again, which essentially functioned like a giant airlock. Its design had always reminded me of the docking bay of the fictional Clavius Base featured in *2001: A Space Odyssey*. Now I found myself wondering if the EDA had borrowed elements from Stanley Kubrick's design. After all, stranger things had obviously happened—and were still happening right now.

Our shuttle touched down on the hangar floor a moment later, and when the engines cut out, an abrupt silence filled the cabin. The others were all pressed to the windows, but I couldn't look. I just sat there frozen in my seat, paralyzed by oscillating waves of anticipation and dread.

Meadows' ATHID emerged from the cockpit and used one of its clawed hands to slap a large green button on the bulkhead. The safety bars around our seats retracted up into the ceiling as the doors opened with a hiss.

"Leave your gear and follow me," Meadows told us over the drone's comm speaker. Then the ATHID turned and exited the shuttle, motioning for us to follow.

Whoadie immediately unbuckled her harness and literally jumped out of her seat. She was already running when her feet hit the floor.

"I can't believe we're on the moon!" she said in childlike wonder, stretching her arms out wide as she leapt through the shuttle's open hatchway. I saw her sprint off and noticed that she didn't bounce as she ran, the way the Apollo astronauts always did in footage of the moon landings, which meant the gravity up here was somehow being altered to match that of Earth.

Chén struggled to get free of his own harness, then scrambled outside after Whoadie. It took Milo slightly longer to extricate himself, but then he exited the shuttle, too, grinning like a little kid on Christmas morning, leaving Debbie and me alone in the passenger cabin. She unbuckled her safety harness and turned in her seat to face me.

"You ready to head out there, Zack?"

I started to nod, but ended up shaking my head.

"I've spent my whole life fantasizing about this moment," I told her. "And now . . . I think I'm too terrified to even go out there."

"It'll be all right," she said. "He's probably just as nervous about meeting you. Maybe even a little more."

Meadows' ATHID stuck its head back into the cabin, with his telepresence monitor now deployed. He smiled at Debbie through the screen, then rotated his drone's head to address me.

"The general is right outside in the hangar bay, waiting to meet you, Lieutenant." He turned to Debbie. "He asked me to escort you and the other new arrivals down to Operations, so that he and the lieutenant can have a few minutes in private. They'll join us there shortly."

"Of course," Debbie said, standing up. She brushed a lock of hair off my forehead, then squeezed my shoulder and gave me another smile. "See you in a few minutes, okay?"

I nodded. "Thanks, Debbie."

She gave me one last smile before she departed with Meadows' ATHID.

I sat there alone inside the cabin for a few seconds, summoning my courage. Then I thumbed the release latch on my safety harness and shrugged it off as I slowly got to my feet.

When I finally stepped outside, he was right there, waiting for me.

15

HE WAS JUST A FEW YARDS AWAY FROM ME, STANDING AT RIGID ATTENTION in a uniform just like the one I now wore. My father, Xavier Ulysses Lightman. Living and breathing.

And smiling.

He was smiling at me—with my own smile, on an older version of my face. The man standing in front of me could have passed for my time-traveling future self, come back to warn me of our shared destiny.

Out of the corner of my eye, I saw Meadows' ATHID escort Debbie through a pair of armored doors at the opposite end of the hangar. Chén, Milo, and Whoadie were waiting for them just inside the tunnel on the other side, along with an EDA officer I didn't recognize, who had a Japanese flag on his uniform. The entire group gaped at us through the open airlock doors until the doors slammed shut again a second later with a dull boom that echoed through the vast hangar.

I was only vaguely aware of their departure, or of my new surroundings, because all of my senses were now acutely focused on my father. The paternal ghost whose absence had haunted my entire adolescence now stood before me, miraculously resurrected. I found myself staring at a drop of sweat that had formed on his brow, and then watching as it rolled down the side of his face, as if this detail were proof this was really happening.

It made me think of a scene in the original *Total Recall*—another movie I knew by heart because he'd once owned a copy on VHS.

I took a long look at him, while he did the same to me. As I drank in the details of my long-lost father's face, my firsthand familiarity with his features made it easy for me to detect the fear he was trying to conceal.

He looked older than I'd expected—but that was probably because he'd never been older than nineteen in every photo of him I'd ever seen. I think part of me was also subconsciously hoping that when I saw him, it would appear that he hadn't aged at all, because the EDA had frozen him in carbonite or subjected him to light-speed time dilation to keep him young for the coming war. No such luck. He would be thirty-seven now, the same age as my mother—but unlike her, he looked a decade older than his real age, instead of a decade younger. He still appeared to be in excellent physical condition, but his once dark hair was now shot through with gray, and there were prominent crow's-feet around his eyes, which were the same exact shade of blue as my own. A hardened weariness seemed to permeate his features, and I wondered if I was getting a glimpse of what my face would look like, if I somehow lived to be his age.

I was still wondering that when I realized he was already moving toward me, closing the narrow distance between us, and then his arms were suddenly wrapped around me.

A dam ruptured somewhere in my chest, and a torrent of feelings came rushing out of me all at once. I buried my face against him, and this triggered a long-dormant sense memory: the sensation of my father holding me just like this, when I was still an infant. It may have even been my memory of the very last time he'd held me, before he'd vanished from my life forever.

No, not forever, I told myself. Until right now.

"I'm so happy to see you, Zack," he whispered, with a slight tremor in his voice. "And I'm sorry—so sorry for leaving you and your mother. I never imagined that I would be gone for so long."

Each word he spoke made my heart swell, until it felt as if it might burst. In one breath, my father had just said all of the things I'd always dreamed of hearing him tell me, back when I'd still allowed myself to fantasize about him still being alive. And I was too overwhelmed to respond. Part of me was still sure that all of this was some sort of precarious dream, and that if I said or did the wrong thing, I would wake up now, at the worst possible time.

I tried again to speak, to tell him I'd been dreaming of this moment my entire life. But I still couldn't find my voice. My father seemed to take my continued silence as a negative sign. He let go of me and stepped back; then he began to study my face, trying to decipher whatever dazed expression he saw there.

"I've been waiting eighteen years to tell you all of that, Zack," he said quietly. "I've practiced saying it in my head a million times. I hope I got it right. I hope I didn't screw it up."

Absurdly, I found myself wishing that my mother were here, so she could introduce me to this complete stranger who was wearing my face.

"You didn't," I finally managed to say, nearly inaudible. Then I cleared my throat and tried again. "You didn't screw it up," I said cautiously. "I'm happy to see you, too."

My father exhaled.

"I'm relieved to hear that," he said. "I wasn't sure you would be." He smiled nervously. "You have every right to be angry, and I know you've got a temper, so—"

He stopped speaking when he saw my smile vanish. Then he winced and contorted his brow—the exact same way I always did when I said something and instantly regretted it.

"How could you possibly know if I've 'got a temper'?" I asked, the anger rising in my voice like mercury. My father laughed involuntarily at the irony of my response, but it was lost on me, and his reaction only made me feel even more hurt and pissed off. Somehow, all of the excitement and euphoria I'd felt upon meeting him had dissipated in the span of a few seconds. "What makes you think you know anything about me at all?"

"I'm sorry, Zack," he said. "But I'm your new commanding officer. I read over your EDA recruit profile, and it contains all of your civilian school and police records."

"All of my private psych evaluation results, too, I'll bet."

He nodded. "The EDA finds out everything they can about potential recruits."

I nodded. "Did my 'recruit profile' mention that my anger-management issues might be linked to the tragic death of my father in a shit-factory explosion when I was ten months old?"

The question clearly hurt him, but I couldn't help but twist the knife a little farther.

"What do you think it was like for me, growing up believing that's how my father died?" I asked. "And having everyone in the whole town believe it, too? Were you trying to ruin my life? Couldn't you have pretended to die in a fucking car accident or something instead?"

He opened his mouth and then closed it a few times before he managed to form any words.

"It wasn't like I had a choice, Son," he said. "It had to be an explosion, so that the body couldn't be identified. They buried a John Doe in my place." He met my gaze. "I'm sorry. I was a kid myself, at the time. I didn't really understand what I was agreeing to do—and to give up."

We stood there staring at each other in silence for a moment; then my father's QComm beeped. He glanced down at its display with a frown, then turned back to me.

"We need to get up to Operations and get you and the other new arrivals briefed," he said. "But we'll have a chance to talk more in private later on, okay?"

I nodded mutely. I'd waited this long—and what choice did I really have?

My father removed a small silver object from his pocket. "Here," he said, pressing it into the palm of my hand. "This is for you."

I turned it over. It was a USB flash drive with an EDA emblem stamped on its casing.

"What's on it?"

"Letters, mostly," he said. "I wrote to you and your mom every single day I was up here." I noticed that he was shifting his weight from one foot to another while he spoke—another of my own nervous tics. "I hope they help explain why I made the decision I did, and how hard it's been for me to live with ever since." He shrugged, still avoiding my gaze. "Sorry there are so many—you probably won't have enough time to read them all."

His voice faltered, and he turned away from me to hide his face. I glanced down at the flash drive, then closed my fist around it protectively, unnerved that so small an object could hold such priceless contents.

My father raised the QComm on his wrist and tapped a series of icons on its display. There was a metallic clank as a row of storage-compartment doors built into the underside of the shuttle's fuselage slid open, revealing cube-shaped shipping containers. My father whispered a series of commands into his QComm, and a few seconds later, a team of four ATHIDs disengaged from a nearby charging rack and marched single-file over to the shuttle. Three of the drones began to unload the cargo, while the fourth climbed into the passenger cabin to retrieve our backpacks.

"Ready, Lieutenant?" my father asked, nodding toward the exit.

"Yes, sir," I replied, slipping the flash drive into one of my uniform's breast pockets so that it rested directly over my heart. Then, together, we continued to cross the hangar, and I finally widened my focus enough to take in the details of my surreal surroundings.

The Moon Base Alpha hangar bay was a breathtaking site. The curved walls of the armored dome around us were lined with hundreds of gleaming Interceptor drones arrayed in the belt-fed launch racks that would fire them out into space like bullets from a high-velocity gas-powered machine gun. These were the drones we had been brought up here to pilot, I realized. We would use these very ships to wage war with the enemy when they arrived here, just over five and a half hours from now.

In that moment, I felt like Luke Skywalker surveying a hangar full of A-, Y-, and X-Wing Fighters just before the Battle of Yavin. Or Captain Apollo, climbing into the cockpit of his Viper on the *Galactica*'s flight deck. Ender Wiggin arriving at Battle School. Or Alex Rogan, clutching his Star League uniform, staring wide-eyed at a hangar full of Gunstars.

But this wasn't a fantasy. I wasn't Buck Rogers or Flash Gordon or Ender Wiggin or anyone else. This was real life. My life. I, Zackary Ulysses Lightman, an eighteen-year-old kid from Beaverton, Oregon, newly recruited by the Earth Defense Alliance, had just been reunited with my long-lost father on the far side of the moon—and now, together, we were about to wage a desperate battle to prevent the destruction of Earth and save the human race from total annihilation.

If this were all just a dream, I wasn't sure that I would want it to end.

But it *was* going to end, and soon—because there was an egg timer strapped to my forearm counting off exactly just how many more hours, minutes, and seconds remained until my rude awakening.

When my father reached the exit, he continued walking through the open airlock doors, into the tube-shaped access tunnel beyond, which—if the layout of this place was as identical to its virtual counterpart in *Armada* as it seemed—led beneath the lunar surface, to the adjacent Daedalus B crater, where the rest of the base was located.

But I stopped just shy of the exit, and turned back to take another look at the thousands of Interceptors racked into the curved dome wall around me, and at the automated drone-assembly plants at its far end, their matter compilers and nanobots working even now to construct more ADI-88s—which they would probably never have time to finish, if what Vance had told me about the aliens' speed was true. I winced as another wave of shame washed over me at the memory of my colossal screwup at Crystal Palace, and the hangar full of drones it had cost us.

But then I recalled one of the final images from the EDA briefing film, of the Europan armada, a massive deadly ring of warships encircling the icy moon, all now headed toward Earth.

Those drones we lost at Crystal Palace wouldn't have made any difference. Nor would all of the drones here, or those stockpiled back on Earth.

My father saw me lingering inside the hangar and ran back to fetch me. "What's wrong, Zack?"

I laughed out loud at the absurdity of his question.

"What's wrong?" I repeated. "Gee, let me think now . . ."

"We need to get moving, Lieutenant," he said. "There isn't much time."

But I didn't move. My father waited.

I turned to study his face, then asked him the question I needed to ask: "How badly outnumbered are we going to be? Once the entire armada arrives?"

"So badly it's not really even worth thinking about," he said immediately, without even pausing to consider his answer. And the lack of concern in his tone pissed me off all over again.

"Then why the hell did you bring me up here?" I asked. "So that you could have a quick father-son playdate before we both die horribly?" I jerked a thumb at the shuttle. "If we're doomed, just tell me right now. I'd rather fly that thing back home and die with my mother. She's all alone now, you realize?"

My father looked as if I'd just gutted him, and I felt a pang of regret—but it was mingled with a twisted sense of satisfaction. It felt good to hurt his feelings—it was payback for the way his choices had irrevocably damaged my own.

It took my father a moment to respond. When he did, his tone of voice had hardened.

"I didn't 'bring' you up here, Lieutenant. You voluntarily enlisted as a solider in the Earth Defense Alliance. You don't get to run home now just because you're scared. Trust me."

"I'm not scared," I said, lying right through my teeth.

"If that's true, then you're a fucking idiot," he said matter-of-factly. "But I know that's not the case." He looked me in the eyes. "I've been fighting this war for half my life now, Zack, and I'm terrified. You don't know how long I've lived in fear of this day, and now it's here."

"You're not making me feel any better right now," I told him.

"I know that, Lieutenant," he said. "I also know how hopeless our chances must seem, given what you've been told and the images you've been shown. But believe me, Son, there are a lot of things about our situation—and our enemy—that you still don't know."

He cast a glance back over his shoulder, toward a large security camera mounted above the nearest exit, sweeping its lens slowly back and forth. Then he turned back to me, and I think that was when I caught my first glimpse of something truly unsettling in my father's eyes. A hint of the very madness that I'd always feared I might have inherited from him.

"We can't talk now, or here," he said, lowering his voice to a whisper. "But things aren't nearly as hopeless as they seem, Zack. I promise you."

He gave me a hopeful smile. "That's why I'm so thankful you're here now. I'm going to need your help."

Despite my better judgment, I went ahead and asked, "With what?"

"With saving the world, Son," my father said. "You think you're up for that?"

I straightened my posture, and for the first time I noticed we were now the same height.

"Yes, sir, General, sir," I replied. "Most definitely."

There was no mistaking the look of pride on my father's face. It was intoxicating.

"I was hoping you'd say that," he said, patting me on the back. "Follow me."

He turned and began to jog back out through the hangar's exit.

I cast another furtive glance back over my shoulder at the gleaming fighter ships stockpiled around me. Then I turned and ran after my father—even though I still wasn't quite sure exactly where he was leading me.

AS GENERAL LIGHTMAN LED ME THROUGH THE DIMLY LIT CARPETED CORRIDORS OF MOON Base Alpha, I kept biting the inner wall of my cheek every few minutes, because each subsequent flash of pain was proof that I was wide awake, and that this was all really happening.

As we took a circuitous route down to the Operations level, I marveled at how strangely familiar my new surroundings were, and at how perfectly *Armada*'s simulated version of the moon base matched the real thing.

When I mentioned to my father that it looked like certain elements of the base's exterior design had been "borrowed" from the fictional Clavius Base seen in the film *2001: A Space Odyssey,* he was delighted to confirm that they had.

"The team of engineers who designed and built this place were in a huge hurry, so they borrowed from a lot of existing designs," he explained, motioning to the carpeted corridors around us. "They stole a lot of ideas from Syd Mead and Ralph McQuarrie, like everyone else. Other people, too." He grinned. "The access corridors down on the maintenance level look like they were stolen right off the set of *Aliens,* I swear—wait until you see them."

Once he told me all of that, I suddenly began to see evidence of sci-fi design theft everywhere I looked inside the base. Everything was sleek, ergonomic, and vaguely retro-futuristic in its design, which often appeared to favor form over function.

There were also a lot of vintage rock band and movie posters taped up everywhere, but I was pretty sure those had been added by the base's current residents—as had the graffiti spray-painted in red on one of the corridor walls: THE CAKE IS A LIE.

We also passed one corridor lined with dozens of framed photos of men and women in EDA flight officer uniforms, wearing hairstyles from at least four different decades. Each photo was accompanied by a small plaque with the officer's name and two dates, indicating each individual's "Term of Service in the Earth Defense Alliance." This was followed by "Made the Ultimate Sacrifice to Protect Us All."

"All these people served up here?" I asked my father.

He nodded. "And they died up here, too," he said. "Those are officers who lost their lives in the line of duty."

"But they were just drone pilots, right?" I said. "How did they all die?"

"During previous attacks the enemy has made on this base," he said. Then, before I could ask him to elaborate, he said, "I'll explain in the briefing."

When we reached the end of that corridor, my father led me onto a turbo elevator that carried us down to the Operations level, located over a mile beneath the lunar surface, in just a few seconds. Then my father led me through a series of cavernous chambers carved into the lunar bedrock, which housed the cold-fusion generators, life-support systems, matter compilers, and the enormous gravity-distortion array.

"I don't know how most of this stuff works," my father confessed. "Or even how to operate most of it. But I've never needed to, because all of the base systems are completely automated. And all of the maintenance is done by drones operated by real people back on Earth."

When we passed the glass-walled med bay, I saw that it, too, was staffed entirely by drones. The base doctor appeared to be a specially equipped ATHID with a pair of articulated human hands that allowed a surgeon back on Earth to operate them remotely.

"A doctor in London used one of those med drones to remove my appendix a few years ago," he said. "The procedure went flawlessly."

The crew quarters were packed onto the same level—fifty modular dorm rooms, each designed for two residents.

"Since only three of the rooms are currently occupied, everyone gets their own private digs," my father said. He pointed to a door labeled A7. "These are your quarters. The door has already been coded to your biometrics, and your pack should already be inside."

I held up my QComm and checked the countdown timer.

"Why even bother giving me a room?" I asked. "The vanguard arrives in just a few hours—it's not like I'm going to try to take a nap between now and then."

"No," he said, smiling. "But you might want some privacy later on, once you're able to call your mother."

I stared at him until he met my eyes. "Are you planning to call her?"

He shook his head. "I doubt that would be a good idea," he said. "Why would she be interested in speaking to me, once she finds out I'm alive and that I . . . abandoned you both?"

"Of course she'll want to talk to you!" I told him. "She'll be overjoyed to find out you're alive." Then without thinking, I added, "Just like I am."

He studied my face. "You really think so?"

"I *know* so," I said, although I was trying to convince myself as much as him. "She never got over losing you. She never fell in love again after you. She told me so."

My father suddenly turned away, and I heard a small noise escape him—like the sound of a wounded animal, caught in a trap. When he made no other attempt to reply, I motioned to the other doors lining the corridor.

"Which room is yours?" I asked.

He pointed to the first door at the end of the hall, labeled A1.

"But that's not part of the tour," he said, attempting to steer me in the opposite direction.

"Just let me peek inside for one second," I said, standing my ground. "Please? Sir?"

"There really isn't that much to see," he said, still interposing himself between me and the door.

But judging by his reaction, there was clearly a lot to see—and I was determined to see it. I didn't move. Our standoff continued for a dozen or so seconds before the general finally stepped aside and palmed open the door, his face already flashing red in embarrassment as I squeezed past him to peer inside the tiny modular room.

The entire back wall of my father's quarters was covered with photos of me and my mom, including all of my yearbook photos going back to grade school. A photo of my mother in her nurse's uniform, which he must have found on her hospital's website, was hanging over his bed. The rest of his walls were completely bare.

Before I could examine his living space further, he prodded me back out of it into the hall, then locked the door.

"Hurry," he said, trying to hide the unsteadiness in his voice. "Every second counts."

16

NOTHER TURBO ELEVATOR HURTLED US DOWNWARD AT AN UNSETTLING speed, then slowed to a stop just a few seconds later. A screen embedded in the wall displayed a 3-D map of the base, and it indicated that we'd just arrived at its lowest level, at the very bottom of the egg-shaped structure nestled into the Daedalus crater. When the doors hissed open, we stepped out into a short, blue-carpeted corridor that terminated in a pair of sliding armored doors with DRONE OPERATIONS CENTER neatly stenciled across them. Above these doors, spray-painted on the wall in stylized graffiti, was the name THUNDERDOME.

The doors slid open as we approached, and I followed my father through them into a large circular room with a domed concrete ceiling that was painted a bright iridescent blue, like the screens that were used on movie sets as placeholders for digital effects that would be added later.

"Welcome," my father said, stretching out his arms, "to the Moon Base Alpha Drone Operations Center. We call it the Thunderdome."

"Why?"

"Well, because it has a dome," he said, pointing up. "And we fight inside it, just like Mad Max." He shrugged. "And because 'Thunderdome' sounds cooler than 'Drone Operations Center.'"

In the center of the room, on a raised platform, was a rotating command chair with curved ergonomic touchscreens built into its armrests.

It was encircled by ten oval-shaped pits sunken into the stone floor, each containing an individual drone controller pod. Unlike the multifunction stations we'd used back at Crystal Palace, these pods appeared to have been designed to control Interceptors exclusively. Each pit contained a simulated ADI-88 Interceptor cockpit—a pilot seat, flight stick, and all of its familiar control panels and system indicators arrayed beneath a wrap-around display canopy that slid into place over you when you climbed into the pilot seat.

My father tapped a button on his QComm, and the bright blue dome over our heads switched on, like the screen of a high-definition television, providing a 360-degree view of the cratered landscape surrounding the moon base that made it seem as if we were standing in the observation deck on the base's top level instead of in a reinforced bunker far beneath the lunar surface.

As he led me across the enormous domed bunker, I glanced inside each of the drone controller pods at my feet. I could see through their semi-transparent canopies, and four of the pods were already in use: Debbie, Milo, Whoadie, and Chén were inside, giving their new rigs a test spin in some sort of training simulation.

The Japanese EDA officer I'd spotted earlier was standing at the command console with another EDA officer—a tall, dark-skinned man I'd never seen before. Both men looked about the same age as my father, and both had the same weary, battle-hardened demeanor I'd seen in him. As they walked over to greet us, I glanced down at the collars of their uniforms and saw they both held the rank of major.

"Zack, I'd like you to meet two of my oldest friends," my father said. "Major Shin Hashimoto, and Major Graham Fogg."

"*Konichiwa,* Lightman-san," Major Shin said. I saluted him, but he threw me off by returning it with a bow. "It's good to finally meet you. Your father has told me way too much about you over the years." He grinned. "I've gotten pretty sick of it, actually."

"Sorry," I said, just to have something to say.

Shin studied my face until it started to feel creepy; then he glanced over at my father, then back at me, comparing our faces.

"Holy Toledo," he said, whistling. "You really are the spitting image of your old man." He elbowed me in the ribs, grinning broadly. "My sympathies, kid!"

He laughed heartily at his own joke, and my father gave me an apologetic look—the same look I used to give to my mom, when one of my friends came over and broke something. But I laughed politely in return, then turned to shake hands with Major Fogg, who appeared to be the tallest person on the moon.

"It is my distinct pleasure to meet you, Lieutenant Lightman," he said brightly. He surprised me by speaking with a thick British accent. "Welcome to Moon Base Alpha!"

I glanced at the shoulder of his uniform and saw the Union Jack there, instead of a US flag. I also noticed that the word *Defence* on his EDA insignia was spelled with a *c* instead of an *s*.

"It's just the three of you?" I asked. "No one else is up here?"

"Just us," Shin said. "A resupply shuttle comes up twice a month, but the rest of the time we're all alone. Not counting all of the drones, of course."

Graham nodded. "The Alliance used to have dozens of people stationed up here, to help keep all of the different systems running smoothly," he said. "But once the QComm network came online, almost everything could be done remotely with drones, so they cut back to just a skeleton crew, made up of essential military personnel."

"There used to be a few more pilots stationed up here," my father added, "including Admiral Vance, but now it's just us."

"The Three Musketeers," Graham said, smiling. "Lucky buggers that we are."

A long folding wooden table and three folding metal chairs were arranged against the far wall. The table's surface was covered with a variety of *Dungeons & Dragons* rulebooks, gaming screens, and dozens of oddly shaped dice.

"We play *D and D* four or five nights a week," Graham explained when he saw me eying the setup. "Helps to pass the time. Shin is usually our dungeon master." He smiled at me. "My character is twenty-seventh-level Elven archer."

"Why don't you show him your character sheet, Graham?" Shin said. "That will really impress the kid."

Graham ignored him and continued to shadow me with an enthusiastic smile as I wandered around the control center, like a kid showing off his room. A short distance away, I spotted a large drum kit, two electric guitars, and three mic stands, flanked on either side by a stack of amplifiers. I wandered over to examine the gear.

"What, do you guys have a band or something?" I asked.

"Indeed, we do," Graham said proudly. "We call ourselves 'The Bishop of Battle.' It's the name of—"

"The short film starring Emilio Estevez?" I finished for him. "From the *Nightmares* horror anthology?"

My father and both his friends blinked at me in surprise as goofy grins spread across each of their faces.

I grinned back, then nodded at my father. "I saw it when I was working my way through all of your old VHS tapes. It—"

I cut myself off when I realized how revealing my last statement had been. But none of them noticed. They were all still beaming at me for getting their band name.

"I like this kid, Xavier," Shin said.

My father nodded. "Yeah, so do I."

"We can play some pretty decent Van Halen covers," Graham continued. "Maybe we'll jam for you guys later?"

"Sure," I said uncertainly. "That would be cool."

I glanced back over at my father, but he was staring at his feet and shaking his head in embarrassment. "We're not going to play for them, Graham, I told you," he muttered. "Aliens are invading in a few hours, remember?"

"What better reason to rock out one last time?" Graham replied, throwing up two sets of devil horns.

I stepped over to the edge of the nearest drone controller station pit and peeked in. There was an OUT OF ORDER sign Scotch-taped to its tactical display.

"What happened to this one?" I asked.

"Graham spilled Coke Zero on it, that's what," Shin said. "Cost the war effort millions."

"Stop trying to pin that on me," Graham grumbled back. "You left your sandals lying around and I tripped over them. Those millions are on you, Shin-bone."

Graham laughed, but when I laughed, too, he scowled at me.

"What's so bloody funny, kid?" he said. "I fried one drone pod—that's nothing compared to the zillions of dollars in drones we lost this morning, thanks to your little stunt!"

Shin nodded, and they both continued to scowl at me for a few more seconds before they both burst into laughter.

"I'm joking, lad," Graham said, still laughing. "I must've watched the video clip of you chasing that Glaive into the base fifty times so far today! Priceless, that was!"

Shin shook his head. "How did you stop Viper from murdering you for that?"

"Maybe he realized I'm already a dead man, so there was no point?"

My father frowned at me and seemed about to say something, but Shin changed the subject before he could.

"Care for some snackage, Lieutenant?" he asked. "Your favorite snacks were listed in each of your EDA profiles, so we stocked up on all of them. You're a Lucky Charms man, right? Dry, with no milk? We laid in a few dozen boxes for you, see?"

He pointed over at one of the unoccupied pods across the room, where half a dozen boxes of my favorite breakfast cereal sat stacked up like crates of ammunition. The other new recruits had an assortment of snacks and beverages laid out on the floor around their sunken pods, too. Stacks of nacho cheese Combos and Slim Jims were scattered around Milo's pod, along with a small mountain of Diet Mountain Dew. There were bags of cheddar jalapeño Cheetos and a row of two-liter bottles of Hawaiian Punch laid out for Whoadie, bags of multicolored Skittles for Debbie, and beside Chén's pod, dozens of silver energy drink cans with QI LI printed on the side, surrounded by writing in Chinese.

"How did our favorite snacks end up in our EDA profiles?" I asked Shin. But it was Graham who answered.

"The EDA knows everything about everyone, kid," he said. "Your food and beverage preferences weren't the only things being recorded while you were playing *Armada* and *Terra Firma,* trust me. Your pulse rate, blood pressure, sweat content—the EDA makes the CIA and the NSA look like the PTA."

"Great," I said. "The government has been spying on all of us our whole lives, but at least we get to have our favorite snacks. Bonus."

To my surprise, my father grinned at my remark. Just then the other new arrivals emerged from their pods, and he went over to greet them. Chén snapped to attention when he saw my father approach, and the others scrambled to follow suit.

"At ease, recruits," my father said as he walked over to them. "Welcome to Moon Base Alpha. I'm General Xavier Lightman, your new CO. I apologize for keeping you waiting."

He scanned their faces, waiting for a response, but my new friends all seemed too starstruck to speak. My father walked over to stand in front of Milo, who was grinning like he was about to meet one of his favorite movie stars, his earlier disdain apparently forgotten.

"You're Milo Dobson, right? Better known as Kushmaster5000?"

Milo nodded imperceptibly, caught in the throes of some sort of gamer fanboy aneurysm.

"It's an honor to finally meet you in person, Lieutenant Dobson," my father told him. He turned to the others. "It's an honor to meet all of you. Whoadie, CrazyJi. AtomicMom." He shook hands with each of them in turn, then nodded at me. "And, of course, IronBeagle. You're five of the most gifted pilots I've ever seen in action. We're privileged to have you here."

The others smiled and their faces flushed with pride—and mine may have a bit, as well.

"Thank you, sir!" Chén said, carefully repeating his QComm's translation.

"Yeah, thanks, General!" Milo said, finally recovering from his stroke of paralysis. "I mean, holy shit—that's a huge compliment, coming from RedJive himself! You're the best of the best of the best, sir! I've been studying your moves for years—we all have."

My father seemed genuinely embarrassed by this praise.

"You're giving me way too much credit," he said. Then he pointed to his two comrades. "Shin and Graham were both heavily involved with your simulator training, too. I'm sure you'll recognize their call signs. Shin uses the handle MaxJenius, and Graham—"

"My call sign is Withnailed," Graham finished. "Though these two rarely use it."

"We prefer to call him 'Limes' instead," Shin said. "It's short for 'limey.' He hates it."

Graham nodded. "Indeed I do."

We all smiled in recognition at their familiar call signs. MaxJenius and Withnailed were both mainstays in the top-five pilot rankings, too. Since the first year the game was launched, they had both alternated between second and third place, right below RedJive.

"I don't mean to be rude, General Lightman," Debbie said. "But when are you going to tell us why the EDA sent us up here?" She glanced over at Shin and Graham. "Why couldn't we just remain back on Earth with the other recruits?"

My father exchanged a strange smile with his two friends, then nodded at Debbie.

"I was just about to brief all of you on that subject," he said.

Graham smiled; then he motioned to a row of low, padded leather bench seats behind us. "You guys might want to be sitting down when you hear this," he said, before sitting down himself. Milo and Debbie joined him, but Chén, Whoadie, and I remained on our feet.

My father waved his hand at the view screen covering the domed ceiling, and the image arrayed across it changed. We were no longer looking at a live feed of the lunar landscape outside the base, but at an animated three-dimensional graphic of our solar system, with the spinning planet Earth in the foreground and the moon lazily orbiting it at a distance, both surrounded by a series of concentric rings indicating the orbital paths of the other planets. My father made another gesture at the screen and the animation of our solar system began to speed up, making the planets zoom around the sun like a pack of race cars, each on a separate track.

"One of the things you weren't told during your enlistment briefing is that this isn't the first time the Europans have sent ships to Earth to attack us," the General said. "Over the past four decades, they've done it exactly thirty-seven times."

On the domed screen, the celestial clockwork of our solar system continued to spin forward until the orbits of Earth and Jupiter aligned, bringing the two planets into their closest annual proximity. Then, as the orbit of Jupiter's moon Europa brought it as close as possible to Earth, the animation froze.

"Every 398.9 days, a celestial event known as the Jovian Opposition occurs," the general explained, "when the sun and Jupiter are both on opposite sides of Earth, and Europa is at its closest proximity to us. Ever since our first contact with them, the Europans have used that proximity to send a small detachment of ships to Earth, to conduct surveillance, test our defenses, and abduct live human specimens for study."

He tapped his QComm display, and an image of Moon Base Alpha appeared on the screen, seen from above, nestled into the Daedalus crater.

"Once the Europans began to send scouting missions to Earth, the EDA decided to construct a secret defense base here on the far side of the moon," the general said. "It was originally intended to function as a long-range surveillance and communications outpost. But when it finally became operational in September of 1988, and a permanent human presence was established here, the enemy's tactics changed. When the next Jovian Opposition arrived, the Europans didn't send their detachment of scout ships directly to Earth. This time they came here to Moon Base Alpha first—and attacked it."

Video footage began to play on the domed view screen, showing a large formation of Glaive Fighters streaking down from the starry blackness of the lunar sky to descend on the tiny moon base nestled in the crater below, as Interceptors began to launch out of the base's hangar and fly up to meet them, setting off a massive aerial battle.

"We managed to fight them off, but just barely," he said. "It took nearly a full year to repair the damage. And when the next Jovian Opposition arrived, the Europans attacked again, this time with an even larger force, to match the increased size of Moon Base Alpha's defenses. And once again, our forces were barely a match for them."

"The same thing happened again the next year," Graham said. "And the year after that."

"Each year, they sent even more drones to assault the base," Shin said. "And every year, we increased our defenses here in anticipation of their next attack."

My father nodded. "This escalation continued for over a decade, until the Europans changed the game on us again last year, by unveiling a new weapon—one you've all encountered before during your *Armada* training. The Disrupter."

A collective groan escaped the new recruits. On the view screen, we watched as a cluster of enemy ships appeared, descending toward Moon Base Alpha in perfect formation, creating an image that momentarily resembled a screenshot of the game *Space Invaders*.

A wire-frame diagram of a spinning dodecahedron appeared adjacent to it on the view screen, and I felt the hair on the back of my neck stand up.

"The Disrupter appears to function by coupling itself to a large celestial body, like a planet or moon." On the view screen, an animation showed a spinning chrome dodecahedron making landfall on Earth and then firing a beam of red energy into the planet's core. "The device then harnesses the planet's magnetic field, using it to generate a spherical field that disrupts all quantum communications inside it."

"All of the EDA's drones have backup radio-control units," Shin added. "Unfortunately the Disrupter interferes with normal radio communications, too, so they're useless."

On the view screen, the emerald green Disrupter began to generate a transparent sphere of red energy that enveloped the entire planet Earth, along with its entire atmosphere—causing the EDA's drones to fall out of the sky. But the moon was outside of the Disrupter's range—as was the secret EDA defense base on its far side.

"The quantum-disruption effect only works if the transmitting and receiving ends of a link are *both* contained inside its spherical field," the general said. "If either the drone or its operator are located outside of the disruption field, the quantum link is completely unaffected and remains intact. If the enemy manages to couple their Disrupter to the Earth, only the EDA personnel stationed up here on the moon—that's us—will still be able to control the drones we have stockpiled back on Earth, and vice versa."

My father flipped away from the wire-frame animation and back to the footage of the enemy fighters, revealing a large, onyx-colored dodecahedron—a dark, multifaceted jewel spinning in their midst. The object pulsed rapidly in color from jet black to molten red along its illuminated angular seams.

"Just before the Europans attacked this base during the last Opposition, they activated the Disrupter, coupling it to the moon's magnetic field, which is relatively weak compared to that of Earth."

As he spoke, the pulsing dodecahedron fired a red beam of energy into the moon's core. It began to generate a spherical field of energy around itself, which increased rapidly in diameter until it completely covered Moon Base Alpha, along with large patches of the moon's surface, which I knew from our briefing was in a pattern that matched the moon's inherent magnetic field.

"When the Disrupter switched on, it knocked out our ability to control drones from here inside the base," my father explained. "But all of the EDA drone pilots located back on Earth were unaffected, because they were outside the disruption field."

Shin pulled a different graphic up on the screen, showing Earth and its nearby moon, the far side of which was covered by the Disrupter's transparent field, which was enormous, but not large enough to envelop both the moon and Earth at the same time.

"The enemy's drones continued to function for the same reason," my father said. "Their operators were back on Europa, hundreds of thousands of miles outside the disruption field."

Shin nodded. "This base has a backup hard-line intranet," he said. "So we were still able to defend the base using the surface guns, and with tethered backup drones, which were all hardwired and thus unaffected by the Disrupter."

On the screen, footage showed sentry guns all over the exterior of the base powering on and returning fire as the enemy Glaive and Wyvern Fighters kept right on attacking, raining down a steady barrage of laser fire and plasma bolts on the base defenses. Down on the surface, a few dozen tethered ATHIDs and Warmechs also continued to defend the base, unspooling their fiber-optic tether cables behind them, which drastically limited their mobility, effectiveness, and range.

"The EDA sent several squadrons of reinforcement Interceptors up here from Earth," he explained. "And with their help, we were eventually able to destroy the Disrupter. But the base was badly damaged, and we barely survived the attack."

"Is a real Disrupter as difficult to destroy as the ones in the game?" Chén asked via his QComm.

Shin, Graham, and my father all nodded.

"Then how did you guys manage to take it down?" I asked.

Shin and Graham both grinned, as if they'd been waiting for this question.

"'It takes two, to make a thing go right,'" Shin recited, smiling cryptically.

Graham nodded, then added, "'It takes two to make it out of sight.'"

They looked as if they were about to recite more of the song's lyrics, but my father shook his head slightly and they both fell silent, waiting for him to continue.

"Some people think we got lucky," my father said, glancing at Shin. "Personally, I think the Europans allowed us to destroy it."

"Why would they do that?" Debbie asked.

"Good question," my father said. "Here, watch the footage and decide for yourself."

He tapped his QComm again, and another grainy video clip began to play on the view screen.

"This footage was shot from one of Moon Base Alpha's surface surveillance cameras," Shin said. "Approximately twenty-three minutes into their attack. All quantum and radio communication is still being jammed by the Disrupter. Most of the base, and nearly all of its surface defenses, have been destroyed by this point."

On the view screen, the smoking ruins of the moon base were visible in the background, its orb-shaped exterior crawling with spider-like alien drones skittering across its armored metal skin and burrowing into it with lasers. In the foreground, just beyond the lip of the Daedalus crater, was the mammoth Disrupter dodecahedron, spinning fiercely just above the lunar surface as it blasted its pulsing red coupler beam down into the moon's magnetic core. In the velvet black lunar sky above, hundreds of Interceptors were launching an assault on the Disrupter's shield, firing on it from as many different angles.

"As you'll recall from your training, the Disrupter only has one weakness," Shin said. "A steady barrage of laser fire and plasma bolts will bring down its shields, but the Disrupter's power core is so large that it recovers far more rapidly than any of the enemy's other drones. Its shields only drop for about three seconds, then come right back up at full strength."

"And three seconds isn't long enough to destroy it," Milo said. "At least it never was in the game. That's why no one has ever taken down a Disrupter. Not even the Flying Circus."

"Look!" Shin pointed at the screen. "Here he comes, to save the day!"

On the screen, a lone EDA mech appeared, power-leaping across the lunar surface, fearlessly charging toward the pillar of blinding red light created by the Disrupter's transparent coupler beam.

"Old Viper Vance!" Graham shook his head in admiration. "Watch him go!"

"Admiral Vance is controlling that mech?" Whoadie asked.

"Yes," my father said. "But he was still just a general back then. He used to be in command of Moon Base Alpha. I took over his post when he got promoted to admiral—in part, for the act of bravery we're watching now."

"Although Viper used to do crazy shit like this all the time," Shin added. "That guy was fearless."

"I'm sure he still is," my father said quietly, his eyes still on the screen.

We continued to watch the silent footage of General Vance's charge toward the Disrupter, wondering what would happen when he closed the remaining distance to it.

"How is he controlling that mech, with the Disrupter still in operation?" I wondered aloud, still studying the footage intently. "He's moving too fast to have a tether, isn't he?"

My father nodded. "You're right, he is," he said. "Tethered drones were always too slow and too vulnerable for Vance's liking." He nodded at the screen. "He's piloting that mech from inside it. There's a cockpit embedded in its torso, just above its power core—which Viper is setting to overload right . . . about . . . now."

On the screen, Vance's mech came within arm's reach of the coupler beam and then suddenly went limp and fell to the surface like a giant metal rag doll, throwing up a cloud of dust.

"He set his mech to self-destruct *from inside it*?" Milo said disbelievingly. "Did the old man have a death wish?"

Shin and Graham nodded; then Shin motioned to my father.

"I used to think he and General Lightman here both did."

I pointed up at the screen. "But he isn't going to have time to eject."

My father nodded. "Vance's escape pod launch system was damaged during his charge. So now he's trapped there next to his own time bomb."

I had already started counting down the seven seconds it would take for his power-core overload sequence to complete, but I'd only hit five when two more mechs appeared, running up from the bottom of the video frame. Laser and plasma fire rained down on them from the dogfight still raging in the dark sky above the burning, half-destroyed moon base. Then I heard a familiar classic rock song blasting over Vance's comm—a song from my father's *Raid the Arcade* mix: "Black Betty" by Ram Jam.

"That's one of our nicknames for a Disrupter now," Shin said, nodding at the spinning black dodecahedron on the screen. "A Black Betty. Or a 'ten-sider.'"

I continued to study the view screen. As the two Titan Warmechs bounded toward the motionless one containing Vance, they moved in a strange sort of unison, almost like a pair of synchronized swimmers. They both seemed to dodge and zigzag perfectly again and again, just in time to avoid being obliterated, always in forward motion, seemingly oblivious to the geysers of rock and moon dust erupting all around—and sometimes directly ahead of—them.

Shin paused the video. "Your father is operating both of those mechs. Simultaneously. He's inside the one on the left, and it's connected to the mech on the right via a short fiber-optic tether, inside a titanium-reinforced cable stretching between them."

"Shin would know," my father said, never taking his eyes off the screen. "He finished helping me rig them together about ten minutes before this footage was shot."

Shin pressed Play again, and my eyes were drawn back to the screen. I watched his two mechs lumber forward, unloading their sun guns and laser cannons into the Disrupter's massive spherical shield as they passed underneath its mammoth spinning form and the coupler array at its southern pole.

Then the mech my father was in reached Vance's mech, ripped its escape pod free—with Vance inside—and tucked it under his arm like a football.

A ring of explosive bolts fired around the armored cable tethering my father's mech to the one beside it, severing their connection. My father's drone threw Vance's now-limp drone skyward like a shot put, toward the Disrupter's still-shielded coupler array.

In the same motion he power-leaped in the opposite direction while hurling Vance's escape pod in front of him, a bare second before ejecting his own. Both of their pods flew out of the frame just before Vance's mech finally completed its seven-second self-destruct countdown and detonated. Two seconds later, the drone my father had hurled skyward did the exact same thing—a perfectly timed one-two punch. A nearly impossible shot, like a three-pointer from full court with one second on the clock.

But even that amazing bit of timing wasn't enough. Because just before both mechs would've impacted against the Disrupter's transparent shield, the shield dropped, leaving the dodecahedron unprotected for that narrow three-second window while its massive power core recharged enough to power its defenses back up. It was during this incredibly short sliver of time that both mechs detonated, one after the next.

The first detonation struck the Disrupter's diamond-hard hull, but its armor appeared to absorb the blast somehow, and the triangular facets of the dodecahedron's skin lit up molten orange as the energy dissipated across them. Only when the second mech detonated a half-second later did the Disrupter's weakened armor finally fail, in an explosion that took out the Disrupter itself.

Graham and Shin both broke into applause. I got the feeling they had watched this footage on a regular basis, and that they applauded like this every time. Whoadie, Milo, Debbie, and Chén all applauded, too, but I abstained. I was too busy staring at the screen.

"Can we watch that footage again?" I asked. "At half speed this time?"

Shin nodded and ran it again. Then he ended up running it for us several more times, at everyone's request. The footage became more impressive, and more unsettling to watch, with each viewing. My father had truly pulled off a one in a million shot. If the Disrupter's shields had failed a split second earlier or later, his attack would have failed, too. And studying the time counter on the video clip, it looked as if the Disrupter's shield stayed down a fraction of a second longer than it should have—just long enough for my father to pull off a miracle.

"How many more Disrupters are on their way here right now?" Milo asked fearfully. "You left that little detail out of your briefing."

"Three," my father said. "There's one Disrupter accompanying each wave of their invasion force."

"Three!" Milo repeated. "There's no way we'll be able to destroy three Disrupters, one after the other—not with a massive alien shit storm coming down on us!"

My father nodded. "Yes, I'd say that's a real long shot. But we do have one last card up our sleeves. The Icebreaker."

"But I thought the Icebreaker mission already failed," Debbie said. "It was destroyed before the melt laser even breached the surface of Sobrukai—Europa, I mean."

"The Icebreaker you escorted last night was destroyed, yes," my father said. "But we had a contingency plan. We hoped we might be able to destroy the Europans before they launched their armada, but we knew our chance of success was extremely slim. So we constructed a second Icebreaker, which was hidden inside a hollowed-out asteroid and placed into orbit around Jupiter, to avoid detection by the Europans. As soon as their armada departed for Earth—leaving Europa unprotected—we launched the Icebreaker. It's already on its way."

"When will it get there?"

"It should reach Europa about the same time the second wave of the enemy's armada reaches Earth."

"What if we don't survive the first wave?" Debbie asked.

"Then the Icebreaker won't make any difference," Shin said. "But that's why we have to make sure we do survive! Because then we may finally get our chance to end this war, once and for all."

I waited for Graham or my father to agree with Shin, but both of them were silent.

"Anyone hungry?" my father asked. He held up his QComm. "I just got word the drones have finished preparing our dinner in the mess hall."

"Thank God!" Milo shouted, already moving toward the exit. "I was afraid that Cheetos and root beer would be my last meal. Let's eat!"

Whoadie and Debbie nodded in agreement, as did Chén once he heard the translation.

"I don't have much of an appetite," I said. If I was about to die, I wanted the breakfast my mother made for me that morning to be my last meal— not some Salisbury steak dinner reheated in a moon base microwave.

My father nodded, and he and Shin began to lead the others toward the exit. Graham saw me straggling behind and threw an arm around me.

"Trust me, you'll change your mind once you see the spread up there," Graham said. "They sent up a special five-course gourmet meal for us on your shuttle."

"Why?" Debbie asked. "Because it will probably be our *last* meal?"

"Probably," Graham replied, giving me a grim smile as he quickened his pace toward the exit. "That's why I, for one, intend to stuff my face."

17

THE MOON BASE ALPHA DINING HALL WAS A LONG RECTANGULAR ROOM CON-
taining four circular tables made of brushed steel, flanked by
matching benches bolted to the floor. Several modular food
and beverage dispensers were embedded in one long wall, along with a few
microwaves—but no replicator, as far as I could tell. The opposite wall was
dominated by a large curved window that provided a stunning view of the
massive Daedalus impact crater spread below us, like a monochromatic
Grand Canyon.

As promised, an extravagant meal was already laid out on the tables,
ready and waiting for us—what looked like more than enough food for
several Thanksgiving dinners. One of the steel tables was covered with a
silk tablecloth and set with eight place settings, complete with silver cut-
lery and fine bone china, and off to the side stood a row of four ATHIDs
standing at silent attention, ready to serve us. A paper tuxedo was taped to
each of their chest plates.

I took the last empty seat, between my father and Milo. Graham sat next
to Debbie, and only then did I realize from their body language that the
two of them were crushing on each other in a big way. Milo noticed it, too,
and rolled his eyes, then nudged me and nodded at the two of them, then
at Chén and Whoadie, who were both making furtive eye contact, too.

"This is just great," he grumbled under his breath. "Here I thought I was being recruited for an epic space adventure, but it turns out I'm a guest star on *Love Boat: The Next Generation*."

"Set course . . . *for romance!*" Shin quoted, doing such a perfect Patrick Stewart impersonation that Milo and I both laughed out loud.

Everyone began to pass dishes and serve themselves food—everyone except Debbie, who bowed her head and began to mumble silently to herself in prayer. We all froze for an awkward beat, then bowed our heads in solidarity until she finished.

Even with all of that delicious-looking food in front of me, I still didn't seem to have any appetite. But the day's bizarre events appeared to have left everyone else ravenous, and for a while they were all too busy stuffing their faces to talk. I cast a few sideways glances at my father, but he was shoveling food into his mouth robotically while avoiding eye contact with me.

Chén was the one who broke the silence.

"My phone is still not functioning," he said, via his QComm's translator. "When will I be allowed to call home and speak to my family?"

My father checked the time on his own QComm.

"An hour before the vanguard is expected to reach us," he said. "That's when the leaders of every nation around the world will break the news to their citizens. Once the cat is out of the bag, you'll be able to call home. We won't have long to talk, I'm afraid."

"Why is the EDA waiting until the last minute to tell everyone about the invasion?" Whoadie asked. "That won't give the world much time to prepare for the vanguard's attack."

"The world is already as prepared as it's ever going to be," my father said.

Shin nodded. "The population is already beginning to panic, judging by what's on the global news feeds. People all over the world saw those EDA shuttles with their own eyes this morning when they were flying around to pick up essential recruits. The media has been airing and analyzing footage all day, along with information about their connection to Chaos Terrain's videogames. The whole world wants to know what's really going on."

My father shook his head. "No they don't," he said. "Once people find out about the invasion, chaos will spread like wildfire. Civilization will start to break down."

Graham made a derisive sound. "The EDA knows people will be more likely to stand their ground and fight if they don't have time to turn tail and run for the hills."

I looked at my father. He briefly met my gaze, then glanced over at Debbie, who was staring down at the countdown clock on her QComm. It was superimposed over a photo she'd set as her display background—three smiling, dark-haired boys resting their chins on the edge of a swimming pool in the bright sunshine.

"Handsome boys," Graham said.

"Thank you," she replied. "I'm worried about them." Then she reached out and covered the countdown clock with her finger so she could still see her sons' faces.

"What about you two?" Debbie asked, addressing Shin and Graham. "Is the EDA going to let you contact your families, too?"

"I'm a bit nervous about that, actually," Graham said. "Me mum is still alive, but she thinks I died back in the nineties. My father had already passed by the time I was recruited, so I left her all alone—and she's been alone ever since. The EDA has taken care of her financially, of course, but emotionally, well, what can one do?"

Graham blinked a few times, then swallowed hard.

"I hope she still recognizes me," he said. "And if she does, I hope the sight of me doesn't give her a coronary—that is, if the PM's address doesn't do that first." He shook his head. "The poor old girl is in her sixties now."

I wasn't all that worried about how my own mother would react to the news our planet was being invaded. She had always been the picture of calm in the face of crisis. She seemed to thrive on it. But when she found out my father was still alive, well—that was another story.

"And you, Shin?" Debbie asked quietly. "Do you have any family, dear?"

Shin's smile faded slightly. "Unfortunately, my parents both passed away years ago. About halfway through my tour of duty up here. So I never got to say goodbye to them, which was extremely painful at the time." Then his expression brightened, and he reached over and gave my father's shoulder a squeeze before slapping him on the back. "But my friend Xavier here had already gone through the same thing, and he helped me get through it. He lost his folks, too, a few—"

Shin cut himself off, then shot a nervous glance over at me and then my father, who was again staring intently at the tablecloth.

"Anyway," Shin said, forging ahead, "right now I'm just thankful they got to live out their lives peacefully, and that they're not around for . . . what's about to happen."

Everyone around the table nodded, save for my father, who seemed to be slowly turning to stone. Shin seemed to sense this, and he turned to me.

"How you doing, Zack?" he said. "You holding up okay?"

I nodded. Then I shook my head. Then I shrugged and shook my head again.

"Don't look so worried," Shin said. "The general forgot to mention one thing during his little pep talk earlier." He gave me a conspiratorial smile. "We have a secret weapon—the greatest drone pilot who ever lived." He jerked a thumb at my father. "Did you know that your old man has shot down over three hundred enemy ships? He currently holds the EDA record."

"Your father has also been awarded the Medal of Honor three times, by three different presidents," Shin said. "Bet you didn't know that, did you?" He shook his head at my father. "He's too modest to even tell his own son."

"Seriously?" I asked him. "*Three* Medals of Honor?"

My father nodded, closing his eyes to his embarrassment—the same way I did when I received compliments.

"They were *classified* Medals of Honor," my father said. "It's not like anyone will ever find out about them."

"I just did," I said. "Mom will, too, when I get a chance to tell her."

He gave me a half-smile, then dropped his eyes again.

My mother would be proud of him, but that might not be enough, and he knew it. I could see it in the defeated look that flashed across his face whenever I mentioned her. My father knew as well as I did that all of his noble motivations and heroic sacrifices might not be enough to win her forgiveness—or even her understanding—for what he'd done to us. Not in the limited amount of time she would have to do so. I still wasn't sure if I had forgiven him.

I glanced over at my father. I knew he wasn't planning to call my mother, but I'd do it for him, if I had to. I wasn't sure what he was supposed to say to her, after disappearing for seventeen years—I didn't know what I was going to say when we spoke, and I'd just seen her earlier that morning—or if she'd be willing to listen. But I had to try.

When Whoadie finished eating a moment later, she got up from the table and went over to the observation window, then spent a moment staring down at the radio dish nestled inside the enormous crater far below. "What did you say that thing was again?" she asked.

"That's the Daedalus Observatory," Shin said, with a tinge of pride in his voice. "It's the largest radio telescope ever built—by humans, at least."

"We built it to talk to the aliens?" Whoadie asked.

Shin nodded. "This crater is near the center of the moon's far side, so this location is completely shielded from all of the radio interference created by humans, which makes it an ideal place to send and receive radio transmissions without them being monitored back on Earth." He sighed. "Unfortunately, the Europans have never been interested in talking."

"One of the first acts of the EDA," Graham said, "was to create an internal task force called the Armistice Council, made up of a bunch of prominent scientists, including Carl Sagan—"

"I've been wondering about that," I said, interrupting him. "How did they get Carl Sagan to keep the Europans a secret for so long?"

"He knew the news could create a worldwide panic and upend our civilization," my father said. "He only agreed to remain silent on the condition that the EDA give him the funding necessary to educate the world's population and try to prepare them for the news that humanity is not alone. That was how he got funding for his *Cosmos* television series."

Shin nodded. "Unfortunately, Dr. Sagan passed away before things really began to escalate with the Europans."

"The Armistice Council kept on trying to establish peace talks after he died," Graham added, "but the squids never sent a single reply."

"Squids?" I repeated. "I thought we didn't know anything about the Europans' biology?"

"That's the official story, all right," Graham said, adopting a conspiratorial tone. "But trust me, mate—they're squids. The brass knows a lot more about our enemy than they let on—they always have." He glanced at Shin, then at my father, then back at me.

"What are you talking about?" Milo asked. "The Europeans declared war on us, for no reason!"

Everyone had given up on correcting Milo every time he referred to the Europans as Europeans—even poor Graham, who actually *was* European.

"That's the official story, all right," Graham said. "But does it make any sense? Think it through. If the Europans had attacked us ten or twenty or even thirty years ago, we never would have been able to stop them."

I sat bolt upright, then glanced at my father. But his eyes were locked on Graham.

"We couldn't even have stopped an asteroid or a meteor from wiping us out back then, much less an angry alien species with vastly superior weaponry and technology," Graham continued. "They had the upper hand from the start, so why didn't they use it? Instead, they basically just handed us their technology and then gave us all the time in the world to reverse-engineer it. Then they gave us even more time to build a huge stockpile of millions of drones to defend ourselves against the drones *they* were building."

It was more than a little disturbing to hear Graham vocalize many of the same questions that had been eating away at me ever since the EDA briefing.

"And they built all of their ships and drones in orbit above Europa, in plain view of *Galileo*'s cameras! There's no way they weren't aware that we were watching them. They wanted us to see! It was like they were running a nonstop, year-round episode of *How It's Made by Aliens*."

Graham noticed that Shin was now making a screw-loose gesture with his index finger and flipped him the bird as he kept on talking.

"The Europans had this huge advantage over us, but then they slowly, gradually lessened it on purpose, instead of just slaughtering us over a weekend. Why? Why send a small group of scout ships every year, year after year, to study us, mutilate our cattle, and attack our secret moon base?" He lowered his voice to a whisper. "But they weren't really even serious attacks. They never try to destroy the entire base or kill everyone inside during their annual Jovian Opposition assaults. Instead, they always do just enough damage to prove that they *could* destroy the whole base if they wanted to. Then they leave without actually doing it. Why?"

Shin interrupted him again. "Are you gonna let him spout this nonsense in front of the new recruits?" he asked my father. "Right before the attack? He'll demoralize them!"

My fellow recruits did indeed seem shaken by Graham's speech. As was I—but for a different reason. Everything he'd laid out matched my own suspicions with eerie accuracy, but I didn't want to hear it. Shin was right: Worrying about abstractions and unanswerable questions just hours before the fight of our lives was a pointless—even harmful—distraction.

"You can't stop the signal, pal!" Graham said. "I've also heard, from several reliable sources, that one of their scout ships crashed in Florida in the late eighties, only it wasn't a drone. They recovered it with two dead Europan pilots, floating inside a pressurized fishbowl cockpit. Word is we've still got the bodies on ice in a bunker five miles beneath Wright-Patterson Air Force Base."

"He's just repeating old rumors," Shin said. "Alliance gossip—bullshit stories that have been circulating through the ranks for decades. There's no evidence to support any of it!"

"That's not true and you know it, Shin-bone!" Graham said. "Why do you think the Sobrukai were designed to be aquatic extremophiles in the Chaos Terrain games? Because that's how the Europans really look, man!" He turned to address me and the other new arrivals. "The Sobrukai overlord's design was based on the biology of the real Europans. They just scaried him up for the public."

"Well, it worked," Debbie said. "I have nightmares about that overlord whenever I forget to skip the intro and mistakenly catch a glimpse of him—it, I mean."

"Once again, I'm afraid the Graham Cracker over there is talking directly out of his ass," Shin told us. "We have no idea if they're cephalo-pods or not. That's just a best guess, based on their current habitat. In real-ity, we don't know if they're carbon-based, or if they're even indigenous to Europa." He smiled at Debbie. "Don't worry," he said. "The overlord is made up. He was invented by Chaos Terrain to give the enemy a face—a villainous, slightly humanoid alien that humanity could rally against! Like Ming the Merciless or Darth Vader or Zod or—"

"I get the idea," Debbie said. She shook her head. "For some reason, not knowing what they look like at all is even more terrifying."

Whoadie and Milo both nodded. I glanced at my father again, but he was studying my face, as if trying to gauge my reaction to what I was hearing.

"Do you believe any of this stuff, General?" Debbie asked him. He hesi-tated a moment and exchanged looks with Graham before finally break-ing his silence.

"I'm far more skeptical about those rumors than Graham," he said. "However, I don't entirely agree with Shin's straightforward assessment of things either." He glanced at me. "We've all had our share of arguments about this—with Admiral Vance, as well. We all interpret the limited data we have in a drastically different way." He smiled faintly. "Part of being human, I guess."

"You didn't answer the question, General," Whoadie pointed out. "What do you believe?"

"Yes, General," Shin said. His tone was suddenly derisive. "Why don't you be honest and tell them the truth. Tell your son the truth—about your 'theory.' That should really give morale an added boost around here, just before Zero Hour!"

Shin dropped his silverware onto his plate with a loud clatter, got up from the table, and walked out of the mess hall. My father watched him go.

Graham shrugged and continued eating. "The three of us have been arguing this subject for years," he said. "Our differences in opinion were bound to come to a head today."

"Shin's just under an enormous amount of stress right now," my father said. "We all are."

"What was he talking about?" I asked. "About your theory?"

My father sighed and glanced at the others, who were all watching him intently—including Graham.

"Nearly everyone in the EDA at the command level agrees with Graham, in that the Europans' behavior and tactics over the past forty-two years raise a lot of questions—at least from a human perspective." He shook his head. "The problem is that no one has ever been able to agree on how to interpret them. Most of the people in command—people like Admiral Vance—lost interest in trying to communicate with the Europans after they began sending drones here to attack us."

"Damn straight!" I said. "They declared war on us."

"True," he said. "But what if the Europans waited until now to attack because they have a hidden motive—one we still can't ascertain? Maybe we've misinterpreted their actions? Or maybe they've misinterpreted ours?"

"What the fuck is there to misinterpret?" I heard myself ask. "They're coming to kill us all, just like they've been promising to do since before any of us were born. The time for negotiating has passed, don't you think?"

My father shrugged. He looked cornered. "I don't know, Son," he said. "Maybe."

I stood up.

"Maybe? Did you say *maybe*?"

"Calm down, Zack," my father said. "Let's talk this through—"

"I've heard enough talk, General!" I said. "Shin is right. You're supposed to be leading us into battle and inspiring us! Not—not dumping all of your own fear on us!"

My accusation seemed to detonate on his face like a bomb. His features began to contort, but I turned my back on him so I wouldn't have to see the rest of his reaction.

I walked out of there as fast as I could without looking back.

WHEN I FINALLY STOPPED WALKING A FEW MINUTES LATER, I REALIZED I WAS LOST. SO I pulled up the interactive map of the base on my QComm and used it to locate the nearest turbo elevator. I rode it down to the habitation level and then returned to where the living quarters were located. When I reached my room, I pressed my palm to the onyx panel beside the door and it slid open. The lights came on as I stepped inside.

The interior looked like a dorm room at Starfleet Academy. It had a symmetrical two-occupant layout, with a loft bed on either side, each enclosed in a transparent soundproofed box that could be blacked out with the touch of a button for privacy. Each loft also had a built in ladder, dresser, and uniform closet, and there was a large flatscreen television monitor embedded in the ceiling directly over each bed. There was also a small computer hutch beneath each bunk, with an ergonomic chair bolted to the floor. My backpack was sitting nearby.

I sat down at the computer, and its built-in monitor lit up, displaying a desktop with EDA logo wallpaper and a few program icons.

I took out the flash drive my father had given me and plugged it in.

I held my breath as the file list popped up. There were hundreds of text files saved on the drive, along with dozens of video files, all with similar filenames: "DearZack" followed by a six-digit numerical date. The first file was named DearZack100900.txt. October 9, 2000. A few days after my father was supposed to have died.

Dear Zack,

I'm not even sure how to start this letter. So much has happened in the past few days, and most of it still doesn't seem real.

I'm writing you this letter from the moon. For real, kiddo. Your dad is on the moon!

You see, I didn't really die in an explosion at the plant, like they told you and your mom. The government just made it look like I had died, because they need my help to fend off an alien invasion. I know that sounds ridiculous, like something out of a science fiction paperback or a late night movie. But there's a reason for that! Star Wars, Star Trek—all of those sci-fi movies, novels, TV shows, and videogames I've been playing my whole life—they were all designed to prepare the people of the world for a real alien invasion. I'm still trying to wrap my head around it, but I know it's true. I've already seen the evidence with my own eyes.

We still don't know when the invasion will begin, so I'm not sure how long I'll have to be away from you and your mom. Maybe it will only be a few months. But it could be years before I'm able to come back home. There's also a chance I might get killed up here. If that happens, I don't want you to spend the rest of your life believing your dad was just some loser sewage worker who died in a stupid accident before he ever did anything important with his life.

I want you to know who I really was, and what really happened to me. But more than anything, I need you to know how hard it was for me to leave you and your mom, and how hard it is now to know you both think I'm dead. Please know that I never would have put either of you through all of this if I felt like there was any other choice.

The government has promised to take care of my family while I'm away. They set up some sort of fake settlement for the accident, so you and Mom should never have to worry about money. You'll be able to live a lot more comfortably than the three of us ever could have on a sewage worker's salary, that's for sure. I know it won't make up for me being gone, but it does make me feel a little better.

I really miss both of you, but I have to admit that it's also kind of amazing up here. My whole life, I felt like I was destined to do something important, but I was only ever good at videogames, which I always figured would be completely useless. But it's not useless, and neither am I. I think this is what I was always destined to do with my life. I just never knew it.

My whole existence is classified now, so I'm not even allowed to send you birthday cards while I'm away. But I'm still going to write you, as often as I can, and I'll save the letters until I can give them to you. I'm going to write to your mom, too. It's only been a few days, but I already miss both of you a lot.

I hope you're both doing okay—and I hope my funeral wasn't

too hard on your mom, or you, even though you're not even a year old yet, so you won't remember being there, but she will, and thinking about how hard that must have been for her makes me feel like jumping off a cliff. Of course, I realize now—I already jumped. That's why I'm stuck up here.

Anyway, I promise to write again soon, when I have more time. I'll tell you about everything that has happened to me, and all about this moon base where I live. But right now, I have to go defend Earth from alien invaders.

Love,
Xavier (Your Dad)

I kept on reading, devouring letter after letter.

His early letters filled in missing details of the story I'd already pieced together from reading his old Theory notebook. My father described in detail how he'd begun to uncover facets of the EDA's grand conspiracy in the years before they recruited him, after his encounter with the strange *Phaëton* game at his local arcade. He would later learn that the same prototype was used to recruit Shin, Graham, and Admiral Vance.

After he was inducted, my father's longtime suspicions were confirmed—the EDA had been tracking him ever since he was in grade school. He'd been moved to the top of their watch list after he'd mailed in dozens of fuzzy Polaroids of his record high scores to Activision. But the EDA deemed him ineligible for early recruitment, due to some "troubling results" in the preliminary psych evaluation they did on him. That was why they didn't actually recruit my father until much later, when he was nineteen—shortly after he became a father. One morning, two men in black suits showed up during his lunch break and abducted him from his job. They took him to one of their secret installations and showed him an earlier version of the EDA briefing film I'd been shown and gave him a choice—he could either join the EDA and use his videogame skills to try to help save humanity, or, he could, as he said, "puss out and keep wading through sewage for a living, until aliens show up and destroy our planet, along with my wife, my baby boy, and everyone else I know and love."

What choice did I have, Zack? I didn't want to leave you
two, but I couldn't just sit around and do nothing while that
happened. So I said yes, even though I knew it meant I might
never see you and your mother again. If I died protecting the
two of you and our home, then I figured it would be worth it.

Imprisonment. That was what he began to call it.

In every letter I opened, my father repeated the same apologies, marking and lamenting every single missed birthday or Christmas. For him, every milestone of my childhood and adolescence had been a double-edged sword. Watching me grow to manhood brought him joy, even from such a great distance. But that joy was always tinged with the bitter agony he felt at having missed every last second of it, and the knowledge of the pain caused by his absence.

Once a month, he wrote, the EDA would send him updates about my mother and me. He looked forward to them like holidays. In the interim, he scoured the Internet for any additional scrap of news about us he could find in a local paper or on my school's website. Every time he received a new photo of me, he wrote about it in his letters in endless detail, going on and on about how big I was getting. About how much he'd missed me and my mom, more and more every year.

He wrote to me about his day-to-day life as an elite Moon Base Alpha drone pilot. He recounted the details of the battles he fought each year, during the Jovian Opposition. He wrote about his hopes for victory, and about his fear of "the coming war." My father used that phrase often in his letters. "The coming war." It made me realize how terrible it must have been for him, to have this conflict hanging over his head all these years. He had lived his whole adult life with this terrible burden, knowing that the End of Everything was coming, and that it was drawing closer every second.

In one letter, he confessed that he'd stopped dreading the coming invasion. "Now I long for it to begin," he wrote. "Because, one way or another, it will put an end to my misery—and my imprisonment here."

He wrote: "I miss you and your mother so much I can barely stand it sometimes."

And then, half a dozen letters later, he wrote, "I just can't stand it anymore."

Another letter said he'd gone "a little nuts for a while." He wrote about how they put him on antidepressants. When things got really bad, he took tranquilizers sometimes, too. And he was required to videoconference with a shrink back on Earth twice a week.

He wrote that they kept giving him medals, but they no longer meant anything to him. He just wanted to go home. But he couldn't, because it was his job to make sure humanity still had a home when this was all over. Besides, he knew the EDA wouldn't let him go home now, anyway, because he'd asked them—repeatedly. But they told him he was far too valuable an asset, and that the world needed him right where he was. So instead, he'd started to beg the EDA to give him just a few hours of shore leave, so he could visit his family and remember what it was he was up here fighting for. They told him that would be too big of a security risk, and that if anyone learned he was still alive, especially his family, it could jeopardize everything he had worked for and sacrificed for all of these years.

As difficult as it had been for me to grow up without knowing my father, I now realized that the years we'd spent apart had been even more difficult for him. For the past seventeen years, I'd been living an idyllic life in the suburbs with Mom, surrounded by friends and all of the comforts of home. My father had spent those years here, in this desolate place on the far side of the moon, all alone, and for all he knew, completely forgotten by his loved ones.

FINALLY I GOT CURIOUS AND JUMPED AHEAD TO THE COLLECTION OF VIDEO MESSAGES HE'D recorded. I clicked on the most recent one, dated less than a week ago. The timestamp said it was just after two o'clock in the morning, by MBA time.

My father was sitting in a large dark room—larger than his quarters. It was some part of the base I didn't recognize. His unshaven face was just inches from his QComm, and his paranoid, bloodshot eyes filled half of the video frame. As he sat there in the dark, rambling into his QComm's video camera, he looked and sounded just like a raving, straitjacketed asy-lum patient—more specifically, a lot like Brad Pitt in *12 Monkeys*.

"There's something I have to do," he said. "Something I can't tell you about, until I see you in person. But I don't know if Vance will really honor my request and station you up here with me—if he doesn't, I need you to know something."

He stared into the camera lens, seeming to search for the right words.

"What if figuring out the aliens' true motives is the only way to beat them?" He shrugged and glanced away. "Or at least survive them? At this point, I think surviving might be humanity's best-case scenario." He looked back into the lens. "I hope all of this makes sense to you, if and when you actually ever get to see it. If you do—please forgive me, Son. For everything. And no matter what people call me—no matter what they say about my own actions, I want you to know that I did what I felt I had to do—to protect you and your mom, and everyone else back on Earth. Please know that I did what I did because I didn't think I had any other choice. If you're still alive to see this message, you'll know I made the right one."

He stared expectantly at the camera for a few more seconds, as if he actually expected someone to respond. Then he tapped the screen in front of him, and his image winked out.

I yanked out the flash drive and pocketed it. Then I knelt to grab my EDA rucksack. My old canvas backpack was stuffed inside, along with my father's old patch-covered leather jacket. I slung the pack over my shoulder, then continued out the exit.

I walked down the empty corridor to my father's quarters. The door hissed open for me automatically as soon as I came within range of its retinal scanner, and I saw my father sitting in a chair in the corner of the room, strapped into an *Armada* Interceptor Flight Control System like the one I had at home. He was wearing VR goggles and a pair of noise-canceling headphones, and didn't appear to notice me come in. I could tell that he was playing an *Armada* practice mission with Shin and Milo, because he kept saying their call signs, followed by his trademark RedJive catchphrase, which he uttered each time he blasted one of his opponents' ships to virtual smithereens.

"You're welcome. You're welcome. Oh, and you're quite welcome, too."

I cleared my throat loudly, and he pulled off his goggles and headphones.

I held up his flash drive. He nodded and stood up. Then he glanced over his shoulder at the nearest security camera before turning back at me.

"Let's go," he said. "I know a place we can talk in private."

18

Y FATHER LED ME THROUGH A MAZE OF DIMLY LIT CORRIDORS, THEN onto a turbo elevator. It whisked us upward, to the base's top level, and the doors opened onto the observation deck. I now noticed that the transparent dome overhead was the exact same size as the domed ceiling down in the Thunderdome, and it offered the same exact view. I glanced around until I located the camera array suspended from the dome's armored frame, which captured the 360-degree view of the surrounding landscape in high-definition and projected it onto the Thunderdome's concrete ceiling, deep beneath the moon's rocky mantle.

Without pausing to admire the view, my father crossed to the other side of the observation deck, to another elevator door. Unlike the other doors on the base, this one failed to open automatically when he approached it. Instead he flipped open a panel beside it to reveal a numeric keypad and punched in a long code from memory. The doors swished opened and we stepped inside. There was a single button, with a down arrow on it that lit up when my father pressed it. The elevator carried us downward, dropping us so fast I thought my feet might lift up off the floor for a moment. When the car opened, we stepped out into a narrow service tunnel lined with wires and metal tubing. I followed my father down its length, nearly sprinting to keep up. It was a very long tunnel, with a steep downward grade.

When we finally reached the other end, my father opened a circular hatch in the ceiling with yet another security code. After a short climb up a metal ladder, we emerged into a large, circular room with a clear domed ceiling. It provided a stunning view of the surrounding crater and of the armored sphere that was Moon Base Alpha, visible off to our right—a giant armored orb nestled into the adjacent goblet-shaped crater high above us, just beyond the lip of the larger bowl-shaped Daedalus crater in which we now stood.

"Welcome to Daedalus Observatory," my father said. "Sorry about all the dust and trash—the cleaning drones never come down here, obviously. They closed the observatory down over two decades ago and made the whole place off limits."

I spent a moment gazing out at the barren lunar surface, which stretched to the black horizon in all directions. The sight suddenly drove home the fantastic isolation of the place. It was no wonder my father and his friends behaved a bit strangely. The years of solitude they'd had to endure up here probably would have driven a lot of people nuts.

"You said this place was off limits?"

"It was," he said. "It *is*. But I figured out how to get the power and life-support systems in here back online without alerting anyone back on Earth. And I left all of the hidden microphones and cameras in here disabled, so this is one of the few places in the entire base where the EDA can't monitor or record me."

He leaned toward a small microphone stalk protruding from a nearby security console and then spoke loudly into it.

"Open the pod bay doors, HAL," he recited. "I said, please open the pod bay doors, HAL." He grinned at me. "See? Sweet, sweet privacy."

"Right, we wouldn't want the Cigarette Smoking Man to eavesdrop on us," I muttered. But he ignored the remark.

"Here," he said, reaching over to flip a bank of switches, flooding the dim space with flickering fluorescent light. "This is what I wanted to show you."

The other side of the control room was a chaotic, cluttered mess. Hand-written notes, diagrams, drawings, and computer printouts were taped up everywhere and stacked on every available surface. It looked like the lair of a homicide detective on some TV show—one who had spent decades tracking a serial killer no one else believed existed.

I crossed the room and walked through the paper jungle my father had created, studying his notes and printouts.

"I know how all this stuff must look," he said, as if he'd read my mind. "Like Russell Crowe's garage in *A Beautiful Mind,* right?"

"I was thinking it looked more like a supervillain's lair," I said. I started punching random buttons on the console in front of me. "Which one of these is the self-destruct?"

"The first one you pressed, actually," he said, pointing to an unlabeled red button.

I believed him for a split second—long enough for my eyes to widen in panic.

"Yes!" he said, grinning. "Got you, kid."

"Fine, you got me," I said. "You did all this yourself?"

He nodded. "I've never shared any of this with either Shin or Graham," he said. "Shin wouldn't take any of it seriously," he said. "And Graham—well, Graham doesn't have a very skeptical way of thinking, and I wanted to approach this scientifically." He locked eyes with me. "But from what you said up in the mess hall before, I was sure you didn't want to hear any of this?"

I shook my head. "I've been asking myself the same questions you and Graham mentioned. I just ... didn't think learning the answers could make any difference now." I locked eyes with him. "Tell me," I said.

He nodded and took a deep breath.

"You know who Finn Arbogast is," he said. It wasn't a question, but I nodded.

"The fake founder of Chaos Terrain?" I said, recalling my brief meeting with the man that morning at Crystal Palace—a lifetime ago. "What about him?"

"I was his primary military consultant when he and the Chaos Terrain team were developing *Terra Firma* and *Armada,* as well as all of the early mission packs," he said, and I thought I detected a tinge of pride in his voice. "I always dreamed of making videogames for a living when I grew up, so you can imagine how I felt when I got the chance to help design the videogames that might save the world.

"Arbogast and I collaborated for several months. Not in person, but we videoconferenced several times a week. It was his job to create the videogames that would train the world's population how to fight off the Europans. So his training simulations had to be able to simulate their ships, weapons, maneuvers, and tactics—all with a very high degree of accuracy. To accomplish that, they gave Arbogast unrestricted access to all of the EDA's data on the Europans—everything we'd learned about them since we made first contact."

He sighed heavily. "And I managed to access some of that classified data."

"How?" I asked. "When you were stuck up here and he was back on Earth?"

"He linked his computer network to ours," my father said. "So that he could share new builds of *Terra Firma* and *Armada* with us as soon as they were ready for testing. That allowed me to gain access to his research files on the Europans—which contained a *lot* of the top-secret data about our interactions with them over the years ... and everything I learned from them confirmed the theory I'd already been forming for almost a decade."

I nodded, trying to hide how nervous he was making me.

"Lay it on me," I said.

"Okay," he said. "Here goes." He took a deep breath.

"Ever since we made first contact with them, the aliens have been intercepting our movies and television broadcasts. Then they edit clips from them together and transmit them back to us, once a year, just prior to the Jovian Opposition," he told me. "But only a handful of people have ever been allowed to see the transmissions." He motioned to the screen. "Now I need you to see them, too."

A barrage of these alien-edited video clips began to appear on the screen—and every last one of them depicted some form of human conflict. I glimpsed a lot of World War II newsreel footage, intercut with photos and video of the dozens of other large-scale military conflicts that had occurred in the following decades. But these images of real-life war were intercut with scenes from a lot of old war movies and television series. It almost seemed as if the Europans were unable to differentiate between reality and fiction. Either that, or they were intercutting the two on purpose, in an effort to make some kind of point.

Even weirder—I also began to spot brief scenes taken from dozens of science fiction films—all of them featuring hostile alien invaders of some kind. In the space of just a few seconds, I spotted shots from various films in the *Trek* and *Wars* franchises, mixed with shots from the various versions of *War of the Worlds, The Day the Earth Stood Still, V,* and even—God help us—*Battlefield Earth*. Nothing from the friendly alien movie genre, though. Not so much a single glimpse of *E.T., Starman, Earth to Echo,* or *ALF.*

"Look at these transmissions," he said as the barrage of clips continued to flash on the screen, showing a grotesque menagerie of extraterrestrial invaders plucked from the entire history of science fiction films—Aliens, Predators, Triffids, Transformers—you name it.

"These images, and the way in which they're arranged—I think it's some kind of a message, Son," he said. "An intentionally cryptic one. It's like—like they're holding up a mirror, so that we can see ourselves from their perspective."

The rapid montage of unsettling imagery flashing on the screen suddenly segued into a series of two- and three-second-long clips from summer blockbusters like *Independence Day, Armageddon,* and *Deep Impact,* most of them from scenes that depicted all of humanity uniting as one species, to save itself and its home from a deadly comet, a rogue asteroid, or from a wide variety of hostile alien invaders.

"I think the Europans have been studying us and our popular culture since before we even made first contact with them," my father said, raking his hands through his hair. "I think they watched all of the science fiction films and television shows we've made that depict an alien invasion of our planet, and they realized it was one of our species' worst nightmares. So they set about making it happen. They proceeded to stage an alien invasion just like the ones we'd always imagined. The kind depicted in our fiction, complete with giant motherships, starship dogfights, killer robots—all of it!"

My father stared at me, waiting for me to say something, but I was momentarily speechless. I could only continue to stare at the screen, where the images kept coming. I spotted stills from the reboots of *The Thing, The Day the Earth Stood Still,* and *War of the Worlds,* and then a clip from an older film, *Earth vs. the Flying Saucers.*

"I knew for certain these transmissions were intended to be some sort of a message when I heard this," he said, tapping his QComm. "Each of these bursts of images ends with a series of five tones."

It was the opening of "Wild Signals" from John Williams' score for *Close Encounters of the Third Kind.* The five tones the government has their keyboardist start off with when they play that epic game of Simon with the aliens at the end of the movie.

La-Luh-La-BAH-BAH!

The tones sounded as if they were coming from an old touch-tone pushbutton telephone handset. They began to play, very quickly, on a repeating loop. Then my father muted the audio and turned to study my reaction. But hearing those five notes from *Close Encounters* had momentarily thrown me off balance. I'd never liked that film—probably because of how easy it was for the main character, Roy Neary, to (spoiler alert) leave his family at the very end of the film. It hit a little too close to home.

I stared at the images. I listened to tones. I waited for him to continue.

"Okay," he said, inching forward. "First, just think about the chronology of events. Think about how our first contact with them went down. The Europans orchestrated this entire conflict—they lured and manipulated us into it." He narrowed his eyes. "Why else would they slap a giant swastika on the surface of Europa—it was a trap, and we walked right into it! Just like Admiral Fucking Ackbar!"

Under other circumstances, this might have made me laugh. But not then.

"So," he went on, "humanity discovers this threatening message from an obviously nonhuman intelligence—placed in a spot where they knew humans would find it when our technology advanced to the stage where we were capable of sending probes to our outer solar system—sort of like the monolith buried on the moon in *2001*?"

I nodded—not in agreement, but just to indicate I understood the reference. I'm sure I would have mentioned that I'd read his copy of "The Sentinel," the short story by Arthur C. Clarke that served as the initial inspiration for *2001*'s artifact-left-behind-by-ancient-aliens storyline—but internally, I was wondering if my father was experiencing confirmation bias or observational selection bias, or one of those other biases I'd learned about in my AP Psychology class. Maybe he was seeing patterns where none really existed.

Then again, maybe not.

"The Europans must have known we wouldn't be able to resist sending a probe down to investigate its origin—and the moment we did, they suddenly declared war and their intention to kill off our entire species. According to the official story, the aliens never gave us a chance to explain our actions, or negotiate with them. But they didn't kill us off right away—even though they clearly had the technological means of doing so. No, instead of attacking us, they lured us into some sort of weird arms race. Then they gradually let us close the technological gap between us and them. Over a forty-two-year period. And then this year, they finally decide to invade. Why? Their behavior doesn't make any sense—unless they're testing us. It's the only logical explanation."

"We're not talking about Vulcans here," I reminded him. "You can't impose human logic on alien behavior, right? Why should anything they do make sense to us? Their culture and motives might be . . . you know, 'beyond our human understanding.' "

My father shook his head.

"This human understands enough to know when he's being messed with," he said. "These aliens have coaxed and manipulated us into this exact position for a reason—maybe to elicit a reaction. Or to put us in specific kinds of circumstances, to see how we'll react to them—collectively, as a species."

"As a test?"

He nodded; then he sat down abruptly without saying another word, like an attorney who had finished delivering his closing argument to a jury, and stared at me, apparently waiting for me to respond, his eyes darting back and forth feverishly, hanging on my reaction.

"What is it you think they're testing us on? To see how terrified they can make us? To see how difficult we are to kill or enslave?"

"I don't know, Son," he said, his voice still calm and even despite his expression. "Maybe they wanted to see how our species would handle itself during an encounter with another intelligent species? A potentially hostile one? That's one of the classic tropes of science fiction. Aliens are always showing up to put humanity on trial. *The Day the Earth Stood Still, Stranger in a Strange Land, Have Space Suit, Will Travel*—and a bunch of different *Star Trek* episodes. The Europans might have a million different motives. On the eighties reboot of the *Twilight Zone,* there was this one episode, called 'A Small Talent for War'—"

I raised my hand to cut him off.

"But this isn't science fiction, General," I said, feeling as if I were the adult in this conversation, while he had assumed the role of the starry-eyed teenager who won't listen to reason. "This isn't some *Twilight Zone* episode. It's real life, remember?"

"Life imitates art," he said. "And maybe these particular aliens do, too." He smiled at me. "Does any of this feel like something that could happen in real life to you? Or do events seem to be unfolding the way they would in a story, or a movie? Perfectly timed for dramatic effect?"

He picked up a large whiteboard resting against a nearby console and tilted it toward me so that I could see the two hastily drawn diagrams on it. He'd drawn a picture of the Death Star from *Star Wars* on the left side and a sketch of the Disrupter dodecahedron on the right. Both drawings were surrounded by arrows and notes that appeared to draw a comparison between the two. But it was hard to be sure—because I couldn't read my father's handwriting to save my life.

"Take the Disrupter, for example," he said. "Why is it so difficult to destroy, when we have no problem plowing through their other drones? Why not make all of their drones that hard to destroy? Because the Disrupter is a level boss, that's why!" He pointed to the whiteboard. "The Disrupter is their version of the Death Star—it's a huge, nearly indestructible doomsday weapon, but it has a small Achilles' heel that will allow us to destroy it." He locked eyes with me. "It's like they designed it that way—so that at least one pilot has to sacrifice themselves to destroy it. The shields only drop for a few seconds—just long enough for two perfectly timed core detonations to go off! Why would they engineer it that way, unless it was on purpose?"

I nodded. "I wondered the same thing," I confessed.

"No weapons designer or engineer would build something with such an arbitrary weakness," he said. "The Disrupter is more like something a videogame developer would come up with, to create a big challenge at the end of a level—a boss that requires a huge sacrifice to destroy. And then they send one—just one—to attack this base, instead of sending it straight to Earth. Why? Because they wanted us to see how it worked! Then they let us destroy it! Maybe that was part of their test—to find out if humans are willing to make a heroic sacrifice to save their comrades? To see if our species actually behaves the way we portray ourselves in our books and movies and games?" He stood back up and began to pace, faster and faster. "They could be testing us to see if humanity lacks the courage of its convictions? Are we as selfless and noble as we think we are?"

"But how would the aliens even know about Vance's heroic sacrifice?" I asked. "Or about anything that was going on within the EDA's ranks during those battles?"

He bit his lower lip; then he held up his QComm.

"Think about it. Where did this QComm tech come from?"

I shook my head, not wanting to believe it. But he nodded in disagreement.

"The Europans invented this technology, and we barely even understand how it works," he said. "For all we know, they're using these to eavesdrop on us right now." He rubbed his temples, wincing. "I mean, do you think it was a coincidence that of all the EDA sites around the world they could've attacked this morning, they chose the one where we'd just relocated all of our elite recruit candidates?"

He fell silent and stared at me. My head was spinning. I sat down in one of the leather chairs bolted to the floor.

"Why are you telling me all this?" I asked.

He frowned, looking disappointed that I needed to ask.

"Because you're my son," he said. "Maybe I just want to get your opinion."

"On what, General?"

"On what you think we should do," he said. "Do we ignore everything about the Europans' actions that don't add up and let the EDA launch their doomsday weapon at them? Try to commit genocide against the first intelligent species we've ever contacted?"

"But they're coming here to commit genocide against us!" I shouted. "We have no choice but to defend ourselves!"

"I believe we do, Son. I think that's what they're doing: presenting us with a choice. We can try to destroy them, thereby ensuring that they destroy us," he said. "Or we can take a gamble, based on our deductions and our moral reasoning, and try to stop the Icebreaker."

"But then—won't we just be allowing them to wipe us out when they arrive?"

"If they wanted to exterminate humanity, they could have done it decades ago," he said. "They had the technological capability to wipe us out the day we made first contact with them. The illusion that we can defeat them in this war is just that—an illusion. It always has been."

I didn't respond. He took me by the shoulders.

"No one else knows all of this. No one else could read these tea leaves like you and me, Zack. I feel like there must be a reason the two of us are here right now. We're in a position to decide the fate of humanity." He smiled. "Maybe it's destiny."

I stared into his eyes. He was telling me the truth—or what he believed to be the truth. There was no doubt in my mind of that. It's impossible to have a poker face with someone who has the same face as you.

"This is why you didn't participate in that first Icebreaker mission, wasn't it?" I asked. "The admiral benched you, didn't he? He thought you might try to sabotage it?"

He nodded. "He knows me well," he said. "We were friends a long time."

"You shared this theory with Admiral Vance?" I said. "And he didn't buy it?"

"Archie is a good man. Fearless. Honorable. But the guy doesn't have much of an imagination," he said. "And he doesn't know shit about common tropes in science fiction." He grinned. "Take his call sign, Viper. He borrowed that from Tom Skerritt's character in *Top Gun,* his all-time favorite movie. He hates science fiction. I could never get him to watch *Trek, Wars, Firefly,* or *BSG*!" He shook his head. "The bastard even refused to watch *E.T.*! Who doesn't love *E.T.,* I ask you?"

"Yeah, the man obviously can't be trusted," I muttered.

My father frowned at my sarcasm. "That's not what I meant," he said. "Archie is a fighter at heart. He believes we can beat them, despite their superior technology, because evolution has better equipped us for warfare." He shook his head. "I'm a gamer, Zack. Like you. When I find myself confronted with a puzzle, I can't help but try to solve it."

He began to pace back and forth in front of me again.

"I want to find out what the Europans really are. What's really down there, under all that ice?" He looked up through the dome, at the bright band of stars overhead. "I want to know the truth. I want to reach the end of the game." He turned to lock eyes with me once again. "And I want to save the world, if I can."

"How?"

"I'm not sure," he said. "But I'm going to try, if I get the opportunity." He looked at the floor. "And I wanted to explain myself to you first. So you'll understand any actions I may be forced to take." He shrugged. "Maybe you can explain them to your mother, if I don't get the chance. . . ."

He trailed off. I was too frightened of what he might say to ask him to elaborate.

When it became clear to him that I wasn't going to say anything more, my father reached out and pressed his hand to the scanner beside the exit. The door hissed open.

"It's a lot to process," he said. "I'll give you some privacy to think it all through."

He took a step forward, as if to hug me, but something in my eyes made him change his mind. He smiled and stepped back.

"I'm gonna head back down to the Thunderdome and run a final systems check on each of the control pods," he said. "Meet me there whenever you're ready, okay?"

I nodded, but remained silent. He gave me another forced smile, then disappeared through the exit.

Once he was gone, I sat there alone in the darkened Daedalus Observatory control room, at the center of the giant electronic ear that humanity had constructed to try to communicate with its enemy, thinking about everything my father had just told me.

What if he was right about this—just like he'd been right all those years ago when he scribbled down his theory about the Earth Defense Alliance in that old notebook of his? That theory of his had seemed ridiculous at first, too.

I let the possibility linger in my thoughts for a moment. Then I cast one last glance up through the dome at the starry dynamo stretched out over my head, taking it all in. Then I turned and hurried out the exit, fleeing the solitude of the Daedalus Observatory as quickly as I could. There wasn't much time left. I didn't feel like spending any more of it alone.

19

I RODE THE TURBO ELEVATOR BACK UP TO THE OBSERVATION DECK. THE MOMENT THE ELevator doors swished open and I stepped into the large domed room, the odor of burning cannabis filled my nose. The smell grew increasingly stronger the farther I ventured into the room, as did the familiar strains of Pink Floyd's *Dark Side of the Moon,* punctuated by fits of only slightly suppressed laughter.

In the dim light, I could now make out two figures sprawled out on the floor across the room: Shin and Milo were side by side, lying flat on their backs, staring up through the observation dome at the glowing band of the Milky Way above. They were passing a cruise-missile-sized joint back and forth. The Pink Floyd was cranked up so loud they hadn't heard me come in, so I stood there eavesdropping for a few minutes while they continued a giggle-filled discussion of their favorite *Robotech* episodes.

I tiptoed up behind them, then loudly cleared my throat.

"What's up, fellas?"

Shin scrambled to his feet, looking mortified. But Milo barely even reacted.

"Zack!" Shin said, turning red. "We didn't hear you come in—" He turned to point a finger at his companion. "I was, uh, showing Milo some of the things we grow in our hydroponic garden and, ah—"

"Now you're getting stoned out of your gourds?" I said. "While listening to *Dark Side of the Moon*?" I motioned to the cratered surface out beyond the dome, stretching to the horizon in all directions around us. "On the *far* side of the moon?"

"This is a special strain of Yoda Kush that I myself created," Shin said, holding up his giant spliff. "I thought it might help relax his nerves." Then he took a long hit and inhaled deeply. "Poor Milo is really stressed out, aren't you?"

Milo shook his head. "Not anymore," he said, grinning wide. "Zack, you won't believe this shit!" With some effort, he sat up, then turned to face me. "Shin told me that the EDA spent decades engineering a special strain of weed that helps people focus and enhances their ability to play videogames! Once they had it perfected, that was when the government finally started legalizing it in the States." He raised his arms in victory. "This ganja is part of the war effort! I love it!" He broke into song, and Shin immediately joined him.

"*'America. Fuck yeah. Comin' to save the motherfuckin' day, yeah!'*"

They broke up into another laughing fit.

"Where are the others?" I asked.

"They all snuck off to bone each other," Milo announced. "Whoadie and Chén slipped away first, then Debbie snuck off with Graham."

I had no idea how to respond to this information.

"I can't say I blame them," Milo said. "We're all facing the possibility of imminent death. Why not throw caution to the wind and go out with a bang—so to speak."

"I was just thinking the same thing," Shin said, turning to smile down at him. The two of them made eyes at each other for a few seconds—until my clueless ass finally figured out what was going on.

As my mother was often fond of pointing out to me, my "gaydar" was just plain broken.

"I'll see you guys later," I said, backing toward the exit. "I'm just gonna— you know." I nodded over my shoulder. "Let you guys have some privacy."

Shin grinned at me, amused at how flustered I'd become all of a sudden.

"Thanks, Zack," he said.

"Yeah, thanks, dude!" Milo called after me, laughing. "We could use the privacy!"

As I rode the lift down to the Thunderdome, I found myself wondering where Lex was and what she was doing. Had she too found some handsome stranger to spend her last moments with, while I waited mine out alone up here, a million miles away?

01H33M43S REMAINING.

WHEN I REACHED THE THUNDERDOME, I DIDN'T THINK THERE WAS ANYONE ELSE THERE AT first. Then the canopy of one of the drone controller pods slid open, and my father climbed out of it. He smiled at me, but I turned away as soon as our eyes met and walked over to one of the other pods. Just as I was beginning to lower myself into it, my father crouched at the edge of the oval-shaped pit and looked down at me.

"I'm sorry, Zack," he said. "I shouldn't have dumped all of that on you. It was too much, after everything else you've been through today."

"It's okay," I said.

"Thanks for listening," he said. "You're a good listener, just like your mom." He looked away. "I just—I've been waiting for a long time to talk with you about all that. . . ."

He trailed off. I lifted my eyes to meet his gaze but didn't respond.

"Aren't you going to say anything?" he asked.

I shook my head. "I'm still trying to process all of it," I replied. "I don't know what to believe."

He nodded. I hit the button to close my control pod's canopy. It slid shut between us, ending the conversation—or at least postponing it temporarily.

I sat in my simulated cockpit with my eyes closed, trying to collect my thoughts. I didn't have much luck.

SOMETIME LATER, I HEARD MY FATHER GREET DEBBIE, CHÉN, AND WHOADIE. MILO, SHIN, AND Graham a few minutes after that.

When the countdown clock hit the one-hour mark, we all gathered in front of the command station to watch the president of the United States address the nation from the Oval Office on live television. She smiled reassuringly at the camera, but the fear in her eyes was evident.

"My fellow Americans," she began. "At this very moment, the leaders of every nation around the world are about to show their citizens the same briefing film I'm about to show you, which will explain the alarming situation that now faces all of humanity."

Debbie was standing nearby, staring down at her QComm display, waiting for the moment when she could finally call her boys. But our phones were still locked. I glanced over at Chén, Shin, and Graham, who were each focused on other, smaller display screens mounted nearby—the ones that showed the leaders of their respective countries making a similar introduction. A second later, the faces of the US and Chinese presidents, and of the Japanese and British prime ministers, vanished from the display screens and the Earth Defense Alliance logo appeared on each of them.

"In 1973, NASA discovered the first evidence of a nonterrestrial intelligence, right here in our very own solar system," Sagan's voice-over began, "when the *Pioneer 10* spacecraft sent back the first close-up photograph of Europa, Jupiter's fourth-largest moon."

The eight of us stood there, clustered together in a tight knot, and rewatched the entire film, this time with the knowledge that the rest of humanity was seeing it, too.

When the film ended, the president's face reappeared, and she told the world what Admiral Vance had told all of us at Crystal Palace earlier that morning—which now felt like an entire lifetime ago. Once the president finished revealing the bad news about the approaching alien armada, the networks began replaying her address, with increasingly alarming headlines superimposed across the screen, along with footage showing the stunned and panicked reactions of average people.

As I watched the chaos unfold in the array of video windows before me, I thought about my mother, and my friends, and everyone else trapped down there.

Would the EDA's plan really work? Would our civilization collapse in the wake of the revelation that we were about to be invaded by aliens, or had the EDA subconsciously prepared us enough to deal with it, as they'd hoped?

Would humanity cower in fear, or stand its ground and fight back?

I stared at the screens, wondering which one it would be.

Shin pulled up dozens of different television networks from all over the world and displayed them on the dome side by side, along with more video feeds from the Internet.

We watched as the initial wave of panic spread across the globe— footage of people freaking out on crowded city streets and stampeding out of sports stadiums. But the world seemed to take the news incredibly well. If there were riots, mass suicides, and lootings going on, no one was reporting them—or even posting videos of them online.

Within minutes, it seemed like the same newscasters who had delivered the news were now reporting with total confidence that most of the world's civilian population was already responding to the EDA's call to arms, and that hundreds of millions of people all over the world were already mobilizing themselves by logging on to the EDA's online operations servers to enlist and then receive their combat drone assignments and take up arms and defend the planet. Several networks were showing clips of people abandoning their cars in traffic to run into electronics stores and libraries and coffee shops and Internet cafés and office buildings, thousands upon thousands of people, all in a mad dash to get somewhere with broadband Internet access.

There was no way the news networks could've pulled together all that footage so quickly (and then edited it together for broadcast). And at this stage, it would be impossible to know whether or not a majority of the world's population was prepared to join the Earth Defense Alliance and fight to defend our home. This had to be the EDA at work, convincing media outlets that our best chance at survival was to tell the reassuring lie. And they were right—if people believed that humanity was already uniting itself under the EDA's banner, they were far more likely to join the fight themselves.

I thought again of the note my father had scribbled in his notebook so long ago:

> What if they're using videogames to train us to fight without us even knowing it? Like Mr. Miyagi in The Karate Kid, when he made Daniel-san paint his house, sand his deck, and wax all of his cars—he was training him and he didn't even realize it!
>
> Wax on, wax off—but on a global scale!

Thirty- and sixty-second-long "public service announcements" began to run amid the news bulletins, each designed to inform the world's civilian population of the EDA's plan and show them how to use their computer or mobile device to enlist in the Earth Defense Alliance online and "help save the world!"

The best PSA was one that opened with a shot of a brother and sister sitting on the couch in their living room. The boy is playing *Armada* on their giant television, while the girl sits beside him playing *Terra Firma* on her handheld tablet. On their screens, we can see that she's operating an ATHID infantry drone while he pilots a WASP quadcopter. Both of them are trying to take down a towering alien Basilisk stomping its way through a suburban neighborhood. On the TV screen, we see the Behemoth lurch forward and step on the corner of a house, crushing it under one of its massive metal feet—and at that same moment, the wall of the kids' living room also collapses, revealing that it was their house the giant robot just stepped on. The two kids aren't playing a game—they're defending their home! Their parents cower behind the couch, watching as their two children do battle with the giant alien machine, with the help of hundreds of other drones operated by their neighbors. When the Behemoth explodes under a hail of enemy fire, the parents whip out their smartphones and use them to take control of two more drones and join the battle, too. It reminded me of one of those old toy commercials that ended with the line "And Mom and Dad can play along, too!"

When I couldn't bear to watch the news feeds any longer, I climbed into my control pod and closed the canopy, then made it nontransparent, creating my own private isolation chamber.

I sat there in the darkness for a while, listening to myself breathe. Then I took out my QComm and queued up a song I'd first discovered on one of my father's old mixtapes. It was a great rock instrumental by Pink Floyd that I'd often used to psych myself up before a big *Armada* mission.

I played it over and over, each time mouthing the words to the single lyric spoken in the middle of the song: *"One of these days I'm going to cut you into little pieces."*

01H00M00S REMAINING.

WHEN THE COUNTDOWN CLOCK SHOWED ONLY ONE HOUR REMAINING, ALL OF OUR QCOMMS beeped in unison. A notice on my display told me that the EDA had finally unlocked our QComms' access to the public phone system. Graham, Debbie, Whoadie, Milo, and Chén each climbed into their individual drone controller pods and then closed their canopies, to give themselves some privacy for their calls home.

Shin didn't call anyone. Instead, he picked up his bass guitar, and, in what seemed like an odd coincidence, he began to play a solo version of "One of These Days" while staring up at the stars projected on the dome over our heads. Then I noticed a practice set list taped to the floor in front of him, and saw that several of the songs listed there were tracks I knew from my father's old mixtapes.

My father was off by himself, too, sitting at the command center console. When I walked over to join him, I saw that he was staring at my mother's contact information on his QComm's display screen.

"Are you going to call her?" I asked, making him jump slightly.

He shook his head. "I was about to send her a video message instead," he said. "I recorded twenty-three takes of it, but they're all terrible—so maybe I'll just give up and send her the least terrible one. . . ."

I plucked the QComm out of his hand and began to dial a number.

"Are you going to call her?" he asked, like a nervous schoolboy. "Right now?"

I nodded.

"I need to let her know I'm okay," I said. "And before you send her some psychotic video message, I should probably break the news to her that you're alive first—otherwise she'll have a coronary when your face pops up on her iPhone."

My father gave me a relieved smile, but before he could reply, we were interrupted by Milo's voice, coming from his nearby pod. When he'd climbed inside, he must've forgotten to close his canopy all the way, and now we could hear every word of his conversation.

"Ma, it's gonna be okay!" Milo said. "You know how they've been training everyone to fight with videogames? Well, I'm one of the best *Armada* pilots in the world, and so that's why they recruited me early! Yeah! And guess what? Now I'm stationed up here on the moon!"

"The moon?" she cried. "That's ridiculous, Milo! Don't you lie to your mother!" She raised a giant TV remote. "I need your help with this blasted TV. The same nonsense is on every channel!"

I glanced over and saw Milo raise his QComm's camera, then tilt it to give her a quick look at the Thunderdome, and at the dazzling field of stars projected on its dome ceiling. She gasped and Milo grinned, lowering the QComm's camera and aiming it back at his own face.

"Told ya," he said.

His mother started to wail in fear—there was no other word for it.

"They put *you* in charge of defending us? Now I know we're doomed!"

"Ma, please," Milo said, sounding more and more like a little boy with each word. "Relax. I'm gonna stop these things, I promise. Don't worry. I'll do whatever it takes to keep you and little Kilgore from getting hurt. You're gonna be proud of me when this is all done, you wait and see—"

I didn't get to find out who or what Kilgore was, because my father walked over and closed Milo's pod canopy for him. Then he walked back over and watched nervously as I raised his QComm and placed the video call to my mother.

A second later, my mother's drawn and worried face appeared on the QComm's display. She was at work, of course, standing in one of the hospital's rooms, clustered in front of a TV with a dozen other nurses. Even now, after the announcement, she still hadn't abandoned the people she cared for.

"Zack!" my mother shouted the moment she saw my face. She rushed out into the empty hospital corridor, holding her phone up in front of her. "Thank God you're okay, honey! You are okay, aren't you?"

"I'm fine, Mom," I said. "You know, aside from the impending alien invasion."

"Can you believe it?" she said. "It's all over the news—every channel!" She held the phone directly in front of her face. "Where are you? I want you to get home, Zackary, right this minute!"

"I can't, Mom," I said. "The Earth Defense Alliance needs me."

"What are you talking about?" she said, sounding increasingly hysterical.

"I enlisted," I told her. "In the Earth Defense Alliance. This morning. They made me a flight officer. See?"

I set the phone down on the console in front of me, then stepped back so she could see my uniform. The sight appeared to leave her speechless.

"Honey, where are you?" she finally managed to ask.

"I'm on the moon," I said, panning the QComm's camera around the room, and then up at the dome above. "Moon Base Alpha. It's a secret base on the far side. I'm going to help fight off the invasion from up here." I gave her a smile. "All those years I spent playing videogames weren't wasted after all, eh?"

She broke down into tears then, but she still managed to sound incredibly pissed off.

"Zackary Ulysses Lightman!" she shouted, making the phone tremble fiercely in her hands. "You are not fighting any goddamn aliens! You come home right this minute!"

"Mom, it's going to be okay," I said, as soothingly as I could. "I'm not alone up here, okay? That's the other thing I have to tell you. It's going to be a shock, so brace yourself."

I pulled my father in front of the QComm's camera, then stood just behind him. His legs were shaking so badly I worried he might collapse.

"Oh my God," my mother said, covering her mouth. "Xavier? Is that you?"

"Hello, Pam," he said, his voice shaking. "It's—it's really good to see you."

"It can't be you," I heard my mother say. "It can't be."

"It's really him, Mom," I said. "He's a general in the Earth Defense Alliance. A war hero." I smiled at him. "He's been awarded three Medals of Honor. Haven't you?"

He didn't say anything. He just stared at her, like a deer in the headlights.

"Xavier?" she said. "It's really you?"

"It's really me," he said, his voice breaking after each word. "I'm alive—and I'm so sorry. I—I can't tell you how much I've missed you—and how sorry I am for leaving you to raise our son all on your own. I'm sorry for a lot of other things, too, but . . ."

She started crying again. My father's face contorted in pain, and that was when I turned and walked away, well out of earshot, to let them talk in private—and to avoid a crying jag of my own.

I glanced around the room and saw Shin talking quietly with Milo. Nearby, Graham and Debbie were doing the same thing. Whoadie and Chén were both squeezed into Chén's pod, seizing their last chance to make out.

I climbed into my own control pod and lowered the canopy. Then I took out my QComm and closed my eyes, thinking about what I was going to say to Lex.

I tapped her name on my very short contact list, and her face appeared on my display so quickly that it startled me.

Her name, rank, and current location appeared in the bottom right-hand corner of my display. According to the readout, she'd already somehow managed to get herself promoted to captain, and she was still located at Sapphire Station, the EDA operations stronghold near Billings, Montana.

She was sitting inside a darkened control pod similar to mine, except that hers appeared to be designed specifically to control Sentinels, Titan Warmechs, and ATHIDs and included a pair of "power gauntlets" that let her control the drone's massive hands with her own.

"Hey you! I was hoping I'd get to see your face again before the world ended."

"I considered putting it off until the weekend. I didn't want to seem too eager."

"No, of course not." She smirked. "So, what's it like up on the moon, Lieutenant?"

"Are we being honest?"

"Why not?" she said. "We probably won't live to regret anything we say."

"It's pretty terrifying up here, actually. How are things down there?"

"Equally insane," she said. "But civilization hasn't descended into total chaos yet. People seem to be holding it together. If the news is to be believed, it seems like the whole world is ready to fight back. It's kind of amazing."

It was hard to hear so much hope in her voice and not be able to tell her about the second Icebreaker—or my father's theory. I desperately wanted to hear what she thought, but there was no time.

"You ready to give these aliens what for, Lieutenant?" she asked.

"As ready as I'll ever be, Lieutenant— Excuse me, Captain Larkin." I gave her another salute—then, like a goofball, I pretended to poke myself in the eye as I did, just to hear the sound of her laugh. "How'd you get promoted so fast?" I asked.

"For heroism in the Battle of Crystal Palace," she said. "And I had the high score on the ground, as far as enemy drones downed. Plus I didn't blow up half the installation."

"Yeah, they frown on that."

"Here, I'm sending you a present," she said, tapping at her QComm display with both thumbs. "A playlist of my favorite *Terra Firma* battle tunes. I like to rock out when I'm knocking clocks out," she said. "Helps with my aim."

"Yeah," I said, smiling. "Mine, too."

A FILE TRANSFER COMPLETE message popped up on my QComm a split second later—she'd somehow bypassed the security software, so it didn't even ask me for permission before it transferred the songs onto my device. The music player opened, displaying her playlist—which, at first glance, appeared to be a mix of songs by only Joan Jett, Heart, and Pat Benatar.

"This should come in handy," I said, grinning. "*Gracias.*"

"*De nada.*"

I asked her to show me how to do the file transfer trick myself. When she was done, I managed to successfully send her a copy of my father's *Raid the Arcade* mix.

She scrolled through the track list for a few seconds, smiling and nodding.

"Hey, wanna hear some good news?" she asked.

"Yes please!" I said. "More than I probably ever have in my life."

"I think I'm going to be assigned to help defend Moon Base Alpha from down here," she said. "You know, provided they don't attack Earth first. We've been running MBA defense sims nonstop since I arrived."

I smiled—something I wouldn't have thought possible a few seconds earlier.

"So you're going to have my back, eh?"

She nodded. "Just give me the QComm ID number on your drone controller station," she said. "I figured out a hack that will allow me to use it to pinpoint your location, and tell me which drone you're operating during combat."

"When did you have time to do that?"

"I've been sitting here all day, exploring the QComm network between training sims," she said. "The EDA set it up a lot like a traditional computer network, which made it really easy to figure out and use—that's probably why they did it that way. So what's your QCLID?"

"My what?"

"Your Quantum Communicator Link Identification number?"

I stared at the icons that ringed the edge of my display screen and shrugged.

"I have no idea."

She grinned at me and rolled her eyes. "See that gear icon at the top right of your display? Those are your drone controller station settings."

"Right," I said, tapping it with my finger. "I knew that."

She helped me navigate through menu screens until I located the twelve-digit-long numeric code she needed and read it off to her.

"Got it," she said, as her fingers danced across one of the touchscreens in front of her. "Now I can keep an eye on you."

"I feel much better now," I said. And I did, too.

"You should," she said. "I've got the skills to pay the bills." She winked at me—all smooth, like a movie star. "And I'm going to make sure you keep all of your pieces in one piece," she said. "Until I get a piece. Get me, soldier?"

"Yes, ma'am," I said. "I believe I do."

Then I saluted, and it made her laugh—but a few seconds in, it somehow turned into a strangled sob.

"Fuck, I'm scared, Zack," she said. She bit her lower lip—to stop it from trembling, I think.

"I'm scared, too," I said, suddenly unable to meet her eyes—even through a screen. "My whole life, I always imagined fighting off an alien invasion would be some epic adventure. That it would be like the movies—humanity would triumph in the end."

"*Invasion of the Body Snatchers*," she said. "The pod people always win. That's the smart way to invade—not this *Independence Day/Pacific Rim*-job crap."

Her words brought me back to my conversation with my father, and the doubt he'd managed to instill in me during the course of it. Was he right? Would the Icebreaker save humanity, or only seal our doom?

"I don't want to die for nothing, Zack," Lex said, looking determined now. "Do you think there's a chance we can stop them? All of them? That humans can survive this?"

I nodded my head way too enthusiastically.

"Yes!" I answered, way too quickly. "We have to." I stopped my head from nodding. "Do, or do not, there is no try, and all that stuff."

She laughed and gave me a smile.

"I'm really glad we met, Zack," she said. She was twisting her fingers into knots in her lap. "I just wish . . ."

"Me too, Lex."

She took a deep breath. "'I must not fear,'" she recited. "'Fear is the mind-killer. Fear is the little-death that brings total obliteration.'"

I laughed and picked up the quote where she'd left off. "'I will face my fear. I will permit it to pass over me and through me.'"

"'And when it has gone past, I will turn the inner eye to see its path,'" she continued. "'Where the fear has gone there will be nothing. Only I will remain.'"

She exhaled slowly; then we shared a smile.

"If the world doesn't end tonight, and we're both still alive tomorrow, then I'm taking you out on a date," she said. "Deal?"

"Deal."

0H14M49S REMAINING.

MY FATHER FINISHED HIS PREPARATIONS AT THE COMMAND CENTER AND CLIMBED DOWN INTO his own drone controller pod, which was adjacent to mine. Then the eight of us sat there, each alone in our stations, watching the last fifteen minutes elapse on the countdown clock.

The general still looked as if he was trying to recover from the emotional strain of speaking with my mom. I didn't want to ask what he and my mother had talked about. But I still wanted to say something to him, to try to make peace while there was still time.

I climbed out of my pod and grabbed my EDA backpack, which was resting nearby on the floor. My father's old jacket was still stuffed inside, and I pulled it out and handed it to him.

When my father saw the jacket, he grinned wide and spent a minute looking over each and every patch. When he was finished, he leaned over and hugged me.

"Thank you," he said. "But how is it possible that you have this with you?"

"I was wearing it this morning when they came to recruit me."

He laughed. "Seriously?"

I nodded. He flipped the jacket around and put it on.

"Still fits!" he said, admiring the patches running down each of its sleeves. "I used to wear this when I would hit the local arcades. I thought it brought me good luck." He laughed. "I also thought it made me look like a badass." He shook his head. "Your old man was kind of a dork." He took the jacket off and tried to hand it back to me.

"I bet it looks a lot better on you," he said. "Let me see."

I shook my head. "No way. You earned all those patches. You should wear it."

He nodded and slipped it back on.

"Thank you, Zack."

"Don't mention it."

By the time I walked back over to my own pod, there were only five minutes remaining on the clock.

And then four minutes. Then three. Two. One.

I dropped down into my pilot seat, and the pod's canopy slid closed above me.

"*'All things are ready, if our minds be so,'*" I heard Whoadie whisper over the comm.

Just then, my QComm made its wireless link to the pod's surround-sound system, and the next track on my *Raid the Arcade* playlist began to blare out of its speakers: "Rock You Like a Hurricane" by the Scorpions.

I bobbed my head in time with its opening machine-gun guitar riff as the last few seconds on the countdown clock ticked away.

When it finally hit zero, a klaxon began to wail, and a RED ALERT indicator began to flash on my HUD.

My tactical display lit up, informing me that our remote sensors had just detected the first sign of the Europan vanguard, emerging from the asteroid belt out beyond the orbit of Mars. They were really hauling ass. The Dreadnaught Sphere in the lead was already closing in on the red planet, surrounded on all sides by a phalanx of Glaives.

"Here they come!" Milo cried over the comlink. "They're coming! See 'em?"

"Yes, Milo," Debbie replied. "Our eyes work, too. We see them."

"There's a lot of them," Whoadie added. "An *awful* lot."

"The ones we don't stop will be knocking on our front door in a few minutes, so take out as many as you can before they get here," my father ordered over the comlink. "Your drone assignments are linked and locked! Pilots, prepare to launch!"

"*Wolverines!*" Milo shouted. Then he let out a long, whooping war cry into his comlink, which somehow mixed in perfectly with the war cry the Scorpions were already blasting into my eardrums.

On my display, the distance between Earth and the approaching enemy vanguard continued to shrink rapidly, and I could feel my pulse begin to rise.

"Stay frosty, everyone," my father said. "And may the Force be with you."

"May the Force be with *us*," Shin repeated, with no hint of irony in his voice.

"May the Force be with us!" Graham echoed over the comlink. Debbie and Milo each echoed the sentiment, followed by Chén, who said it in Mandarin.

"*Yuan li yu ni tong tzai.*"

The sincerity in Chén's voice finally convinced me to join in. I keyed my mic and carefully repeated after him. "*Yuan li yu ni tong tzai.*"

Chén laughed and said something else. The somewhat imperfect English translation popped up on my HUD: "We are coming here to kick ass and chew bubblegum, and we have no more bubblegum!"

I laughed out loud, and for several more seconds I couldn't stop laughing. I'd only just learned the term "gallows humor" a few months earlier, from a book we'd been assigned in American Literature about the Civil War. At the time, it wasn't a type of humor I thought I would ever be in a position to experience. But now, as hearing Chén belt out Roddy Piper's battle cry from *They Live* in Chinese struck me as one of the funniest things I'd ever heard in my life, I understood the concept perfectly.

"All drones cleared for launch!" the general announced. "Let's go get 'em."

The eight of us launched our Interceptors, joining the steady stream of drones already pouring out of the hangar, under the control of pilots located back on Earth.

Together, we flew out to meet the alien invaders.

20

OUR INTERCEPTORS MET THE EUROPAN VANGUARD HALFWAY BETWEEN Earth and the edge of the asteroid belt, just within the orbital path of Mars. On my tactical display, the cascade of dark green triangles that represented the enemy vanguard began to slow its speed as it closed in on our forces, represented by an arrowhead-shaped mass of white triangles racing to meet it.

There were a great deal more green triangles than white ones.

But with the fearlessness of drone pilots, we continued to charge forward, straight toward our advancing enemy, until we were just within visual contact. Then, at my father's order, we all slammed on our brakes, and our wing came to a collective, drifting stop. "Bad guys at twelve o'clock," my father announced over the comm. "Fangs out. Prepare to engage, as soon as we're within range. You can bet they will."

A collective reply of *"Weapons hot!"* echoed over the comm channel.

There they were: an impossibly vast swarm of Glaive Fighters, arrayed in a protective grid-like shield around the massive Dreadnaught Sphere gleaming in their midst, the warped reflection of the starfield streaking across its chromed surface as they hurtled toward us. The Disrupter had yet to be deployed—it was still concealed inside the armored skin of the Dreadnaught Sphere, along with hundreds of thousands of troopships, carrying millions of ground-force drones.

"Well, hello there!" I heard my father say over the comm. "This is General Xavier Lightman of the Earth Defense Alliance. Where do you assholes think you're headed?" After a pause, he added: *Klaatu barada nikto,* fellas."

Then, perhaps taking his own stab at some gallows humor, he whistled the five-note message used to communicate with the friendly ETs in *Close Encounters of the Third Kind.* The same tones that bookended each of the Europans' montage transmissions.

The only response to my father's whistled entreaty came a few tense heartbeats later, when the spearhead of Glaive Fighters leading the vanguard finally came within range of our ships and opened fire on us.

The black void around us erupted in a deluge of crisscrossing blue plasma bolts and streaks of red laser fire as ships on both sides broke formation to attack.

Our Interceptors returned fire, and then ships began exploding above and below me, to port and starboard, aft and stern, lighting up the mirror surface of my Interceptor in a horrific light show. A similar cascade of contained atomic explosions began to light up the enemy ranks out in front of me, like tangled chains of Christmas tree lights being switched on, only to short out a second later.

I aimed my rocket eighty-eight right into the torrent of enemy fighters and fanned the trigger on my flight stick to fire off a rapid volley of plasma bolts. The Glaives were packed so tightly in front of me that it seemed difficult to miss, and for a few seconds I felt invincible and unstoppable, like I was using the Force.

But then I was passing through the cloud of arcing, swooping Glaive Fighters, evading their laser and plasma fire, which I did reflexively, almost without thinking—and I smiled because everything had become clear once again, now that I was finally facing off against my true enemy. The doubt and uncertainty my father had planted in my mind were gone. So was the lead ball of fear in my gut. Now, all that remained was primal, territorial rage, and the clear sense of purpose that came with it.

Kill or be killed. Conquer or be conquered. Survive or go extinct.

These were not difficult decisions. In fact, the answers were hardwired into the human brain. The only thing I could think was: *Now for wrath, now for ruin and a red nightfall!*

I continued slicing my Interceptor through the enemy's ranks at sharp right angles, firing first, then moving, always moving and always firing, firing at the shifting pattern of targets cascading across my HUD, overlaying the folding formations of Glaive Fighters in front of my ship, which moved just like they had always moved in our old *Armada* and *Terra Firma* missions.

I began to slip into the zone—the old familiar rhythm I would sometimes fall into when I played *Armada,* where everything just seemed to click. With the help of the music in my headphones, I'd locked into the enemy's patterns of movement, their little digital idiosyncrasies that allowed me to anticipate their attacks and evasive maneuvers. I was on fire. I couldn't seem to miss, while at the same time, nothing could seem to hit me.

For a few seconds, it felt just like playing *Armada* back home.

Why would real aliens behave exactly like videogame simulations of themselves?

The question kept trying to worm its way into my thoughts, but I wouldn't let it. I focused on the bliss of battle instead.

Our Interceptors were getting picked off fast, but the first of our reinforcement drones was already arriving. Each time one of our drones was destroyed, its operator took control of another Interceptor inside the reserve hangar at Moon Base Alpha and flew back to rejoin battle as quickly as they could. Thankfully the trip back to the battlefront was growing shorter every second, because the vanguard was still moving forward, still closing in on Earth. We were losing ships fast.

If it hadn't been obvious before, it definitely was now—we were fighting a war of attrition. We weren't going to be able to stop the vanguard. Not by a long shot. The vanguard was moving too fast, and it was mowing down everything we put in its path.

We were only going to make a small dent in their forces before they reached Earth—if that.

I took out seven enemy ships before my first drone got waxed.

The handful of minutes it took my second drone to get "back in the shit" seemed to stretch on for hours. Once I finally reached the enemy's ever-encroaching front line and reengaged with the vanguard, I got nailed by an overloading Glaive reactor core on my way in and was blasted to bits once again—this time without scoring a single enemy kill.

As my third Interceptor rocketed out of the drone hangar, a warning began to flash on my HUD, informing me that the enemy was already closing in on the far side of the moon.

A second later, I saw them falling toward me, straight out of the black lunar sky above, thousands upon thousands of them, filling the horizon.

"The vanguard is splitting up!" my father said over the intercom. "Dividing itself in two. It looks like the half containing the Disrupter is headed for Earth."

"And the other half is headed here," Shin added.

I checked my tactical display—they were right. The vanguard had split itself in two, like an amoeba, creating two torpedo-shaped clusters of roughly equal size. One cluster had the Disrupter dodecahedron at its center. The other was closing in on us.

On my tactical display, the deluge of green triangles began to rain down on the base, like lava erupting from some Olympian volcano anchored in the stars above.

"Moon Base Alpha is under attack!" my computer helpfully informed me. "Warning!"

An ear-splitting klaxon began to wail over the base intercom.

"Knock, knock!" Graham shouted over the comm. "Our guests have arrived! And they never seemed this pissed off on any of their previous visits. Check the topside feeds!"

I flipped off my VR goggles for a moment and tapped a small security camera icon on my QComm. A dozen thumbnail windows filled its display, each showing a different camera feed from the base. The exterior of the base was crawling with enemy drones, so covered by attackers that it looked like some otherworldly anthill being invaded by a neighboring colony of metal insects. In the background, other drone dispersal dropships continued to make landfall, opening up like metal flowers as they hit the lunar surface, allowing thousands of Spider Fighters and Basilisks to pour out and join the swelling army of alien drones already descending on the base.

"Welcome Wagon activated!" my father announced. The base's automated sentry guns sprang to life and began to unload a steady barrage at the hundreds of Glaive Fighters descending on the base like angry hornets.

The Fighters' first volley of plasma bombs detonated against the base's defense shields. The explosion erupted and crackled across the shield's transparent surface as its energy was deflected back out into space, creating a dazzling light show across the display over our heads, briefly lighting up the darkened Thunderdome. The accompanying transfer of energy shook the entire base, and the lunar surface beneath it.

As the moonquake—my first—subsided, I had to resist a panicked urge to scramble up out of my control pod and run to safety—wherever the hell that might be.

Instead, I gripped my flight stick even more tightly, pulled my newly launched reserve Interceptor into a steep climb, and firewalled the throttle, blasting straight upward into the deluge of Glaive Fighters descending toward me. Other drones were launching and forming up below me, adding their fire to mine.

I took out five more enemy fighters. Then a sixth, and a seventh. My comrades were doing equally well. I heard Debbie mutter "Easy-as-can-beezy" to herself over the comm.

Then, just as I was swinging my crosshairs over my next target, a hail of enemy laser fire finally converged on my drone from several different angles, and it was blasted to smithereens.

I cursed and took control of another ship, but before I could even launch it, the enemy ships had reached the surface and blasted their way into the base's drone hangar.

When I fired the launch release on my drone, nothing happened, because the catapult mechanism had already been blasted in half. As the towers of unused drones around me began to crumble and collapse, my display flashed bright white.

At the same moment, I heard a thunderous, booming explosion up on the surface, followed by a shockwave that shook the Thunderdome violently.

I opened the canopy of my pod and stuck my head up, then looked around. One at a time, the others emerged, too.

"Damn," my father said, far too calmly for my liking. "One of them breached the hangar's defenses and self-destructed. The whole place went up, along with all of our remaining reserve drones."

"What are we supposed to do now?" Debbie asked, echoing my own thoughts—though she sounded a lot calmer than I was currently feeling.

"The EDA is sending more Interceptors up from Earth," Shin told us. "But they're all going after the Disrupter. We're probably on our own here now."

He and my father exchanged a brief glance, before the general turned to address the rest of us.

"Everyone get back in your pods, now!" my father shouted. "Shin will give each of you control of one of the base's laser sentry turrets. Try to keep as many of them from advancing down here to the op center for as long as you can! Hold them back, okay?"

Before he'd even finished speaking, he leaped down into one of the dual-ATHID control rigs he'd constructed and powered it on. He slipped his hands into its power gauntlets as the display screens arrayed around him all lit up simultaneously.

Another violent tremor shook the Thunderdome as we all scrambled back into our control pods. As I closed the canopy and settled back into my seat, a simplified HUD appeared on my screens, laid over a high-definition video feed from one of the base's sentry turrets, along with a targeting reticle, a range finder, and a power meter for its laser cannon.

"Keep firing!" my father said. "Hold them back as long as you can!"

I picked off as many drones as I could, but they just kept on coming in a never-ending assault. Within a few minutes, the inevitable happened: a group of drones concentrated their laser fire on the hangar airlock long enough to break through the blast doors to the corridor beyond.

The enemy now had free run of the base.

"Breach! That's a breach!" Shin shouted over the comm channel.

"They're inside the base! I can see them on levels five and six, and they're already making their way down here! Mostly Spider Fighters—hundreds, maybe thousands of them!"

We all remained inside our control pods, each of us now taking control of an ATHID in different locations through the base. I don't know about the others, but I was getting my ass kicked. Each time I took control of a new ATHID, it was torn apart by Spider Fighters even more quickly than the last.

"Okay," my father said. "Abandon stations. We're evacuating, right now! Chén, Whoadie, Zack! Do I have to pull you guys up out of there? Because I will! Come on! We're *leaving*!"

I scrambled up out of my pod just in time to see my father make good on his promise. He reached down and grabbed Whoadie around the waist, then lifted her up out of her pod, away from the controls. My father passed her off to Debbie, then turned and prepared to do the same thing to Chén, who complied on his own at the last second—leaping up out of his pod like Superman, then snapping the general a salute as he landed on the deck in front of him.

"Sir, yes, sir!" Chén shouted.

Shin remained inside his pod. I ran over to check his pod display screens—he was operating a whole squadron of ATHIDs posted outside the turbo elevator shaft leading down to the Thunderdome. On the security camera feeds, we could see an angry horde of Spider Fighters in the process of breaking down the armored door that now separated them from our current location. Each time they slammed into it, we could hear the muted, repetitive clanking transmitted through the stone walls around us.

When he saw that Shin wasn't leaving, Milo jumped back into his own pod, saying, "Shin and I will hold them off; then we'll catch up with you!"

My father opened his mouth to protest, but another explosion shook the base, cutting him off. Graham shouted both their names over his shoulder and headed for the exit.

"You're already wasting seconds, General," Shin said. "Milo and I can hold them off a lot longer than the automated sentry systems. But if you don't leave now, you'll never make it!"

"Go ahead, sir," Milo shouted over his own comm. "We got this."

While he deliberated with my father, Shin was dragging the fingers of both of his hands across the screens in front of him, highlighting groups of drones and assigning them to attack certain enemies or defend certain sections of the base. I could see him struggling to effectively manage the base's dwindling defensive resources—all while he was simultaneously controlling half a dozen ATHIDs, fighting alongside other infantry drones controlled by operators back on Earth who weren't nearly as skilled or lethal.

Shin glanced over at Graham, then back at my father. Something unspoken passed between the three men. Then my father nodded, and his fingers began to dance across the control panels in front of him.

"I'm setting all of the unmanned sentry guns to auto-fire," he said. Then he turned and ran toward the exit. "The rest of you follow me! Now! Hurry!"

He tapped the QComm on his wrist, and a hidden door opened in the curved stone wall, opposite the entrance, revealing a narrow staircase. The six of us sprinted down it just as another series of tremors rocked every level of the moon base.

The staircase led down to a large cube-shaped room with a pressurized hatch embedded in its stone floor. There was a rack of visored space helmets mounted on the wall, and my father ordered us each to put one on before donning one himself. After I put mine on, I felt the helmet retract in size slightly to form an airtight seal around my face, just below the chin line. Then a HUD appeared, superimposed on the interior of the visor, with atmospheric readings and a gauge for the small oxygen tanks mounted on its collar.

Once Graham made sure everyone had their helmets on properly, my father pressed his palm to the scanner beside the hatch, which hissed open, revealing the interior of a tube-shaped capsule about the size of a VW microbus, with ten passenger seats inside. Through the capsule's porthole-like windows, we could see that it was nestled inside a spherical underground tunnel, like a bullet inside the barrel of a gun. Once we strapped ourselves in, my father smacked the red button mounted on the bulkhead and the capsule rocketed forward, pressing each of us back into our seats.

As our capsule hurtled through the darkened tunnel, we could hear Milo and Shin shouting a mix of insults and words of encouragement at each other over our QComms as the two of them continued to hold the Spider Fighters at bay.

"The base is completely overrun," Shin told us over the comm. "Every level. They're concentrating outside the Thunderdome now. They'll break inside any second!"

"Get out of there!" my father shouted back. "We'll send the capsule back for you!"

"Sorry, boss," he replied, raising his voice over the sound of rending metal and laser fire. "It looks like we're gonna have to make our last stand right here." He said something else, but it was drowned out by an explosion.

All of the video feeds to the Thunderdome on our QComms went dead, but we could still hear audio.

"Godspeed, old friends," Shin said a second later, shouting to be heard over the chaos unfolding around him.

My father tried to reply, but he couldn't get any words out. He nodded; then I saw his face contort into a mask of pure anguish just before he buried his face in his hands.

"Hey, do me a favor, too, will you guys?" Milo added. "After we win this war, tell everyone back home in Philly that my last request was to have my old high school named after me, okay? My mom went there, too, and I think she'll really like that. You hear me?"

I took my father's QComm and answered for him.

"Yeah, Milo," I answered. "Sure thing. We'll take care of it."

"Thanks, man!" he replied. "Kushmaster High School. I love it!" He laughed maniacally again, and I could hear that he was still relentlessly firing his laser turret. "Oh wait! One other thing! Tell them to erect a bronze statue of me in downtown Philly! Just like the one they made for Rocky! But make mine bigger than his, okay?"

Before I could reply, another explosion rocked the base, distorting the QComm's audio channel. This explosion sounded far louder than the previous ones.

"Shit! Shit-shit-shit!" we heard Shin yell. "Here they come, Milo! Brace yourself!"

"Come get some!" I heard Milo shouting, his voice strangely gleeful. I could hear the sound of him rapidly firing his QComm's wrist laser. "Who wants some? From hell's heart I stab at thee, assholes! By Grabthar's hammer, you shall—"

Milo's voice was drowned out by another series of massive explosions, followed by what sounded like a hailstorm of incoming enemy laser fire, and by the terrible hurricane-like howl of the Thunderdome being breached and depressurized, as its atmosphere—and everything else inside—was sucked up and out into the dark vacuum outside on the lunar surface. But the silence that followed was somehow even worse.

21

S THE CAPSULE HURTLED US THROUGH THE TUNNEL, I STARED AT MY QComm screen in silence, watching video feeds of the final moments of the Last Battle of Moon Base Alpha.

There were still a few scattered ATHIDs duking it out with alien Spider Fighter drones up on the surface, while a lone Sentinel grappled with a Basilisk in a fire-scorched crater nearby. A handful of Glaive Fighters were still dive-bombing the base, now completely unopposed by EDA forces, hammering it mercilessly until nothing remained.

We were watching all of this happen on our tiny QComm display screens, as if it were some televised event occurring far away, when a massive tremor shook our escape capsule. A second later, the roof of the tunnel ahead of us collapsed and artificial light poured in from above, as if a bank of stadium floodlights had powered on.

It was a Basilisk—sort of a giant metal praying mantis with enormous scythe-like blades in place of its front legs, along with an extra pair of clawed, telescoping robotic hands, and twin plasma cannons standing in for its mandibles.

One of its massive metal arms snaked into the tunnel, barely missing us as we passed beneath it, bringing its fist down like a wrecking ball, smashing the length of track our capsule had passed over a split second earlier.

A pack of eight-legged Spider Fighter drones detached from the Basilisk and began to skitter toward our capsule as yet more Spider Fighters poured into the tunnel behind them. The capsule continued to accelerate, moving just fast enough to stay ahead of the giant metal claws as the Basilisk struck again and again, tearing into the lunar surface and destroying the tunnel piece by piece just behind us.

Another tremor shook the tunnel ahead as the Basilisk power-leaped to catch up with us. At the same time, its right arm telescoped forward, and its clawed hand smashed through the capsule's rear porthole. My father slammed on the brakes as the interior of the capsule depressurized, and our helmets switched on automatically to supply us with oxygen. Graham spun around to fire at the flailing Basilisk claw with his QComm laser just before it lashed out and closed its massive metal fingers around him.

Before Graham even had time to scream, the alien drone crushed the life out of him, right there in front of us. Then it yanked his lifeless body outside, through the smashed porthole, and hurled it against the tunnel wall like a rag doll.

Debbie let out an earsplitting scream over the comm just as the Basilisk reached back toward Whoadie. Chén moved to try to block its path, while my father fired at it with his QComm laser.

The Basilisk's other arm smashed through another porthole behind me, but Whoadie yanked me clear of it just in the nick of time. The remaining five of us retreated to the front of the capsule, out of its reach. It flailed its insect-like arms for a few seconds, then suddenly retracted both of them before standing upright, towering over our damaged, depressurized capsule. My father jammed the throttle forward, to try and get us moving along the track again, but I could already see he didn't have enough time to get us clear.

The Basilisk raised one of its massive clawed feet, preparing to crush us.

This was it. There was nothing we could do. We were going to die.

But then, just as the foot descended, a Sentinel tackled the Basilisk to the cratered surface. The two drones grappled with each other up on the surface, beyond the lip of the gaping hole above us, in eerie silence. There was a volley of laser and rocket fire between them, a blinding white explosion, and then more silence.

A few seconds later, when the smoke cleared and the lunar dust settled, the massive humanoid face of the Earth Defense Alliance Sentinel swung into view, blotting out the black sky. Then a voice crackled over the comm channel.

"Told you I had your back, Lightman," I heard Lex say.

"Th-th-thanks, Lex," I stuttered, my voice cracking over the QComm. "Thank you. You saved our asses. I owe you one."

"You bet you do," she replied. Her Sentinel reached out toward our exposed escape capsule with one of its massive hands, and I had a sudden moment of panic. But she used both of her mech's hands to delicately lift our escape pod up out of the rubble, then place us back into the tunnel just beyond the section destroyed by the Basilisk.

After she set us down, Lex waved goodbye with a massive hand.

"Everyone here at Sapphire Station has already been reassigned to drones back on Earth," Lex said over the comm. "I stuck around to see if you guys needed any help, but Shanghai is getting totally hammered. I have to roll!" There was a whine of servos as she stood her Sentinel perfectly upright. "Good luck!"

Her Sentinel powered itself down and fell dormant, like a giant metal puppet abandoned by its puppeteer.

"Who was that?" Whoadie asked.

"Captain Alexis Larkin of the Thirty Dozen," I said. "She's a friend of mine."

She nodded; then I saw her nod at Debbie, who was shuddering and weeping silently, staring through one of the smashed portholes. My gaze followed hers, and only then did I realize that my father had already scrambled out of the capsule and was now outside, cradling Graham's dead body, with his helmet's clear faceplate pressed to his friend's cracked and bloodied one.

His comm was muted, but through his fogging faceplate, I could see his face contorted in anguish. His mouth was open in a silent wail as he hugged Graham, rocking his lifeless form back and forth. Back and forth.

That was the only time I ever saw my father cry.

I DON'T KNOW HOW MANY SECONDS PASSED LIKE THAT. I DO KNOW THAT I WAS STILL TRYING to muster the courage to yell at my father, and tell him we had to get moving, when he finally stood up and scrambled back inside the capsule. Then he hit a button on the bulkhead. Armored shutters irised closed over the capsule's smashed portholes, sealing the leaks in the hull. As the cabin repressurized, my father got us moving forward again.

Debbie was still weeping silently in her seat. Whoadie put an arm around her.

"'Oft have I heard that grief softens the mind,'" the young woman recited. "'And makes it fearful and degenerate; Think therefore on revenge and cease to weep.'"

Debbie nodded and took a deep breath. Then, in what seemed like the space of a few seconds, I saw her expression transform from grief into pure, unbridled rage.

Our escape capsule reached the opposite end of the darkened tunnel a few minutes later, and we pulled into a pressurized arrival dock, and the capsule's doors hissed open. We followed my father to the armored doors of what was clearly an emergency bunker the EDA had constructed in the Icarus crater.

I saw my father hold his breath when he placed his palm against the scanner beside the station's armored front entrance. The faceplate beeped and turned green a second later, and the doors to the Icarus bunker slid open, revealing a narrow tunnel beyond. My father ushered us all inside, then punched a button on the wall. The armored doors slammed shut behind us, sealing us safely inside. We found ourselves in a small hangar bay nestled at the Icarus crater's base. Inside it, eight Interceptors stood gleaming under the halogen floodlights.

"We have to hurry," my father said. "Everyone take a ship. Quickly now!"

I hurried down the catwalk to examine the nearest one. These ships weren't like any of the drone Interceptors we'd already seen: They had cockpits, and were designed to be piloted from inside, rather than remotely. "These are AI-89s," my father shouted to us. "Special manned Aerospace Interceptor prototypes."

As he spoke, he was reaching into a large metal tool chest bolted to the wall of the hangar. He took out some sort of pistol-shaped power tool, like a motorized ratchet, then ran over to the first Interceptor and opened a hatch on the underside of its hull, revealing a mess of wires and circuitry. As he dug around inside, he said, "We didn't have access to this bunker until the invasion began, to prevent us from using them to go AWOL." He smiled. "But the base security protocol fail-safes just granted me emergency access."

He used the power tool to remove a small cube-shaped component from the ship's underbelly, tossed it on the floor, and closed up the hatch. Then he ran over to the next Interceptor and repeated the process.

"What are you doing?" I asked him. "We've got to get the hell out of here!"

"Don't you think I know that?" he said. "This is important. Sixty more seconds."

True to his word, a minute later he had pulled the same cube-shaped component out of all eight ships. I picked one of them up off the floor to examine it. Stenciled on the side of its gray plastic casing was a long serial number followed by some letters: EDA-AI89-TAC-TRNSPNDER.

His task complete, my father ran up the metal gantry platform and over to a darkened command console that lit up at his touch. The fingers of both his hands began to dance across its touchscreens as he tapped icons and navigated submenus—almost as fast as Commander Data. In seconds, he had powered up all eight of the AI-89s. Their fusion engines began to hum and then whine, their exhaust ports glowing with orange energy.

My father tapped another icon, and five of the eight cockpit canopies slid open. As I ran over to the nearest Interceptor, a panel slid open in the aft side of its hull and a metal stepladder unfolded to the stone floor at my feet with a metallic *clang*. I heard the same sound three more times in rapid succession on either side of me, as Debbie, Whoadie, and Chén each approached a ship.

It was the first time I'd been inside a real cockpit of any kind—much less that of an interplanetary spacecraft. But it didn't feel like the first time. The controller setup inside was identical to those in the drone command pods, and those hadn't been all that different from the simple plastic flight stick and throttle rig I'd been using in my bedroom for years.

Sitting in our open cockpits, we were now at eye level with my father, who remained behind the command console on the elevated command platform in front of us, so I was able to see the array of display screens in front of him.

"When these ships are in flight, each of them is enclosed in a spherical no-inertia field," he said. "So flying these ships from inside won't seem any different than piloting them remotely. Except for one thing, of course—if you get shot down piloting one of these, you won't be able to take control of another drone. Because you'll be dead."

When he saw our reactions to this statement, he showed us their main safety feature. "Don't worry. The cockpit module inside each of these ships is actually a self-contained ejection pod. It's supposed to deploy automatically in the event of a direct hit, like airbags."

"Supposed to?" I said.

"These ships are all prototypes," he said. "I don't think they got much testing." My father's hands continued to fly across the control panel. From my vantage point in the cockpit, I could see the control screen over his shoulder, and it seemed that he was pulling up the flight plans for the three remaining Interceptors—the ones we were about to leave behind. He pulled a wrinkled piece of paper from his pocket, consulted it, and began typing, as if he was punching in a route for the unmanned Interceptors, using the paper as a reference. Then he began to access a series of hardware configuration menus I'd never seen before.

When my father finished working at the bunker's command console, he powered it off, ran down the metal catwalk, and jumped into the cockpit of his own Interceptor, sliding down into the leather pilot seat like a kid sliding down a banister.

The canopies of our five cockpits slid closed with a pressurized hiss, our engines screamed in my ears as they powered up to full readiness—and then the small hangar itself depressurized and its armored doors slid open above, revealing a rectangular swath of the starry lunar sky.

We blasted out of the crater and rocketed around the moon's opposite side, and the fragile Earth became visible to us once again, hovering in the blackness ahead.

Over the comm channel, I heard my father gasp at the sight—one he hadn't seen with his own eyes in an entire lifetime. My lifetime.

"There it is," he said softly. "Home sweet home. Man, I really missed it."

I'd missed it, too, I realized. And I'd been gone less than a day.

As our five ships moved into formation and turned homeward, toward Earth, I checked my scope and saw that the three unmanned Interceptors were heading in the opposite direction, out into space, toward whatever destination my father had programmed into them.

I turned my gaze back to Earth and watched it begin to grow in size as we approached, until its blue curve completely filled the view outside of my spacecraft.

My father sent a tactical map to the display screens inside our cockpits. "They're dividing their forces in half again," my father said over the comm. "See?"

He was right. Half of the vanguard's remaining forces appeared to be descending on mainland China, while the other half continued to escort the Disrupter, which was heading off in a different direction, along with the alien drones that had survived the assault on Moon Base Alpha.

"Command thinks the Disrupter is probably going to make landfall somewhere along the Antarctic Peninsula. They're sending every Interceptor they can spare to try and take it down. The rest of our aerospace forces are currently defending Shanghai."

"Shanghai!" Chén repeated, followed by something in his native tongue. A second later, my QComm translated: "My family lives just outside the city limits. But my sister is stationed at a drone operations base in the center of downtown. I have to go help her!"

"No, we have to go after the Disrupter," my father said. "They'll activate it as soon as they reach the surface, and then only manned ships like these will continue to function. All the EDA's drones will fall out of the sky."

"What about the conventional air force?" Debbie asked. "Can't they help?"

"They'll try," he said. "But the Disrupter knocks out all wireless and radio communications, too. It alters Earth's magnetic field and plays havoc with GPS satellites, too. Our conventional aircraft will all be flying blind. And they might as well be going up against Godzilla. Conventional fighters won't stand a chance. It's up to us."

Just as my father finished his sentence, we received word that the Disrupter had already made landfall, before our ships even reached the edge of Earth's atmosphere.

But the Europans didn't activate their ultimate weapon then, even though they could have.

For some reason, they waited.

They waited until the five of us got there to switch it on.

WHEN OUR TINY SQUADRON OF FIVE INTERCEPTORS REACHED THE DISRUPTER'S LAST KNOWN position, just off the Antarctic Peninsula, the battle was kind of hard to miss. The massive black dodecahedron hovered just above the landscape like a floating mountain, spinning like a top as it finally activated its pulsing coupler beam and fired down into the melting ice below. The powerful beam sheared away huge chunks of glacier and sent them plunging into the icy water.

The clear blue arctic sky around the Disrupter was a chaotic cloud, packed with thousands upon thousands of enemy fighters locked in fierce aerial combat with an even greater number of Interceptor and WASP drones, all swarming and diving to strafe the transparent deflector shield that surrounded the skin of the spinning Disrupter in their midst. The Disrupter's protective shield was already beginning to pulse and flicker on my HUD, indicating that it would soon fail. Of course, when it did, there was still the escort of Glaive Fighters orbiting around it, dogfighting a steady onslaught of gamer-controlled drones.

Fusion reactor detonations kept firing off every few seconds like popcorn, further weakening the shield. It flickered and pulsed more rapidly, and I thought the timing of our arrival just might turn out to be perfect.

Then the Disrupter activated itself.

Every one of our thousands of drones froze, and then, in unison, they began to drop out of the sky like pieces of leaden ash.

Meanwhile, of course, the thousands of alien fighters kept flying, unaffected—with their operators safely back on Europa and out of the Disrupter's range, its field had no effect on them.

A few seconds after their links went dead, the EDA drones' emergency fail-safes activated and their autopilots kicked in, attempting to right the drones and land them safely on the nearest patch of ground—or in this case, the crumbling ice shelf. Most of the drones I saw got picked off by enemy fire before they could make it to the ground safely, and most of the others crashed into the ocean or the ice and were lost.

In a blink, the Disrupter had rendered every single drone in the Earth Defense Alliance's entire global arsenal inoperable.

I knew the same thing must be happening at that same moment over Shanghai, Karachi, Melbourne, and everywhere else around the world as the millions of videogame-trained civilians who had been waging drone warfare against the alien invaders from their laptops and game consoles just a few seconds earlier now found themselves staring at a "Quantum Link Lost" error message.

Earth's mighty gamer army was out of commission, unable to do anything now but sit and wait for the end.

I saw a few other manned Interceptors continue to attack the Disrupter, along with several squadrons of conventional military fighter aircraft. But they were now vastly outnumbered, in addition to being outgunned, and they were getting massacred.

The sky surrounding the Disrupter now contained only enemy ships—an unopposed swarm of Glaives and Wyverns. The now-dormant ATHIDs and Sentinels standing on the ice shelf below were being picked off like beer cans by the Spider Fighters and Basilisks marching on them from all sides.

Our five Interceptors continued to dive into the heart of the enemy's forces as a few other stray manned Interceptors formed up just ahead of me, on my father's wing—only to get blasted to smithereens a few seconds later, lighting up the sky on either side of him. But my father piloted his ship through the onslaught, untouched—and so did I. Miraculously unharmed.

I pitched into a barrel roll as I flew through the flaming debris, silently cursing my father. He'd planted the seeds of doubt in my head, and now I suddenly saw evidence to support his theory everywhere I looked: My father, my friends, and I continued to streak and loop through the chaos, effortlessly blasting enemy fighters out of the sky one after the other while laser fire and plasma bolts streaked past us on all sides—just like we used to when we played *Armada* together.

But these were real aliens we were fighting—sentient beings with highly advanced technology, intent on destroying us. And we were outnumbered thousands to one. We should've been dead a hundred times already. Were humans really just better at war than they were, or all this time, had the aliens been throwing the game?

A volley of photon bolts nailed my shield, knocking its power down by two-thirds and snapping me out of my reverie. I shook my head to clear it, then accelerated to catch up with my father and the others. We all locked into attack formation, tearing along the ragged edge of the ice shelf, which continued to crumble and collapse into larger and larger pieces, melting rapidly under the intense heat emanating off the spinning dodecahedron above.

The Disrupter now hung about a hundred meters above the ocean's wrinkled surface, like a diamond chandelier suspended from nothing at all. Its escort of Glaive and Wyvern Fighters continued to swarm and dive over and around it, circling it like a cloud of silver flies.

There were still more enemy fighters than I could count—so many that my Tactical Avionics Computer was having a hard time estimating their number, too. There appeared to be a few hundred of them now, with more circling farther out, on the periphery of the battle. And according to my HUD readout, there were thousands more enemy ships on their way—hundreds of thousands of more.

"Where are those reinforcements coming from?" Whoadie asked. "Did they stop attacking Shanghai?"

"No," my father said. "According to the EDA command, the city has already fallen. Now they're diverting more of their ships here. In a few minutes, the odds of us being able to destroy this thing are going to be a lot worse."

"Then let's get it done right now," Debbie suggested. "No time like the present."

"Ready to rock shit from my cockpit!" Whoadie declared. "What's the plan, sir?"

Just then, I saw Debbie's ship get hit by a barrage of plasma fire. One of her engines erupted in flames.

"Eject!" the rest of us all yelled over our comms. But Debbie had already beaten us to the punch. Her cockpit module shot away from the rest of the ship's smoking fuselage like a bullet casing being ejected from a gun port. It flew upward for a few seconds, then began to arc back down toward the wrinkled surface of the icy sea below.

As I steered my Interceptor into a dive to try to go after it, Whoadie's ship swooped in out of nowhere and caught the pod in mid-fall, using the magnetic retrieval arm slung under her ship's nose. When the metal pod locked into place on the underside of her fuselage, she let out a cry of victory—but it was cut off in mid-yawp when a barrage of laser fire streaked across her hull, nearly hitting Debbie's pod.

"I got you!" Whoadie cried. "I got her, General! But I don't think I'll be much good in a fight now."

"Get out of here, Whoadie!" my father ordered. "Get Debbie to safety. Now!"

"Yes, sir," she replied, firewalling her throttle. Her ship streaked away in a blur.

"And then there were three," I muttered over the comm. "And all three of us are gonna be toast in a few seconds, too, if we stay where we are."

"Just keep watching the birdie," my father said as I saw his ship swoop and make another pass over the dodecahedron surface, blasting two Wyverns in the process. "According to my HUD, that shield is already pretty weak. Keep firing at it— Chén, what are you doing?"

The comm channel was drowned out by the sound of Chén, screaming "Seven!" in a voice choked with tears. Then he yelled "Six!" And then "Five!"

Only then did I understand. Chén was reacting to the news of

Shanghai's destruction in the worst possible way—a nervous breakdown, right in the middle of combat. And who could blame him? He wasn't a soldier. No one had prepared him—or any of us—for the horrors of war.

I located Chén's ship on my tactical display and saw that he was already turning into a steep dive toward the Disrupter, with his guns apparently set to auto-fire. His shields took a direct hit and failed, and then a second later, his weapons failed, too, followed by his engines. But his ship's momentum continued to hurtle it forward, toward the Disrupter, and on my HUD, his ship began to flash red, indicating that its reactor core had been set to overload.

Over my comlink, I heard Chén cursing and shouting in Chinese. The English translation popped up on my HUD: *They killed my sister! Now I'm going to kill them!*

I watched in paralyzed horror as Chén continued his dive toward the Disrupter's spinning faceted surface, and I saw my father spiral his ship over into a sharp dive to pursue him. As Chén's Interceptor closed in on the spinning dodecahedron, I winced and held my breath, expecting his ship to impact on its deflector shield. But a millisecond before his ship reached it, its reactor detonated, lighting up the sky.

The explosion's energy dispersed across the Disrupter's deflector shield—and then it flickered and failed. The transparent blue shield around the Disrupter had vanished, leaving its faceted skin exposed to attack.

Of course, by the time I saw this, it was already too late for me to do anything about it. Even if I'd been willing to overload my own ship's power core, to join Chén in his kamikaze run, there wasn't enough time for me to react now. The shield would only be down for three and a half more seconds. You had to be both psychic and suicidal to get the timing right, and at that moment, I was neither.

My father, however, appeared to be both.

Because he was still streaking toward the Disrupter, right on Chén's tail. He had seen the rash decision Chén had made, and then immediately made one of his own.

"Are you nuts?" I shouted. "The shield won't be down long enough!"

"It will, Son," he said. "Because they're watching, and they want my heroic gambit to work. Just like I told you. Watch—I need you to see this."

"I don't want to see anything, you fucking asshole!" I screamed. "Eject, now! You can't do this to me!" I said, voice cracking. "Not again!"

My father's ship righted itself, but didn't change course.

"I love you, Son. And I'm sorry. Tell your mom—"

Time slowed down to a crawl. Everything seemed to be happening in slow motion.

I finally thought to begin counting—*one thousand and one, one thousand and two, one thousand and three, one thousand and four.*

The Disrupter's shield remained down. Was I counting too fast?

On my tactical display, my father's ship closed the remaining distance to the still-exposed Disrupter like a bullet streaking toward a bull's-eye, as the Glaive Fighters closed in, firing on him from all sides—all of them conveniently missing our hero.

Stormtrooper Syndrome, I thought to myself absurdly. *These guys couldn't hit water if they fell out of a fucking boat.*

A split second before my father's ship self-destructed, I saw the armored shell slide down over his cockpit canopy as it had Debbie's, transforming it into a sealed escape pod. The pod fell like a stone, plunging into the churning ocean below—just as his power core imploded and the whole world went white.

Somehow I had enough presence of mind to jam my flight stick forward, diving my own ship into the ocean below just as the overlapping blast waves emanating from the massive explosions above slammed against the surface, throwing up steam and making the sea boil and evaporate.

My tactical display showed me what was happening on the surface. My father's reactor core detonation had torn apart the unprotected Disrupter, and its faceted skin exploded into a cloud of triangular debris that blanketed the ocean surface, mingling with pieces of human and alien spacecraft. I could hear the largest pieces of debris as they thudded again the watery ceiling above me, like dirt raining down on a coffin lid.

It was completely quiet down there, beneath the waves, floating inside my watertight spaceship as I gazed up at the fiery apocalypse erupting above the surface. The silence was so total that for a moment I wasn't sure if I was alive or dead. Then I heard the panicked cadence of my own breathing and realized that yes, I was indeed alive, at least for the moment.

But I wasn't sure about my father. I wasn't getting a signal from his pod's emergency beacon, and the scopes in my ship's sensor package were useless—the ocean was so littered with the wreckage of hundreds of drone Interceptors, Glaives, and conventional fighter aircraft that picking out a single escape pod from the detritus was impossible.

He would drown down here, if he hadn't already.

I powered on every external light my ship had, and then the internal ones, too, just for good measure, but I was still only able to see five or six feet into the murky waters, and there was nothing there, nothing—and the deeper I went, the muddier the water.

I stared helplessly at my blank scopes, trying desperately not to assume the worst, but doing just that.

Could Fate possibly be so cruel as to take my father away from me, on the very same day I'd found him? I didn't like the answer my subconscious spat back at me, of course. But it was my fault for asking, really. I should've known better.

Warnings began to flash on my HUD, telling me that my hull was leaking and that I would need to surface now, or risk having my engine and life-support systems fail.

But I didn't surface. I kept on looking for him, even though it was pointless.

He couldn't vanish on me again, not now. Not before I had a chance to tell him what I'd seen during the battle. What he'd shown me.

He was right; I was wrong. I understood that now. If he would just come back, I would tell him, I would help him, I would do whatever he wanted. He didn't need to punish me like this—by letting me get to know him and learn to love him, only to break my heart all over again.

A voice in my head was saying, *At least he died for what he believed.* But that only made me feel worse, because it didn't ring true.

I knew what was happening up there, above the water's surface. As soon as my father destroyed the Disrupter, all of the Earth Defensive Alliance's quantum communication links would've instantly come back online, everywhere around the world. Now all of the Earth Defense Alliance civilian recruits were back in the fight, controlling the millions of drones stockpiled around every heavily populated area in the world.

Thanks to my dad, humanity had a fighting chance for survival once again. He'd given everything to save the world.

But I didn't care about the world just then.

The world could go to hell and take everyone and everything with it, if only that meant I could have my father back.

I swung my Interceptor across the darkness of the ocean floor, peering into the emptiness, ignoring the increasingly loud warnings from my TAC telling me to surface, and to do it now, or I would die, too.

Because that sounded fine to me. Just fine.

EARTH DEFENSE ALLIANCE

PHASE THREE

If we don't end war, war will end us.

—H. G. Wells

22

SITTING THERE IN THE DARKNESS, WAITING FOR IT ALL TO JUST END, I FOUND myself thinking about Lex. I wondered where she was, and if she was still alive.

Then I remembered my conversation with her, and the QComm hacks she'd shown me. My father's QComm number was on my contact list. If he had the device in his flight suit and if he hadn't powered it off, I might be able to use that to find his escape pod.

Feeling a sudden burst of hope, I fumbled my QComm out and pulled up my short contact list. Then I repeated the steps Lex had shown me to perform her "remote location hack." It involved pressing several icons on my display in rapid order, like the old Konami code. It took me several tries to get it right, because my hands were shaking and the hull-integrity and leak warnings from my computer kept frazzling my nerves.

Finally, a GPS program appeared on my QComm's display. My QComm appeared as a green dot—and my father's appeared right on top of it, as a flashing red dot. I rotated the display to show our relative depths.

My father's pod was directly below me!

I blindly circled my ship around in a corkscrew, using my QComm to close in on him. As I pulled up to avoid the tangled wreckage of two Glaive Fighters, I felt a jolt and heard a loud crack as my father's escape pod appeared out of the watery darkness outside, slamming right up against my cockpit canopy. As the two acrylic domes collided, I caught a horrifying glimpse of his limp and lifeless face, just a few inches away from mine.

It was covered in blood.

Once I'd stopped screaming, I maneuvered my Interceptor around his pod and activated its retrieval arm. A second later, its magnetic seals locked into place with a thud and the arm retracted, fusing my father's escape pod to the underside of my ship's hull.

My computer linked to the pod's occupant diagnostics, and my father's vitals appeared on my HUD. He wasn't dead! He was merely unconscious, and the computer calculated a sixty-seven percent chance that he had suffered a concussion. He was also bleeding from a deep laceration on his scalp. A dialog box popped up on one of my cockpit screens, providing me with a running list of the treatment and drugs that the pod was administering to its occupant. A video window popped up on my display, showing my father's unconscious form from the shoulders up, and I winced as the pod dosed him with a cocktail of painkillers via a needle gun mounted on one of its many robotic arms. I hoped to hell the drugs in that pod didn't have an expiration date.

I watched the drone work on him for a few more seconds; then I finally snapped out of my daze and gunned my ship's throttle, blasting up out of the ocean, then on up into the clouds above, still flooring the gas.

My computer informed me that my passenger needed medical attention immediately, and the autopilot set a course for my ship to the nearest EDA med center, at the southern tip of South America.

I ignored it.

Instead, I flew us home.

AS I GUIDED MY INTERCEPTOR OVER PORTLAND'S CHARRED AND SMOKING SKYLINE, I FELT tears come to my eyes. Here was my first glimpse of the devastation the vanguard's attack had caused on our cities, and it was as bad as I'd feared. The whole city looked like a scene out of *Deep Impact* or *World War Z*. Every street, road, and highway leading out of Portland was clogged with all manner of vehicles, none of them moving. Pillars of black smoke rose from half a dozen fires all over the city, and the sky was filled with news helicopters and small-engine, fixed-wing aircraft, most of which appeared to be fleeing inland.

I tuned my QComm to one of the big cable news networks, so that I could listen in to the broadcast—and heard the last thing I expected.

"In addition to the Earth Defense Alliance's decisive victory in Pakistan," one male news anchor was saying, "news of dozens of other victories are pouring in from other cities around the world. The tide began to turn after the aliens' surprise attacks on Shanghai and Cairo—"

I frowned and switched to another network, showing live coverage from New York City. The Big Apple looked just like it did in every apocalyptic disaster movie I'd ever seen. The skyline was a smoking ruin, and the streets of Manhattan had been flooded by a tsunami created by one of the many artificial earthquakes resulting from the attacks.

"—dozens of epic battles were raging over the city just moments ago, but as you can see, the skies are clear," another newscaster reported. "The EDA's army of civilian-operated drones has won another decisive victory here. Humanity has successfully defended itself against the first wave of the invaders' attack. We managed to fight them all off—it's incredible!"

The beautiful female anchor beside him nodded enthusiastically.

"In every engagement we've had with the enemy so far, it has become obvious that humans are naturally more adept at combat than the creatures who are operating all of these invading ships and drones," she said. "In every battle they seemed to have us outmatched, but despite their vastly superior numbers and technology, the Europans appear to lack our reflexes and natural predatory instincts—"

I switched newsfeeds again and saw Admiral Vance, addressing the troops via his handheld QComm, wearing his trademark expression of grim resolve. The man looked downright heroic.

"—but even though we managed to fight off the first wave of the invasion, we suffered heavy losses in the process," Admiral Vance said. "The enemy didn't lose a soul—just equipment. And two-thirds of their forces are still en route to Earth." He paused to let this sink in, then continued.

"The *second wave* of their attack will reach us just over two hours from now, and we need all of you to be ready."

Just as he finished making that statement, a new countdown clock appeared on my QComm display—just over two and a half hours to go until the second wave arrived, bringing twice as much devastation as the first.

I switched to another channel, and then another, but it was the same war propaganda on every station. Newscasters of every nationality were claiming victory and imploring their viewers not to give up, to hunker down and keep on fighting, because there was still hope—we could still win this.

I put my QComm away, wishing that I could bring myself to rally to the Earth Defense Alliance's global battle cry. But it was obvious to me that our remaining forces wouldn't be able to withstand another assault of equal magnitude, much less two more attacks, delivered by a force of double and then triple the size of the first wave.

I tried to forget about the news, and thought again of my father's heroic act of self-sacrifice, performed in the wake of Chén's kamikaze run. It shouldn't have worked. But it had—just as my father had predicted it would.

I shouldn't need any more convincing—and, I decided right then, I didn't.

"I'm sorry I doubted you, Dad," I said to him over the comlink, while I stared at his unconscious face on my monitor, his eyes closed and his forehead caked with dried blood. "And I'm sorry I couldn't bring myself to call you 'Dad' before now, too, okay? Do you hear me? Do you, Dad?"

His eyes stayed closed, and he remained perfectly still—the ship's inertia-cancellation field kept him from even being jostled slightly, even though we were flying through Earth's atmosphere fast enough to set the ship on fire.

"You were right and I was wrong, okay?" I told him, raising my voice, as if that would help him to hear me. "And I'd really like it if you would wake up now, so that I can tell you that in person. Would you do that for me?

"Please?" I said. "General? Xavier?"

When he didn't answer, I tried again.

"Dad?"

But he still didn't respond.

He was dead to the world.

I FLEW HIM STRAIGHT TO THE HOSPITAL IN SOUTH BEAVERTON WHERE MY MOTHER WORKED, but when I swooped down looking for a spot to land, I saw that all the roads surrounding it were jammed with abandoned vehicles and frightened people. If I landed my Interceptor nearby it would draw all kinds of attention, and it was doubtful I'd be able to take off again.

I was circling back over the city, looking for a quiet place to set down, when I spotted my high school down below. There were only a few cars still parked in the student lot, and mine was one of them. I could also make out the burn marks on the school's front lawn left by the EDA shuttle when Ray had arrived to pick me up this morning—a whole lifetime ago.

I considered landing my ship in the lot right next to my car, but then I thought better of leaving it parked out in the open. A few seconds later, I spotted the perfect parking spot.

I swung around and flew back over the school, but this time I strafed the roof of the gym with laser fire. Then I made another pass and strafed it again, until the whole roof collapsed. Once the dust settled, I lowered my Interceptor down into the gym, concealing it perfectly from view, except from directly above.

The school superintendent was going to be pissed about the damage, but he could bill me.

I was sure someone must have spotted my ship during its brief descent, or heard the noise I'd made. But when I climbed out of my cockpit and ran back outside the gym to take a quick look around, I didn't see anyone rushing toward the building to investigate. I figured that the people who weren't too busy fleeing the city or looting were probably inside their homes, glued to their TV and computer screens, waiting for news.

I sent my mother a text message, asking her to meet us at home with a first aid kit, as soon as possible. Then I pulled my car around, up to the gymnasium's exit. I ran back inside, opened up my father's escape pod, and—staggering under his weight—carried him out to my car.

The jolt of pain he must've felt when I finally managed to flip him into the passenger seat brought him to a state of semiconsciousness.

"RedJive, standing by!" he said drunkenly, slurring his words. He blinked a few times and looked around the car, his eyes widening in recognition.

"Hey, I know this car. This is my old Omni! This shit heap still runs?"

I couldn't speak for a moment. I was too overjoyed to see his eyes open.

"Yeah, it still runs," I finally managed to say. "But just barely." As I gently removed his jacket, I noticed there was blood on some of its patches. I balled the jacket up and shoved it under his head for a pillow. "Try to stay still, okay? Just rest. We'll be home soon."

"Wow, really?" he said, smiling faintly. "I've never been home."

LUCKILY MY HOUSE WAS ONLY A COUPLE OF MILES FROM SCHOOL, AND MOST OF THE STREETS were still passable. I only had to make one detour, to get around a five-car accident blocking an intersection. During the trip, my father drooled and mumbled in the passenger seat, obviously riding high on whatever pain meds the escape pod's emergency systems had injected into his bloodstream.

As I turned down our street and saw our empty driveway, I clenched my teeth in disappointment. My mom wasn't here.

I was still helping my father out of the car when I heard an engine behind me and turned to see my mom's car pulling in. I made a second's worth of eye contact with her through the windshield, saw her eyes widen as she recognized me—and then she was leaping out of her car and running to mine, covering her mouth with her long fingers.

My father opened his eyes in the passenger seat beside me as she peered in.

He didn't speak. He just stared at her, as if paralyzed. I put a hand on his shoulder.

"Hey, Mom," I said, getting out of the car. "I'm home. We're home."

She took me in her arms and crushed her face against my shoulder as tightly as she could. When she finally let go, she turned back to look at my father, still inside the car. "Xavier?" she said. "Is that really you?"

Somehow he managed to pull himself up out of the car, onto his feet.

Then he took a step toward her, and she threw her arms around him. He buried his face in her hair, inhaling deeply.

As I watched them embrace, there on the front lawn, my heart was rocked by waves of unbridled joy. It occurred to me that up until this moment I'd only ever experienced the bridled kind. Having the reins slipped off my heart after a lifetime of wearing them was a bit overwhelming—in the best possible way.

I heard barking, and a second later, Muffit burst out of his doggie door. The old beagle barked and bounded down the front steps and across the front lawn, moving faster than he had in years.

"Muffit!" my father cried, breaking off his embrace with my mother to greet the ancient dog, just a second before Muffit somehow summoned the strength to bound into my kneeling father's lap.

"Oh, it's so good to see you, boy!" he said as Muffit showered his face with kisses. "I missed you, boy! Did you miss me?"

Muffit barked happily in reply, then continued to shower my dad with saliva. It had never once occurred to me to wonder whether our dog remembered my father—after all, Muffit had been just a puppy when he disappeared.

My father began to laugh under the beagle's barrage of kisses—but then he glanced over at my mother and me and his features suddenly contorted into a mask of pain. He turned away and tried to hide his face by burying it in Muffit's graying coat. My mother put her arms around both of them, and *I* saw that there were tears running down her cheeks—and I knew they were the same sort now welling up in my own eyes. Tears of joy.

Through my increasingly blurred vision, I watched my father and my mother and my dog, all holding each other, just a few feet away from me— my family, impossibly reunited, after all this time.

Suddenly, I wanted very much for the world not to end. I wanted it to keep going, more than anything.

My father set Muffit down and scratched his silvery muzzle. "You got old, didn't you, buddy? That's okay. I did, too."

My mother examined the cut on my father's forehead and winced.

"Help me get him inside," she said. "Christ, what did you give him? Bourbon?"

"The med computer in his escape pod dosed him with some sort of painkiller," I explained. "Will he be okay?"

My father burst out singing—some old song I didn't recognize.

" '*I haven't got time for the pain!*' " he bellowed.

My mother let out a laugh, then nodded at me.

"He's definitely suffered a concussion, but yes—he'll live." She let out another laugh, which turned into a sob halfway through. "That's funny, considering he's been dead for seventeen years." She gave me an unsteady smile. Her lower lip was trembling.

"It's gonna be okay, Mom," I said, just to have something to say.

We got my father into the living room and lowered him onto the couch. Then I turned to my mother and hugged her as hard as I ever had in my life.

"I need to run over to Diehl's house, Ma," I told her, breaking off the embrace. "There's something I promised Dad I'd do."

"He didn't promise me anything!" my father shouted—but his face was buried in the couch cushions, and Muffit was sitting on his head, so I may have misheard him.

"Zackary Ulysses Lightman, you are not going back out there!" my mother said, pointing her finger at me. "I've been worried to death! You can't do that to me again!"

"It's okay now," I told her as I headed for the door. "The first wave of the invasion is over. Nearly all of the alien drones from the vanguard have been destroyed."

My mother smiled with relief, clearly mistaking my meaning.

"But that was just the first wave, Mom," I said. "A lot more are on their way."

"Two more whole waves of them," my father mumbled, lifting his head long enough to dethrone Muffit, then dropping it facefirst into the cushion again.

Her eyes shifted back and forth between the two of us uncertainly. I went over and hugged her a last time.

"I'll be back before then," I told her. "I promise." I glanced at my father. "Try and sober him up, will you?"

THE DRIVE TO DIEHL'S HOUSE WAS EASIER THAN I'D FEARED—I HAD TO USE SOME SIDEWALKS and lawns to avoid pileups and downed power lines, but there was no traffic, so the detours didn't take long.

When I reached Diehl's house, I saw over a dozen dormant ATHIDs standing guard around the perimeter of his lawn like robotic sentinels. I saw the omnidirectional camera eyes swivel to follow me as I approached, but they made no move to stop me. I scaled Diehl's backyard fence, climbed up onto his roof, and then tiptoed over to his second-story bedroom window to peer inside.

To my relief, Diehl was in there, he was alive, and he was doing exactly what I'd expected to find him doing—sitting at his computer, talking to Cruz via a video window on his computer.

Diehl had the soles of his feet propped against the edge of his desk, and he was leaning his metal chair back, balancing it on its two rear legs—an old habit of his. When I tapped on the windowpane and he looked over to see me standing outside in my EDA uniform, he jerked backward in surprise, the chair tipped over, and he fell to the floor with a thud. But he recovered quickly, scrambled back to his feet, and ran over to throw open the window.

"Zack!" he said, leaning out the window to give me a hug before pulling me inside. "Jesus, man!"

We hugged each other; then I turned to wave at Cruz in his monitor. He was sitting at his computer in his own cluttered suburban bedroom, just a few miles away.

"Holy shit," I said. "It's really good to see both of you guys."

"Yeah! We had no idea what happened to you!" Cruz said. "Sweet EDA uniform!"

"Thanks," I said, collapsing into a beanbag chair in the corner, suddenly feeling the heaviness of my exhaustion weighing me down like a suit of medieval armor.

"We weren't sure we'd ever see you again, after you flew off in that shuttle!" Diehl said, sitting back down at his desk. "Oh, that reminds me—" He leaned over and punched me in the shoulder. Hard.

"Ow!" I said, recoiling as I raised my own fist to feign retaliation. "What the actual fuck, Diehl!"

"That's for leaving without me, Biggs," he replied, leaning back. "Don't ever do that again."

I sighed, rubbing the site of my future bruise. "Like I had a choice," I said, laughing. "Asshole."

"School was canceled right after you left and they sent everyone home," Cruz added. "That's where we were when the news hit earlier this afternoon. So we jumped online and helped fight off the first wave."

"We've been glued to our consoles since," Diehl said, still in shock. "We helped defend Shanghai and Karachi—until the Disrupter activated and disabled everyone's links. We would have been hosed if the EDA hadn't taken that thing out."

"The EDA's Drone Operator Assignment System switched both of us to local defense once the enemy began to spread out and attack everywhere," Cruz continued. "And since we're two of the highest-ranking drone drivers in the greater Beaverton area, we got first dibs on local drone access! We used our ATHIDs to help defend Beaverton from the drones that landed here."

"Yeah, did you see that Basilisk we took out?" Diehl asked. "It was right down the street from your house."

"You two did that?"

They both nodded proudly.

"We couldn't let that thing stomp your house!" Diehl said, slapping me on the back and then hooking his arm around my neck.

"Thanks, fellas," I said. "I appreciate it." I pointed back outside, at the ring of ATHIDs encircling his house. "How did you manage that?"

"Their operating system software has zero security installed," Cruz said. "I guess the EDA decided not to bother—but that makes them incredibly easy to hack. People all over the world have been figuring out all sorts of hacks to make them do stuff the EDA never intended, then they post 'How To' videos on YouTube, showing everyone else how to do it, too." He pointed outside. "That's how I disabled the recall subroutine on those ATHIDs out there, so they didn't leave for reassignment after the first wave." He beamed proudly. "Now they'll be here to protect my mom and little sisters when the second wave arrives."

I nodded, impressed. I was about to ask if he'd tried making them line dance when Cruz shouted at me from the laptop screen.

"So spill it," he said. "What happened to you after that shuttle picked you up at school this morning? Where the hell have you been all day?"

I considered how to answer.

"On the far side of the moon," I replied. "With my dad."

On the monitor, I saw Cruz's jaw drop open.

To my left, Diehl leaned back a few inches too far in his chair and fell over again.

ONCE I CAUGHT MY BREATH, I TRIED CALLING LEX TO MAKE SURE SHE WAS OKAY. SHE DIDN'T answer, but a few seconds later she texted me: *I'm OK. Will call U ASAP.* <3

Then, as quickly as I could, I told the Mikes everything that had happened since we'd last seen each other. Eventually I worked my way up to telling them my father's theory about the Europans' true motives, and the observations he'd made that supported it. It took a while for me to get to our battle with the Disrupter, and to explain how its conclusion seemed to be proof of my father's theory.

When I'd finally laid everything out, I asked the question I'd come here to ask.

"What do you guys think?"

They both stared at me in silence for a long time. Diehl was the first to speak.

"I think your dad is probably right," he said. "Why would the Europans bother to send robots and spaceships to attack us?" He shoved a handful of corn chips into his mouth, then chewed thoughtfully. "If their primary goal was to wipe out the human race, they could have just hurled an asteroid at Earth. Or fired a bunch of long-range nukes. Or poisoned our atmosphere, or—"

"Maybe they're precursors!" Cruz shouted from Diehl's computer monitor. "Maybe they seeded life on Earth millions of years ago, and now they're here to punish us for turning out to be such a lame species and inventing reality TV and shit?" He raised an index finger. "*Or* maybe they're omnipotent beings who have grown bored with immortality, and they're just tormenting us for their own twisted amusement? You know, like whenever Q would pop in from the continuum to fuck with Picard!"

"This conversation was an intelligent one, right up until you joined it," Diehl said.

I didn't chime in. I just let them debate the issue, as if we were all back in our high school's cafeteria, arguing some trivial facet of pop culture over cardboard pizza. This was why I'd come here, I realized—to get the opinion of my two most trusted friends, gauge their reaction, and see if their conclusions mirrored my own. And in a way, they did. They seemed to be just as confounded by all of this as I felt, and yet were also just as intrigued by the mystery as my father.

I checked the time. It was still running out. And I realized that I'd already made my decision.

"I appreciate you talking through this with me, fellas," I told them. "Now I've got a phone call to make."

I raised my wrist and activated my QComm. Both of my friends' eyes lit up.

"What the holy sweet hell is that?" Diehl asked. "A tricorder?"

FINN ARBOGAST ANSWERED AFTER THE THIRD RING, AND HIS SMILING FACE APPEARED IN high-definition video on my QComm's display. Judging by the view behind him, he was sitting in some sort of command bunker, with giant display screens bolted to its thick concrete walls each displaying icon-littered maps of various regions of the world.

"Zack!" he said. "I'm glad to see that you're alive! You and your father were reported missing in action just after you took out that Disrupter. Congratulations, by the way. I watched the whole thing!"

"Then you know that my father just risked his life to save us all," I said. "So I think you owe him a favor, don't you?"

He smiled uneasily. I waited for him to ask about my father, but he said nothing.

"Did my father ever tell you his theory, about the Europans' true motives?"

His smile vanished and he let out a heavy sigh.

"You mean his theory that this invasion is all a ruse?" Arbogast said. "That the Europans orchestrated this whole conflict as some sort of test for humanity? Yes, I know all about it. I'm sorry, Lieutenant. Your father is a great man—a hero. And we all owe him a huge debt. But all these years at war have addled his brain. He's become delusional."

"No, he hasn't," I replied, too forcefully. "I've seen the evidence myself, when we were going up against the Disrupter in Antarctica—it dropped its shield on purpose. They let us destroy it! Look at the footage—you can see it happen for yourself!"

He didn't respond, but his eyes shifted evasively. He looked as if he spent most of his time in front of a computer instead of with people, and he wasn't used to being interrogated or put on the spot like this.

"I don't see the point in this conversation," he said. "We debated all of this with your father years ago, and I'm not going to go through it again now with you, kid. I mean, look around you! Our enemy's motives are obviously no longer in question!" He pointed to the giant map of the world behind him. "The Europans just killed over thirty million people—and that was just the first wave of their invasion. The second wave is arriving just over an hour from now. So if you'll excuse me, I need to prepare for it—"

"Sir, if you'll just let me speak to someone who—"

Before I could say another word, he ended the call.

I lowered my phone and turned to look at my friends.

"Okay," Diehl said, leaning forward. "That was a giant ball of fail. What now?"

I smiled and held up my QComm. All the names I'd just lifted from Finn Arbogast's phone were listed there. I scrolled down to highlight the one labeled *Armistice Council Members—Conference.*

"He already gave me all the help I need," I said.

"You hacked his future phone?" Diehl said. "How? You can barely use apps!"

"If you must know," I said, "that super-hot mech driver I met at Crystal Palace showed me how to do it. She also kissed me, FYI."

"Really?" Cruz said, laughing. "Is she from Canada? The Niagara Falls area, perhaps?"

"I want to know if they boned in zero gravity," Diehl said. "Spill it, Lightman."

I ignored their questions and called my father on his QComm. It rang and rang. As I continued to let it ring, I grabbed Diehl's phone off his desk to dial my mother's number—only to discover that it was already programmed into his contacts as "Pamela Lightman."

"Why do you have my mom's number saved in your phone?"

"Oh, you know why, Stifler," Cruz muttered from his video window, his voice dripping with innuendo—this was his version of "that's what she said."

"I've had your mom's number in my phone since I was twelve, psycho!" Diehl said. "You have my mom's number in your phone, too. Get over yourself."

I nodded, then shook my head vigorously. "Sorry," I said. "Sorry, man."

I put his phone to my other ear. My mother's number rang and rang, too, while my father's continued to ring in the other. A minute passed. Neither of them picked up. Probably not good. I wondered if my dad's condition had gotten worse and she'd decided to take him to a hospital after all.

After Crom knows how many rings, I finally gave up and canceled both calls. Then I pulled up Arbogast's contact for the Armistice Council again and tried to make a decision.

I badly wanted to have my father on the line before I called them: The Armistice Council would be made up of world-renowned scientists or

EDA commanders or both, and they probably wouldn't listen to some eighteen-year-old kid. But there was a good chance my father was unconscious, and the clock was ticking down. What choice did I have?

I summoned my courage and tapped the Armistice Council contact on my QComm. I watched as the device dialed five different numbers all at once and then connected all of them simultaneously. Then my QComm switched into "conference mode," and my display screen was divided into five separate windows, each containing live video of a different person, each of whom appeared to be in a separate location.

There were four men and one woman, and all of them looked familiar to me, but I only recognized two of them by name—the two men whose faces appeared in the last two video windows on my screen. The first was Dr. Neil deGrasse Tyson, and the second was Dr. Stephen Hawking, slumped in his motorized wheelchair. I heard Cruz and Diehl gasp behind me just as my own jaw dropped open like a castle drawbridge.

Dr. Hawking spoke up first. I saw the familiar heads-up display for an ATHID on the computer monitor behind him—it appeared that Dr. Hawking had been helping defend Cambridge from its alien siege when he answered the call.

He spoke using his famous computer-generated voice, which now, ironically, reminded me of Chén's translator instead of the other way around.

"Who are you?" he asked. "And how did you get this number?"

I opened my mouth to answer, but no words came out. I'd just recalled the names of the other three scientists on the call—I'd seen each of them interviewed on countless science programs and documentaries. The Asian gentleman was Dr. Michio Kaku, and the other two people were famous SETI researchers, Dr. Seth Shostak and Dr. Jill Tarter. I recognized Tarter because she was a former colleague of Carl Sagan's, and she'd served as the primary inspiration for Jodie Foster's character in the film *Contact*.

I was on the phone with five of the world's most prominent scientists, and they were all waiting for me to say something.

"Doctor Hawking asked you a question," Dr. Tyson said, rolling his eyes slightly. "This is not a good time to be wasting our time."

I shook my head, and forced my voice into action.

"I'm sorry, sir, of course," I said, clearing my throat. "My name is Zack Lightman. I was stationed at Moon Base Alpha with my father, General Xavier Lightman, until it was hit—and the fate of human civilization depends on what I have to tell you."

They all stared at me, waiting.

I told them, as quickly and succinctly as I could, everything my father had told me, along with what I'd seen for myself in our last Disrupter battle.

To my shock, none of them hung up on me. So I kept on talking until I had told them everything—and probably a few things more than once. I also used my QComm to transfer the data my father had obtained from Arbogast, including all of the raw *Envoy* mission footage and the transmissions we'd received from the Europans. It only took a few seconds before they were each scanning the data on their own QComms.

"Some of the things you've just told us are extremely unsettling," Dr. Tyson said. "But unfortunately, they're not entirely surprising. Since it was first formed, this council has encountered a fair amount of secrecy and military bureaucracy in our dealings with the Earth Defense Alliance command—especially pertaining to the release of classified information about the Europans. We were never given unrestricted access to that data."

"Lieutenant, would you mind if we put you on hold a moment?" Dr. Tarter asked. "So that we can discuss the information you've just given us in private?"

"Sure," I said, glancing at the countdown clock in the corner of my display, now ticking off the remaining minutes until the second wave attacked. "Take all the time you need. It's not like the world is about to end."

I don't think they even heard my snarky reply, because they put me on hold before I'd finished making it. Their video stream windows froze and grayed themselves out. I also noticed tiny arrow icons linking their five video windows, to indicate that they were all still talking to each other on the call while I was temporarily excluded. That was when Cruz caught a glimpse of my QComm screen, which was now divided into over half a dozen windows, each with a different person's face, just like the opening of *The Brady Bunch*—so he decided to belt out an impromptu parody of the opening line of the show's theme song: *"This is the story, of an alien invasion, by some fuckheads from Europa who are—"*

That was all he managed to get out before Diehl snapped his laptop shut, cutting him off. He winced at me apologetically.

"It's okay," I told him. "The council has me on hold."

Diehl exhaled and reopened his laptop. Cruz was still singing away.

"All of them have tentacles, like their mother! The youngest one in curls!"

Diehl laughed. Cruz laughed. I laughed.

Gallows humor.

23

AS WE SAT THERE WAITING, MY QCOMM RANG, STARTLING ME SO MUCH that I nearly dropped it. My display informed me that, in addition to the five other calls on hold, I had a new incoming call—from my father.

I hit the answer icon, and my father face's appeared in another video window, along with the five grayed-out ones.

He was smiling—an unbridled, rapturous smile, even bigger than the one he'd been wearing when we first met. I half expected to see an animated bluebird alight on one of his shoulders before he broke into song. My eyes went to the gash on his forehead, which my mother had bandaged, and I wondered if his uncharacteristically upbeat mood was somehow due to his head injury. After a few seconds he managed to force the smile down—but his mouth snapped back into a goofy grin a second later. He shrugged, as if to say *I just can't hide how I feel inside.*

That was when I finally noticed that the wallpaper in my mother's bedroom was visible behind him, and I suddenly understood—and immediately wished I could pull and somehow yank the knowledge back out of my brain. No wonder my parents hadn't answered their phones earlier. They'd been too busy boning each other like teenagers.

"Zack!" my father said, way too brightly. "How are you doing, Son?"

I wanted to reach through the phone and strangle him—then I stopped to wonder why. It's not like it was their first time, right? And hey, the world was probably about to end. Half the people on the planet were probably going at it right now, just like everyone up on the goddamn moon! Everyone was jumping at their last chance to jump one another. And if anyone deserved a moment of happiness, it was my father, who had just risked his life for the zillionth time to prevent the extinction of the human race.

If I'd still been my old Bruce Banner self, I would have Hulked right the fuck out on him, then and there. But I didn't. I smiled back at him.

"Hey, Dad. I'm on hold with all five members of the Armistice Council," I said. "I just told them everything—to the best of my ability, anyway."

He laughed, assuming I was making a joke. But then his smile abruptly vanished.

"Wait," he said. "Are you being serious with me right now?"

"As a heart attack," I said, tapping at the menu on my phone. "I just added you to the conference call."

His eyes widened when he saw the names of the other people on the call.

"But—how did you get in touch with them?"

"You aren't the only one with a few tricks up his sleeve, Dad," I said. "I'll explain later, if we have time."

My father's face changed—he looked as if he was trying not to panic now.

"What did you tell them?" he asked. "I mean, how did they react?"

I noticed that Diehl was staring over my shoulder, holding up his laptop so that Cruz could eavesdrop, too.

"Holy shit!" he whispered. "Is that your dad?"

I nodded. I was about to introduce my father to my two best friends when the Armistice Council took us off hold. They all seemed a bit surprised to see that my father had joined us—but not nearly as shocked as he was when he saw who was on the call. "Who is this gentleman, Lieutenant?" Dr. Shostak asked.

"This is my father, General Lightman," I said. "The officer I was just telling you about."

My father was still staring into his QComm's camera, dumbfounded. "Well, first of all," Dr. Tyson said, "we would like to commend you both for your service, and for being brave enough to bring this information before the Armistice Council."

"You're welcome?" I said uncertainly.

"We've only had a limited time to consider the evidence," Dr. Tarter said carefully. "But we believe there's a strong possibility your theory about the Europans is correct."

"You do?" my father and I both asked in unison, making the scientist smile.

"This council has access to classified information about the Europans that adds further credence to your theory, gentlemen," Dr. Shostak said. "The official story is that when NASA's *Envoy* probe landed on Europa to investigate the swastika-shaped anomaly on the moon's surface, it attempted to make contact with the extraterrestrials who created it by burrowing down through the moon's surface ice with a melt probe to reach the subsurface ocean below. But that cryobot's mission wasn't to make contact with the Europans—its mission was to destroy them."

"I knew it!" my father said. "President Nixon ordered NASA to strap a nuke onto that probe, didn't he?"

Everyone but Hawking nodded grimly.

Shostak continued, "Nixon didn't believe the swastika could be anything but a threat. He and a few advisors decided that we had no choice but to take preemptive action."

"So it was us," my father said. "We attacked them first. And then they came here to attack us. That's how it started. And both sides have been slowly escalating the conflict between ever since, for forty-two years—"

"Until a few days ago," I said. "When we escalated things to the breaking point by launching a doomsday weapon at them."

Dr. Tarter nodded. "In light of everything you've told us, it's entirely possible that our use of the Icebreaker was what prompted them to finally deploy their armada and invade after waiting so long."

I shook my head. "This whole time, it's been us. We're the ones who've upped the stakes every step of the way."

My father nodded. "And now there's nowhere else for things to escalate. We've reached the endgame—the point of mutually assured destruction. If we attempt to destroy them, they'll destroy us."

"And you believe the only way to prevent that is for us to recall the Icebreaker and declare a cease-fire?" Tyson asked. "After these beings have already attacked us and killed millions of innocent people?"

"If we continue to escalate this pointless conflict with them, they're going to exterminate all of us in a few hours anyway," he said. "Admiral Vance is wrong. Launching the Icebreaker at Europa won't stop the second or third wave of their armada from attacking us—quite the opposite. It will seal their decision to destroy us!"

"He's right," I said. "We have to take this chance. Humanity has nothing to lose—nothing we're not going to lose anyway. We can go down fighting, but we'll still end up extinct."

Dr. Tyson nodded. "Unfortunately, it may already be too late for us to convince the EDA command to act on this information," he said. "Admiral Vance still isn't answering our calls, and the second wave of the attack is only minutes away."

"The Icebreaker will be within firing range just a few minutes after that," Shostak added. "Perhaps the Europans timed it that way?"

"Don't bother contacting Admiral Vance," my father said. "He won't listen."

"You're damn right, I won't," Admiral Vance said as his face appeared in a video window alongside the half dozen others on the call.

I blinked in surprise. Apparently Vance knew a few QComm tricks of his own.

"I've listened to about as much of this treasonous talk as I can stomach," he said, and reached up and tapped his QComm screen several times in rapid succession. One by one, each member of the Armistice Council was disconnected from the conference call. When he was done, only my father and I remained on the line with him. His haggard face grew to fill half my display, scowling at us in crystal-clear high-definition.

"Don't bother trying to call the council back," he told us. "I've just locked all of their QComms, so don't hold your breath for them to call you either."

My father didn't respond right away. He just glared at his old comrade in silence over the video link for a long moment.

"How long have you known about that weaponized *Envoy* lander, Archie?" my dad finally asked. "How long have you known that we're the ones who started this war?"

"I found out when they put me in charge," he said. "And by then, it no longer mattered. And it most definitely does not matter now." He paused. "Whether or not they lured us into this war is irrelevant at this point. Can't you see that, Xavier? We're fighting for the survival of our species! Informing the world that humanity may have accidentally incited this conflict wouldn't help the situation."

"Accidentally?" I said. "Nixon had NASA send a nuke as our first olive branch, Dr. Strangelove!"

"You and your son need to give up on this nonsense, General," Vance said. "I need you both back on the front lines, right now, before the second wave makes landfall."

My dad shook his head. "No, Archie," he said. "We're done fighting. Both of us."

Vance frowned. "Funny. I never pegged you for a deserter—or a coward."

"The Europans know about the Icebreaker, Admiral," my father said. "They have to. Their technology is slightly more advanced than ours. You noticed that, right?"

Vance snorted. "If they've spotted the Icebreaker, why haven't they destroyed it?"

"Because they're waiting to see if you'll actually use it, you obtuse prick!" my father shouted back. "That's the whole reason they're attacking us in waves instead of all at once! Don't you see? They're testing us!" He lowered his voice. "Archie, listen to me, man. This is how we survive. They're giving us a chance to reconsider—to think all of this through, instead of blindly retaliating, just like we've always done in the past!"

"We've had this argument before, X." Vance shook his head. "Many times. You know I'm not going to risk the survival of the human species on some big fat maybe that you cooked up because you've seen too many old movies." He pointed up. "Those things—whatever they are—have already killed millions of innocent human beings, and I'm not going to recall our last chance to destroy them before they destroy us. I don't care who else you've convinced of your asinine fairy tale. The decision is made."

"Archie," my father repeated, struggling to remain calm, "I'm telling you right now, if you launch those nukes at their home, you're ensuring the destruction of ours!"

Vance studied him for a moment, then tapped his wristwatch.

"I guess we'll find out who's right in about twenty-three minutes," he replied. Before my father could reply, Vance hung up, leaving the two of us alone on the line together. My father's face enlarged to fill my whole QComm display. He looked utterly defeated for a second. But then he broke into a broad smile.

"Oh well," he said. "I guess this means we go to Plan B."

I shook my head. "Remind me what Plan B was again?"

"You and I stop the Icebreaker all by ourselves."

Before I could reply, a single tone sounded, and three other video windows popped back up on our displays as Lex, Whoadie, and Debbie all joined our call simultaneously, each from a different location.

"Hey, fellas," Lex said. "Count me in."

"Me, too!" added Debbie, just before Whoadie shouted, "And me three!"

"What the hell?" my father said. "Where did you ladies come from?"

"Dad, this is my friend Captain Alexis Larkin," I said. "We met at Crystal Palace. She figured out how to jailbreak the QComm operating software. I asked her to set things up so they could all listen in on the conference call. She also installed software on our QComms to prevent the EDA from remotely disabling them."

My father raised his eyebrows, impressed. "Outstanding, Captain. Thank you!"

"You're welcome, General!" she said, returning his salute.

He froze, seeming lost in thought for moment. "Is there any chance you can tell me what Admiral Vance's location was when he broke in on the call?"

She nodded. "He's in Pennsylvania. At an EDA base code-named 'Raven Rock.'"

My father grinned and then saluted her. She returned it.

Diehl leaned in over my left shoulder, holding Cruz on his laptop screen. "We want in on this operation, too!"

My father studied the faces arrayed before him in silence.

"So what's the plan, General?" I asked.

24

WE RALLIED AT STARBASE ACE.

     I drove Cruz and Diehl there in my car, and we pulled up in front of the store just a few minutes before my mother arrived in her own car. My father wasn't with her.

"Where's Dad?" I asked. "What happened?"

"He drove separately," she replied, before pointing up at the sky overhead. A second later, my Interceptor swooped into view. My father brought the ship in for a perfect landing in the strip mall's crumbling parking lot and ran over to greet us. After my mother and I each gave him a quick hug, I introduced him to Cruz and Diehl, who had watched his arrival in awestruck silence.

I unlocked the store and led everyone inside. When my father saw the store shelves, lined with high-end *Armada* and *Terra Firma* flight controllers, he broke into a broad smile.

"This is perfect!" he said as he began to grab items off the shelves and hand them to each of us. "I need each of you to build the best rig you can, as fast as you can."

The moment I finished setting up a makeshift drone controller pod for myself in the store's War Room, my father called me back into the tiny, cluttered room that served as Ray's office. He was ransacking the place.

"What are you looking for?" I asked.

He nodded at the QComm on his wrist. It displayed a map of the local neighborhood, with an EDA icon hovering over the location of Starbase Ace.

"There's a secret access node for the EDA's hard-line fiber-optic intranet hidden somewhere at this location," he said. "But I can't find it."

I remembered something Ray had told me during our shuttle ride to Crystal Palace. That Glaive Fighter I'd seen outside my classroom window—he'd said it was a scout ship conducting surveillance on the EDA's hard-line intranet. When I'd spotted it hovering over Beaverton, it had probably been in the process of scanning the "secret" intranet access node hidden here in the store.

But if the Europans knew about the EDA's backup intranet, why hadn't they bothered to destroy or disable it before they invaded?

Because their actions have never made any sort of tactical sense, I thought. *Why start now?*

My father continued to tear through the office. He began to pull books off a nearby shelf one at a time, then suddenly raked the remaining ones off with his arm in frustration. "It'll be concealed behind an armored access panel—like a safe? Any ideas?"

I shook my head. "We don't have a safe," I said. "We never needed one." I held up my QComm. "But I've got Ray's number."

"Be careful what you say," he warned. "Vance could be monitoring your QComm."

"Not anymore," I told him. "After Vance broke in on my conference call with the Armistice Council, Lex helped me turn on my QComm's hidden security mode—the same feature that Vance uses to prevent his own QComm from being monitored."

"Captain Larkin appears to be something of a genius, doesn't she?"

I caught him studying my face for a reaction, and blushed involuntarily. I nodded in reply, then pulled up my contacts and tapped the last name listed there: Ray Habashaw. His face instantly appeared on my display. His name, rank, and current location appeared across the bottom—he was at an EDA base in Arizona called Gila Mountain.

"Zack!" he shouted. "Where are you? Are you okay?" He lowered his voice and moved his QComm camera a bit too close to his mouth. "I heard you and your father went missing in action after you took out the Disrupter. I was afraid you bought it."

I shook my head and tilted my QComm so that he could see my current location.

"You're back at the store?" he said, brightening first, then scowling at the sight of his office. "What the hell, man? Who are you letting ransack the place? Looters?"

I shook my head, then positioned the QComm so that Ray could see my father, too. His eyes widened.

"General Lightman," he said, awkwardly saluting his QComm. "It's an honor, sir."

My father returned the salute.

"The honor is all mine, Sergeant," he said. "I owe you a huge debt for watching over my boy while I was gone. Thank you."

"You're welcome," he said, blushing visibly.

"Ray, we don't have much time," I said. "We need to access the EDA intranet node hidden here in the store. It's an emergency."

Ray only hesitated for a split second. "Behind the UFO poster on the back wall."

I turned and located the one he was talking about—a framed reprint of Mulder's "I Want to Believe" poster from *The X-Files*. I took it down, revealing what appeared to be a small titanium safe embedded in the brick wall behind it, with a keypad at its center.

"The combination is 1-1-3-8-2-1-1-2," Ray said.

My father grinned and punched in the numbers. The lock disengaged, and he opened the door. The only thing behind it was a row of ten Ethernet cable ports—just like those on the back of our cable router at home.

"Thank you!" my father said. He turned to me. "You guys got RJ45 cable here?"

I nodded. "On the wall opposite the register!"

He ran out, and I looked back at Ray on my QComm.

"Thanks, Ray," I said. "But now I have to ask you for another favor. A big one."

"You better make it quick, pal," he said. "The second wave is minutes away."

I gave him the short version of the story. It still took way too long. Thankfully, Ray took even less convincing than Lex or my other friends. Once I finished telling him everything my father had told me, he paused for a few moments, then nodded.

"Tell me what you need," he said.

AS SOON AS WE GOT OUR MAKESHIFT DRONE CONTROLLER RIGS CONNECTED TO THE HARD-line intranet node back in Ray's office, my father laid out the plan. Cruz, Diehl, my mother, and I all watched my father's chalk talk there in the store, while Lex, Whoadie, and Debbie listened over their QComms.

I wasn't a fan of several aspects of his plan, but there was no time to argue, or to come up with another solution.

My father wished everyone good luck. Then the others stayed inside while my mother and I walked outside to bid him farewell.

"What if you can't delay the Icebreaker long enough for me to get there?" I asked, once we were far enough outside that my friends wouldn't hear his answer.

"Don't worry," he said. "I'll take care of it. Okay?"

"Okay."

He grabbed me and pulled me into a fierce embrace.

"I love you, Son," he said. "Thank you for helping me do this. Thank you for believing in me. You'll never know how much—how much that means."

He kissed my forehead, then walked over to say goodbye to my mother. She wasn't crying—she'd put on her bravest face, for both of us.

They spoke to each other briefly, but I stayed out of earshot. I don't know what they said to each other. But my mother nodded before she kissed him goodbye, and he smiled at her.

Then he turned and climbed inside my damaged Interceptor, and my mother and I watched as he flew off, bound for the Raven Rock command center. After his ship had vanished over the horizon in a blur, we continued to stare up at the sky for a few more fearful moments, dreading what we knew would soon descend from it. Then we ran back inside the store and prepared to carry out our own part of the mission.

25

THE SECOND WAVE ARRIVED JUST MINUTES AFTER MY FATHER DEPARTED, AND a swarm of Glaive and Wyvern Fighters descended from the sky to attack Portland and the surrounding suburbs. Our drone reserves were heavily diminished, and consequently we were far more outnumbered than we had been during the first wave. But the EDA's civilian gamer forces continued to put up a valiant fight, and a fierce battle raged in the streets of the city and in the sky above while we carried out our mission inside the store.

During his chalk talk, my father had explained how the EDA's hardline intranet worked. It was an underground fiber-optic cable network directly linking all of its drone controller outposts together, creating a Disrupter-proof communications system that the Alliance had prepared in anticipation of the invasion. It would allow the EDA to keep communications open between its command outposts, and allow drone operators to help defend other installations remotely while the Disrupter was active, via hardwired defense turrets and tethered drones.

If everything went according to my father's plan, we would be able to use our intranet connection at Starbase Ace to help him infiltrate the Raven Rock outpost during the chaos of the Disrupter attack.

If not, well—then he was going be totally hosed.

———

WHILE MY FATHER PILOTED HIS MANNED INTERCEPTOR TO ASSAULT RAVEN ROCK, WHERE Vance's team was located, I sat inside Starbase Ace piloting the three Interceptors my father had commandeered from the Icarus crater and sent off toward massive Jupiter, its tiny moon Europa—and the Icebreaker closing in on it.

Cruz and Diehl took control of four new ATHIDs from a nearby EDA drone cache and redeployed them in the Starbase Ace parking lot, to defend us during the second wave of the attack.

Lex was at Sapphire Station, and Ray was at Gila Mountain. Both were connected to the hard-line EDA intranet from inside their assigned drone controller pods—and both were already preparing to help my father execute his infiltration plan.

While Cruz and Diehl used their giant robots to help defend Starbase Ace from the incoming swarm of Spider Fighters and Basilisks, my mother, Debbie, and Whoadie all used WASP aerial drone quadcopters to defend the store from above.

Whoadie was fighting from an *Armada* sit-down arcade game located in the game room of her uncle Franklin's bowling alley in New Orleans. Debbie was back home in Duluth, controlling her drone from her own living room while her three sons continued to stand guard outside their home by controlling EDA drones with an Xbox, a laptop, and a touch-screen tablet, respectively. We knew that Debbie and Whoadie would both lose control of their drones when the Disrupter switched on, but there was nothing we could do about that. They intended to help out for as long as they could.

While my friends kept the enemy drones at bay, I continued to pilot my drones toward Jupiter, trying to make it to Europa in time to stop the Icebreaker—while my father attempted to prevent Vance from launching the weapon before my ships even got there.

That was when we got word via a public EDA command broadcast that the second Disrupter was about to make landfall back here on Earth, in the unlikeliest of locations. At first, I couldn't believe what I was seeing. Instead of activating the Disrupter in a secluded spot like Antarctica, this time the aliens picked a far less subtle location—the national monument at Devils Tower, Wyoming. The same spot where humanity makes first contact with the alien visitors in *Close Encounters of the Third Kind*. An "intergalactic game of Simon," featuring those same five tones the Europans had used to bookend their cryptic transmissions to us.

"Oh, that's not cool!" Diehl shouted, staring at a live video image of the Disrupter taken by an orbiting satellite. "Are these alien pricks openly mocking us now? Christ!"

WHEN THE DISRUPTER ACTIVATED, THE DRONES MY FRIENDS WERE USING TO DEFEND STARbase Ace were disabled and went limp or fell out of the sky—as did every untethered EDA drone around the world.

But the Europan drones continued to attack, closing in on Starbase Ace as if they somehow knew it was of strategic importance.

Lex, Ray, Debbie, and Whoadie all lost control of their drones as their links went dead. So did Cruz and Diehl, but they both ran outside and activated the hard-line controllers on two dormant ATHIDs. They detached the small Xbox-like game controller from each ATHID's back and then ran back inside, unspooling their drones' carbon-fiber-sheathed tether cables to their maximum length.

My mother, always cool during a crisis, ran over to guard the door behind me with an aluminum baseball bat, apparently with the intention of using it to fight off any killer alien robots that attempted to get past her. I took off my QComm, strapped it onto her right wrist, and showed her how to fire its built-in laser. She tossed her bat aside, then aimed the device at the floor and activated its beam for a split second—long enough to burn a hole in the carpet and the concrete foundation beneath.

"I got this," she said, smiling with satisfaction. Then she aimed her new weapon back at the door, continuing to stand guard over me.

I focused my attention back on the array of monitors and controllers spread out around me. The three Interceptors my father had launched from the Icarus crater were finally closing in on Europa.

Even though I was located inside the Disrupter's cancellation field, these three ships were millions of miles outside of it, so my quantum communication link to them was unaffected. And so, unfortunately, were the EDA's links to the Icebreaker and its fighter escort, under the control of Vance and his underlings at Raven Rock.

I took control of the lead Interceptor, and through its cameras I could see the Icebreaker closing in on the icy moon, surrounded by its escort of two dozen drone Interceptors. I knew that those ships were under the control of the best pilots the EDA had available, and that would almost certainly include Viper and Rostam, who were both listed above me in the *Armada* pilot rankings for a very good reason—they were better than me.

Even with three ships, there was no way I could take them all on at once, no matter how badly I wanted to. So instead, I did as my father had instructed. I sat tight, out of sight, and waited for him to even the odds.

WHEN HE REACHED RAVEN ROCK, MY FATHER CIRCLED HIGH OVER THE BASE, WAITING UNTIL the moment the enemy activated the Disrupter. He knew exactly when it happened, because the EDA fighters and drones protecting the installation down below deactivated instantaneously.

I also lost the audio and video feeds from inside his cockpit, but a few seconds later Lex executed some further computer wizardry, and a live video image of my father's ship reappeared at the edge of my HUD. The feed appeared to be from one of the base's external security cameras, fed back to us through the hard-line intranet.

With the base's defenses momentarily disabled, my father had turned his Interceptor into a steep dive, and now he appeared to be making a suicide run at the base's armored blast doors, which were still very much closed.

As he raced toward the base, I realized he was aiming for one of the drone launch tunnels, just as I had earlier during my colossal screwup at Crystal Palace. But here, instead of being disguised as grain silos, the launch tunnel openings were camouflaged as rock formations embedded in the mountainside.

I sat in Starbase Ace, watching his progress over the base's network of security cameras. Once his ship was inside the Raven Rock drone hangar, my father set it to hover on autopilot, then used his ship's laser turret to cut a large hole in the ceiling. He raised his Interceptor up to the opening, opened his cockpit canopy, and jumped out, scrambling into the dust-filled level above the hangar ceiling.

Then he drew his sidearm and took off running, even deeper into the base.

I EXPECTED THE CORRIDORS TO BE EMPTY, OR FILLED WITH INERT DRONES. BUT WHEN THE Disrupter activated, some of the base's internal hard-wired defense turrets had remained operational, along with a few dozen tethered ATHIDs, all controlled by operators linked to them through the EDA's hard-line intranet. They were already converging on my father's position, under orders to stop him at all costs.

If it hadn't been for Lex and Ray, he wouldn't have had a chance. Thankfully, Lex was already inside the EDA's security firewall, so she was able to access the base security system to guide my father and use it to help him avoid or evade as many of the tethered ATHIDs as she could while throwing up blast doors around his route to keep defenders away. Meanwhile, Ray used his own hard-line network access to seize control of the laser defense turrets positioned along my dad's route and used them to blast a path through the drones stationed ahead of him.

But just when there seemed to be no stopping him—they stopped him. His luck ran out, and a pack of tethered ATHIDs got the jump on him. He managed to take them all out, but not before a stray plasma bolt hit him in the chest, and he went down.

I watched helplessly as he struggled to get back on his feet, but he couldn't. So he began to crawl.

He pulled himself down the corridor, until he reached a charging dock where five dormant ATHIDs were stored. He opened up the maintenance access panels one at a time and entered a long code on each one, and then all four of them powered up. My father detached the tethered controllers from each drone and used them to command the four ATHIDs to lift his injured body off the ground. Then he had them interlace their eight arms and legs around his body, forming something that looked sort of like a walking spider tank. This contraption lifted him up and continued to carry him forward.

He rode inside as he blasted his way farther into the base, firing four sets of ATHID weapons as he came.

He also hijacked all of their external speakers, and then used them to play a song I recognized immediately from his old *Raid the Arcade* mix— "Run's House" by Run-D.M.C.

"Archie really hates hip-hop," we heard him say. "I bet this will throw him off balance. Like 'Ride of the Valkyries'!"

He cranked the song up to an earsplitting volume. I could see him mouthing the lyrics as he continued to fight his way toward Vance, lumbering forward like a Terminator that was never going to stop until it had completed its final mission.

My father piloted his makeshift tank down one last corridor, then finally arrived at his destination—a pair of armored doors labeled RAVEN ROCK DRONE OPERATIONS COMMAND CENTER.

Then, to my horror, I watched as he set the power cells on all four of his ATHIDs to manual overload. In a panic, I asked Lex to patch my voice through to him.

"I already did," she said. "He can hear you right now."

"Dad, what are you doing?" I screamed.

But it was a rhetorical question. I knew exactly what he was doing.

He glanced up at the security camera mounted nearby—the one we were watching him on. He smiled, but he didn't answer me. He just turned his makeshift spider-tank around and then used it to crash through the armored doors, into the command center itself. Several of the drone drivers had already climbed out of their pods and were now standing there in the middle of the room waiting for him—including one I recognized, Captain Dagh, aka Rostam, the teenage officer who had asked for my autograph. He looked completely starstruck in my father's presence.

Admiral Vance was standing in their midst, waiting, too.

The admiral ordered his men to open fire on my father as soon as he stumbled forward into the room, but only a few of them actually obeyed. The majority of them—including Rostam—didn't even raise their weapons, and most of those who did couldn't seem to bring themselves to fire— not with General Xavier Lightman in their sights.

Then Vance started shooting, firing his nine-millimeter Beretta. First he took out the speakers on each of my father's drones, silencing the music blaring out of them.

Then he turned his weapon on my father. I saw Rostam avert his gaze.

"You're a damn fool," Vance said, just before he opened fire on my father. Several of his men opened fire, too. Most of their shots were deflected by his shield of ATHIDs, but not all of them. A bullet grazed my father's left leg.

He still didn't stop coming, though.

He continued to lurch forward, piloting his makeshift ATHID spider-tank farther into the room, as more laser fire and bullets struck him and his drones, until he finally collapsed a few yards away from Admiral Vance, trapped inside the tangled wreckage of the four ATHIDs. That was when Vance finally spotted the power core overload countdowns ticking away on each of them. All of them had about ten seconds remaining.

"You guys all need to get out of here," my father said.

Rostam and the other men turned and ran for the exit as fast as their legs would carry them. But Vance didn't move.

"You better get going, too, Archie," my father said. "Six seconds. Five . . ."

Vance shook his head and then ran to the exit before turning back.

"This was pointless!" he said. "This won't stop us from deploying the Icebreaker, you know."

Then he turned and ran, and the op center doors hissed closed behind him.

"I know," I heard my father mutter to himself. "I was just trying to delay you." Then he laughed. "My son is going to stop you."

Then my father's four makeshift bombs all detonated in unison, and the video feed went black.

———

I SCREAMED. I DON'T KNOW FOR HOW LONG.

When I finally got ahold of myself and returned to my senses, I checked the camera feeds from my three drones orbiting Europa. The squadron of EDA drones escorting the Icebreaker had broken formation. They were now drifting around the Icebreaker, which had discontinued its descent toward the moon.

At this very moment, I knew Admiral Vance and the other pilots who had been in control of the Icebreaker's fighter escort were evacuating the Raven Rock installation. But I also knew that it would only be a matter of seconds before they reached a safe location and retook control of their drones and the Icebreaker. I probably had less than a minute before they started to come back online.

I left two Interceptors orbiting at a distance, took control of the third, and swooped in to attack the defenseless drones drifting helplessly in front of me.

I destroyed half of the Icebreaker's fighter escort before I came to my senses and forgot about the rest to focus all of my fire on destroying the Icebreaker.

But I was still struggling to knock out its shields when Vance and his men seized control of their drones once again, from some new location—possibly using their QComms.

Suddenly, I found myself outnumbered and outgunned, locked into a dogfight with six Interceptors. As I moved to engage, the song "One Vision" by Queen cued up on my father's old *Raid the Arcade* playlist. That finally managed to put me in the zone.

I took out four of their ships in as many seconds, leaving only two Interceptors remaining—the ones piloted by Rostam and Viper Vance.

I went after Rostam first, recklessly ramming his drone with mine. The impact set his drone careening off at an oblique angle, right into the path of one of the Icebreaker's automated sentry guns. It exploded in a collapsing fireball.

Now it was just me and Admiral Vance.

The two of us were now locked in a fierce duel around the Icebreaker as it hovered above Europa. Muffled through my headphones, I could hear the chaotic sounds of real-world combat somewhere close by—and they were growing ever closer. Spider Fighters had surrounded Starbase Ace. Cruz, Diehl, and my mother were fighting to keep them at bay, and a Basilisk was closing in on the store.

Then, at the last minute, Whoadie swooped down out of the sky in her own manned Interceptor. When the Disrupter had activated and she'd lost control of her drone, she'd decided to jump back into her prototype Interceptor and had hauled ass here from New Orleans to help us. She took out the Basilisk on her first pass with a shot right between the eyes, then swung around again and strafed the Spider Fighters, allowing me to focus my attention back on my duel with Admiral Vance, halfway across the solar system.

I knew that Vance had flown on my father's wing at Moon Base Alpha—but he turned out to be even better than I expected.

Before I knew what had happened, Vance had swung around on my tail and blasted my Interceptor to pieces.

Then he turned and continued to escort the Icebreaker to its target. But Vance didn't know that I still had those two last Interceptors in reserve, waiting in a holding pattern nearby.

I took control of another ship and went after Vance. I managed to strafe him with a barrage of plasma bolts, but his shields held and his ship remained undamaged.

He killed me again. He was really good. Almost as good as my father, but not quite.

I took control of my last ship, and once again intercepted Vance and the Icebreaker—just as it came within firing range of Europa's surface. It was now or never.

I pushed aside my grief and paralyzing rage and focused on what I wanted now, more than anything else in this life—to make my father proud of me, and to make certain that his sacrifice had not been in vain.

I firewalled my Interceptor's throttle and locked horns with Vance's drone, which was still flying in a protective pattern around the Icebreaker.

But his ship's power core was running low now, while I had a fresh ship with a full charge.

There was no time now for subtlety. I put my fighter into a dive and came straight at him with all guns blazing while he did the same, the two of us playing an outer-space variation on a game of chicken, unloading all of our weapons at one another simultaneously.

A split second before we collided, his depleted shields failed—but mine held, allowing me to destroy his ship with a well-placed plasma bolt. It incinerated his ship, just as mine flew straight through the ensuing fireball.

I didn't stop to celebrate. I swooped down to take out the Icebreaker, too—just seconds before it launched its nukes at Europa's surface.

"Don't do it, kid!" Vance screamed over the comlink channel, now powerless to stop me. "If you do this, you'll be personally responsible for the extinction of the entire human race."

I went ahead and did it anyway.

When I fired a last burst from my sun guns, the Icebreaker went up in a brilliant, soundless explosion of light.

26

THAT WAS ALL IT TOOK.

In that one moment, it appeared that I had negotiated a cease-fire. The news was already coming in over all of the EDA comlink channels. All around the world, the alien drones and ships had just suddenly deactivated, allowing themselves to be easily destroyed.

I sat there, listening to the news the war was over, trying to make myself believe it. Then, just as I was about to disengage from my Interceptor and remove my helmet, I saw the surface of Europa crack open beneath me, breaking apart like an eggshell as a giant chrome orb rose out of the hidden ocean below, ripping a massive, circular hole in the surface ice as it zoomed up into orbit and began to hover in space directly in front of my ship. Upon closer inspection, I saw that the object was actually an icosahedron, with twenty symmetrical, faceted sides—a "twenty-sider," Shin would have probably called it.

The icosahedron hovered in front of my ship. Then it began to speak to me.

"I am the Emissary," it said. "I am an intelligent machine created by a galactic community of peaceful civilizations known as the Sodality."

The Emissary quickly explained to me that there were never actually any extraterrestrial beings living on Europa at all. Only microbial life had evolved in the moon's subsurface ocean. No intelligent beings—indigenous or otherwise—had ever lived there.

"Then who built the armada that just attacked Earth?" I asked. I felt like a character in someone else's dream. "Who have we been fighting this entire time?"

"I built the Armada," it said. "And this entire time you were fighting against yourselves.

"The Sodality has been monitoring your species' radio and television broadcasts for as long as you've been transmitting them into space. But we didn't begin to take a special interest in humanity until 1945, when you created your first nuclear weapon and then used it for warfare against your own kind. At that time, we used all of that data we had collected to create a detailed profile of your species and ascertain its evolutionary strengths and weaknesses. In 1969, when your species became technologically advanced enough to reach another world, in this case your own moon, you became a potential threat to the other members of the Sodality. And that was when I was sent here, to deliver the Test."

"So it *was* a test, after all?" I said. "What for?"

"A test that we use to gauge whether or not your species is capable of existing peacefully within the Sodality," the Envoy said. "It was initiated when your probe first discovered the swastika on Europa's surface. We selected a symbol that your culture most associates with war and death, and then we re-created an enormous replica of that symbol on the nearest celestial body in your solar system with conditions capable of harboring intelligent life.

"We knew your discovery of such a symbol would eventually prompt you to send another probe down to the surface to investigate its origin," the Emissary said. "As soon as your probe landed on Europa, the next phase of the test began. I simulated a standard first-contact scenario for your species, in which a cultural misunderstanding leads to a declaration of war."

The machine's declaration didn't ring true to my ears, but I was in no mental condition to start a debate.

"You built all of those drones yourself?" I said. "And you controlled them in combat?"

"Affirmative."

"So this entire time, it was just you?" I said. "One artificially intelligent supercomputer pretending to be a hostile alien race for the purpose of testing humanity's character?"

"In very simple terms, yes. That is accurate." The machine paused. "It was your time to be tested. The Sodality found it necessary to ascertain how your species would handle a common first-contact scenario with a neighboring civilization. As I said, it was a test. *The* Test."

"Your 'test' killed millions of innocent people," I said through clenched teeth. "Including several of my friends. And my father."

"We are sorry for the losses you have suffered," the Emissary said. "But know that many other species have passed the Test with no conflict or loss of life."

I was nearly sobbing now. "What did you want us to do? What were we *supposed* to do?"

"There is no right or wrong way of taking the Test," the Emissary told me. "Using human psychological terms, it was a projective test, rather than an objective one. It presents the subject civilization with varying sets of circumstances intended to gauge your capacity for empathy and altruism, and your ability to act and negotiate as one collective species. It allows the Sodality to see how your species navigates first contact with a species of similar temperament."

"Isn't there an easier way to do that?" I asked. "One that wouldn't have involved killing millions of us and trashing our whole planet?"

"The Test reveals things about a species that cannot be ascertained any other way—what your Earth scientists refer to as an 'emergent property.'"

I didn't know how to respond. I was almost too upset to form thoughts or words.

"You should not feel too remorseful about how the Test played out," the machine said. "Your species' primitive warlike nature made a certain amount of conflict inevitable, as it often does. Regardless, your species should be pleased with the outcome. You passed the Test."

"We did?"

"Yes. The result was uncertain for a while, but you did well at the end. Many species lack the ability to defy their own animal instincts and allow their intellect to prevail. Such species are usually declared unfit for survival, much less membership in the Sodality."

"So you're saying that if I hadn't destroyed the Icebreaker, you would have exterminated the entire human race?"

"Correct," the machine replied. "But thankfully you made the correct choice, and knowingly disengaged from the cycle of warlike escalation with your imaginary enemy. That is why I'm speaking to you now. Once the Test has been passed, the Emissary makes contact with the individual most directly responsible, to inform them that their species has been invited to join the Sodality."

"How many other civilizations are there—in the Sodality?"

"At present, the Sodality has eight members," it replied. "Your species will be the ninth, if you accept our invitation."

"How do we do that?"

"You may accept the invitation on your species' behalf right now," it told me. "You have earned that right."

"What if I—what if *we* decline to join?"

"No species has ever declined to join the Sodality," the Emissary told me. "There are many benefits to membership. The sharing of knowledge, medicine, and technology, among other things. Your species' longevity and individual quality of life will increase drastically."

I didn't spend a whole lot of time thinking it over. I just went ahead and said yes.

"Congratulations."

"That's it?"

"Yes. That is it."

"What happens now?"

"Now we will begin the process of inducting your species into the Sodality," it said. "The first step is for us to share certain beneficial aspects of our technology with your species that will help you rebuild your civilization. Very soon your people will also be free from sickness and hunger. But this is just the first step. The Sodality will contact you again when you're ready for the next one."

"When will that be?"

"It depends on what you do with what you are given."

Before I could sort out my next question, the Emissary probe departed, warping out of our solar system in a blink. I never saw it again.

I parked my Interceptor in orbit around Europa and disengaged the link, leaving it there, possibly forever. Then I turned around and saw my mom standing behind me, along with Cruz and Diehl. All three of them had been watching, and I saw that Cruz and Diehl had both recorded my entire conversation with the Emissary on their phones.

I asked Diehl to post my exchange with the Emissary on the Internet, but he told me there was no need—the aliens had been broadcasting it all around the world, on every TV channel and device connected to the Internet. The truth about the Envoy and existence of the Sodality had already been revealed to the entire human race.

When the third wave of the alien armada arrived a few hours later, the drones didn't attack. Instead, they landed and began to help humanity rebuild its civilization, as well as its planet's fragile environment. The alien drones also began to dispense miraculous life-giving medicine and technology, along with an endless supply of clean, abundant energy. It seemed like they gave humanity everything it had ever wanted.

But while the world celebrated its victory, all my mother and I could do was go back home, and begin the process of mourning everything we'd just lost.

EPILOGUE

Y FRIENDS AND I EACH RECEIVED A MEDAL OF HONOR FROM THE PRESI-
dent, on the lawn in front of the newly rebuilt White
House in Washington, DC.

And my mom thought it was just as hysterical as I did when they decided to rename the gym I'd destroyed at my high school after me.

As promised, Lex took me out on our first date, but we spent most of
it in a state of traumatized disbelief, talking over everything that had just
happened to us. It wasn't until our fourth or fifth date that we were able to
focus on something other than the invasion. Then we did our best to stop
discussing it altogether.

With Ray's blessing, I decided to take over the operation of Starbase
Ace. Lex moved to town with her grandmother, and they both helped me
run the place. It quickly became the most popular secondhand videogame
store/historical battlefield in the world.

ON THE ONE-YEAR ANNIVERSARY OF HIS DEATH, A COMMEMORATIVE STATUE OF MY FATHER
was erected in the Beaverton town square, and we all attended the unveiling ceremony, during which my father was posthumously awarded military honors and medals from dozens of different nations.

Admiral Vance gave the closing address, during which he spoke at length about my father's bravery and their long friendship. He spoke honestly, as he always had, about how my father had prevented him from making the worst mistake of his career. His shame and regret were evident, even though he was far from being the only political or military leader guilty of the same mistake.

My dad had been right about Admiral Vance. He was a good man.

AFTERWARD, AS WE WERE ADMIRING MY FATHER'S STATUE, SOMETHING STRANGE HAPPENED. A young man stopped me to ask for an autograph. That in itself wasn't a strange occurrence at all, now that the Sodality had made me an international celebrity; what was strange was that this particular young man happened to be Douglas Knotcher, my old high school nemesis.

He was wearing an EDA uniform with the rank of sergeant. He was also standing on a pair of artificial legs, which were heavily in fashion this year. His right arm was a robotic replacement, too. For a moment I almost didn't recognize him. His self-satisfied smirk was long gone.

He held out a pen, along with a copy of our senior yearbook, open to my photo. Because of the war, our class had never even had a proper graduation ceremony. They had mailed us our diplomas, along with our yearbooks.

I took the yearbook and scrawled my name beneath my photo. Then I paused a moment to study the clueless, smiling teenager in the picture. For a moment I almost didn't recognize him either.

I handed the book back to him. He tucked it under his lone arm.

"I was sorry to hear about your father," I told him.

He glanced at his shoes and nodded.

"Wish I could say the same," he muttered. "The world is a better place without him."

He gave me a sad smile, then motioned to the statue of my father, looming over both of us. "You must be really proud of him."

I nodded. "I am."

"If he was here now, I'm sure he'd be proud of you, too," he said.

I opened my mouth to respond, but no words came out. Knotcher had obviously done a lot of growing up—maybe even more than I had. I wondered if he'd heard about Casey, the boy he'd bullied mercilessly throughout most of high school. He'd died during the first wave, along with his whole family, and millions of others.

I decided to not bring Casey up. I'm sure he knew.

We stood there in silence for another moment, staring at my father's statue. Then Knotcher turned to go. But first he offered me his left hand—the real one.

I reached out with my own left hand to shake it. Then, without another word, he turned and walked off, into the crowd.

I never saw him again.

AFTER THE CEREMONY, THE FOUR OF US WENT TO VISIT MY FATHER'S GRAVE—ME, LEX, MY mom, and my three-month-old baby brother, little Xavier Ulysses Lightman, Jr.—the kid whose name ensured that he would never have to pay for a drink as long as he lived.

We'd visited my father's tombstone many times, of course, but his empty casket had been exhumed a few months after he died, and we'd had another funeral for him. And this time, we'd filled his casket with old mementos before they buried it again. I'd put a few of his old mixtapes in there. I'd thought about burying his old high-score jacket with him, but then decided that I should keep it to give to my little brother. He must've sensed this, too—because whenever I wore the jacket, like I did today, Xavier Jr. was constantly reaching out to grab hold of its patches, then would refuse to let go.

"No, J. R.!" I would tell him (he seemed to prefer these initials over "junior"). "Mine! You can have it when you're big enough to wear it, little man." And then he would gurgle happily back at me.

When we reached my father's gravesite, we discovered the ground around it piled high with flowers, notes, and gifts from well-wishers around the world, as usual. My mother added her handpicked bouquet to the pile; then we stood there in silence for a while, admiring the sunset and paying our respects.

When we finally bid my father farewell and turned to go, I paused to admire the inscription on his new headstone, which I'd had a hand in writing:

HERE LIES
XAVIER ULYSSES LIGHTMAN
1980–2018
BELOVED HUSBAND, FATHER, AND SON
HE SAVED HUMANITY FROM TOTAL ANNIHILATION
"YOU'RE WELCOME."

I stood there, staring at his headstone, thinking over everything that had happened over the past year. Soon after the war ended, I'd received an offer from the EDA to take on an ambassadorial role to the Sodality, but I'd turned it down. I wasn't interested in helping either the asshole aliens who'd devised such a horrible "test" and murdered my father—or the human powers-that-be who had lied to all of humanity for decades and nearly brought us to extinction.

As the Emissary had promised, things on Earth were changing for the better, thanks to the Sodality's advanced technology and medicine. My mom had to find a new nursing job for the best possible reason—we now had a cure for all forms of cancer, which had eradicated the disease in a matter of weeks. And most other diseases, too. The Sodality had also gifted us a new form of cheap, clean, fusion energy technology. It looked as if humanity had begun a new age of wonders and miracles.

Perhaps it was my late father's influence, but despite all of their generous gifts, I still felt mistrustful of the Sodality. In hindsight, their "test" seemed like more of a trap—one they had set and baited for all of humanity. How benevolent could the beings behind such immoral machinations really be?

Yes, they had shared all of these technological advances with humanity, but they still hadn't revealed any real details about themselves, or the different alien species they claimed made up the Sodality, always using the excuse that "humanity wasn't ready for that knowledge yet" and that it was "beyond our primitive understanding."

Whenever I read about this in the news, I heard the echo of my father's words: *This human understands enough to know when he's being messed with.*

Now I couldn't shake that same suspicion. They had messed with us, and they clearly weren't finished messing with us.

How long would their generosity last? What would happen if and when it ended?

I looked over at my loved ones. Lex. My mother. And little Xavier Jr. I wondered what sort of world he was going to grow up in—what sort of world we were going to allow the Sodality to impose on us.

That was the moment when I realized I couldn't stay at Starbase Ace. There was no going back to the life I'd had before, because it was gone—for everyone—along with the world in which we'd lived it.

I couldn't just sit on the sidelines and remain disengaged from the world. Not after everything that had happened—and everything that might be in store for humanity.

When I got back home that evening, I took out my QComm and dialed my friend Dr. Shostak. I told him I had decided to become one of Earth's ambassadors to the Sodality after all. In time, I hoped my new job would eventually put me in a position to learn the truth about our new alien benefactors' true motives.

For the time being, I intended to try to follow Master Yoda's timeless advice—to keep my mind on where I was, and what I was doing. And to do everything I could to protect what was now most important to me. It wasn't as hard as I thought it would be. After all of the things that had happened to me, after everything I'd been through, I no longer found myself staring out the window and daydreaming of adventure.

maxell UR

POSITION
IEC TYPE I • NORMAL

UR

Raid The Arcade Mix

A DATE 8·8·89 N.R. ○YES ✗NO — Hell

B DATE 8·8·89 N.R. ○YES ✗NO — Hell

Side A:
1. One Vision - Queen
2. Crazy Train - Ozzy
3. Chase the Ace - AC/DC
4. Hair of the 🐕 - Nazareth
5. Get it On - Power Station
6. Old Enough 2 R/R - R. Hawes
7. Danger Zone - Kenny Loggins
8. Vital Signs ⌁⌁⌁ Rush
9. Barracuda - Heart ♡
10. T.N.T. 💣 - AC/DC
11. You Really Got Me
12. Another 1 Bites Dust - Q
13. One of these Days - Pink Floyd
14. TOP GUN Anthem - H.F.

Side B:
1. I Hate Myself 4 ♡ U - Joan Jett
2. It takes two - Rob Base
3. Hammer to Fall - Queen
4. Twilight Zone - Golden Earring
5. We're Not Gonna Take It
6. Rock y/1 Hurricane -
7. Black Betty - Ram Jam
8. D.T. - AC/DC
9. Delerious - ZZ Top
10. Iron Eagle (NSD) - King Kobra
11. Run's House - Run DMC
12. WW Rock U / Champ - Q

Bonus Track:
🐤 vs. ✠ The Royal Guardsman

ACKNOWLEDGMENTS

There are times when writing a novel—or just living your life—can make you feel like you're waging a one-person war against increasingly insurmountable odds. I'm grateful to have had a lot of wonderful people on my wing and watching my six during the writing of this book. My sincere thanks and appreciation go out to:

My younger brother Eric, for inspiring me and this story. And his son, my enviably named nephew Talon, for teaching me about the unique brand of courage that can stem from being the son of a soldier.

My best friend, Cristin O'Keefe Aptowicz, for her love, life support, and constant encouragement throughout our long friendship, and most especially during the writing of this novel. I couldn't have done it without her.

My beautiful and brilliant daughter, Libby Willett-Cline, for inspiring me every day to be a better father, writer, gamer, and human being. And her mother, Dr. Susan B. A. Somers-Willett, for helping me raise the coolest kid in the world, and for bringing her into it in the first place.

I am also extremely grateful to my long-time manager, friend, and Hollywood partner in crime Dan Farah (aka "The Jersey Jedi"), and to my fantastic literary agent, Yfat Reiss-Gendell, along with Kirsten Neuhaus, Jessica Regel, and all of the other miracle workers at Foundry Literary and Media.

I also want to extend a special note of thanks to my tireless, brilliant editor, Julian Pavia, who deserves a Medal of Valor from the Earth Defense Alliance for his contribution to this work, and for putting up with me during its creation. And thanks also to Sarah Breivogel, Jay Sones, Jessica Miele, Molly Stern, Maya Mavjee, Robert Siek, and all of the other super cool cats at Crown Publishing.

I owe a Wookiee Life Debt to the amazing artist Russell Walks for creating the EDA insignia, to Mark Duszkiewicz for his blueprint design, and to the brilliant Will Staehle and art director Chris Brand, for creating our incredible front cover.

I am extremely grateful to my friend Wil Wheaton, for once again lending his voice and his talent to my story. Thanks also to Amy Metsch and Dan Musselman at Penguin Random House Audio for their work on the audiobook.

Mad props to my astrophysicist pal Dr. Andy Howell, for his attempts to help me get at least some of the science in this story correct. (Whenever it's not, know that it is because I chose to ignore Andy's suggestions for my own twisted ends.)

I also need to thank:

Mike Mika, for allowing me to benefit from his reality distortion field and for helping me transform the fictional videogames in my novels into the real thing, one line of code at a time.

Katherine Europa Welch, for her awesome middle name, her wicked web design mojo, and for answering my endless questions about working in the modern videogame industry.

Bruce Aptowicz, for sharing his expertise in the surprisingly perilous profession of working in wastewater treatment.

Astronaut Kjell Lindgren, for giving me a guided tour of NASA, for sharing his patriotism and enthusiasm with me, and for taking the cover of my first novel up in outer space. I want to be him when I grow up.

The late, great Aaron Allston, for giving me advice on this story and for his work that helped inspire it. He is missed, and always will be.

My humble thanks and gratitude also go out to George Lucas, for creating the mythology of my youth and for filling my young heart with a deep yearning for adventure among the stars, and to Steven Spielberg, for the role his work also played in inspiring this story and for buoying my spirits while I was writing it with the life-changing news that he had chosen to direct the adaptation of my first novel. Nothing gives you the courage to dream big dreams like one of your lifelong heroes deciding to quite literally make one of your biggest dreams come true.

Speaking of dreams come true—I also want to thank Scott Stuber, Jeffrey Kirschenbaumm, Alexa Fagan, and everyone at Universal Pictures, for believing this story would also make a great movie and for making so many of the movies that inspired it.

For their advice, assistance, encouragement, and friendship, I am also eternally grateful to Craig Tessler, Matt Galsor, Trevor Astbury, Deanna Hoak, Elena Stokes, Jack Fogg, his father, Tony Fogg, Zak Penn, Hugh Howey, Andy Weir, George R. R. Martin, Patrick Rothfuss, John Scalzi, Erin Morgenstern, Felicia Day, Daniel H. Wilson, Richard Garriott, Jeff Knight, Chris Beaver, Mike Henry, Harry Knowles, Dannie Knowles, Giovanni Knowles, Aaron Dunn, Chris Nine, Phil McJunkins, and Jed Strahm. And to Hildy, my canine Girl Friday, who lay curled at my feet during the writing of this book and the last. *Cave lupum.*

I also wish to extend my sincere gratitude to Dr. Neil deGrasse Tyson, Dr. Stephen Hawking, Dr. Jill Tarter, Dr. Michio Kaku, Dr. Seth Shostak, and the late Dr. Carl Sagan, for inspiring my lifelong interest in science and the search for extraterrestrial intelligence, and for allowing me to pay tribute to their work by giving them each a cameo in this story.

Finally, my sincere thanks to all of the scientists, writers, filmmakers, musicians, and artists whose work helped inspire this novel, and to all of my friends, family, fans, and readers, for the boundless enthusiasm and patience they showed me while I was writing it.

MTFBWYA,
Ernest Cline
Austin, TX
April 30, 2015

ABOUT THE AUTHOR

Ernest Cline is a novelist, screenwriter, father, and full-time geek. His first novel, *Ready Player One,* was a *New York Times* and *USA Today* bestseller and appeared on numerous "best of the year" lists. Ernie lives in Austin, Texas, with his family, a time-traveling DeLorean, and a large collection of classic videogames.

For more information, please visit ernestcline.com.

35674055849914